Hitler's Brothel

Steve Matthews

16pt

Copyright Page from the Original Book

Big Sky Publishing Pty Ltd
PO Box 303, Newport, NSW 2106, Australia
Phone: 1300 364 611
Fax: (61 2) 9918 2396
Email: info@bigskypublishing.com.au
Web: www.bigskypublishing.com.au

Cover design and typesetting: Think Productions
Printed in China by Jilin GIGO International

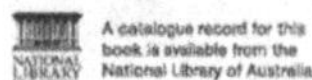

A catalogue record for this book is available from the National Library of Australia

For Cataloguing-in-Publication entry see National Library of Australia.

TABLE OF CONTENTS

To the memory of Martyn Isbell
1955-2016

PART 1:
ANNA AND
STELLA

1

7 February 2000
Paterson, New Jersey, USA

Stella Lombardo was fifty-nine years old when it happened. She would never work again, never fully recover, and would always be asking herself and God why such a dreadful thing had happened and if there was anything she could have done to prevent it.

A small crowd of reporters had gathered around her front door later that day and she told them she had *never seen anything like it in her life before,* then she felt stupid because of course she hadn't-who had? They asked Stella how well she knew the woman concerned and she held her face in her hands and said, "Know her? She's like a sister to me, like a sister!"

Stella and Anna had worked together at the Paterson Manor Rest Home in New Jersey for well over forty years-as long as they had been neighbours, in fact. Stella would tell the reporters that Anna and her husband, Leo, had actually been at her house the evening before, the sixth of February, helping celebrate her wedding anniversary.

Stella's husband Joe was also very fond of Anna and as his wife was being interviewed at the front door he appeared in the background, fresh out of the shower, clean shaven, wearing his work pants and a spotless white singlet. One of the reporters called out and asked Mr Lombardo what he thought about it all, and he said, "Listen to me, I tell you. I tell you this: she was a good neighbour, a good worker and a good woman."

***

"It's not silver, gold or diamond, it is what is known as our plastic anniversary," Joe said during his little speech at the party the night before. He produced a cheap ring with a red plastic jewel stuck to it-purchased from the kids' dress-up section in the local Five and Dime discount store- and slipped it onto one of Stella's fingers. Everyone thought it was hilarious, but Stella knew that the toy ring was all she was going to get from Joe. He had always been careful with his money, especially where she was concerned. Joe ended his little speech by turning towards Stella and saying that above everything else, more than being a wonderful mother and a caring wife, she was his best friend. Everyone sighed and nodded in agreement and a few women even squeezed their husband's hand affectionately-everyone except Stella. If you did not know her well enough you would forgive her by thinking that perhaps she had not heard everything that Joe said; but she had, and the truth was, she did not think of her husband as her best friend.

Anna was Stella's best friend; always had been, right from the start. Her husband, Joe? He was father and provider, nothing more. It was Stella's opinion that only women knew what real friendship was. *You cannot be a parent and a friend to your kids, any more than you can be a husband and a friend to your wife.*

There were things that Stella shared with Anna over the years that she could never have told Joe. Not just intimacies, but gossipy stuff about their respective families; things that would have caused great upset if Joe had known that his wife actually felt the way she did.

Stella often said that Joe always told her where she was going wrong. "He can't help giving me his opinion before telling me how to fix things. I don't want his opinions or his solutions; if I did, I would ask for them, wouldn't I?"

As much as Anna was always there to listen to her friend, so too was Stella. Whenever Anna needed an ear, Stella was there. And the need was frequent because Anna's husband Leo was as bad as Joe!

Stella had not had the easiest life, but compared to Anna? Stories of Anna's war years always left Stella aghast and ever grateful that she had never had to endure such terrible times. It appeared that Anna had seen and done things that most people would find hard to believe, and Stella knew that she had not heard the worst of it-Anna always held something back.

The two women frequently joked to each other that they had made the local priest redundant because neither of them needed him or the confessional-they had one another, and that was what being best friends was really all about.

***

Anna and Leo had remained childless and Anna took great delight in borrowing Stella's kids when they were young. If she was not taking them to the movies during the school holidays, they could usually be found at the beach. Anna loved having the kids to spoil because she claimed that she had no one else to spend her money on-Leo did not count.

Anna was in fact Stella's kids' second mum, and there was nothing she enjoyed more than embarrassing them. She loved to dance to the background music at the mall or dress up and take them trick or treating on Halloween. Even though they only lived next door, the kids sometimes had a sleepover at Aunty Anna's place, renting Disney videos, eating popcorn, reading scary books by torchlight. Sometimes Anna would help with their homework, and when Joe Junior was four and a half he developed an interest in numbers, it was Anna who encouraged him the most. He very quickly learned how to identify a four and a three, also seven, nine and eight and Anna used to giggle and complain that he tickled as his tiny fingers traced around the tattoo on her left forearm.

When Stella's kids grew into troubled teenagers, it was Aunty Anna they turned to for guidance, and it was the same Aunty Anna who marched them back home and made them apologise to their mum for the way they had treated her. Anna seemed to have so much wisdom and common sense that what happened at the nursing home the day after Stella and Joe's anniversary party seemed even more puzzling.

***

There was no doubting that for her age, Anna was still a remarkably attractive woman; five feet six with mid-length silver hair that was once shiny and black, and a figure that still carried the hallmarks of having been quite something back in the day. She had filled out a little here and there as women do when they age, but her hourglass shape and voluptuous curves were still evident, and she remained perfectly proportioned-just a little rounder. Her skin was flawless despite the time she spent in her garden under the hot New Jersey summer sun, and the lines on her face only showed when she smiled. It was no surprise that she could still turn heads when she wore a swimming costume, but Anna hated the remarks and stares she attracted from men at the beach or swimming pool. Someone once said she would give her left arm to have a man look at her the way men looked at Anna. "You are blessed!"

Anna smiled wistfully. "Me? Blessed? If you just knew..."

It appeared that one of the few concessions Anna made to growing old was the wearing of contact lenses. Strangely, one was brown and the other clear. Of course, Anna's vision was much improved by the lenses, but the real reason she chose to wear them was to hide-the last thing she wanted to see when she looked in the mirror every morning was her true self. However, there were times when her mask slipped, and for no apparent reason her eyes would lose their sparkle and the corners of her mouth would drop like an upturned 'U'. That usually happened when something triggered a distant memory from a time when life had been very different.

Anna Brenewski had secrets.

***

The tiny house that Anna and Leo shared was austere but always spotless, and if Anna had not been the one who mowed the grass or cleaned the windows it was doubtful that they would ever be done.

The place was frugally furnished because Leo did not think furniture was all that important. The pieces they had when they first moved in did the job until they fell into disrepair, and then Leo tried his best to fix them up rather than shell out good money on replacements.

There was only one vase, always in the centre of the kitchen table, usually bursting with roses from Anna's garden. Window ledges and shelves were spotlessly clean and free from the usual household clutter-there were no dolls, teapots or painted plates-nothing superfluous to gather dust.

Things that were not in use on a daily basis were stored away out of sight. For instance, there were only two knives, two forks and two spoons in the kitchen drawer. Two coffee mugs stood alongside two dinner plates and a pair of dessert bowls in the cupboard. When additional cutlery or crockery was needed, it was taken from the stackable plastic storage bins beneath the sink.

As well as being devoid of unnecessary furniture, there were no rugs on the floor and no pictures, photographs or paintings on the walls. The only exception was in the kitchen (the parlour, as Anna called it), where there was one framed photograph above the small laminate sideboard; Stella and her kids standing alongside Anna at Coney Island, their eyes scrunched up in the sun's glare. Both kids had ice-cream dripping down their faces and Stella and Anna wore colourful hats and the smiles of happy tourists. On the back of the picture was an inscription, in Anna's handwriting-*my family and me, summer 1992.*

Stella's kids were forever curious about Anna's past life, and the question was once asked as to why there were no other pictures in her house. The kids wanted to see what Anna looked like as a child, when she was their age. Anna told them she had never been their age because of the war-her life only began the day she arrived in America as a refugee, after the hostilities finished.

"Is that why you don't have any photographs or stuff in your house, Aunty Anna, because of the war?" Joe Junior had always been the kind of child who was never backwards in coming forwards.

Anna took a deep breath and dismissed her initial thoughts about dodging the question, so she sat the wide-eyed boy in front of her and took both his hands in her own. She explained that she had lived in Europe during the war years, and when it ended the place was completely trashed. *Whole cities and towns had been reduced to rubble. In some places there was simply nothing whatsoever left standing—not one single building.* "Most people had no job to go back to after the war, and many of them never even had homes."

"What, no house at all?"

"That's right, not even an outhouse or a doghouse."

The boy screwed his face up and tried to grasp the enormity of it all. He opened his mouth to ask another question, but this time words failed him. Anna continued. "It's hard to imagine, Joey, but after the war the only thing some people had was the clothes they were wearing. Everything was destroyed."

As she spoke a small tear gathered in the corner of Anna's right eye and then trickled down her cheek. The little boy reached up to wipe it away, and she gripped his tiny hands and whispered, "Some of us lost everything in that war, Joey."

2

While Stella and Anna rarely disagreed, there was one subject that they constantly debated: which country produced the laziest men, Italy or Poland? They agreed that it was a close-run thing because they both had useless, good-for-nothing husbands!

Joe worked in something to do with construction, Leo found his vocation behind the wheel of a cab and they both chose to work off the books whenever they could. Leo kept his cash in an old tea tin in the kitchen and Joe had his stashed in his sock drawer *(the very last place a burglar would look, I promise you, I know this thing!).* Another common bond between the two men was their love of traditional, home-brewed alcohol. Joe's grappa was much sought after and appreciated, while Leo made vodka from potatoes that Anna grew in her backyard vegetable patch. It was a family recipe, known to be over one hundred years old, *and it still tasted like Drain-o,* according to Anna.

Leo had another reminder of his homeland-a backyard smokehouse. As a child in Poland before the war his father would sometimes go to the markets and buy a small pig, which Leo watched him slaughter and smoke. Over many years, Leo perfected his own smoking technique, switching his expertise to fish. Now on special occasions he would get up early and head to the Fulton Fish Markets in the Bronx, buy the best salmon, and cook it to perfection in the backyard. Leo's food became famous throughout the neighbourhood and there were times when people willingly drank his disgusting vodka just to get access to the magnificent fish.

While Leo stubbornly retained a few traditional ties to his homeland, he appeared to be strangely uncomfortable with his heritage, and even considered changing his last name at one stage. He was most offended when Joe referred to him as Polish-American. "I am American, for God's sake. No different from the Lone Ranger or John Wayne!"

"Being called Polish is not an insult, my friend. Hey, you should hear what they call the English where I work—Limey bastards! Mind you," he paused for effect, "most of them are bastards..." then laughed aloud. "Get over yourself, man. What the fuck's up with you? Anyone would think you are ashamed to be Polish!"

3

Stella and Joe had arrived in America as children before the war. Their penniless parents worked wherever they could, including neighbours' backyards where they grew vegetables that they sold on the roadside. They met through the usual channels in those days-introduced through friends of Italian friends whose family knew their Italian friends and their friends' Italian families.

Now, so many years later, Stella and Joe were holding their wedding anniversary party in the tiny backyard of their own home in Paterson, New Jersey. Joe had gone all out with the preparations and even gave the concrete a fresh coat of green paint the day before. Just as he finished, from out of nowhere a stray cat jumped the back fence and ran across the wet paint. Despite Joe's protestations, at Stella's insistence, the paw prints remained to mark the occasion.

The day of the party was unusually mild, so everyone gathered on the back porch, which saved on the utilities because they never had to use the air-conditioner, pleasing Joe no end. Stella had been cooking for a week, but was still concerned that there may not be enough food to go around. Thankfully, as tradition dictated, everyone arrived with a plate.

Stella and Joe's two kids were there, of course, with their partners, and Anna arrived with something stuffed with cabbage, which most people only picked at, because Italians do not eat Polish food. Leo also brought something wrapped in foil, and two bottles of his disgusting potato vodka, which Joe opened because Italians *do* drink free alcohol.

Joe spoke after the first glass. "No wonder you Poles look so sour-you eat those insipid cabbage rolls of yours, and you drink camel piss!" Everyone laughed, glasses were clinked together and wide smiles quickly turned to grimaces when Leo's disgusting vodka found its way down unsuspecting Italian throats.

Leo pretended to be offended by the comments that followed and made a great drama out of leaving. "I am going and I will take my food with me, at least I will be appreciated in my own house!" And he waved his foil package under Joe's nose.

"What do you have there? Not more cabbage I hope?"

"No no, nothing to interest you. It is just a couple of trout I got from the Bronx yesterday. I smoked them through the night!" He placed his thumb and forefinger together and kissed them into the air.

Joe's tone immediately changed. "Leo! Leo my friend, I beg you, don't take your trout away. Please! *You* can go and so take your vodka with you, you miserable Polish fuck, but leave your wonderful fish! Leo, please, I beg of you!" He put a large hairy arm around Leo's shoulder and guided him and his parcel of smoked fish into the kitchen, both men grinning broadly and everyone else laughing.

The party was a great success, and at seven o'clock Joe insisted on having a bridal dance. "With my missus, like our wedding." The smiling couple shuffled around the veranda as Dean

Martin sang, 'That's Amore.' Guests sang along and swayed to the music as Joe and his bride smooched even closer. Stella was touched by the moment, albeit briefly, because it *did* take her back to her wedding day, to the accordions, the laughter and the sunshine in her parents' garden. As well as the dancing, she remembered having to kiss her brand-new husband every time someone tapped a knife on a plate-it was either that or drain her glass, which somehow always seemed to be full! What a wedding it had been, all those years ago.

Magic moments like the ones Joe and Stella had shared on their wedding day had since evaporated, replaced by the familiarity and boredom of a long, unexciting but faithful marriage. The fact that Joe wanted to dance at their anniversary party was a welcome surprise and Stella felt once more the spring in his step as he unexpectedly placed his hand on her ass as they smooched. "Hey, Giuseppe Lombardo, if you think you're gonna get sex tonight, you'd better think-a twice!" she yelled, much to everyone's delight, including her own. Even the kids laughed. Mamma and Papa were so cute when they were drunk.

A few drinks later, after the music was turned down and the chitchat resumed, Anna was reluctantly talked into reciting her party piece, her famous 'Owstralia' story.

"You have three choices. America, Australia or Canada. What is it to be?" The British Officer addressing her in 1945 was in a hurry-there was a long queue and it seemed that most of those who survived the war wanted to get out of Poland before the brutal Russians took full control.

There was a rumour going around that married couples were being given preference for migration, so Leo and Anna joined in the queue after Leo introduced himself. No record of their 'marriage' was available, of course, but that was not uncommon in war-ravaged Poland. It was easy enough to convince the officer in charge that they were husband and wife, as he was more interested in shortening the queue than he was in substantiating everything he was told.

Leo had seemed pleasant enough to Anna's way of thinking. As far as he was concerned, bumping into her was convenient, and, of course, she was rather easy on the eye. He also knew about her involvement with the Germans and that did not sit well with him. However, he felt they had a better chance together, starting a new life in a place where Communism was just a word in the dictionary.

"Alphabet," Anna had said to the British officer. "We go with alphabet."

"Good. OK. Done. "The two of you will be on your way to Australia within three weeks Mr and Mrs Brenewski. Now go and join the queue over there and give the officer this document when he calls your names." He rubber-stamped a single-sided sheet of paper, signed it at the bottom and held it out at arm's length. Anna and Leo never moved.

"There. The table over there!" The irritable officer nodded towards the table, but Anna and Leo were seemingly rooted to the spot. "What now? Is there something wrong? You do understand English, don't you?"

Anna was angry. "Owstralia? No Owstralia. I said alphabet. America is first alphabet!"

"Madame, allow me to explain how the King's English works. The United States of America comes after Australia. The letter 'U' has always followed the letter 'A' in our language, though it may be different in Polish for all I know and for all I care. So please go and join the queue over there!"

He flicked the document between his thumb and forefinger and Anna snatched it from his hand, mumbling as she walked away, "Owstralia, what the fuck is Owstralia?" It was apparent that she did, in fact, have a reasonable grasp of some parts of the King's English after all.

The only time Anna ever swore was when she told the Owstralia story, and she always blushed, but it was not the same without the f-word, so at Stella's request she kept it in. But for some reason she was not herself when she told everyone her story that night, and despite the laughter and the spontaneous burst of applause that followed, Stella could tell there was something else on her best friend's mind. Anna had been distant at work all week, and Stella was convinced she had been avoiding her. Why?

The story about Owstralia was not finished yet, and someone yelled above the din. "Hang on, hang on. You said you were sent to Australia, how come you ended up here in the States?"

Anna continued. "We thought we were stuck with Owstralia but when we arrived at the docks there were two ships and thousands of people trying to get on them. We figured out which ship was going where, slipped up the gangplank and waited for the right moment to squeeze past the authorities and mingle with the crowds on deck. Before we knew it, we were on our way to America! Each cabin had six bunks and it did not take long before people were doubling up for a cuddle at night, so we took advantage of the space. A few weeks later we found ourselves standing in a queue at Ellis Island."

"But surely they checked your documents when you arrived?"

"Of course they did. But it was the end of the war and there were so many refugees to process. Thousands and thousands of us! We had all been crammed into a boat for a couple of weeks with barely enough facilities, then we were shoulder to shoulder in the processing hall at Ellis Island, all those people-it got mighty hot and terribly stinky in there, I can tell you. They discovered that Leo and I had the wrong paperwork but they also saw we had come from a concentration camp.

"We played dumb and pretended we couldn't speak much English. Initially they were going to send us back to Poland, but I burst into tears and Leo started ranting and raving about the Germans and how they would never have surrendered without the Americans' involvement. *God Bless America!* Then, with a real tear in his eye, Leo started talking about democracy. Of course, neither of us knew much about the United States in those days, but Leo had heard of President Lincoln, the New York Yankees, Mickey Mouse and hotdogs, so he gave them all a mention in a rousing speech. I was crying, Leo was crying, there was all kinds of a hullabaloo and the place was in turmoil.

Everyone joined in. *Let them in for God's sake, haven't they been through enough already?* There was uproar so the customs people gave in. It would have been chaos otherwise. Someone shook our hands and said, 'Welcome to the United States of America' then stamped our documents. It was that simple!"

***

At eleven o'clock that night after everyone had gone, Stella found Anna alone in the kitchen washing up, a thoughtful, far-away look on her face. Stella finally thought she had an opportunity to ask Anna why she had been acting so strangely recently, but just as they started to talk Joe stumbled in, and it was clear that he was still feeling sentimental. He crept up behind his wife and put his hands around her waist then gave her a big sloppy kiss on the neck.

They were still smooching when they finally said goodnight to Anna half an hour later. Joe had to virtually shove her out of the door and despite Stella's concern for her friend, Joe would have none of it. The women could talk tomorrow. Right now, there was some men's business that needed taking care of.

No sooner had the door closed than Joe started to manoeuvre his wife towards the bedroom. Stella had no choice but to give in, so she agreed to leave the rest of the clean up until morning and go to bed with her adoring, drunk husband. By the time she got undressed and slipped between the sheets Joe was almost asleep. He farted, and said, "Was that you?" Before she could reply he was gone-snoring like a locomotive with a smug, self-satisfied grin plastered over his face. It had been a great night and a memorable party, but it was going to pale into insignificance when the events of the next day emerged.

4

Anna had been forced to retire from Paterson Manor when she reached the grand old age of seventy. However, she was invited to return a short while later, when management decided, in their wisdom, to set up a library trolley service. They needed reliable volunteers to run it, and there was only one person to approach. It saved Anna's life, or so she claimed, because she could not cope being around Leo so much. He was still driving his cab but only did local runs a couple of days a week, so he was home and under her feet more often than not. Anna claimed to be near suicidal after the second week, so the phone call about the new library trolley was indeed a godsend.

Anna felt as if she had been away on vacation. The smell of disinfectant in the hallways, the lack of air-conditioning in summer and the clawing damp of the old grey stone building in winter; Anna loved it all. There was no doubt about it: even though Anna had only been gone a few weeks, Liberty Wing had not been the same without her. '*Part of the furniture*' was how she was described when the shift manager spoke at her farewell, and '*you should always keep quality furniture*' was what she said a few weeks later when Anna returned.

***

"Oh no! Not again! Who left the goddam locker room open?" This statement was quickly followed by, "Oh Jesus Christ all mighty, that old bitch has gone too far this time!" Stella made a beeline for the room and stood mesmerised at the door. One of the other auxiliaries, Sharron Ward, was holding a bright red purse between her thumb and forefinger at arm's length. Her face was scrunched up in disgust as a small stream of brackish liquid trickled from the bottom corner.

The doors on several of the lockers were open (unusual, as they should all have been locked), and dear old Joan Nevin, the resident from room three, was sitting at the table in her nightgown, looking decidedly shifty.

At the subsequent enquiry, no one admitted responsibility for failing to lock the staffroom. This was typical of the staff at Paterson Manor-refusing to be accountable when things went wrong. "I be paid to clean, not to t'ink," a Jamaican cleaner said when questioned about the incident. "Anyway, what she doin' wid a bag like dat at a place like dis? Ain't no fashion show here."

The cleaner was right, of course, but Sharron Ward wanted the whole world to know that she had a relationship with money-through her ex-husband. She claimed not to have to work, *but a woman has to do something useful with her time, now doesn't she?* Her wage provided a little fun money, and her frequent trips to Vegas and the old lop-sided Cadillac she parked in the car park every day were indeed confirmation that she may once have had money to burn. Problem was, she appeared to be running a little short on fire-starters right now but did not care to admit it.

Sharron often made mention of her property in fashionable Tribeca-part of her divorce settlement, she said- and she was only renting residential space above someone's garage in Jersey on a temporary basis. Her loft was being renovated and she would soon be moving back in. At least, that's what she said two years ago, and as far as everyone at work was concerned, it must have been one hell of a renovation! Sharron arrogantly walked around the hallways and public areas as if she owned them, her nose in the air, jet-black hair (it had to be a wig) and a heavily powdered face with beady eyes and a puckered mouth that looked like a dog's rectum covered in red lipstick.

***

The Paterson Manor Rest Home had new owners in 1995. They promised to redecorate and get rid of the dreadful flaking pale green paint that had been on the walls since the place was built in the 1942. Most of the floors were covered in cracked grey linoleum that had been continuously repaired over the years, and it was hard to find a bathroom without damp or mould in at least one corner of the ceiling. The new owners introduced a Charter and what they called a Mission Statement, both neatly framed and hanging in the foyer at reception where they were ignored by everyone.

Most of the staff went about their work with a reasonable amount of care and consideration, some more diligently than others. However, Sharron Ward had a spiteful streak, and there were times when she went a little too far with the old folks in Liberty Wing; but she always seemed to escape scrutiny. She managed to hang on to her job because, as she rightly often said, "Who else would do such work for under fifteen bucks an hour?"

An incident happened a while ago, when Sharron was changing Joan Nevin's diaper. Just as the soiled garment was removed, Mrs Nevin realised she had not completely emptied her bladder, and she had no control whatsoever over that particular bodily function. The unfortunate mishap resulted in Sharron having to change her own uniform, Joan's nightdress and the bed. Dealing with such matters outside the documented weekly routine did not sit well with Sharron Ward, and neither did the smell of urine.

The language that came from room three at the time was certainly not mentioned in the company Charter, and the old lady was in tears by the time Anna checked to see what the fuss was all about. Anna later discovered several nasty bruises on Joan Nevin's upper right arm, which, according to Sharron Ward, were the result of a misunderstanding when *the stupid old biddy almost fell in the shower.*

It was a few days later when Mrs Nevin seemed to have mistaken the staff locker room for the toilet, though why she might have chosen Sharron Ward's brand new, bright red leather Coach purse to urinate in was a mystery to some folks at Paterson Manor ... but not everyone.

***

"I heard, I heard what she did!" A cackle came from the hallway as a gangling stork of a man loped into the room as Anna tucked Joanie into bed. "Wonderful news! I saw it on CNN just now! Been naughty again have we, old girl? They said it was a damned good shot too, bullseye first go!" And he made the sound of a bomb falling from a great height.

During his first month at Paterson Manor, Les Howell had been found in bed with three different, very confused old ladies on three separate occasions. The next week he was found in a compromising position with yet another female resident, who seemed far less concerned than the other women. She vehemently refused to let him leave until she had been given *a darned good seeing to*—her words not his, as disclosed in the incident report that was waiting to be reviewed by a visiting clinical psychologist. Mr Howell claimed it was all a misunderstanding and he was having problems with his orientation. Anyway, he was far from capable of giving any woman a 'good seeing to', though he did admit to being willing to try.

Most of the residents at the nursing home were from middle-class backgrounds, their fees coming from limited personal resources and supplemented by generous families. A few dollars a month was a small price to pay to keep the irritating old relics at bay.

The loneliest of them spent their time staring into the garden looking for lost memories and past loves, while others pretended to read their newspapers or do crossword puzzles, but they too were lost in the moment. Among them were the card players and jigsaw assemblers, the chatterboxes and gossipmongers, the quiet types who enjoyed knitting or painting by numbers, the sparky women like Joanie Nevin and boisterous old men like Les Howell. They were a mixed bunch and Anna loved them all, and they all loved her. She never failed to find time to chat or help look for a dropped stitch or missing piece of jigsaw. She willingly sat and watched their soaps with them and loved to listen to stories about happier times. No one seemed to have a bad word to say about Anna. No one that is, apart from the new resident in room twenty-four, Pawel Michalik, who went by the name of Polak.

5

Pawel Michalik had survived life inside a concentration camp for the last two years of World War II, when the extermination of the Jews was at its height. It seemed that he was a hero of some repute, and he loved to talk of his exploits to anyone willing to listen, though it was not unusual for his frail audience to fall asleep as he droned on about the hardship and misery of those terrible years.

After the initial excitement of having a war hero in their midst died down, most residents gave Polak a wide berth. He was hard work, a little too brittle and full of himself for most folks' liking, so he eventually gravitated back to his bedroom and spent most of his days in bed, where he continued to research his memoirs.

Polak did, however, make an effort to appear at dinner sometimes, because he knew he had a captive audience. Apart from his ego, his other regular companion was a silver hip flask; his so-called survivor reviver. Having alcohol in an unapproved receptacle was strictly forbidden at Paterson Manor, and Polak was convinced the staff had no idea about his cunningly concealed tipple. He was wrong-they knew, but they chose to ignore it. The shift manager wanted to cut Polak some slack; not only was he a war hero but his file also mentioned possible dementia and onset of early memory loss.

Polak was new to the New Jersey area, having previously been living with his family in a large home in an exclusive part of Florida. It was not clear how or why he came to reside in a damp, dilapidated old nursing home at Paterson, given that Florida was considered the retirement capital of America. It was put down to a matter of finance, and people wrongly supposed that he could no longer afford the good life in the Sunshine State.

Within days of Michalik's arrival at Paterson Manor, an article about his concentration camp experiences was circulated by management, who considered it might be of interest to other residents. The story had appeared in the *Florida Times* several months prior, complete with photographs and the modest headline of 'Concentration Camp Hero.'

Polak claimed to have been a hard-working factory hand when he was detained by the Germans, and the newspaper said he was a Polish Jew. Sharron Ward was quick to point out to interested parties that according to his medical records Pawel Michalik was not circumcised. "Perhaps his parents were not practising Jews," she concluded.

Despite his decline into old age, there was still something distinguished and authoritative about Michalik, and you could tell that if it weren't for his failing health, he would still have what could be described as a military bearing.

He barely moved his lips when he spoke, making people concentrate when listening, which in turn made him feel important. His complexion had become grey and sallow, almost corpse-like at times, and if ever a young child happened to visit a relative in Liberty Wing they either gawped at him from a distance or ran away scared-usually the latter.

Anna avoided him as much as she could, and when Stella said she had noticed that he always sat with his back to the wall and seemed to stare a lot, Anna secretly watched for a day or two and realised her friend was right. Being in Polak's presence became quite unsettling for some.

The Florida newspaper had stated that Polak's amazing story would be told in two parts and in the following week's edition there he was again, holding a document that he had apparently rescued from a smouldering pile of records the German guards were attempting to destroy prior to liberation. Polak claimed to have obtained the document by stealth, and it held not only a grainy picture of his haunted face when he first arrived at the camp, it also detailed his town of origin, hair colour, complexion and so on. His occupation was for some reason shown as 'clerk,' not 'factory worker.' The document was over-stamped with the word *Juden,* in ominously large block letters.

According to Ellen Randolph, the freelance journalist who wrote the article for the *Florida Times,* Polak's time in captivity had been spent at a camp called Wysznica, one of the service arms to the giant Auschwitz-Birkenau complex in Poland. Wysznica supplied timber, lime, gravel and, more significantly, labour. Research confirmed that Wysznica was not much different from many other camps at the time, a place designed for the punishment of enemies of the Reich, intellectuals, artists, the occasional prisoner of war, Gypsies and homosexuals. As the war deepened and Hitler's 'Final Solution' solidified, Wysznica tripled in size to help cope with the massive influx of European Jews. Just like Auschwitz, Wysznica became a death camp.

Pawel Michalik said he was at the camp when thousands of Hungarian Jews started to arrive. He proudly boasted that he was not at all like them; in so much as they met their fate *silently and ignorantly, without so much as a struggle.* He took the self-appointed role of 'agitator' in an attempt to disrupt the Germans as much as possible, and stay alive in the process.

Michalik said he hid among the daily hordes of arrivals, ducking and weaving his way around the camp, sleeping in a different hut every night, avoiding roll call whenever he could, doing whatever it took to stay alive. He became an expert at making sure he was never in the wrong place at the wrong time, though admitted to knowing his luck probably would have run out eventually. "The Germans had too much to handle," he was quoted as saying. "In the end there were just too many prisoners. For every one thousand who were sent to the gas chambers, another two thousand arrived the next day. It was not hard to lose yourself amongst the masses, if you had a mind to."

Michalik said he spent every waking hour sabotaging his captors' efforts. It was highly dangerous work, but he did *whatever it took* to slow the German killing machine. At least he had been able to give some of his fellow Jews time to breathe a little longer, even if only for a few hours.

"God in his infinite wisdom had deserted the Jews at Wysznica," Polak said in the article. "He left us to our own devices, to die with his name on our lips. Maybe he forgot us? I decided that He was going to hear my voice in that pit of misery." He went on to claim that before the camp was liberated, he killed several of the guards who had made his life so miserable. "It was time for a little payback," he said.

After the second article was published, several national dailies picked up the story and ran features, and even CBS's *60 Minutes* started poking around to see if there was a segment there for them. It was all evidenced by the little stash of press cuttings, letters and documents Polak proudly passed around the dinner table a few weeks after his arrival. His fame had spread far and wide.

However, out of the blue one day, Ellen Randolph received a mysterious letter from Poland that cast doubt on the validity of Polak's story. Ellen did what any good journalist would do-she started digging. The first thing she did was visit her subject again to ask a few more questions. She was not without experience, so she hid behind the possibility of a further article with even more in-depth revelations. However, her tactic failed and when Miss Randolph arrived for the meeting, Pawel Michalik's children told her he had suddenly decided to go on a trip back to his old haunts in Europe, for old time's sake, and they had no idea when he was going to return. Ellen did not believe them. Michalik was far too frail to travel from Florida to Poland without someone by his side, yet they said he was travelling alone, and for an undisclosed period of time ... Impossible.

A little more digging confirmed that there was no trace of anyone with the name of Michalik leaving the United States by ship or aircraft during the last three months. The mystery deepened. Where was he, and more importantly, why had he disappeared?

The chase was on. If only Miss Randolph knew the real story behind Pawel Michalik's life, she would have sold her soul for the scoop-it was going to set the whole world talking. However, it was not the ambitious young journalist from Florida who wrote the last page of Polak's story; it was a seasoned campaigner from the *New York*

Times who produced the words that summed the whole thing up: *Pawel Michalik's life is so amazing, I doubt that even Stephen King or John Grisham could have come up with a story like this!*

6

Stella was still laughing at Joan Nevin pissing in Sharron's purse that morning when she noticed the old lady smiling. Joanie was a consummate giggler, with red-rimmed, bright blue watery eyes that still showed the mischief that had kept her husband captivated until he died shortly after his ninety-fourth birthday. Joan raised a frail, almost claw-like hand and twitched her index finger, indicating that Stella should come closer. "What is it, Joanie? What do you want?"

The old lady's whispered words floated through the air on unseen butterfly wings. "She deserved it!"

"Who deserved what, dear? Are you talking about Sharron?"

"Yep. That nasty Sharron bitch. She has always hated me, but I got her this time, eh? I got her real good and she don't know the worst of it yet!" The comment was followed by a wicked, cackling laugh. Stella asked herself what could be worse than someone urinating in your purse?

"Just you wait till she puts her shoes on tonight," the old lady continued. "Wait till she takes those dirty old trainers off and slips her stinking corn-encrusted feet into them fancy new shoes of hers!" Sharron Ward had also purchased a pair of expensive-looking ankle boots, and she took them to work that very morning with her new purse to show everyone. They were made from bright red, patent leather and suede, a perfect match for the Coach bag.

The frail old lady leaned forward and told Stella her secret. "The left shoe."

"What, dear? What about the left shoe? What on earth are you talking about, Joanie?" Stella looked at Mrs Nevin's face and immediately wished she had not asked the question.

"I couldn't help myself; it had to be done, so I took a dump in those brand-new shoes of hers-the left one, like I said. I laid that turd myself, I did, just before I got caught piddling in her purse!" The old lady hunched her bony shoulders and her head sunk between her collarbones as she bobbed up and down, giggling about her disgusting secret like a naughty child; which was exactly what she was and always had been.

Stella screamed with a mixture of shock and delight. "Oh, my good God, Joanie! You are incorrigible! I wish you hadn't told me that!"

***

A few minutes later Stella was in the staff lunchroom hoping to bump into Anna to tell her about Joan Nevins latest act of revenge. If anything was going to break the ice between Stella and Anna, the story about Joanie crapping in Sharron Ward's posh new shoes would do it!

Stella hummed 'That's Amore' to herself as she took a mug from the cupboard above the sink, and popped a spoonful of instant coffee into it. Then she opened the refrigerator and took out the leftover cake she had brought from home that morning. It was as she waited for the kettle to boil that the whole dreadful business began.

It started with a shout so loud that it sent every bird outside into the air;

in the building, people's words froze on their lips.

It was a man shouting. No doubt about it. Loud and very angry. Stella immediately ran into the hallway to see where the ruckus was coming from. It was room twenty-four, Polak's room.

"Don't do it! Put that down, you Polish bitch or you'll live to regret it. Put it down I tell you!" The little hairs on Stella's arms stood on end and she sprinted towards room twenty-four and burst in, unannounced.

The first thing she saw was Polak sitting upright in bed, still in his pyjamas, visibly shaking. His mouth appeared to be stuck open and a string of saliva stretched from the top set of his dentures to the bottom. His nostrils were flared and his skin was deathly white. The room smelled strongly of urine and for once Polak's eyes were completely still, as round as saucers, fixed onto someone standing in front of him, at the end of his bed.

Stella followed his gaze, that was when she saw Anna and the gun for the first time. Strangely, Anna never moved when Stella entered the room;

she did not take her eyes from Polak for a single moment. It was as if she was expecting Stella to appear. Stella did not know at the time, but she learned later that the gun Anna was holding was a Luger, standard issue to the SS during World War II. For all she knew it could have been a toy, but judging by Polak's expression and the problem Anna appeared to have with the weight of the thing, it most definitely was real.

Anna spoke quietly to Stella, over her shoulder, as if she knew by instinct who had just entered the room. "It's him, Stell. I knew it was him all along."

"What do you mean *him?*" Stella asked.

"Him. Polak! The Greyhound! He is Polak *and* the Greyhound, don't you see? He's one and the same person." Anna was speaking in riddles.

Polak intervened, his voice faltering. "Now why don't you put the gun down? I am a war hero and if you kill me you will have gained nothing, and you will go to prison for the rest of your life."

Anna waved the gun around and started to laugh,-a lunatic's laugh that frightened Stella as much as the weapon. "I *have* been in prison, you stupid old fool, since January 1940!"

Stella said, "What's this all about, Anna? Can't you put the gun down? I'm scared, Anna, please. Do it for me, put the gun down."

Polak seemed to relax a little, and he shuffled into a more comfortable position and pulled the sheets around him. His chest rose and fell inside his pyjama jacket and his eyes had now narrowed to a squint. His lips curled upwards at both ends, as if he was mocking Anna.

Stella's heart was thumping. Beads of sweat formed on her top lip and her palms were damp with perspiration. Why was Anna pointing a gun at Polak? She would not have a clue how to use it; but she did look very determined. "Please, Anna, please put the gun away. Surely we can sort this out. Whoever Polak is, he's not worth this, is he?"

"Oh, you are so wrong, Stell. He's worth it alright; he is worth every single moment, and more." Tears started to trace their way down Anna's beautiful cheeks and she wiped her face with her sleeve. Then for some reason she suddenly froze, as if an idea had just popped into her head. Then she sniffed loudly and blinked her eyes a couple of times, bracing herself for a decision just made. Surely she wasn't going to do this, she was not going to actually pull the trigger, was she?

In one deliberate movement, almost in slow motion it seemed, Anna raised and fully extended her right arm—a firm grip on the weapon, her hand no longer shaking. She deliberately rested her chin on her collarbone and with one eye shut, squinting down the length of her arm to the sights on the far end of the gun which she appeared to line up with Polak's head ... then she flicked the safety switch off with her thumb.

PART 2:
KILL AND
CAPTURE

7

9 January 1940
Zwinbrzych, Poland

The killing was easy according to the German soldiers travelling through Poland after the blitzkrieg of 1 September 1939. They had been discussing it during the journey as they bounced and rattled along the bleak grey landscape towards the German border and the Polish villages beyond. The general consensus was that once you had started, it was difficult to stop killing. The first time was the hardest, after that it was *like shooting rats in a bucket'*, someone said, and everyone laughed at the analogy because rats was exactly what Minister Goebbels called the Jews and the Poles.

The SS were surprised by the lack of resistance during the second wave, and they paid no mind to the fact that they were only dealing with peasant farmers and their families, not trained army personnel. It was so easy being involved in the clean up, running behind the elite storm troopers after they had bulldozed their way into Warsaw like an unstoppable machine just a few weeks before. Everyone was so proud to be German.

And now they were mopping up, dealing with petty local government officials and making lists—always the interminable lists. Every single matter had to be documented and rubber-stamped because it would ultimately be lodged with Berlin. The Fuhrer had stated that he wanted things recorded because they were making history. They had been told they were invincible and the way everything was collapsing before them, it seemed that they were.

No one had said how many phases there were before victory, but it was becoming clear that there would be many. The quicker they got on with the job in hand, the sooner the war would be over. Things had to be done swiftly in this second phase as well; the SS were told to deal with the petty objections and silly complaints (there would be many people upset by the changes) and not let anything or anyone stand in the way.

Berlin came up with the excellent idea of using prisoners for labour, saving German troops for exactly what they had signed up to do-fight for the Fatherland. Conquered lands provided many resources, and from what had been seen of Poland so far, the Fuhrer was right-the Poles would be good for labour but not much else. They were a step above the Jews, but it was a small step.

Having plenty of time during the long journey, the men in the truck covered a variety of subjects, and their mood was buoyed even more when they talked of the perks associated with the 'second wave.' You inevitably received the best accommodations, for instance, especially if you were an officer. Also, it was good to have a friend in the Gestapo because that would speed things along, and there was nothing better than taking over an apartment that had recently been vacated by some rich Jew, because they always had the finest properties and inevitably left good quality possessions behind. They were only allowed to take whatever they could carry, which was very much to the benefit of the incoming occupant.

The biggest issues associated with the second wave were resources and time. It was typical of Berlin, the home of faceless bureaucrats who filled in the detail between the lines of the Fuhrer's speeches; they had no idea of the practical problems that those on the ground had to face every day. At least there were very few operational rules. Sure enough, everything had to be documented and reported and there were audits, checks and balances, but you had the scope to do what you needed to do to get the job done. It was as simple as that and those were the orders. Get it done!

And that is where the killing came in. You had no choice sometimes, or else you would have fallen behind and then there *would* be hell to pay. If someone caused an unnecessary delay they had to be dealt with then and there so you could move on to the next objective. That was all that mattered.

Rolf Schroder, being the most senior German in the truck, talked about correspondence he had received regarding problems some of the younger SS recruits were having despatching large groups-shooting unarmed old people and children hour after hour could get a bit galling for some. The matter was gaining traction in Berlin after the lodgement of a great many field operational reports. Instead of telling his troops to 'harden up' and do their duty, Reichsfuhrer Himmler, who was in command of the SS, and even Obersturmbannfuhrer Eichmann (commander of all camps) were looking at different methods of despatch to ease concerns.

It was clear that volume was going to increase as news of the establishment of ghettos to temporarily house Jews spread. There was even talk about founding an adult euthanasia program to help work out the practical issues associated with such matters. Everyone felt reassured that Berlin took their concerns seriously.

Russian prisoners of war and Polish dissidents were dispatched quickly because they were potentially the most disruptive. Despite their obviously dire circumstances, for some ridiculous reason they still had fire in their bellies. It was clear that the harder you hit the troublemakers the more stubborn they became, the fools. There were more Jews than all the others put together, but fortunately they were so passive and compliant that it was easy to manage them. They had been bullied and downtrodden, systematically beaten and dehumanised to such an extent that they even agreed to police themselves!

Those that were chosen were formed into groups of Kapos-trusted prisoners-to maintain discipline among their own kind. The Germans had to laugh when they discussed the fact that the Kapos would willingly beat anyone with a yellow Star of David on their sleeve! It was the genius Adolf Eichmann who worked out exactly how these people ticked long before they were moved into their ghettos. They never put up a fight; they stood to attention when they were told to, worked until they could work no more, dug their own graves and even filled in the ones around them before it was their turn to be shot. It could not have been easier. If only there were not so many of them!

Mind you, there was no sport in dealing with the Jews according to some SS; where was the chase, the hunt? The lack of combat made it boring, so the troops had to keep focussed using whatever means they could. It was hard to have respect for an enemy who did not fight back.

Karl Braun was the one who expressed most concern about the 'lack of sport.' The others in the truck that day had already seen him in action and did not doubt that he enjoyed killing. Sometimes it showed in his eyes-they seemed to glaze over when the shooting started. But it was good having him around. You could get on with your day when you had the Greyhound at your side.

8

The early morning sun was trying to announce its arrival through naked trees and a slate-coloured sky. A heavy frost coated the grass and a layer of ice crunched under the tyres as the truck lurched through frozen mud and potholes. Rolf Schroder stared into the beginnings of yet another bleak Polish winter day. He hated Poland with its grey skies and insipid landscape. The night before he had met with the argumentative mayor of a large town, eventually got the names he needed and rested there for the night. Before he departed the next morning, he decided to leave an example of why it was best not to argue with the SS at such times. The example was hanging from a tree outside the town hall. In fact, there were three such examples.

Then it was time for a one-hour drive through narrow back roads to the tiny village of Zwinbrzych, ten kilometres inside the German-Polish border.

Schroder allowed himself the briefest of smiles. Life as a second lieutenant in the SS had not turned out to be as bad as he or his parents originally feared. There was no frontline fighting for him. The dice seemed to have rolled his way and he was confident that if he kept his nose clean, he could sit the war out and return to a normal life, all the better for the experience when the conflict was over.

***

Lez Burczyk lifted his aching body out of bed, stretched and walked bare foot across the cold floorboards to the window. His breath hovered in front of him, a light cloud of yet unspoken words as he pulled the hessian curtains aside to reveal another freezing morning. It had been a long winter so far, an eventful time but for all the wrong reasons. The German invasion, long talked about and feared, excruciatingly fast in its execution, had heralded the year in, in the worst possible way.

Usually at this time of the year Lez was thinking about spring and the coming season's planting. But spring was still two months away and two months could be a very long period of time when so many people depended on you, and your fate was in someone else's hands.

Lez, who was now almost in his eighties, had been born in that house, and his father before him. Generations came and went and now the house was home to Lez and his wife Zlota and their daughter Roza, whose two teenage girls Danuta and Ania were with them. The place was crowded once more and worse for Lez; it was crowded with women! That was one of the reasons he broke with family tradition and made sure he was first up at daybreak-for the peace and quiet of an early start.

Roza had been a wild one, the worst of Lez and Zlota's five children, and she brought shame to the family in the worst possible way. She had been living with her husband Lech (a lazy, good-for-nothing loser, like most of the men from Lublin, according to Lez) and their first child Danuta on a rented smallholding in the middle of nowhere, somewhere just outside Lodz. When

Roza announced that she was pregnant for the second time Lech did not greet the news with much joy. Another mouth to feed. It had better be a boy this time; at least when he grew up he could help on the farm. As a family they got by, but only just, and they would now lose the income they had from their lodger, whose room would soon be needed for the expanding family.

Lech was going to miss the lodger. The two men regularly played cards or chess and drank together most nights-Lech and the quietly spoken farrier who stayed longer than originally envisaged, after they had been introduced by a friend at the market. The farrier had an odd look about him, the look of a Gypsy perhaps, with long black curly hair and different-coloured eyes. It was hard to work out if he was shifty or exotic (men at the market thought he was shifty but their women said he was exotic). But what did it matter? He could drink with the best and laugh when caught cheating at cards. He was able to supplement his income with a bit of horse-trading on the side and always paid his rent on time. More often than not he would do little jobs around the house too, jobs that Lech never got around to because he was either too busy or too drunk. The small amount of money the lodger brought in and the help he provided soon made him indispensable.

But the farrier was told that he would have to leave soon after the new baby's arrival. However it transpired that he left far quicker than anyone expected-a few hours after the baby was born, in fact. Lech left also, ten minutes later-in pursuit of the lodger.

Lech caught up with him on the outskirts of Lodz and almost beat him to death, then went back home, punched Roza in the face, packed a bag and had not been heard from since. Roza took her two children back to her parent's farm in Zwinbrzych, reverted to her maiden name and got on with life as a single parent.

The new baby, Ania, became quite a novelty in the small market town; after all, it was not every day that you saw a child with jet-black curly hair, one blue eye and one brown in a Polish farming community.

As she matured and moved into her teens, Ania's beauty became more and more apparent. She definitely did not have the same look about her as most of the gangly, blonde-haired, blue-eyed farm girls who attended the local school. While it was thought by some that she was carrying a little prepubescent puppy fat, it soon became evident that this was not the case. Ania had been blessed with the voluptuous body and ravishing looks of a Gypsy Queen and that gave her a real edge when it came to the boys, but she spent more time warding them off than encouraging them.

Danuta, Ania's elder sister by two years, was very much like her mother—a real Polish girl. Her hair was cropped and blonde, her face long and her nose noble. Her legs appeared to start beneath her armpits, and she had the slim, wiry look of an athlete. She was clearly destined for great things in the sporting arena, but she could also hold her own in the classroom, just like Ania, especially when it came to languages. The two girls were inseparable.

Danuta was by far the most experienced when it came to matters of the heart. By the time she turned nineteen she had already been in love twice and had long forgotten when she lost her virginity and who took it. Somehow, Ania had managed to preserve hers, but at the age of seventeen she was under great pressure from several suitors, two of whom were fathers of her friends. For the time being, she preferred listening to her sister's exploits as the two of them lay in bed talking late into the night.

Neither girl was afraid of a bit of hard work and they did more than their fair share around their grandfather's farm. They were strong limbed and equally strong willed, and no one messed with the Burczyk girls, and those who dared try always ended up worse-especially the boys.

While Danuta could be stubborn, Ania was always the realistic one, though she had a flippant side that they said could one day get her in trouble. Lez and Zlota thanked God for blessing them with such delightful grandchildren, while at the same time they cursed their daughter Roza for the shame and hardship she had brought upon them and herself. At the end of the day, though, family was family, and the whole family was as close as dirt on a shovel. Lez felt truly blessed.

***

Working on the land had taken its toll on Lez over the years. Growing sugar beet had been the centre of his universe for as long as he could remember. But now? Things seemed to be changing on a daily basis and the Germans had already imposed strict dietary regulations in Poland.

Polish citizens were now limited to six hundred and fifty-four calories a day, about twenty-five per cent of the normal recommended intake, and Jews were permitted only one hundred and eighty-four calories. Audits were threatened, rationing imposed and the majority of food grown by farmers like Lez was taken for the German army. And that was why he was certain they were safe. Why would the Germans do anything to harm farmers who were working hard to feed their lords and masters? The gossip at the village market made no sense.

***

Lez pulled a patchwork quilt around his shoulders then turned and left his thoughts at the window. He puzzled for a moment at a noise somewhere in the distance outside. It sounded metallic, a clatter almost, and he put it down to the locks and chains on the barn door, which often rattled for no apparent reason. He made yet another mental note to look at them soon.

Zlota mumbled something in her sleep when Lez returned to the bedroom, and he stood by the bed staring affectionately at the woman who had been his wife since she turned fifteen. He had been only sixteen himself when they married. A life of hard work had taken its toll, but she had been a good wife and a wonderful mother to his children, an even better grandmother. Other men in the village (who Lez drank and played chess with from time to time) constantly cursed their wives, but he could find no real reason to complain about his Zlota-no matter how strong the vodka or how late the hour!

Zlota was an excellent cook and like all Polish women, she ruled indoors. She had a hard side that was not unusual in Polish women, and together, she and Lez had done alright, better than many thought when they first got together all those years ago, that was for sure.

As always, the gossips at the market had Zlota in a panic and she had not had a decent night's sleep since first hearing of the German invasion. Lez had to work hard to reassure her that they would be fine. It was the Jews they were after. "Poland has been invaded before and probably will be again, and all things considered, Hitler needs people like us to feed his army," he said, not for the first time. Here was an opportunity to make some money at last, albeit out of someone else's misfortune, but such was life.

Lez permitted himself a little smile as he made his way into the kitchen and remembered the conversation over dinner the night before. Zlota was full of doom as usual and had ruined the bigos for the second time that week! He put more timber into the stove, blew until a flame rose up and engulfed it, then placed a saucepan of water on top. The sun had been up less than thirty minutes but there was enough light for him to be able to see what he was doing. Zlota's arthritis was worse in winter, so Lez was happy to take his wife a hot cup of tea while she took her time to get out of bed and start her day.

He was looking forward to the day passing quickly. At seven o'clock that night he and some other men from the village would gather at his cousin's house and play chess, talk of politics, sport, the invasion, smoke and drink homemade vodka. This was his favourite time of the week because it was *his* time, away from the women.

As he sat at the old wooden table engulfed in the quilt that Zlota had hand sewn for him on their tenth wedding anniversary, he heard the rattling noise from outside again. This time he was certain it was not the chains on the barn door. It was too loud and too mechanical, as if a vehicle had just arrived at the front of the house.

The sound of a door slamming confirmed he was right.

Lez did not know anyone who had a car. In fact, the only time anyone had ever visited him in a vehicle of any kind was when some local government officials came to confirm his annual sugar beet quota a few days ago. Maybe they had come back for more information or perhaps there was a question they had failed to ask. But they would not do it just after dawn. They would come during office hours-unless, of course, there was a problem.

Lez rose from the table as he heard two sets of heavy boots tramp down the pathway towards the cottage. By the time he was halfway down the hall someone was already knocking at the door.

Lez had lived in the village of Zwinbrzych all his life. He went to the big city of Krakow occasionally, to the markets and apart from his spell in the army he had only ever heard Polish spoken. And now, as he hurried towards the front door for the very last time that morning, he heard a German voice. "Offnen. Open up, schnell, hurry up now, schnell!"

9

The damned door stuck like it always did in winter and when Lez finally managed to wrench it open, he was confronted by a German soldier pointing a rifle at his chest and another holding a clipboard. Lez froze in the moment.

The one with the clipboard appeared to be in charge, though he looked more like a pale civil servant than a commanding officer in the German army. "Herr Burczyk?" Lez nodded in reply. The German with the list was full of his own importance, standing there with his pencil, ticking off names, trying not to let Lez see that his ungloved right hand was shaking from the cold.

It was the skinny one, the one with the rifle that Lez did not like the look of. The cold would not bother him; he looked as if he enjoyed a spot of trouble and his deep set, black eyes confirmed it. Lez felt that with a bit of luck and the element of surprise, he could take them both if he had to, despite his age. But in the background, smoking cigarettes at the rear of the truck he spotted two more armed SS. He knew he had no choice other than to cooperate. As the freezing air sneaked into the hallway and rushed past him, Lez stood patiently waiting for the one in charge to speak again. It was one of those lingering moments that seemed to last forever but in reality was over and done within a matter of seconds.

When the German did speak, there was a level of indifference in his tone, and even though Lez had no idea what he said, the hackles rose on the back of his neck. He had no time to think because he was instantly stunned by the deafening roar of a gun discharging, which was followed immediately by a blinding light as something exploded in his chest, sending him crashing backwards. He slid to the floor, leaving the remains of his life on the wall behind him in the form of a thick red smudge.

The two Germans stepped over the inconvenience that was Lez's body and advanced down the bare hallway, striding purposefully towards the door at the far end.

The sudden disturbance had woken Zlota from a deep sleep, and the frightening sound of a gunshot echoing in the small hallway had her springing upright and staring at the bedroom door. And now the water in the glass on her bedside table trembled as heavy footsteps shook the floorboards on the approach to her room. Two men burst in and she instinctively pulled the bed sheet up under her chin to protect her modesty. There was the briefest of eye contact, but when Zlota turned her gaze to the open door she saw the bloody body of her husband lying in the hallway beyond.

It was to be the last time she saw him or anything else as death burst out of the skinny soldier's gun for the second time in less than a minute. Zlota lay on the bed, her head split open while the feathers that had been dislodged so violently from her pillow drifted gently through the air and landed softly on her blood-soaked body.

Time was of the essence, and Schroder was frustrated that he could not find the two young girls on his list. The idiot mayor he dragged out of the town hall the previous night was now hanging from the tree in the town square along with two other officials. The mayor had eventually reluctantly provided a list of all the families with girls of the required age in the outlying villages, and for the sake of his own family, he had better have been honest about the names. The Burczyk's were first on the list.

Orders were shouted and the skinny soldier with the gun marched into an adjacent room and moments later another gunshot echoed through the house. Roza's naked body was left draped over the side of her bed like a discarded toy.

One door remained.

Karl Braun burst in and at last discovered seventeen-year-old Ania sitting upright in bed, white faced and shaking. He marched across the room and pulled her out by her hair, screaming. "Rasch, rasch, hurry!" He dragged her down the hallway over the top of her grandfather's lifeless body, through a pool of his blood and dumped her onto the frozen doorstep outside. He then picked up the quilt that was lying next to the old man's body and threw it to where she lay, wide eyed and shivering like a frightened puppy.

The one in charge, the one who Ania would learn later was called Rolf Schroder, double-checked his list-there was one girl missing. As he was about to order a more thorough search he heard a noise from Ania's bedroom. He nodded towards the room, instructing Braun to go back and check. Maybe it was the other girl. *She was holding things up, damn her.*

The skinny soldier moved swiftly into the girls' bedroom, and immediately realised someone was in the wardrobe. It had to be the other girl. He ordered her out. Nothing, though he did hear a noise of some kind. Maybe a whimper. The truck started up outside, so he knew he had to get a move on. He raised his rifle, discharged several rounds into the wardrobe and heard the muffled sound of a body collapsing inside.

A trickle of blood made its way from beneath the corner of the door and started to pool on the timber floor.

Back at the truck Schroder asked what had happened. "She didn't want to come, so..." Braun shrugged in explanation as he climbed into the cab.

"Did you check? Did you confirm it was her?"

"Of course it was her, who else could it be? Anyway, there was plenty of blood."

"Scheisskopf!" Schroder angrily climbed out of the cab and signalled Braun to join him. They needed to know for sure that it was the second girl! No problem if it was-she was hiding, resisting arrest and had to be dealt with-but there would be paperwork and it had to be correct. That was why Schroder was a lieutenant and Braun was just a corporal. The brains and the muscle, it had always been that way, ever since they teamed up in the Hitler Youth.

Schroder approached the wardrobe carefully, his pistol at the ready. He saw the large puddle of blood on the floor beneath the door and slowly opened it. In front of him lay a pile of blood-soaked fur. The family dog! He turned and gave Braun a look of disgust, and out of the corner of his eye he saw the figure of Danuta running across a field towards the forest beyond. "Your rifle, quick!"

Danuta, who never failed to win the one hundred metres in the school athletics competition every year, was no longer running for a trophy—she was running for her life. Her heart was pounding in her chest and her arms pumped by her side as she strained every muscle to get as much distance between her and the house as she could. Several times she nearly slipped on the wet grass but ahead of her, less than fifty metres away now, was the forest and the possibility of somewhere to hide.

With the rifle stock wedged firmly against his right shoulder, Schroder soon had Danuta in his sights. As he flicked the safety catch off" he slowly let a breath out and gently squeezed the trigger.

The loud bang sent birds fluttering up into the sky and at that precise moment Danuta lost her footing and slid on the grass, crashing to the ground in a tangle of arms and legs. She could feel warm blood on her shoulder and raised her head slightly to see just how close the trees were, and then everything went black.

The two soldiers had been watching from the bedroom window. They clearly saw the plume of blood splay into the air as the girl tumbled to the ground, and they also saw her raise her head momentarily, before falling back again.

"*That* is how it's done, scheisskopf!" Schroder said to Braun officiously.

The two men made their way back to the truck. Braun did not like being called shithead. A man had his pride after all, and his eyes were blazing as he jumped up into the cab again. It was typical of Schroder to put him down by shooting the girl himself. He could have dispatched her just as effectively himself, but it seemed that Schroder always had to remind him who was in charge.

Ania had heard the shooting as she lay shivering on the doorstep at the front of the house. She was too frightened and too cold to cry and her mind was now numb with fear as another German grabbed her by the elbow and yanked her to feet, shoving her up into the back of the truck. Her nightmare was to continue as she sat at the tailgate, staring out blankly, sniffing occasionally and blinking rapidly, her grandfather's bloodied quilt around her shoulders and her head full of the frightful sights and sounds she had just witnessed.

The sudden hiss and roar of a flamethrower made her jump, and she saw one of the Germans standing with his legs astride just a few metres from the front door of the house. The weapon suddenly roared to life, spewing a line of burning tar and petrol into her grandparents' home. She watched in horror as the flames licked their way over her grandfather's body and down the hallway like the tongue of an insatiable dragon. Within a minute the whole property was engulfed in flames and the fire feasted greedily on a structure that had stood there for generations.

A few moments later the German soldier put the flamethrower into a metal box on the side of the truck then joined Ania in the back, a look of complete disinterest on his face. He slapped the tailgate twice and the vehicle clanked into gear then started to slowly rattle back towards the road.

Behind Ania lay her past life, a plume of smoke taking her childhood memories up into the cold morning air while the blackened skeletal remains of the building crackled noisily as the fire finished its feast. As tears slipped down her face, she mumbled her sister's name ... *Danuta...*

***

Ania sat sniffing and shaking as the soldier who had used the flamethrower lit a cigarette and stared at his feet. He appeared interested in his left boot all of a sudden, raising it slightly, turning it this way and that and muttering to himself, "Cow's shit, fucking typical of my luck!" Then he stretched his leg forward and scraped the boot onto the floor of the truck until the mess was gone. Satisfied, he then looked at Ania and took a long slow drag on his cigarette.

The truck suddenly lurched forward. Ania and the soldier held on to the tailgate as they rattled and bounced onto the main road, heading towards the next farm on the list. It was not long before they slipped into a gap in a convoy of German army vehicles. The ground shook and small stones bounced onto the grass verge as low loaders carrying tanks and artillery snaked their way east towards Krakow.

Village gossip had proved to be right. Germany was on the move and Hitler's worst threats were now being realised. Great Britain had declared war on Germany and the lives of most people on earth would never be the same again. Either they would be directly affected by the thoughtless indifference of war or they would watch horrified from a distance, unable to grasp the magnitude of what was happening.

The village of Zwinbrzych and its population of two hundred and twenty-six? By that evening, it was no more.

10

Danuta painfully raised herself onto her right side when she regained consciousness. Judging by the silence around her, the Germans had gone. She could smell an unusual copper-like odour coming from the wound on her neck, then a light breeze replaced it with the acrid stench of burning wood and when she looked towards her house all she could see was a pile of smouldering timbers and ash.

Her eyes filled with tears as the events of the last few hours flooded back: the Germans bursting into the house and the noise from the hallway as they shot her grandfather. Then the footsteps; heavy army boots stomping along the wooden floorboards towards the room she shared with her sister-but they stopped at the door of Babcia's bedroom. Muffled voices next, it was hard to be certain, but she knew for sure she heard a scream followed by shooting. Momentary silence. A terrible pause. Then those heavy boots on the floorboards again.

She closed her eyes at the moment when she leapt from her bed and dived into the wardrobe, grabbing the dog, which was still half asleep. Perhaps it was intuition, but her grandma, Babcia, insisted the dog sleep with the two girls that night, and Cabbage had no objections. He was virtually crippled with arthritis and deaf, but he had more than paid his keep on the farm over the years, and he relished the opportunity to enjoy a little comfort and attention. It had been fifteen years since a neighbour turned up with the runt of the litter but Lez could not afford to pay for him. *All we have is vegetables. I can give you cabbages, as many as you can carry in exchange for the mutt.* So the dog was named Cabbage after the currency they used to buy him-a fitting name.

As she stood shaking in the wardrobe that morning, Danuta suddenly realised that Ania was still in bed. Danuta had always been a light sleeper and Ania was the exact opposite-she would sleep through an earthquake. Every morning Danuta was up first, the minute her eyes opened, but her sister loved her bed and liked nothing more than cuddling Cabbage and stealing a few extra minutes of warmth, especially in winter.

The door to the room had burst open just as Danuta pulled the wardrobe door shut behind her. She held it closed with one hand and placed her other over Cabbage's muzzle. She heard the German soldier shouting as he pulled Ania from the bed. The last time she heard Ania's voice was when she screamed as she was dragged down the hallway. Ania, her Ania, was gone and Danuta did nothing to help her.

Danuta waited in the wardrobe for what seemed like an eternity, wondering what to do. There were no more footsteps in the hallway, but she could still hear voices at the front of the house. German voices. Evil voices. As quickly as she could, she clambered out of the bedroom window then realised she had left Cabbage in the wardrobe. She was about return for him when she heard someone making their way towards her bedroom again. She ducked out of sight and moments later heard more gunfire. When she plucked up enough courage to look through the window all she could see was Cabbage's blood seeping under the wardrobe door.

In a daze, she sat back on her heels just outside the window, and then from the front of the house she heard raised voices again. She was still in her nightdress, bare foot, and it was bitterly cold, but her instincts told her it was time to run. Being nimble and athletic was very much to her advantage, and she soon found herself halfway across the field. It was not far to the trees and she could still see the rotting remains of the last few autumn leaves on the grass around her-a pathway of red orange and yellow laid down by the overnight winds, guiding her to safety. But the leaves made the grass slippery, and with the early morning frost and the ever-constant cowpats, it felt as if she was running on ice. More than once she thought she was going to lose her footing and finally she did, at exactly the same moment she heard the crack of a rifle behind her.

Something zipped through the air and she felt a stinging sensation in her shoulder, around the base of her neck just as she skidded on a cowpat. Her feet went up in the air and she fell in a dazed tangle onto the cold damp grass.

She remembered that something in the woods caught her eye, and she raised her head to see what it was-an animal, a deer, more soldiers? Then she felt the terrible pain in her shoulder and passed out.

She had no idea how long she had been lying there, but the sun was higher in the sky when she woke and behind her, her grandparents' house was a blackened, smouldering ruin. The only part still recognisable was the stone chimney.

Then she felt movement. She could hear the pounding of heavy feet on the ground and she was jiggling and shaking in time to the movement. And everything was upside down. *She* was upside down, over someone's shoulder, so it seemed. Then she felt herself being lowered to the ground, heard someone breathing heavily by her side. The pain made her grimace and cry out as she stared up at the canopy of the branches above. It was dark in this place, musty, and the smell of pine needles and mould filled the air. She was now on a blanket of rotting leaves and bracken that prickled through her nightdress. As she tried to turn her head to see who had put her there, an intense pain shot up through her shoulder into her neck again. Then everything went black for the second time that morning.

***

Wherever the truck went that day, the events seemed to follow a similar pattern. They would leave the main road and trundle down a narrow potholed lane towards another farm, and the Germans were greeted by several nervous, enquiring faces. Schroder would be there with his clipboard, accompanied by the skinny Braun, and words would be exchanged in both Polish and German. Whoever was not on the list was liquidated immediately. There was no waiting around, no negotiation, no haggling and certainly no mercy. Women, children, old people, it seemed to matter little to the SS and Ania found herself with her head in her hands all too frequently as the slaughter continued in front of her. It was impossible to drown out the pleading and the inevitable sound of gunfire; the dreadful silence that always followed.

Karl Braun attended to the job at hand with a degree of efficiency and detachment that was as frightening as it was ruthless. He acted no differently than someone at a fairground shooting gallery, but instead of pinging rows of ducks he was killing innocent, unarmed Polish farmers and their families.

He occasionally arrived at the rear of the truck and looked up at Ania as if seeking approval-*look what I just did!* She managed to control her urge to abuse him and he laughed aloud at the expression on her face.

He was complaining of the cold at one point, and after the shooting finished, he went back inside the house, coming out moments later wearing a pair of gloves and throwing several knitted scarves and cardigans into the back of the truck next to Ania, though she could not bring herself to touch them.

At the next stop, Ania watched in horror as Schroder dragged a frail old woman out of her house into the front garden. It was Mrs Paulowski, a well-loved great-grandmother whose family had farmed the same land for over one hundred years. Schroder left the old lady on her knees in the cold and went back into the house, leaving Braun to watch over her. Ania stared at Mrs Paulowski's torn stockings, shaking hands and trembling blue lips, but she could not look her in the eye. Nothing could have prepared Ania for what happened next.

As the old lady knelt and prayed, Braun casually strolled behind her and shot her in the back of the head. A spray of blood arced into the air, the old woman's head jerked violently backwards in recoil and then her whole body slumped forward, legs folding beneath her body as she bled onto the cold ground.

Braun turned and his eyes met Ania's for the briefest of moments. They were darting around somewhere inside his skull; a sparkle of light playing hide and go seek with her emotions as the corners of his mouth curled upwards in a smirk that turned her blood cold. As he walked away, Ania vomited over the back of the tailgate.

The horror was not over, as moments later another German appeared with Mr Paulowski at the front door. The old man managed to break free when he saw his wife's body. He quickly hobbled down the pathway and, shaking visibly, threw himself upon her body. With tears streaming from his eyes he looked into Braun's face and cried like a baby. "Please, please."

For the second time, Braun casually raised his weapon and pulled the trigger. A small red smudge appeared between Mr Paulowski's eyes, and then his mouth seemed to twitch into what was almost a smile of appreciation, before he joined his wife forever.

Ania had seen these dreadful things with her own eyes and if someone had told her the day before that she would be witnessing such atrocities she would never have believed it possible. Until then she thought sin involved telling lies, stealing an apple from a market stall, back chatting her mother, but this? This was beyond sin.

As well as the Paulowski's, Ania knew a lot of the families whose farms and cottages were visited that day. Some she knew from the markets or school, and others her grandparents and mother had gossiped about, mostly fondly, for they were good, honest hard-working Polish farmers. The backbone of the country.

As the journey continued, Ania was joined in the back of the truck by more young women, each ticked off the list on Schroder's clipboard. After the selections, their homes were burned, always with a flamethrower. Several times it was clear that people were still alive inside the buildings, and Ania once witnessed an old man engulfed by flames come crashing through a window. She saw what she could only describe as confusion on his face, and he crouched on the ground in front of her, bent by pain, his clothes still burning, his smouldering skin bleeding and blistered.

The Germans seemed completely unconcerned. They stared at him dispassionately and left him to die where he lay, his blackened limbs painfully moving with the slow jerky actions of an insect while they went about the rest of their important business. It was madness.

When darkness fell and the cold started to creep through the canvas cover at the back of the truck, there were twelve young women inside. Throughout their journey they had hardly spoken or acknowledged one other, each numb with her own thoughts and fears. The only communication between the women had been by way of looks and fearful glances. What was going to happen next? Even when one of the younger girls started to vomit because of motion sickness, nothing was said, but a woman did change seats so she could cradle the girl's head and perhaps provide some comfort.

It had been a harrowing day for the women, and apparently a hard day for the Germans as they pulled up outside yet another farmhouse just after darkness fell, relieved that they could now take a well-earned break.

11

One of the soldiers made his way around the back of the truck, dropped the tailgate and lit a cigarette, which he shared with a colleague who had climbed down from the seat opposite Ania. As the two men talked and smoked, occasionally looking at the women, sometimes smiling, sometimes nodding.

Ania had managed to retain her position at the tailgate all day. The countryside had flashed behind her in a cold grey blur, the main roads choked with military convoys and the blur of diesel fumes. She occasionally saw the bizarre sight of a horse-drawn cart stacked with a family and their possessions, plodding along in line with armoured vehicles; troop carriers and huge cannons towed behind low loaders weighed down with tanks. Despite the nightmare around her, her mind sometimes drifted back to her grandfather's house and her sister. Where was Danuta?

Schroder suddenly appeared by the side of the truck with his now familiar clipboard tucked under his arm. He stopped to speak to Braun then stretched and yawned, straightened his uniform and made his way towards the front door of the farmhouse.

Braun stubbed his cigarette out and tagged along a few paces behind Schroder. The front door opened when they were just a few paces away.

Two people were silhouetted in the yellow light that glowed inside the house. There was a brief exchange before Braun marched back towards the rear of the truck. He spoke to one of the guards and a moment later Ania and the rest of the women found themselves being herded onto the roadside.

Once unloaded, they were moved into a small enclosed area inside a large barn, where several cows stared at them with detached interest.

Ania found herself next to a woman she recognised, a teacher called Emilie. "You taught my sister, Danuta, didn't you?" Ania asked as they shuffled the hay around, trying to make a comfortable place to lay for the night.

"Yes, Danuta was one of mine," Emilie said. "She was gifted in most track and field events, but it was the 100 metres where our hopes lay for her. We thought she could make it to the Olympics one day."

The conversation petered out and the two women snuggled up to each other for warmth, beneath Ania's grandfather's bloodstained quilt. As well as the cold, hunger and thirst were also having an effect on the women, but no one dared approach the Germans to see if there was any food or water available.

One of the guards remained at the open barn door and scouted around for something to sit on. He lit a cigarette and sulked while his three colleagues made themselves comfortable inside the warm farmhouse.

Meantime, Schroder was enjoying the fine beef stew that Mrs Lipchitz had already prepared for her husband Jacob that night. The Lipchitz's sat at one end of the long pine table in the kitchen while Schroder ate alone at the other end, seemingly amused by their presence. Mrs Lipchitz's eyes followed Schroder's spoon as it dipped into the bowl then rose up to his mouth. They followed it back down as he took the next mouthful. What was going to happen when her guest's plate was empty? She had been reading the papers over the last six months-she knew what the Germans thought of the likes of her and her husband.

Mrs Lipchitz decided to offer Schroder a top-up. "More stew, sir, can I offer you more?"

"You can. It is very good indeed." And he smiled as he pushed his bowl forward and spoke to Mr Lipchitz. "Your wife is a very good cook, Mr Lipchitz!" The German's apparently pleasant disposition did nothing to ease the discomfort in the room. "May I ask, what is this meat, Mrs Lipchitz?"

In their anxiety the Lipchitz's replied together, Mr Lipchitz saying 'cow' too quickly and Mrs Lipchitz at the same time saying 'mutton.'

The German laughed. "A moolamb, eh? We don't have them in Germany, but here in Poland with your in-breeding, it does not surprise me!"

He laughed expansively again, while Mr Lipchitz stared harshly at his wife, encouraging her to join in the hilarity and more importantly, to leave him to do the talking.

Braun and the driver were sitting in front of a roaring fire away from the table, eating the cheese and pastries they found in the pantry. They had already taken some outside to their colleague on guard duty at the barn, and at Mrs Lipchitz's suggestion it was agreed that she could take some stale bread and other scraps to the women. "They will need water. They are women. Women need to wash," she said respectfully to the guard, but he waved her away with a sweeping gesture of his arm as he tucked into his plate of food.

Mr Lipchitz managed to lighten the atmosphere by producing a bottle of brandy, which he waved in the air almost joyously. "We do not imbibe ourselves, but we understand the need at times like these, sir. Here, take it. Enjoy it, please. Please."

Schroder took the bottle and opened it, sniffed the contents, poured some into a cup then handed it back to his host. "How do I know you have not put poison in this, Herr Lipchitz?"

"Why would I do such a thing to our new masters, sir? We are supporters of the Fuhrer. Heil Hitler!" His right arm shot out in front of him in the most ridiculous manner, making his wife scowl and Schroder smile.

Schroder slid the cup of brandy across the table towards Mr Lipchitz. "After you, I think."

Mr Lipchitz looked at his wife for support, but she was still fuming over the Hitler salute. It appeared that he had no choice. Schroder signalled him to drink up. "Come on, prost, prost!" The old man looked into the cup, blinked nervously and slowly raised it to his lips. Schroder placed his index finger beneath the cup, tilting it towards Mr Lipchitz's mouth.

The old man gulped the liquid down as instructed. Looks were exchanged then Mr Lipchitz's eyes rolled and he looked up at the ceiling before a fit of coughing overtook him and rendered him helpless. "As I said, we don't drink, sir. We don't use alcohol except for religious or medicinal purposes," he wheezed. The old woman slapped her husband's back a little too hard and he coughed even more. Schroder could not help but laugh.

"Gutte? It is gutte, ya? How do you say ... good, is that it?" Mr Lipchitz nodded between coughs and sips from the glass of water his wife handed him, while Schroder poured himself a large cup of brandy and waved the bottle at his two colleagues.

A quick search of an adjacent room revealed an old Bakelite radio and after twiddling the dial for a moment or two, Schroder managed to tune in to some rousing music. The scratchy sounds of an orchestra broke the tension inside the kitchen, which now seemed to have a cosy yellow glow from both the fire and warmth of the brandy.

Ten minutes later, Schroder appeared at the door of the barn, a second cup of brandy in his hand and a big smile on his face. He told the guard about the brandy, suggesting he go inside and help himself, "Before that pisspot Braun finishes it; but don't be too long!" The guard was gone in a flash and Schroder took the opportunity to survey the women.

He waved his arms around. "Line up now, kommen, line up for me please, ladies!" When he spoke Schroder oozed confidence; he did not have to shout or threaten the women. He was authoritative and they immediately organised themselves into two lines which he walked between on slightly unsteady legs. The women did their best to avoid eye contact, but Schroder stopped occasionally, looked someone up and down then nodded as if he were making their acquaintance at a party.

After having completed his inspection he threw his now empty brandy cup away, removed his pistol from its holster and walked directly towards Ania. She had been jockeyed into a vulnerable position in the front row by several older, much wiser women and she realised she was exposed. Schroder had smiled at her during the inspection and she knew she had caught his eye. Now he was standing in front of her.

"Name?"

"Ania Burczyk." She replied almost too abruptly and shivered visibly as he raised his gun and placed it under her left breast, slowly raising it up and down as if he were assessing the quality. He nodded appreciatively, and then turned his attention to her face. "You have strange eyes, Ania Burczyk. One blue and one brown. You have feline eyes."

She stared at her feet and ignored his comment.

"I like that. I like that a lot. Now! It is time to do your duty for your country, my little Polish pussy cat." Ania's eyes widened with fear as Schroder took her by the crook of her elbow and started to lead her away. A woman's voice unexpectedly came from behind them.

"Excuse me, sir, but I have to speak up. I need to advise you of something that may affect your choice tonight." Emilie looked at Ania first, then back at Schroder. "I have to tell you, she has her period."

Schroder stopped in his tracks. "She does?"

"Yes, sir," Emilie stepped forward and raised the hem of Ania's nightdress to show a large reddish-brown stain on the fabric. Schroder was not to know it was Ania's grandfather's blood, smudged onto her nightdress as she was dragged over his body earlier that day, but it was enough to put him off. He let go of Ania's elbow and stepped in front of Emilie. "And who might you be, her gynaecologist?"

"My name is Emilie, sir. Emilie Karpinski. I am her cousin," she lied bravely. "She is young, sir; she doesn't understand and is scared to speak up. I don't want you to have your evening ruined because she has her period."

"I suppose I should reward you. What did you say your name was?"

"Emilie, sir, Emilie Karpinski." And her mouth twitched at the side, leaving Schroder unsure if it was a nervous smile or something seductive.

"Then her loss is your gain, Emilie Karpinski, cousin and gynaecologist to the girl with the cat's eyes. Come with me!"

12

The next morning, an hour after the sun had managed to break through the heavy clouds that filled the sky like huge lumps of cotton wool, Emilie returned to the barn. She ignored Ania and headed straight to a water pump.

Another girl had been taken from the barn that night, a girl much younger than Emilie and far more inexperienced; the one who suffered motion sickness. She was pulled from the crowd of women, taken kicking and screaming towards the house by Braun. "I don't want to go with the stinking German bastard!"

The girl was slightly built with a sickly disposition and a pallid complexion, but she managed to put up quite a fight as Braun tried to drag her away. He ended up slapping her around the head several times in an effort to persuade her to join him, but she continued to struggle so Braun punched her heavily in the face, which did calm her.

With the girl bleeding profusely from her nose and a cut to her lip, Braun dragged her inside the house. She looked so frail, but had put up one hell of a fight, and judging by the noise that came from the house, she continued to object for several hours. Her screams and his yelling could be heard well into the night, until everything suddenly went quiet. The guard looked towards the upstairs window of the house and shrugged as Ania and the women who were still awake exchanged anxious glances.

It was seven o'clock the next morning when Schroder made his appearance, adjusting his uniform, staring at the sky to check the weather. Mr and Mrs Lipchitz were standing nervously by the door, as if to wish him safe travels and thanks for visiting.

The truck rattled to life and clouds of diesel fumes filled the air as the women were herded into the back. Braun arrived with the young girl at the last minute, her face pale, bloody and bruised. She winced with pain as he marched her around to the tailgate and pushed her up into the back. The same woman who had comforted her the day before gathered her up and cried when she realised how broken the young girl was. Ania took her position at the tailgate, with Emilie, silent, by her side.

Schroder sounded so decent when he said his goodbyes to his hosts. He clicked his heels together in the usual way, straightening the peak of his cap, and smiled. "Mr and Mrs Lipchitz, I have to thank you for your hospitality. My friends and I enjoyed our stay very much."

Ania saw the relief spread across the faces of the old couple. They had survived. They would live to tell their family and friends about this one day, the bombastic and cruel behaviour of the Germans towards those poor young women.

"It was an honour having you as our guest, Herr Colonel." Mr Lipchitz had got the rank wrong, but at least he had gone in the right direction, and Schroder genuinely smiled at the mistake.

"No, no, Mr Lipchitz, the pleasure was mine. Thank you again." He clicked his heels once more, gave a crisp Heil

Hitler salute then turned and nodded at Braun, before marching away to the front of the waiting truck.

From her position at the tailgate Ania could tell that Braun was having trouble with something-a piece of equipment maybe. He was facing away from her, bending at the knees and struggling with his rifle. She could hear metallic clicks and clacks as he cursed under his breath. In the meantime, she looked over the top of him and saw the terrified expression on the faces of the old Jewish couple. Mrs Lipchitz's eyes were wide and her jaw slack. Her husband's hands visibly shook as he placed a reassuring arm around his wife's shoulder.

Braun finally stood to his full height. "Ah, got it!" Ania could now see that Braun had been attending to the mechanism of a machine gun, and with a sudden slap of his hand followed by a loud metallic clunk, he slotted the magazine into place. This was immediately followed by a deafening roar as the Lipchitz's danced a grotesque jig as bullets ripped through their frail bodies and shattered the doorframe behind. The roar of the weapon was accompanied by the sound of wood splintering and the stink of smoke from the muzzle.

It was less than one minute later when Braun made his way back to the truck. As he walked past Ania, he saw her open mouth and the question in her eyes-*why?* He knew what she was thinking-there was an explanation-of course, there was. "Juden," he said, shaking his head from side to side, "Juden."

***

When Danuta woke a second time, it was late afternoon. There was a chill in the air, the kind of damp she associated with the river. The floor beneath her seemed to be gently rocking as she turned to look around, bracing herself for a surge of pain from her shoulder. It was then that a shadow fell across her and she heard the click of a safety catch being released on a rifle, followed by a German voice. "So, what do we have here, eh, a Polish maiden perhaps ... if ever there was such a thing?"

She looked along the length of the weapon that was pointing at her head and much to her relief saw a familiar face at the other end. "Krzys Paderewski?"

The reply was in Polish this time. "Yes."

"What's with the fake German accent?"

"You can never be too safe, can you?" Krzys laughed as he helped Danuta sit upright. The Paderewski's had been known to Danuta's family for many years, having farmed the adjacent property and shared equipment and water during difficult times. "How is that shoulder of yours now?" he asked.

"It hurts," she said as she moved her arm and winced.

"You're lucky it was me who found you."

Krzys told Danuta he had been stalking a deer through the forest when he heard the gunshots and had seen everything the Germans did, from a distance. He was alone and unable to do anything but watch.

"I saw you running towards the trees then there was a shot and you fell. I took you into the woods and patched up the wound as best I could. I was certain you were safe so I ran back home to warn my parents about the Germans, but I was too late." He lowered his head at this point and seemed to talk to his feet. "I watched them drive away, and that was when I found my" parents.

Krzys started to cry, and Danuta moved beside him, placing her good arm around his shoulder as he continued in a whisperquiet voice. "They were hanging from an apple tree in the orchard. Can you imagine that? They planted that tree over fifty years ago, on their wedding anniversary." He sniffed loudly and closed his eyes, the vision of his parents' bodies swinging beneath the gnarled old apple tree embedded in his mind.

Krzys was full of guilt for not being at home before the Germans arrived. Perhaps he could have helped, maybe talked them out of whatever it was they wanted. He could have at least tried something, but his absence had left his aged parents exposed and vulnerable. The Germans had been looking for his sister, but she was away at the time. The only thing that helped ease Krzys's grief and guilt was the fact that he had been able to do something practical when he found Danuta in the forest, and he took her to the houseboat. Danuta's mind started to drift back to when she hid outside her bedroom window as the Germans searched the house for her. Should she have given herself up? If she had, she might well be with Ania now. Or dead like her grandparents. Instead, she ran away and the guilt hung over her, obscuring the calls of birds in the trees along the riverbank and the gentle slapping of water on the side of the boat.

"It's not as bad as it first appeared." Krzys sniffed away his tears as he examined Danuta's wound again. "It looks as if the bullet just missed your shoulder blade and I think everything will be OK in a few weeks. We have to be mindful of infection, that's all." The bullet had passed through soft tissue only, in and out, nice and clean. It was slightly deeper than a flesh wound but not serious. There was no major damage-nothing that time could not heal.

His fingers ran across her bare flesh as he adjusted the dressing, and his hands rested a little too comfortably for a moment. At another time something may have happened between them, but shock and grief overwhelmed them both. Krzys broke the uncomfortable silence. "Danuta, I'm going to Krakow to join the Armia Krajowa. There's nothing for me here now."

"The what?"

"The Home Army, the Polish underground, in Krakow. I have to kill Germans."

"Oh yes, and how do you propose getting there? Are you going to hitch a ride with a German convoy?" she said with a trace of sarcasm.

"I'll go by the river."

"But won't you be a bit conspicuous in a houseboat?"

"This old tub wouldn't even make it to the next bend. No, I will row. There is a rowboat moored behind us. I'll use that. And I will stick to the tributaries. There's a route I know, where the river splits into small backwaters that wind across country towards the city." The pain of the loss of his family had filled Krzys with steely determination. "It's a long way but I know I can make it."

"And you're going to do that alone are you? You're going to save Poland on your own?" Danuta's voice was gentler now. She had a degree of common sense that was unusual in such a young woman that would serve her well in the coming weeks. It was clear that she wanted to join Krzys.

"My family's ancestors fought the Russians in 1813, Danuta, and you can be sure they're fighting the Germans now. It's what we do and it's also my duty, my calling."

Danuta's eyes sparkled. "Ah, but you forgot one thing in this grand plan of yours. "You will need someone to cook and share the rowing. Two can travel better than one, and there is safety in numbers."

"And you have someone in mind?" Krzys knew what was coming.

"I can cook, and when my shoulder is better I can row. I'm good company too."

"This is not a holiday on the river—"

"And I can shoot. Probably better than you!" Danuta was lying. The nearest she had ever been to a gun was holding her grandfather's old .22 for him, when he took her rabbit shooting a few years ago. But she was convincing when she looked at Krzys with those bright blue eyes of hers-he would have believed anything she said at that moment.

"Do I have a choice?" he asked.

"Not if you know what's good for you," she replied.

"Then I surrender!" He threw his arms into the air and inadvertently hit Danuta's shoulder, making her yelp. "I think we should wait a few days, here at the river. We should be safe for a little while but we must begin our journey soon. If you want to join me, you have a lot of recuperating to do in a short period of time."

13

On the eastern side of Krakow, thirty kilometres outside the Polish city that history says was founded in AD 700, Wysznica labour camp was beginning to make an impact on the local economy and its inhabitants. Established to service the giant Auschwitz-Birkenau concentration camp, Wysznica was also providing a huge boost to the local black market.

In addition to providing timber and lime, the camp was to supply labour to Auschwitz, a commodity that while not in short supply, was always in demand if it was highly trained, fit and ready to work. A number of well-heeled industrialists had already established factories in and around the town of Auschwitz, with the promise of abundant labour, at no cost to them apart from a modest stipend to the local SS commanders.

Before the camp at Wysznica was complete, an architect arrived to supervise a team of local tradesmen who built a luxurious two-storey house on the perimeter of the camp, and it was from there that the new commandant, Obersturmbannfuhrer Baldric Fischer, was to run his empire.

The lieutenant colonel's wife arrived soon after the house was finished to give the place and its staff the once over. But when she saw the whole area, the idea of her and her darling children spending the next few years living so close to those disgusting prisoners was not something that appealed to her sensibilities, so she returned to Berlin the very next day. Twenty-four hours later, exactly according to plan, the commandant's Polish girlfriend, Krystyna Bylok, arrived.

Most German officers serving abroad took local girlfriends. There was no objection to this in France and Belgium, for example, as relationships with such women were sanctioned by Berlin. However, in Poland, fraternisation was strictly forbidden, thanks to German ideology. Jews were at the very bottom of the list, and just a notch above them sat the Poles, who were regarded as mere imbeciles, capable only of serving the Reich in the most menial ways. A

German officer having a relationship with a Polish woman was frowned upon and considered by many to be disgraceful.

Of course, rules were broken here and there, and those with a high enough rank who happened to find themselves in Poland, worked hard to keep their whores and girlfriends under wraps. Finally, with an amendment to the Nuremburg Race Laws, sexual activity between Germans and Poles was considered to be not only acceptable but also a necessity-a business transaction of sorts, in fact. This also opened the door for German soldiers to legitimately visit Polish brothels. Fischer called the new amendment the 'ways and means act' and was pleased when the High Command in Berlin agreed to bow to the pressure he and other senior ranking officers placed upon them. Krystyna 'Tina' was immediately put on display.

The master bedroom suite of the new house had conveniently placed French doors along one wall, opening onto a large veranda that provided shelter from the chill winter winds that slipped across the river and filtered through the nearby forests like thieves. In addition, the veranda also caught the sun's rays for the best part of the day, and even during the early stages of autumn, Tina was able to sunbathe topless there.

She was given the nickname of Titsy Tina by the guards who manned the perimeter watchtower that overlooked the house, and they sometimes paid for the rights to day shift duties if the forecast promised warm or clement weather. Tina enjoyed the attention, though she always pretended to be unaware that she could be seen. After all, her main role was to be beautiful and available at all times, to ease the stress that came with the job of camp commandant. Baldric (or Baldy as she sometimes affectionately called him) was her preoccupation.

Like most Polish girlfriends during such times, Tina kept a little 'something' in reserve, as a bargaining chip. She promised Baldric that she would participate in a particular sexual activity when she felt ready and comfortable enough to try it herself but not before.

Of course, the occasional extravagance might help soften her resolve, and if she was eventually persuaded to participate, she assured her beau that he would not be disappointed. It was all a matter of timing. *Be patient, Baldy, my darling, be patient and generous...*

Fischer lavished gifts on Tina, kept a car and a driver at her service twenty-four hours a day and established accounts at the best boutiques and haberdasheries that Krakow had to offer. He knew a good thing when he saw it, and there was no doubting that Tina was indeed a good thing.

Fischer's wife was very different to Tina, and from the very beginnings of their relationship she made it plain that she considered all forms of sexual activity to be vile, but necessary if one was to do her duty. She was stoic and conventional in her lovemaking, but theirs was a marriage of convenience, for Mrs Fischer had connections that her husband was keen to leverage.

Obersturmbannfuhrer Fischer was something of an anathema to most of Hitler's inner circle. His rank was considerably above that usually associated with the commandant of a small service camp; indeed, Rudolf Hoess, the commandant at Auschwitz was a mere captain when first appointed. In addition, to add to the insult, Fischer had been personally awarded an Iron Cross first class by the Fuhrer himself, even though such glories were usually reserved for those who served at the front. According to some, Fischer had never served in a cafeteria let alone a battlefront, but such comments were usually said in select company, with a smirk.

There was something about Fischer that confused Hitler's closest aides, and they treated him with cautious respect at all times. On his desk and bedside table, Fischer had personally signed photographs of himself with Eva, the Fuhrer and his dog Blondi, relaxing at Berghof—Hitler's private residence in the Bavarian Alps. That was evidence enough, if any was needed, that Fischer was exceptionally well connected. Himmler, Goering, Goebbels, Speer and the others also had the obligatory photographs of themselves standing alongside the Fuhrer, but none were as intimate as Fischer's, and that was something of concern to them all.

Adolf Eichmann was irritated the most, as the Fuhrer had placed him in charge of all camps in Europe and expressly told him to *look after my close friend, Baldric.*

As far as Eichmann was concerned, Fischer was a constant irritation, *like a pebble in your shoe that you can never dislodge.*

It appeared that sometimes even the Fuhrer himself did not know whether to smile or scowl when Fischer's name came up in planning or strategy meetings. Even a highly secretive investigation by the Gestapo failed to find the reason for Fischer's rapid ascendency and unique relationship with the Fuhrer. They never would know because the reason was safely locked away in a place that only Fischer himself knew.

***

In an attempt to distance himself from the task of babysitting Fischer, Eichmann deliberately changed the reporting lines so Fischer had to go through Hoess at Auschwitz and not directly to him. Fischer was infuriated and immediately phoned Hitler to have the directive changed, but the Fuhrer would have none of it. He said he could not and would not reverse Eichmann's decision. It would be seen as favouritism and upset 'Berlin.' If there was one thing that the Fuhrer believed in, it was the bureaucracy he had worked so hard to establish.

Fischer realised that the rest of the 'inner circle' were keen to put him down at every opportunity, so he started to protect himself from repercussions during his reign at Wysznica. Important matters were not always documented by him-he had others sign the execution warrants and if anything contentious was put in writing, he made a point of telling his secretary to sign it on his behalf-he could always claim he knew nothing of it at a later date, if things backfired. And he stopped being directly involved in summary executions wherever he could-after all, killing was a tawdry and messy business, one that was best handled by those more suited to it and there was seemingly a never-ending supply of men with cold eyes and even colder hearts in the SS.

***

Fischer's office walls were lined with oak panelling, decorated with swastikas and a magnificent oil painting of the Fuhrer. The artwork was copied by a well-known Polish artist, from a photograph taken during one of Hitler's many rousing Munich speeches. When Tina first saw the painting she was amazed. "It looks like a photograph, Baldy! You can almost see the pores in the Fuhrer's skin!"

"You can indeed see the pores, but they are not the Fuhrer's." Fischer said, in a matter-of-fact tone.

"Oh..." Tina took a deep breath to stop herself dry retching. "Oh, Christ!"

The artist who painted Hitler so accurately was there at the unveiling. He killed himself the same night, knowing his name would live forever in the bottom right-hand corner of the canvas, which was made from human skin.

Fischer was an avid pipe smoker, joining that elite and sometimes despised club that counted such luminaries as Einstein and the famous German theologist Rudolf Bultmann amongst its glorious list of unofficial members. National boundaries did not exist for pipe smokers, although during dinner parties, eyebrows were raised when Fischer mentioned that Stalin, Alexander Graham Bell and even the British fictional character Sherlock Holmes were well-known pipe smokers.

On the mantelpiece above the fireplace in his office was a rack holding his six most revered pipes, with only one German-made Vauen among them. He was particularly proud of his British Royale Supreme, hand carved from briar, complete with a hallmarked sterling silver ring at the point where the mouthpiece connected with the bowl. A pipe gave Fischer a point of difference; people remembered 'that man with the pipe' from dinner parties and that was a good enough reason to participate.

Several days a week, Fischer sat like judge and jury behind his huge oak desk, calmly puffing great clouds of Virginia tobacco smoke around the room as he dispensed sentences, ordered executions, gave commands, sent directives and fired off missives in every direction. To some, he appeared to be a bumbling old fool, but those who crossed his path or looked his way at the wrong time quickly came to fear the commandant.

What really mattered to Berlin was statistics; at the end of the day, it was all about the numbers. He had to shift so many tonnes of lime every month, he had the figures on his desk somewhere, so he broke them down to a weekly target, then daily, then doubled them. The same applied to the timber mill. Trees (mostly pine and birch) were cut from the forests that proliferated in the region, and they were defoliated outside the camp. The trunks were then dragged into the mill where they were cut into planks or posts or whatever had been ordered.

Labour was Fischer's main product, and he consistently turned out the fittest and strongest workers for the factories and industrial complexes that surrounded Auschwitz, manufacturing armaments and rubber products for the war effort. The hard labour at Wysznica produced good workers; there was no doubt about that. Fischer watched them himself sometimes, everything done on the run to avoid beatings, sprinting up ramps, their barrows filled with lime, loading waiting railway carriages. If a prisoner slipped or became too frail to continue at the required pace he was immediately 'processed' and replaced.

Fischer's high standards produced the best stock-it was his trademark. He had been known to visit the loading area at the rail yard on occasion, order one or two summary executions, and then move on to the timber mill where the level of activity miraculously increased as word quickly spread of his pending arrival.

He enjoyed his tours of the camp and the fear they instilled. "I feel so powerful. They look at me as if I am God," he once said to Tina.

"But here you are God," she said.

Somehow it never failed to amuse Fischer to see a rabbi or a great Polish scholar, a teacher or artist, struggling to come to terms with a real day's work. Wysznica was a great leveller for the Polish and Jewish people, but nothing brought them down to earth as much as their uniforms. Wandering around in their striped pyjamas they looked for all the world like human versions of the animals in children's natural history books. It was no wonder the locals called them 'zebra people' when they saw them during their deliveries at Wysznica.

Visitors were not so amused when they got up close to the prisoners and saw lice scuttling around their clothing and bodies.

And their disgusting teeth. My God, how they stank, those zebra people! They were Jews, of course, most of them-Polish Jews it was true, but Jews nonetheless- and the locals treated them accordingly. For some, the war was a disaster and for others, a mere inconvenience. But there were also people, and they were not isolated, for whom the war presented great opportunity. It was simply a matter of whom you knew and whose palm you were prepared to grease.

***

Fischer had been spending a great deal of time studying the processes within his camp. Production figures (tonnage of lime, metres of timber) were first class and he was quietly confident that they would be hard to better. But when it came to labour, he was not so comfortable with his statistics. Every time a unit 'failed' it had to be 'processed' and replaced-it was an expensive business! New units required training, discipline ... it took time to get them into a working regime and time cost money. What irritated Fischer the most was the cost incurred when a unit failed. Food had a nominal cost, of course, and clothing could be recycled, but processing? Processing was expensive. To take a unit out of production and process it-the gas chamber, crematorium, then the matter of disposal. It all had a cost! It was far better to sell an active unit to one of the local industrialists because they would have to carry the cost of disposal when it eventually failed. But the industrialists were not stupid when they negotiated for labour. "Let's face it, they all fail in the end, don't they, Baldric? That is the idea, isn't it?"

It was a numbers game and out of every one thousand units that arrived on any given transport, Fischer had first to deal with at least eight hundred that were of no possible use at all! That in itself was a major problem as the size of transports seemed to be increasing daily and unlike Auschwitz, he was judged on what he produced, not what he disposed of.

Of the two hundred or so units that remained after selection, less than fifty eventually made the grade and went on to work at the Auschwitz factories. A less than five per cent success rate was too low as far as Fischer was concerned.

At odds with a lot of his colleagues in the SS, Fischer considered himself to be a New Order thinker. Hoess, like most, believed in discipline when it came to getting the best from workers, and Fischer had no problem with that-to a point. After all, there was nothing wrong with the occasional summary execution-he used that tactic himself from time to time. It kept workers on their toes. But why would you want to beat a man who was an exemplary worker? Why sacrifice his efficiency and carry the cost of disposal afterwards? Why not *reward* your best workers? Offer them a carrot instead of a stick.

There were ways that it could be done, and Fischer was convinced that output would increase as a result. A radical new idea was beginning to form in the commandant's mind, one that would have a profound impact on the whole concentration camp network in Europe. And if he could prove to the Fuhrer that it was working, his place in the Berlin Bunker would be assured.

14

Danuta and Krzys stayed at the houseboat for a few more days. They spent their time fishing, eating, talking, recuperating and trying to come to terms with the recent past. Their tales of happier days occasionally had them laughing, but mostly their minds were shrouded in gloom. It was hard to believe that in such a short period of time their lives had been so radically altered. Things would never be the same again and there was no longer such a thing as 'normal'.

While he could find no real evidence to support it, Krzys was convinced that all of Danuta's family had perished at the hands of the Germans. He was yet to find any bones in the fire-ravaged remains of Danuta's family home, but then, he found little of anything except dust, carbonised fragments of wood and shattered bricks. The fire must have been intense; the debris was still smouldering two days later, making it impossible to search properly. But Danuta refused to give up hope;

somewhere, deep inside her heart, she knew that Ania was still alive.

***

Krzys had been a keen cross-country runner, the school champion in fact. "We never did race against each other did we?" he asked Danuta.

"No," she replied. "It was against school rules for us girls to race you boys because of the humiliation we would have brought upon you!" There was something about Danuta's feisty attitude that sat well with Krzys. It was well known throughout the village of Zwinbrzych that the Paderewski family were decent, fair-minded people who went about their lives treating others as they themselves wished to be treated. But do the wrong thing by them? It was at your own risk, because the Paderewski's never forgave, never forgot and certainly never gave in.

As far as he knew, Krzys was the only male survivor from the village and the responsibility weighed heavily. In a strange way, it seemed that his father had unknowingly prepared him for what was to come. But Krzys was still young, with little life experience. He may have been determined and angry, but was that enough?

***

Winter was well and truly upon them now, although the usual late flurries of snow seemed to be a long time coming. It was as if the sun wanted to linger just an hour or two longer above the cold mists that gathered about the river during the latter part of the day. Danuta had been spending her time rugged up on the deck of the boat recuperating, as Krzys scouted around the remains of the village, sometimes returning with food, occasionally with drink and always with sad stories.

The scene was one of utter devastation. Most of the homes had been burned to the ground, dead pets and livestock lay everywhere. But the worst sights by far were the bodies of people that Krzys knew, those he loved and respected, indiscriminately riddled with bullets, lying in their own blood, horror etched on their empty faces. It all seemed so senseless.

Krzys had buried everyone he could find, the ache in his back and the blisters on his hands making him even more determined to seek justice. It took several days before he was satisfied that he had done all he could do, then he took Danuta to the site of her old house, where he had finally found evidence of the murders. He buried a few charred bones and three skulls. Was one of them Ania's?

They stood by the small wooden cross and stared in disbelief at the ruins. No tears came. Krzys looked up at the sky. "The Germans will pay for this. I promise you, my God, as I stand here before you with Danuta as my witness, the Germans will pay."

The next afternoon, after another visit to the village, Krzys raced back to the houseboat, breathless and anxious. A small German patrol had been cruising around on a motorcycle and sidecar. They had stopped and examined several new graves, looked around, realised that someone was still about. "It is time for us to move on. I am sure that the Germans will return soon. I shall row but will need you to help me. Do you think you can manage?" Chris said.

"Of course," Danuta replied, revolving her injured shoulder in its socket. For such a young woman, Danuta showed a resolve that many older would not be able to match. Her young athletic body was already recovering, helped by her need to avenge the injustices she had been exposed to. She knew that some people were born to do great things, to right wrongs and to leave their mark. She wanted to join them.

The night before they commenced their epic journey Krzys opened a bottle of vodka. The evening sky had an unusual glow to it, heavy snow clouds clung to the horizon, trapping what little warmth remained and holding the bitterly cold winds at bay, seemingly just for them. The young couple snuggled beneath a tarpaulin on the deck of the houseboat and Krzys raised a glass and clinked it against Danuta's. "Na Zdorovie!"

"Cheers! Here's to our journey, during which we shall immortalise the memory of the Jagiellon Dynasty. Death to the Teutonic Knights, I say!" Danuta said.

"The who? What? I haven't a clue what you're talking about," Krzys said. "But I salute them and you regardless!" He emptied his glass with another rousing "Na Zdorovie!"

Danuta followed suit, as is the tradition. The vodka had an immediate effect. Danuta was determined to teach Krzys some history despite slurring her words and seeing two of everything. "You don't know about the battle of Tannenberg? What did they teach you at school, you ignorant Polish pheasant?"

"How dare you call me pheasant? I am a *peasant* not a pheasant, and proud of it!"

"Presactly!"

"So here's to an ignorant Polish pheasant and his highly educated knight, Danuta Burczyk!"

"Na Zdorovie!"

Danuta fell sideways. Krzys put his arms out to break her fall and they found themselves in a brief embrace. Krzys reddened with embarrassment. "I'm sorry," he said softly.

"There's no need to be," she said, avoiding his eyes as she pulled away.

15

The truck carrying the women rattled on in an easterly direction, before suddenly turning south at Opole. The journey had been broken occasionally so their guards could stretch their legs, relieve themselves, smoke and refuel the truck. If there was a stream or an abandoned house by the side of the road the women were allowed to see to whatever it was that women saw to at such times.

That morning they had driven through several shattered towns. They saw stunned people wandering aimlessly through the streets or just sitting at the side of the road with a distant look in their eyes as they gazed hopelessly down at their feet or up to the heavens.

But the place where they were now refuelling, whose name had been removed from the signposts during the initial Blitzkrieg, had not been completely devastated. Some buildings remained intact though they stood next to others tottering on the brink of collapse, peppered and pockmarked from bullets and shells. Silent wisps of smoke could be seen escaping from nearby chimneys as hunger-ravaged dogs sniffed around the piles of bricks and grim-faced people searched for lost belongings, pets and loved ones amongst the rubble of dismembered buildings.

On a piece of wasteland between two shattered buildings the women caught sight of a pile of bloodstained corpses, all higgledy-piggledy like a giant game of human pick-up-sticks. Limbs sprung out from the stack, an arm here, a leg there, finally a face with blank eyes-*what do you think you are staring at?* It was only then that the women saw the rest of the bodies. Hanging from trees, piled in front of a wall, lying among smoke-blackened ruins, frozen into macabre poses; a hand protruding from a pile of rubble, halfway towards forming a fist in its last anguished moments before death. So many dead people. So many bad dreams to come.

They also encountered dead animals by the side of the road, bloated and gorged, ready to burst, most lying on their sides or backs with legs rigid and pointing upwards, locked by rigor mortis.

The few stray dogs they saw no longer chased the scabby emaciated cats that still roamed the shattered remains of buildings that were once their homes. A fine layer of brick dust covered everything-trees, plants, animals, people- and it seemed that the whole town was numb. Even the birds were quiet. The women in the truck did not discuss what they witnessed in that anonymous place; it was enough that they knew the sights and smells would revisit them every time they closed their eyes, until they did so for the last time.

As the guards busied themselves emptying cans of fuel into the truck, Ania caught sight of a makeshift gallows in the grounds of a nearby school, five freshly hung corpses gently swaying in the mid-morning breeze. "I need the toilet," she said to the guard.

"Too bad," he replied without looking up.

"Look, I need it, and I need it now. If you want me to shit in the back of the truck that is up to you. You will have to put up with the smell as much as me."

He rolled his eyes and nodded towards a bush. "Over there where I can keep an eye on you."

She jumped down from the tailgate and ran behind the bushes, crouched on her haunches and lifted her nightdress. Here she was, defecating in a public place; her mother would be so ashamed. Ania was ashamed. She looked up to find a wild-haired, snotty-nosed girl in a battered yellow dress staring at her. The child was no more than five years old.

As Ania turned away, shamefaced and embarrassed, she realised the girl was not staring at her at all. She was looking past her towards a line-up of men, all of them dressed in similar black clothing. They were standing behind a trench or a ditch, which, judging by the mud around their shoes and lower legs, they had dug themselves. Each of them held a shovel clogged with thick grey clay.

The men appeared somewhat unusual to Ania. Foreigners, she

assumed. Some had beards; some had peculiar looking hats with curls hanging down the side of their heads. They all had fear in their eyes. A few of them were swaying as they stood, muttering or chanting some strange words that she could not make out, though she was certain it was not her native tongue.

She found herself swaying too, picking up their silent rhythm as she crouched behind the hedge. And the child also, she was swaying, her mouth moving to her own silent words as she stood wide-eyed and unblinking, staring at the scene before her.

Another man appeared, formally dressed in a business suit. Judging by his demeanour, he was some kind of official. He ran along the row of strangers, bobbing and bowing in a seemingly comical manner as he collected the shovels. He then placed the shovels at the feet of a German officer who stood resplendent in his greatcoat and hat, buttons and badges gleaming proudly, a huge Doberman panting at his side. The German looked 'all business', his mouth tight and his nostrils slightly flared. Then, for some unknown reason, Ania noticed his gloves: immaculate, smart, soft, beautifully tailored black leather gloves.

The man who had delivered the shovels to the officer stood to attention and yelled officiously. "Equipment returned as ordered, sir." He actually did a Heil Hitler salute, which looked quite comical, and Ania could not help but smile at the ridiculous scene.

Then the German started to slowly and quite deliberately remove his wonderful gloves. One hand at a time. One finger at a time. Resplendently. Starting at the thumb and working his way out to the little finger on each hand, it took him several minutes to go through the ritual of removing both gloves. And all the time the foreigners stared forward, still swaying, still mumbling their unheard prayers or songs. When the German was finally ready he handed his gloves to the little man, who took them in a most business-like manner, still standing to attention, waiting for his next instruction.

What happened next was so dreadful that the shock made Ania want to turn her head, to close her eyes and blink the scene away, but it also said to her *look ... look at this will you?*

She could not believe what was happening. It was one of those things that she could never imagine seeing, and therefore, when she did see it, she could not bring herself to look away, no matter how terrible it was and no matter how much relief diverting her eyes might have brought. *Please, God, tell me this isn't real, tell me I am dreaming and wake me up back home in bed with Cabbage keeping my feet warm.*

Surely Ania was not a witness to this? No. It could not be! It wasn't actually happening; it was an imagining, a bad dream. Surely she did not see the German officer move along behind the line of strange looking foreigners, raise his handgun and fire one shot into each of their skulls.

She never saw that did she? She never saw their heads jerk backwards as the bullets blasted into them, and they never tumbled into the ditch they had just dug. Why had she imagined such a terrible thing? Why had she dreamed this terrible dream? When would she wake up?

As the German reached the last but one man he paused, slowly undid his overcoat and reached into the inside pocket and removed a new clip of bullets. Then he took the empty magazine from the handle of his gun and placed that into his pocket. After he had rebuttoned his overcoat he pushed the new clip into place, pulled it out again once more before ramming it home hard, a second time.

During all this, the comical little man in the business suit stared ahead as if in a trance, ignoring everything. One of the last two foreigners turned around and said something, then turned back and made the sign of the cross on his chest. Ania could see him shaking-his lips were moving rapidly. She could see his eyelids flicker and his face twitch, and she could almost see the beads of perspiration on his top lip as he prayed and rocked backwards and forwards on his heels. He did not attempt to run or fight back. In fact, he looked strangely resigned to what was going to happen. A resounding bang made Ania jump as the German shot the man in the back of the head. His victim seemed poised on the brink of collapse, so the German raised his right foot and nudged him headlong into his pre-dug grave.

The officer finally moved to the last man and competently despatched him in the same manner as the others. All the foreigners were now in the trench. Ten shots. Ten men. Ten men gone. All that remained was the space they had been standing in, just a few moments before.

The comical looking man in the business suit waited patiently as the German placed his weapon back in the leather holster at his side, then clipped several press-studs into place to secure it. He held his right hand out, palm up: a signal for the little man to slap the beautiful leather gloves onto them with a loud crack. The German inspected the gloves closely, and upon finding them to be satisfactory he put them back on as slowly as he had removed them, as if it were again, part of the important ritual.

Ania was still in a state of disbelief, her mouth locked open and her eyes open wider, when a menacing shadow crept over her. The guard from the truck had come to find her. "Rous, rous!" She continued to stare at the strange scene in front of her; the German officer, the little official and the dead men in the ditch. The guard's eyes followed her gaze and his voice softened slightly. "Kommen," he said as he pulled her to her feet.

As she made her way back to the truck Ania realised that the little girl had gone but the man in the business suit was still fussing over the German officer. It was then that he turned and she saw that he was wearing some kind of medallion or Chain of Office. He was the mayor of the town.

A short time after Ania took her seat in the back of the truck, she said to Emilie, "I am so ashamed."

"You have nothing to be ashamed of Ania. It's not your fault that you are here. It's none of our faults."

But it wasn't the shame of being held captive by the Germans that was haunting Ania. It was the shame of being a person; a witness to what other human beings were capable of. "When all of this is over, Emilie, what will we make of ourselves? Tell me please? Will this terrible time be worth living through if afterwards we are not better people?"

The truck suddenly rattled back to life and moved away with Ania in position at the tailgate. Her mouth was now set straight, and a look of determination had fallen across her eyes. She had to stay alive for Danuta. They would need each other after the war and she was certain that Danuta would be thinking the same. Danuta had to be alive-she just had to be. Ania would never give up hope.

16

The journey continued in silence for several hours. Sometimes the truck tagged along as part of a large convoy; sometimes they were the only vehicle on the road. Most of the time, though, there were a few vehicles in front of them; one or two small transports maybe, a motorcycle and sidecar or staff car full of uniformed officers. But always refugees. Some pushing barrows loaded with possessions, old women with their heads covered with shawls, others with perambulators loaded with children and chickens, a goat once, a baby pig. Did they think they would be better off moving east, away from the Germans? Was it safer in Kielce than it was in Poznan? Or perhaps Lublin would be the better place?

Anywhere was better than where they were, that was the thing. They had no men to look after them so they had to do what they thought was best for the little ones and the old people. They would get as far away from Germany and the border as they could, that was the plan. How were they to know that wherever they went, the Germans would be there too?

After three hours of silence, Ania was the first to speak. "If I ever have to do anything for the Germans, I shall refuse."

"Pride like that could get you killed, Ania." Emilie was older. She understood.

"It's not pride, it's decency. It's the difference between right and wrong and my grandparents always told me that was what made you what you were; a good person or a bad person. Now I understand what they were saying."

"It can also make you a dead person, Ania. Remember that as well. One day soon you may find yourself in the position of having to do what you *have* to do. When that day comes you will have no choice but to leave your morality behind, because the Germans are not principled people and these are not ethical times."

Both women stared silently at the dust that clouded up from the rear wheels of the truck as it bounced and rattled along the road to who knows where. The sky was still heavy with cloud, but the snow was steadfastly refusing to come. The air was warmer than it had been for a while and the land was waiting for winter's blanket to fall. The guard who was seated opposite Ania looked on implacably, no longer concerned about the condition of his boots. He sniffed deeply then spat over the back of the tailgate.

***

The young girl who had been beaten by Braun the night before was in a bad way. Both her eyes were swollen and her jaw appeared to be broken. She was being comforted by several women, but it was obvious that her injuries consisted of more than just a split lip and a few bruises. At the next stop they would try to find some medical assistance. Perhaps there was a first aid kit in the cab?

The truck finally clattered to a stop on a potholed dirt road in the middle of nowhere. Ploughed fields stretched as far as the eye could see and hedgerows lined the road. The women were allowed to disembark. Braun had been staring at Ania at every opportunity, and he was staring at her again now. It was not *that* he was staring that scared Ania. It was *how* he was staring. There was something menacing about his eyes, something that made her feel very uncomfortable and extremely wary.

Schroder had spread a map over the engine cowling, and was talking and pointing animatedly to Braun. The remaining Germans kept a watchful eye on the women and smoked. They laughed when one of the older women asked for medicine, a headache tablet maybe, some disinfectant, something to cover the injured girl's wounds. Another woman ripped a strip of fabric from the hem of her dress, dipped it into a puddle then placed it upon the girl's forehead while someone else tried to clean up the vomit in an attempt to reduce the stench in the truck.

The guards handed around a few dried biscuits for the women to divide amongst themselves. The injured girl's portion was snatched away by a fat, voracious-looking woman with short black hair and an angry disposition. Some of the women cupped their hands to drink the water from a nearby stream and others washed their faces or dabbed at their clothing, rarely speaking, eyes nervously darting everywhere. A few of them, like Ania, were still dressed in their nightclothes with quilts and knitted blankets wrapped around their shoulders. What they would not do for a hot bath!

They stood around in silence, shivering and fearful as the Germans smoked, drank hot coffee from flasks, laughed with each other and ate the remaining pastries they had taken from Mrs Lipchitz's kitchen.

It was about ten minutes later when the rumble of a distant engine caught their attention. The women stared at a small cloud of dust as it moved slowly towards them. A truck eventually rattled into sight and a few minutes later it pulled up behind them and clattered to a stop as the dust settled. There were three Germans inside the cab and another who was watching over women of varying ages, who sat uncomfortably in the uncovered rear of the large vehicle.

The driver of the new truck jumped from the cab seemingly full of enthusiasm. He was decidedly overweight with sweat stains under his armpits and thick black tufts of hair protruding from every visible orifice. He walked past Ania and the women from her truck, looking at each one in turn, a lascivious smile on his unshaven face. He reported to Schroder, and after a brief discussion returned to his vehicle, stopping in front of Ania and Emilie. When he spoke he revealed a mouth full of stained teeth and a tongue that wormed its way around them like a slimy pink slug. "Tonight we will be having a party, and you are invited, my little Polish princesses!" Ania could actually see the blackheads in the creases of his nostrils and smell the tobacco on his breath.

"You disgust me!" she said through clenched teeth.

The German held his stomach and laughed. "You are so right. I am disgusting and I like to do disgusting things to Polish princesses, especially ones with strange eyes like you!" He pinched Ania's cheek then walked back to his vehicle where his colleagues greeted him with raucous laughter and backslapping.

Ania saw the injured girl slouched up against a truck tyre for warmth. One side of her face was raw and swollen, her left eye now completely closed. She was sobbing quietly when someone placed a piece of damp cloth on her forehead. "Isn't there something we can do for her?" Ania asked.

"I don't suppose there is. They don't care, that's for certain," Emilie said, nodding towards the guards. The fat driver waddled over and held his hand out. "Here, for you and your friend." He unfurled his hand to reveal a bread roll. "Get your strength up for tonight, eh, princess?"

"I don't want your bread," Ania said sternly, pushing him away.

Emilie snatched it up before the German could withdraw his hand. "Thank you, sir."

One of the guards yelled from the front truck. "Come on, load up, it's time to go!" As Ania stepped up to the tailgate the fat driver pushed her from behind, his hand sliding inside her nightdress, on her naked bottom. She kicked out wildly but missed.

"Ah, you like it, I thought so!" he said with a leer. "Very nice, princess, very nice indeed," he nodded appreciatively as he looked up her clothing. Emilie pulled her into the truck before she could spit at him.

Ania looked down from her position at the tailgate, smiled at the fat driver and said, "You know, my mother used to tell me that you should never window shop where you can't afford the goods."

"Ah, but this is Poland and I am German. I don't have to pay for the goods here!" He rolled his head back and let out a disgusting laugh as he slammed the tailgate into place.

"Hey! You fat bastard, get out of my way!" The guard who normally sat opposite Ania arrived and wanted to get into the back of the truck. "And don't try to feel my arse or I will kill you!" he said as he pulled himself up over the tailgate.

The lecherous driver walked away as the guard took his usual position. He looked at Ania, shrugged, then said by way of explanation, "Don't take any notice of him. He is from Hamburg."

The two vehicles rumbled to life and were soon bouncing through the potholes and partly frozen puddles. "We are going across country. It will be quicker and we avoid the convoys," the guard said, looking at Emilee.

"Where are we going?" she asked, but there was no reply. He had said enough and decided to stare into nowhere again.

Ania was still sitting at the tailgate, and found it impossible to avoid looking at the fat driver in the truck behind. He was wrestling with the steering wheel and bouncing up and down, waving at her like an over-enthusiastic child on a fairground ride. One of the men beside him was hidden by the map he was studying and the other was resting, a cigarette lodged in the corner of his mouth.

With a loud mechanical clank, the truck suddenly dipped at the front end, the suspension bottomed and it thudded into a huge pothole before lurching back out. Several women flew into the air and landed on their hard, wooden bench seats with a sickening thud and the air was peppered with screams as the injured girl vomited over several occupants. She was now bleeding from one ear and her partly open eye had rolled back so only the white was visible. There was nothing that could be done except to hold her.

The women in the second truck were still exposed to the elements, the effects of the cold showing on their faces. Ania pulled her quilt around her shoulders and recalled the time when as a child she fell from a horse and hurt her shoulder. She was feeling very sorry for herself when Babcia gave her a useful life lesson. *No matter what, there will always be someone worse off than you, my child.*

The two-vehicle convoy seemed to be going deeper into Poland and the bleak winter countryside flashed past them hour after hour. At times they saw nothing except ploughed fields and startled, naked trees; occasionally a cow, sometimes a lone farmer repairing a wagon or tending his livestock. Most of the buildings bore evidence of a recent conflict and they passed the ruins of many barns, overturned carts and the bloated carcasses of dead horses and cows. By the side of a small mill they came upon the terrible sight of a grotesquely twisted body, blackened beyond recognition by anybody except the dog that stood guard over it.

Ania leaned her head against Emilie's shoulder and tried to sleep for a while. The diesel fumes lay heavy around the back of the vehicle and the chug of the engine and the bleak surrounds added to her wretchedness. She could no longer feel her feet and the cold had started to creep up her legs like the hand of an unwelcome suitor. Hopefully her dreams would help her escape the fear and misery that was building inside her. Where were they going and more significantly, what was going to happen to them when they arrived?

17

The small rowing boat moved smoothly and quietly across the inky black river, the sun having decided to remain behind the heavy snow filled clouds all day. Fortunately, Krzys had packed many blankets, a tarpaulin, plenty of food and some medical supplies. He seemed to know what he was doing, and whenever they came upon a tributary he knew exactly which direction to take, rarely finding the need to consult the map by his side.

Most of the time, Danuta reclined against the pile of clothing and equipment she stashed behind her and watched the scenery drift by. When she was bored, she stared at Krzys-the best scenery of all. It would have been easy to forget why they were there if they hadn't heard the rumble of nearby military vehicles. Occasionally she had to pull a blanket up over her shoulders to keep the damp air at bay as her wound was still aching. Krzys told her the pain was a sign that it was healing. At another time she may have enjoyed the river, but for now the grey clouds and the cold matched her heavy mood, the memories of her family's suffering at the hands of the Germans filling her mind. Grief seemed to have given Krzys resolve, but Danuta felt weighed down by her losses. And her only hope lay with Ania; she had to be alive.

Before they had set off Krzys had traced their route onto a spare map so Danuta could follow the almost one hundred-kilometre journey. By staying with the smaller tributaries, they avoided most main roads and, more importantly, bridges. The only bridge of consequence was on a minor road between two market towns about halfway through the journey. It was large enough for the Germans to transport weapons and troops between the towns, or for locals to take contraband and illicit goods. He was confident in his assumption that the Germans would be more interested in the road than the small river that flowed beneath it, and his hopes of sneaking past the bridge lay very much with that in mind. If he was right, they could be on their way without any drama. If he was wrong, they would have to deal with whatever was there.

The first half of the journey took them through fields and alongside back roads, conveniently avoiding most major transport routes, therefore minimising their risk. They were, after all, in a small rowing boat on a backwater, and even if the Germans did spot them it was doubtful that they would have looked upon the two young lovers apparently enjoying an outing on the river as much of a threat, even though it was a somewhat unusual sight in winter. Most of the roads were set back from the river, but when they did occasionally run parallel, the water was always at a lower level. Krzys managed to slip under the cover of reeds and overhanging branches several times as vehicles thundered past above them. It slowed their journey somewhat but kept them out of harm's way.

There was one occasion when Krzys got the timing wrong, and he found himself rowing parallel to a main road for a short time. He briefly lost concentration and failed to notice the German munitions truck that was now cruising alongside them. The driver had spotted Danuta in the rowing boat and was yelling something to her. He may have been speaking in German, but it was clear from his tone of voice and expression that he was not just wishing her 'good morning'. Both Krzys and Danuta were relieved when the truck finally accelerated away.

Before they reached the town of Wieliczka they turned into a narrow offshoot that Krzys knew would lead them to the river Wisla, eventually taking them into Krakow-but they had to get past that bridge first.

As a child Krzys had spent a lot of time around the Wisla, fishing, exploring, camping on its banks with his father. His childhood had been idyllic, with many warm summers spent on the river. He could still remember the soft light that filtered through the branches of the overhanging willows, and the sound of his father's voice, lubricated by homemade vodka, as Krzys sat by the campfire listening to his father talk of his own childhood.

The old man had seen and experienced things in the first war that he cared not to talk about until the drink got into him, then he chatted passionately about his country's constant struggle with Germany and Russia. Borders came and went over the years; Krzys's father knew exactly how many times, and which towns had been affected. "That's why Polish people have flat heads," he would slur, "because the Germans or Russians are always pushing us down!" Thanks to the German invasion, the days of Krzys listening to his father were gone, as were those watching him silently fishing from his favourite spot on the river. Life would never be the same again.

Krzys was hungry. "I am famished, but I think I shall die if I am forced to eat another one of your damned golabki-I hate cabbage at the best of times, but eating it cold? Can't you find something else for us?"

"I think we still have some pierogi somewhere," Danuta said as she searched through the small hamper at her feet.

"But they are made from cabbage as well!"

Danuta shouted, "There is a war on you know!" then she realised that Krzys was smiling. "How about we tie the boat up on the riverbank tonight and see if we can find a few spare eggs or maybe a chicken from one of the farms around here?"

"That sounds fine to me, but no cabbages, OK?" Krzys said.

"OK" Danuta replied, A moment later a soggy golabki landing with an audible 'plop' on Krzys's forehead.

***

Just before dark Krzys checked the surrounding land. "There's a small road just off to the right behind that row of trees; you see that building there? That will be a farmhouse. I think we should head over there and take a look around."

As soon as the sun set, they made their way towards the lights of the farm with a spark of adventure in their eyes. It was good to be on dry land again. Their boots were soon covered in clods of brown mud and Danuta said she felt as if she was wearing clown shoes. They both laughed as Danuta told Krzys about the time as a child when she saw a touring Russian circus. The clowns terrified her with their green and orange wigs and exaggerated, painted mouths. Krzys smiled at Danuta's giggling chatter and shifted his rifle from one shoulder to the other. *Were girls always this talkative?*

They skirted along the ditches and small hedgerows that bordered the field adjacent to the stone house, their senses heightened as they walked along in silence. The hoot of an owl had them both ducking as it sprang from its hiding place and silently slipped through the night above their heads. Moments later they found themselves behind a small stone wall, watching the farmhouse for any unusual movements or activity. When Krzys was satisfied that everything was OK, they cautiously moved forward.

A dog suddenly charged out of the darkness, heading straight towards them, baring its teeth. Krzys held his hand out and offered a golabki, which the animal devoured greedily. "The poor thing will be dead by morning," he whispered to Danuta as he dropped more food on the grass.

To the side of the property was a large timber barn, and they could hear the sound of pigs inside. They could also make out the shadows of sties and troughs dotted about the paddocks that surrounded the property. There would be plenty to eat here.

They already had a plan. Danuta would do the begging. A good-looking young country girl like her would certainly appear less threatening than an unshaven young man with a rifle and rucksack, so Krzys remained at the side of the barn and kept the dog company. His father's old .22 rifle was loaded and ready as Danuta approached the front door.

After looking over her shoulder for encouragement, Danuta plucked up enough courage to knock on the door. Moments later she heard muffled voices, then the sound of a lock turning. Someone was shuffling around inside and to her horror, when the door finally opened she found herself face to face with a German officer, a pistol in his right hand.

Several hours earlier, a small convoy of military vehicles was driving along the main road to Krakow, when one of the staff cars got a puncture. The officer in charge ordered the convoy to continue, saying he would catch them up shortly. Unfortunately, his driver found it difficult to remove the wheel nuts as the mechanics in the garage at Wroclaw had over tightened them when they put new tyres on the vehicle the week before. It took two hours to complete the ten-minute wheel change, so the officer consulted his maps and ordered the driver to take a short cut across country in an effort to catch up with the convoy. As night fell, he realised they were lost.

The thought of a nice hot country dinner appealed; somewhere warm and comfortable to spend the night before looking for the convoy in daylight. So the officer told his driver to pull into the nearest farm, where he ordered the occupants to cook for him.

Almost an hour later there was a knock at the door and a pleasant-looking young girl appeared. She was cold and shaking, her boots were caked in mud and she asked if she could borrow some cabbage.

Danuta disappeared inside the house and it was then that Krzys stumbled upon the staff car parked behind the barn, on the blind side. The vehicle was unlocked and unguarded, and he found a first-class example of a standard issue Sturmgewehr 44 rifle, complete with ammunition in the back. A great improvement on his father's old rabbit hunters .22.

With his new rifle set and primed, he positioned himself behind a large oak tree where he got an excellent view of proceedings through the kitchen window. He could clearly see a uniformed German talking to Danuta at the kitchen table, apparently having been easily convinced that she was from a neighbouring farm in search of cabbage to make her elderly parent's dinner. The officer was pushing a glass of wine towards her while his driver looked worse for wear, a few feet away, an empty bottle of wine in his hand.

A nervous woman worked at the stove stirring a large stew pot while an old man was tied to a chair by the wall.

Through the rifle sights Krzys could see that he was gagged and bleeding from the nose. There did not seem to be anyone else around.

While Danuta was busy trying to convince the German that she was too young to drink she saw a bright flash through the kitchen window, which was followed by a loud crack and the tinkle of breaking glass. The officer in front of her stopped talking mid-sentence, and as he looked up at the ceiling she noticed a small red circle on his forehead, right between his eyes. A dribble of blood made its way down the bridge of his nose and he collapsed face first onto the table with a resounding thud.

The woman dropped the soup ladle and put her hand up to her mouth to stifle a scream, and before the driver realised what had happened, he too was lying head first on the table with a hole in his temple.

It took only a few minutes for Krzys to reassure the couple that they were safe and he meant them no harm. While Danuta untied the elderly man, Krzys scouted the house and its surrounds, to ensure there were no surprises lurking elsewhere.

Considering what they had been through, the couple were remarkably stoic. The old man and Krzys carried the German bodies into an outbuilding, and when they returned the woman served everyone a splendid hot pork and cabbage stew.

Two hours later Danuta and Krzys were ready to depart. The rucksack was full of vegetables, two loaves of bread, a freshly skinned and gutted rabbit and half a ham, personally selected from the meat cellar by the man.

As they readied to leave, Krzys nodded towards the outbuilding where the German's bodies lay. "What about them?"

The old man's eyes narrowed and he made a guttural noise in his throat and spat on the ground. "Pigs," he said.

Krzys nodded in agreement and added, "The German bastards."

The woman intervened. "No, no," she said. "Pigs. He will feed them to the pigs tomorrow!"

"German sausages; that is what I shall be producing here for the next few months!" The farmer spoke without any humour in his voice.

"And the car?" Krzys asked incredulously.

"I will hide it in the barn and cover it with straw bales. It will make a nice vehicle to take my pigs to market after the war!" the old man smiled, breaking his leathery face in two.

Danuta was still laughing an hour later when she and Krzys arrived back at the rowing boat. They now had plenty of fresh food. "No more cabbage. Thank you, God!" Krzys said as they checked the rucksack. "We also have two new weapons and enough ammunition for a decent confrontation." He showed Danuta the rifle and a handgun he had taken from the officer.

A duck quacked from its nest in the reeds and frogs croaked alongside them as the moon made a brief appearance, its reflection floating on the surface of the river.

"I'm cold," Danuta said, and Krzys raised his side of the cover as she slid across and snuggled next to him, his arm around her shoulder and her head resting on his chest. She felt secure for the first time in many days as sleep washed over her and took her to a place somewhere far more comfortable than the old rowing boat. Krzys remained awake, his hand resting on his new rifle and his thoughts on the bridge up ahead.

18

After another six-hour drive the two trucks stopped on the outskirts of yet another nameless town. The women were permitted to drink from a large puddle, after one of their guards broke the ice with his rifle butt. Strangely, despite the cold, it was not hunger that the women felt most, it was thirst and they willingly scooped the dirty water into their shaking hands.

The sky was threatening to finally release its load of snow; the heavy clouds fluffed up, full and ready to burst. The women huddled in small groups and spoke in whispers as the smell of cigarette smoke drifted across from the guards at the front of the truck. Ania talked of slipping into the forest when the Germans were busy. After all, there must have been over thirty women in both trucks and only six or seven Germans watching over them. They could not chase everyone.

"That's fine if you are one of the ones who gets away, but what of the repercussions for those who don't run or who are caught?" someone asked.

"She's right. You can't do that to them, Ania, the price would be too high," Emilie concluded. "I don't fancy another night like last night, let me tell you that, but the alternative of a freezing night alone in the forest is not much better. And who will help us? People will think we are Jews on the run and who in Poland wants to risk helping a Jew?"

The fat driver suddenly sprang up from nowhere, like a jack-in-a-box, a thin black, foul-smelling cigar wedged between his clenched teeth. "Ah, my strange-eyed princess!" He gripped Ania's jaw. "Tonight ... your prince awaits!"

"I can hardly control myself, you fat German pig. As soon as I get back from the synagogue I will be all yours!" Ania spat on the ground and the driver instinctively slapped her face, a stinging smack that left its mark. He had never thought about the women being Jews; were they not supposed to be Polish farm girls-is that not what the orders said?

The German glared at Ania as he stomped away in disgust. The Burczyk girls were known for their cheekiness, Ania more than Danuta. But being given detention or extra homework was the worst that could happen to them in those days. This was a far more serious situation and Emilie told Ania to be careful, not to be so smart, or she would come to regret it.

The ground floor windows in what appeared to be a derelict building on the other side of the road suddenly lit up, revealing a large two-storey timber building that looked like a village hall of some kind. The women were ushered through the front door where they were greeted by several old ladies dressed warmly in long woollen clothing and shawls. Their faces were weathered and their hands twisted by arthritis, but their eyes were bright and sympathetic.

They saw the way that the truck women were dressed; how young they were, how they shivered and whispered their thanks through purple lips as they were ushered upstairs and given knitted quilts and blankets for warmth.

The room was empty apart from a few chairs stacked at one end. It appeared to be an assembly hall that had perhaps been used for dance classes or public meetings before the war. It smelled strongly of floor wax with every window crossed with tape, in the shape of an X.

One of the old ladies showed the women a sink at the far end of the room. The taps no longer worked but several buckets of water were made available, and there was a flushing toilet behind a screen. Such luxury!

The old women soon found the sick girl, who now looked as grey as the blanket they had wrapped around her. She was seriously ill, shivering and mumbling deliriously as they fussed around her. A bowl of hot water appeared from downstairs, along with a clean towel and some tablets that the girl was encouraged to swallow. One of the Germans sat smoking on a small wicker chair by the only door, a rifle by his side, completely disinterested in the goings-on.

Less than half an hour later the old ladies reappeared, and they gave the women warm beetroot soup and homemade bread along with metal mugs full of piping-hot milky tea. As the truck women ate, an old man with one arm appeared, a bag of nails hanging around his neck and a hammer tucked into his belt. He proceeded to somehow nail every window shut around the perimeter of the hall, and as he moved amongst the women they whispered their questions.

"What is this place, grandfather, what town are we in?"

"Do you know where they are taking us?"

The old man went about his task competently despite his handicap, all the time keeping a watchful eye on the guard at the door. "I heard them talking," he said quietly. "You are going to some place near Krakow tomorrow; a camp I think. Beyond that I know nothing, my children."

The guard yelled from the doorway. "Come on, you stupid cripple, get a move on! You're taking too long." The man looked up and nodded apologetically, then returned to his task, seemingly with more enthusiasm.

"Young woman," he said under his breath to Emilie, "good luck and may God bless you."

His voice was soft and warm, reminding her of her own dear Grandpa. "You too," Emilie replied respectfully. "You too, Dziadek."

It had been a long time since the old man had been spoken to so affectionately, and his eyes filled with tears as he pretended to have a problem with the window frame above the spot where Emilie lay.

Schroder appeared at the door with a napkin tucked into his shirtfront, striding around the room, examining the windows. The old man waited nervously for his approval. At the last window Schroder said, "Hurry up and make sure it's as secure as the rest. Not a bad job considering your situation!" He flicked the empty sleeve that hung from the old man's shoulder and grinned. "Very good. Hurry up now, we need you in the kitchen downstairs to help." And he was gone.

The old man banged the final nails into place and gathered up his tools, but as he made his way across the room he seemed to stumble against Emilie's legs. "Get out of my way," he said loudly.

The guard was quickly out of his chair, scanning the room to see what the fuss was about. When he realised what had happened he settled back down and lit a cigarette. "Fucking cripples!" Then he shouted at the one-armed man to hurry up again.

"I am sorry, sir!" the old man called back. As he pulled himself onto his feet he discreetly pushed something towards Emilie. She saw it immediately-a six-inch galvanised nail- and carefully slid it under the folds of her skirt as he hobbled away.

The old ladies reappeared to collect the empty cups and soup bowls, and distribute more blankets. They stopped at the injured girl and tried to make her more comfortable, but shook their heads and talked among themselves in grave tones. Later that night the girl disappeared from the room as the other women slept; she was never seen or heard of again.

It was around three in the morning that Ania awoke to the sound of a scuffle at the door. The fat driver, clearly drunk, was arguing with the guard. There was an angry exchange between the two men and the driver pointed at Ania and shouted. "You, queer-eyed Jewish bitch!" The guard stepped in front of him and pushed him away, but the fat driver had not finished. "You'll regret this, Jew girl!" Ania could hear the driver yelling as he stumbled back down the stairs and out of sight. She did not feel too concerned about the fat driver's interest in her; he was a slob and a drunk, and it was clear that his colleagues despised him as much as she did. But Braun, the skinny one, he was very different. He was sly, ruthless and brooding and Ania could feel his eyes boring into her every time she saw him. There was something very unsettling about Braun.

***

"Ladies. Good morning to you all! I hope the arrangements were to your satisfaction and you slept well. For those of you who do not know who I am, my name is Obersturmfuhrer Schroder. You will no doubt be pleased to know that today we will reach our destination and you will soon have the honour of serving our beloved Fuhrer and the Fatherland. This is a great day for you, ladies! I understand there are facilities here where you may wash, a bathroom of sorts. Please, look your best. Good times await those of you who are willing to embrace them!" Schroder clicked his heels and left the room.

A murmur of suspicion buzzed through the room. Some women made their way towards the facilities as others sat tight and talked to their neighbours. Fifteen minutes later more hot soup and tea arrived. There was plenty of conversation now, as the women speculated about Schroder's change in demeanour.

An hour later they were marshalled downstairs and despite their uncertain circumstances, they seemed to enjoy the scene as they crunched through a fresh layer of undisturbed, crisp white snow on their way to their transports. The back portion of the second vehicle was now enclosed, and the women were told they could keep the quilts, shawls and blankets they had been given by the old ladies in the village hall. There was a mixture of anxiety and relief as the journey to their final destination began.

Ania's day got off to a good start when she realised that Braun and the fat driver were no longer around, and many of the women were chatting comfortably for the first time. Several actually smiled and the occasional sound of muted laughter was heard above the rumbling of the truck's engine.

But this was not like the times when the women gathered in the town square to gossip. There was no talk of cooking, sewing or drunken husbands. There was, however, a growing degree of confidence with some of the women; *look how they are treating us, we are safe, they want us!*

Ania and Emilie were the only two not involved in the chatter. Instead they exchanged silent, anxious looks, their faces grim, their minds deep in the reality of their situation. They were not blinded by false hope; they had already seen and experienced enough to know not to trust the Germans. Emilie sat quietly with her thoughts and Ania closed her eyes and listened to the rumble of the truck as it made its way onto a tar road again. Once again, her thoughts were of Danuta. Where was her sister?

19

Danuta woke to see heavy clouds moving across the sky from the west. *"The snow is coming at last—let's hope the Russians are coming with it!'* she mumbled as she sat up and watched Krzys put a pot of water on the boil on the riverbank. Her confidence had started to return because she felt safe around him-he had not attempted to take advantage of her or their situation the night before and she knew he would look after her, and make sure she came to no harm. Her family would have approved of Krzys Paderewski.

Danuta was not without experience, and when she did decide to lie with a man, it was always someone older. Younger men of Krzys's age behaved like silly children; they rolled around in the grass, wrestled each other and drank too much in their attempts to gain her approval. But Krzys was different from other village boys. He was more mature, and Danuta was thankful that she had found herself with him and not someone else. When Krzys saw that Danuta was awake he took her a cup of warm tea, which tasted of the river. They sat in silence for a while, each with their own thoughts, blowing on their tea, slurping occasionally. Danuta shivered as the morose feeling that had consumed her earlier in the journey started to return. Feelings of guilt sent her mind off to a darker place...

She had been in bed when the Germans arrived. She heard the gunshots and the screams, so she hid. She only thought of herself during those terrifying moments. Then, as soon as the opportunity presented itself, she ran away and left everyone else to fend for themselves. What kind of person would do that? Had the war already changed her? Or perhaps it brought out the real Danuta, the one who was inside her all along. Christ! She had even participated in the killing of two human beings-the Germans at the farm. They were someone's sons, husbands, brothers, lovers ... Then something in her head reminded her that the killing of the soldiers had helped free two other people-the pig farmer and his wife. She gave them back the opportunity to live. It was like a game in a way-*lose one, save one.* She was so young; she did not ask for this kind of responsibility!

But it was hers nonetheless, and Danuta knew that if she wanted to again enjoy the simple things in life-the musty odour of a wet dog as it steamed by the kitchen stove, skating on the village pond in winter, pounding around the track leaving everyone in her wake-or best of all, sharing gossip in bed with Ania-she may well have to participate in killing again.

***

As the boat slipped through the smooth grey water the only sound that could be heard was the slap of the oars just before the backwards pull. Krzys had been watching Danuta as she sat deep in her thoughts in front of him. He was not used to women's ways, their sudden tears and their wide-ranging emotions. He did not yet know when it was time to give Danuta space or when to talk and engage in what to him seemed like pointless conversation most of the time. Women were a mystery to Krzys. The greatest gift of all would be to unravel their secrets-how much would that be worth to a man? A small fortune, no doubt!

Just before dusk they moored the boat on the riverbank, two bends away from the bridge. The reeds were thickest there so it gave them a perfect place to sit and wait for night to fall. Krzys left a corner of the tarpaulin open so he could keep an eye out for any activity before darkness descended.

As soon as it was safe he would slip out and check the bridge; would there be Germans there? If there were, would he try to get past them in the early hours of the morning when hopefully, the moon would be concealed by cloud and they might be at their least observant. Would they be watching the river or the road, or both?

As Krzys prepared to scout out the bridge, he turned to Danuta and asked, "Do you think you can do it?" She knew what he meant. Could she kill a German? Could she be face to face with someone and pull the trigger?

She replied after a moment's thought. "I don't think I have a choice.

I *won't* have a choice, will I?" Krzys had tried to teach Danuta to shoot a handgun the day after they took the German officer's weapons at the pig farm. Her aim had been erratic at best. First, a bullseye but the next shot didn't even hit the target, and she was only a couple of metres away! He had decided then that the only way she could be successful would be at very close range. Even she could not miss if she was less than a metre away-assuming she had the courage to pull the trigger.

He asked her again, and she replied, "I will do it, Krzys. I can do it." And she smiled for the first time that day-a tentative smile.

PART 3:
THE
COMMANDANT'S
CLUB

20

Obersturmbannfuhrer Baldric Fischer puffed on his favourite pipe then checked his pocket watch. Ten o'clock precisely. It was a Swiss piece, so he knew it to be always correct. German engineering was superior in every way except time keeping; he was happy to acknowledge that.

Fischer had cancelled all hearings, submissions and requests for clemency that day. Even the weekly budget meeting was postponed. It was an important day; the new facilities had to be inspected and the stock was scheduled to arrive that afternoon. Knowing that Obersturmfuhrer Rolf Schroder was responsible, he had no doubt that the stock would be there at the allotted time. That was why he charged him with the task-Schroder was reliable. Nothing must go wrong. Nothing would go wrong.

Fischer had first suggested the idea in writing, through the usual channels, only to receive a reply from Eichmann that was nothing less than derisive.

Eichmann used words such as '*idiotic*' and '*ludicrous*', but Fischer was not going to let such an ingenious idea fall by the wayside. He immediately sought a private meeting with the Fuhrer, who did actually admit that the idea 'had merit.' "*The only reason Eichmann does not like it, is because he did not think of it himself Baldric, that is all!*" the Fuhrer had said, laughing broadly and slapping his old friend on the shoulder.

That had been a good visit for Commandant Fischer, when he pitched his idea to Hitler. It was handled over dinner, just him, the Fuhrer, Eva and Blondi in front of a roaring fire at Bergdorf. "Baldric, my friend, I want you to call me Adolf when we are alone like this," the Fuhrer had said. It was the finest night of Fischer's life, after which he no longer cared what Eichmann thought.

The next morning was back to business as usual. Several members of the High Command arrived at Bergdorf for a breakfast briefing. Himmler, Hermann Goering, Minister Goebbels and Eichmann. Fischer was invited to stay but as soon as the Fuhrer left the room to take a phone call, Eichmann personally let him know that he thought the idea was ridiculous. The two men came close to exchanging blows.

As far as Fischer's innovative new concept was concerned, Eichmann was not the only person who thought it foolhardy and irresponsible. Minister Goebbels did not like the idea either, although the Fuhrer stood firm and told his minister for propaganda that after a good deal of thought, he had decided that Fischer's plan would not only succeed, it would also provide a wonderful opportunity for some first-class propaganda.

"Mein Fuhrer, I fail to see how anyone would see any benefit in this ... this ... farce! Berlin would be seen as a laughing stock if you approved it!" Goebbels was furious. Perhaps he had overstepped his mark with such an outburst. The room immediately went silent and the Fuhrer reacted in what was for him, a most unusual way.

Calmly, and in a very measured way, he asked everyone to leave the room except for Minister Goebbels. Then Goebbels sat listening as the Fuhrer spent fifteen minutes of his valuable time selling Fischer's concept. He made it plain that he supported the initiative, and come what may, this revolutionary plan was going to proceed. Nothing, and he emphasised his next few words, *and no one,* would prevent it from happening. Goebbels seemed to understand after that.

Goebbels had lied, of course; he did not buy the idea. What sane person would? But it did serve to prove beyond doubt yet again that Fischer was a danger. If he had managed to persuade someone like the Fuhrer to accept an idea such as this, what else did he have up his sleeve and where did his power come from? What was it that he was holding over the Fuhrer's head? What secrets did he have?

***

The Commandant was expected at ten minutes past ten precisely. The area needed to be ready to receive the stock or heads would roll. Fischer turned to his personal assistant of four years, Rapportfuhrer Fritz Schole, and handed him his pipe, which Schole then placed on the rack above the fireplace.

"Ready, Fritz?"

"Ready."

The two men then stepped into the square outside the house where a small guard had already assembled to escort them to the inspection point. They marched at breakneck pace towards the gate at the side of the main entrance. It opened when they were five steps away. Heels clicked, prisoners scurried out of sight and supervisors shouted extra loud to ensure the Commandant knew they were doing their jobs.

A brisk walk across the parade ground then four steps up a small flight of stairs and Fischer was inside the building being inspected, and out of the cold. Using the same stance that he had often seen the Fuhrer use. He clasped his hands behind his back and said, "Mhhm," as a curtain was pulled aside so he could view a room. "Small but no doubt sufficient. Next!" On to the adjacent room. Same size, about four metres long and three wide. A double bed along one side, sink and toilet on the short wall at the far end.

"I have taken the liberty of ensuring the Fuhrer's picture is in every room, Obersturmbannfuhrer, and for the sake of pleasantry, a picture of some scenery from the Fatherland. A different one for every room. Discreet, and as I say, pleasant." Rapportfuhrer Schole had done a fine job, and next to the light switch Fischer was pleased to see two documents on display: 'Rules of Conduct' and 'Health Regulations.'

"A good touch," Fischer said as he tapped the notices. The boss was happy. So far, so good. "I want to see the Premier Room next," he said. The two men stepped into the hallway. On the right-hand side, opposite the kitchen was a room with a green door, which Schole opened. Fischer stepped inside.

"Wunderbar!"

"Fraulein Tina oversaw the decorations, sir, as instructed. The colours are to her orders. Same with the bed. All the linen, everything meets her exacting requirements."

Fischer's hands were still clasped behind his back. "Gutte. This is very gutte indeed."

Schole continued. "Fraulein Tina was behind every design aspect, except the picture of the Fatherland; that was my idea, as I say."

Fischer stopped. "But Fraulein Tina approved of the picture?"

"Very much, Herr Obersturmbann-fuhrer!"

"Then everything is gutte."

When Fischer stepped back into the hallway, he found it lined with people. Schole explained. "These are the tradespeople, Herr Commandant. Those responsible for the work. They are here for your consideration."

Fischer sniffed the air. "Very well, if I have to." He walked down the line of workers, nodding appreciatively here and there, hands still clasped behind his back. Some of the men were prisoners, dressed in their zebra uniforms, and Fischer avoided their stench by moving past them quickly. Everyone stood cap in hand, head bowed, having been told not to look the Commandant in the eye unless he addressed them personally.

Fischer was bored before he reached the fifth man. "Enough. Time to move on. Get these men something meaningful to do and reward them with extra soup tonight." He managed a smile for one of the workers, even tapped another on the shoulder. "Maybe a voucher for you, if the reports say you are up to it, eh? You lucky man!" Then he turned to Schole and said, "The vouchers are ready, Fritz?"

"Everything is ready, mein Commandant."

The voucher system had been devised by Schole. Exemplary behaviour, duty above and beyond the call, a higher work rate, pleasing supervisors with exceptional commitment-all these aspects garnered points, and points led to vouchers!

"Now that is what I call motivation, Fritz! Eh? If that doesn't lift output around here I don't know what will!"

Eichmann and Goebbels had been horrified by the voucher system. The Fuhrer was mystified, but could see a possible benefit and anyway, he wanted to keep Fischer happy, quiet and out of the way. Promoting him to lieutenant colonel had worked up to now, but it was beginning to look as if the Fuhrer may have created a monster when he sent Fischer to the outer reaches of Poland to run this little sub-camp at Wysznica...

Fischer dismissed everyone except Schole as he reached the front of the building. "Fritz, I have a problem. Walk with me so we can talk this thing through." The two men strolled casually back towards the gates. "I have told you before that Herr Goebbels does not like this concept of mine. I am told he would close it tomorrow if he could. But the Fuhrer is with me all the way. He sees the value of rewarding the best workers for a job well done."

"The Fuhrer is right, of course, mein Commandant."

"Indeed." Fischer was in a thoughtful mood. He patted his pockets then realised he had left his pipe in his office. Schole extended his right hand, palm up like a magician. "I thought you might want this," he said, handing the pipe over.

The thing about Fritz Schole was that he always knew what Fischer wanted when he wanted it. The commandant had made him his right-hand man for that very reason. And there was a time recently, when Fischer returned from his last visit to Bergdorf, that he pulled Schole aside and told him he could call him Baldric. "Only when the moment is right, you understand? Never, and I repeat, never call me Baldric if anyone else is in earshot-including Fraulein Tina. You understand?" Schole did, and he was delighted to now be on first name terms with the commandant. It was a level of intimacy that no one else enjoyed at Wysznica, except of course, Tina.

"What would I do without you, eh, Fritz?" Fischer took the pipe and set about lighting it. "We need a name, Fritz, a name for this new venture that confirms its significance. A dignified name that makes people feel proud and honoured to be associated with it. I like the name for the room with the green door—the Premier Room-I like that. It is classy. But what do we call this project, this special place, eh?"

"Have you any ideas yourself, Baldric? Perhaps name it after Herr Goebbels or the Fuhrer even?"

"No, no, no. Absolutely not. Can you imagine the Fuhrer finding out that this place has been named after him? My God, no! What are you thinking of, Fritz? Come now, you are my ideas man; I depend on you at such times. Think, man, think!"

"How about calling it..." Schole paused for a moment, as if to appear deep in thought, then he came up with the name he had been quietly thinking of all the time. "The Club? That sounds discreet enough doesn't it? It may even make the men feel a little status conscious, Baldric; give them something to boast about amongst themselves? Like being a member of a country club for instance, a place of stature."

"The Club, is that it? They will be able to say they are a member of *the Club.* Is that your point?"

"Indeed it is mein Commandant."

"I like it... The Club ... I like it very much! Congratulations, Fritz! The Club it is! A great name for the first brothel to ever be established in a Reich concentration camp!"

21

It was dark when Krzys first heard the German voices, from the riverbank up ahead, about one hundred metres away. He carefully nudged Danuta awake, his index finger pressed against her lips, "Shhh." The voices came nearer and Krzys could now hear the conversation. Someone said, "What's that? Over there, in the reeds. What is it?"

Krzys carefully reached out and tapped around beneath the tarpaulin, trying to locate the rifle.

The German voice again. "Shall I shoot, or what?"

"It's up to you. I can't see a thing anyway, it's too fucking dark." Krzys heard the dreaded sound of a bolt sliding a bullet into place and without further warning, a round discharged somewhere into the black night. Immediately, from the other side of the river bank there was a huge fuss. The air was full of the sound of screaming and wings flapping as several wild ducks fluttered noisily off their nests and scattered in all directions.

"Did I get one Klaus?"

"Who knows? Like I said, it's fucking dark, dummkopf; we'll have to check in the morning. Come on, let's get back. We are supposed to be on guard duty, not on a duck shoot."

Krzys sighed and Danuta closed her eyes; it had been a close call. The German voices were growing faint now, and within five minutes they could no longer be heard so Krzys moved the tarpaulin aside and peered through the reeds. All clear.

"What do we do now?" Danuta asked anxiously.

"Well, it sounded as if there were just two of them, so I think we need to take a closer look and see exactly how many there are. If there are too many we will just have to take our chances and try to get under the bridge without being seen or heard later tonight."

With nothing more said between them, Krzys slipped along the riverbank and disappeared into the dark night. Danuta remained in the boat, the sounds of the river all around her. A croaking frog heralded his return ten minutes later. He was a little breathless but clearly buoyed. "There are only three of them! If we play our cards right we can knock them all off and be on our way tonight."

"Kill them all?" Danuta sounded distinctly nervous.

"That's right. All of them. You have a better idea?"

Danuta gulped and shook her head; *no.*

The plan was simple enough. Danuta was to row herself across the river, hide the boat on the opposite side and scramble up the bank, and then make her way to the road. On a predetermined signal she would approach the bridge and engage the guards in conversation, with the handgun in her pocket. Krzys was confident he could pick off two of the Germans before they realised what was happening, using the German rifle he found at the farmhouse. The third guard would be down to Danuta: a close-range shooting with the handgun. Risky, but it was their best option.

"What do I talk to them about? I can't just walk up to three German guards from out of nowhere and make a conversation, can I?" Danuta's anxiety was a concern for Krzys. He needed her to be solid and confident, not full of doubt, and they didn't have time to write a damned script!

"What did you talk about at the farm, when that German answered the door?"

"Cabbages."

"You've got it then; talk about cabbages!" Danuta made a noise that sounded something like *hmmph;* Krzys shrugged and sighed, then went over the plan one last time.

They agreed on the signals and set their watches. He had to be in position first, and would let her know when he was ready with an owl hoot. Then it was up to her to walk across the bridge and engage the guards in conversation. When he got two shots off in quick succession, she would have to take care of the third guard. No hesitation. No messing around. One or two close range shots and that would be the end of it. Krzys explained that the light above the sentry box was critical. From his little sortie he discovered that he could see reasonably clearly and had spotted a tree further up the riverbank where he felt certain he could manoeuvre himself into the best possible position. Danuta had to ensure that all three guards were under the glow of the lamp; her cabbage talk had to keep them engaged long enough for him to hit his marks, and for her to hit hers.

She wanted to go through it again but he stopped her. If she didn't know now she would never know. She had to figure it out, act intuitively if necessary. She would be fine. Krzys didn't want her to think too hard about it, and he knew if she did she might stumble at the wrong time and alert the Germans that something was going on. If she did not manage to shoot the third guard after Krzys had bumped off the other two, the whole plan could fall apart.

It was now or never. They said their goodbyes, sealed them with a hesitant hug and before Danuta knew what was happening Krzys had pushed her and the boat out into the river. He watched her slip silently away into the darkness, then he scampered back to collect his rifle and make his way to the tree, up river.

Five minutes later, Danuta found herself moored amongst the reeds on the opposite riverbank and had already started to scramble up the embankment.

Krzys could just about make out her dark form as she struggled to the top, quickly reaching the roadside, where he saw her crouch down in the shadows and tidy herself up. Once he was certain she was safe, he got himself in position. The branches from the willow were just as he hoped, hanging low enough to tickle the water's edge, providing him with a veil of cover. He was positive that he could not be seen from the bridge, yet he still had an excellent view of everything. And then he felt the first snowflakes land on his face. Small puffs of cotton wool drifted down from above, increasing in volume as the seconds ticked by.

Despite the snow, Krzys could still see the three German guards at the sentry box, and as agreed, he made the sound of an owl-a muffled kind of hoot that had made Danuta laugh when he initially tested it, but now made her gulp anxiously because she knew Krzys was in position and things were about to happen.

She braced herself, took a deep breath and stumbled up the final slippery patch of grass, where snow was already starting to settle. She passed through a wire fence and found herself on the road, still hidden by the undergrowth. The bridge was ahead, no more than one hundred metres away. She could see the three Germans talking under the light of the sentry box. The night was silent, calm and surprisingly beautiful because of the snow, which was now floating in large white flakes, as gentle as feathers drifting down to earth.

Krzys double-checked his weapon, flicked off the safety catch, rubbed the snow off the muzzle then focussed carefully through the sights, lining up one of the Germans on the bridge in the cross hairs.

Danuta gave herself no time to dwell on things. Krzys was absolutely right-she must just get on with it.

"Don't give your nerves a chance to play games with your mind", he had said; there was no room for hesitation. She thought of herself in a track and field event, jogged on the spot for ten seconds then stepped out of the shadows and started to walk towards the sentry box on the far side of the bridge. The handgun felt cold and heavy in her pocket and she kept her trigger finger in place as she walked towards the Germans with billowing snow clogging her eyelashes, making her blink.

More than ever before Krzys was grateful that his father had taught him to hunt in the forests around their village when he was a young boy. Initially they shot rabbits, but they soon moved up to deer. Stalking was the best part-getting an animal in your sights without it knowing you were there. It had started as a game, but soon Krzys learned how to disguise his smell and camouflage his body to such an extent that he became virtually invisible to his quarry. They kept score of their kills and by the time he was fourteen, Krzys had a better strike rate than his father.

By his sixteenth birthday he could venture alone into the forest, stalk, shoot and skin a beast and live off the land for several days. He had learned about the forest and its ways, the creatures that lived there, their habits and their habitats. His greatest talent was shooting and he had the best teacher, his father being a highly decorated sniper from World War I. Krzys called him Pa or Tata, but when his mother was around, always Ojciec. She was so traditional, as was typical of her generation, and Krzys, unlike many of his contemporaries at the time, had nothing but deep admiration and respect for his parents.

Aided by the light from the single yellow bulb on the sentry box roof, Krzys watched Danuta approach the bridge. The snow was swirling like moths around the light, but he still had excellent vision.

There they were.

Three Germans.

All in overcoats, all with weapons in easy reach.

And they were completely unaware of what was about to happen.

Clouds of steam came from the guards' mouths when they spoke. One was drinking from a tin cup; the others had their rifles slung over their shoulders, hands in their pockets, stamping their feet for warmth. Very relaxed. Krzys patted his new German rifle confidently. He knew he could get two of them in quick succession; the coffee drinker and the one to his left. No doubt as soon as the first one went down, the others would go for their weapons. Before they reached them, the second would be blown apart with a head shot. While all this was going on, Danuta had to shoot the third guard. She would be close enough, around a metre. Even she could not miss at that range and if she only disabled him for a moment, it would be long enough for Krzys to get him in his sights and finish him off.

Krzys adjusted his position under the tree: body flat, legs spread-eagled behind him, elbows bent, chin nuzzled into the stock of the rifle, head up, left eye closed, the other focussed through the sight and on to the target. The snow was heavier now, and he prayed that none of the Germans would move into the sentry box for shelter. At the moment they were laughing and seemed unperturbed about the weather. Then Krzys saw Danuta approaching from the right-hand side of the bridge. His heart rate jumped. The Germans still had no idea what was happening.

With every step, Danuta felt her pulse quicken. At rest it was unusually low at 45 beats per minute, but after running one hundred metres it shot up to around one hundred and eighty beats-exactly where it was now. She glanced across the river downstream to the dark outline of the huge willow-there was no sign of Krzys.

The Germans watched her approach. She stared straight ahead, blinked the snow from her eyelashes, blowing flakes away from her mouth and slipping a little girl lost smile onto her face. Why was she shaking so much-the cold- or fear? All of a sudden the air seemed to penetrate her clothes, reaching right through to her bone marrow. Her teeth were chattering and the gun felt like a block of ice in her pocket. She flexed her fingers several times to warm them up then slipped her index finger back inside the trigger guard.

One-step ... two steps ... three, four, five. One of the Germans was smiling at her, another had a cup of hot coffee raised to his mouth and the third was stepping out from behind the other two to check out the beautiful girl approaching. The snow had already settled on their shoulders and helmets, and the ground was covered in a thin layer of glistening white flakes that twinkled under the light from the sentry box.

All Danuta needed now was that first shot from Krzys. As soon as she heard it there would be panic and she would dispense with her target from point blank range. She was even going to try to get in an extra shot or two, just in case Krzys only wounded one of his targets. She steeled herself for the moment and then she was there, face to face with the three German guards at the sentry box.

She glanced quickly to her left, down the riverbank. Krzys was under that tree, just sixty metres away. Everything would be over soon, thank God ... One of the guards spoke; the one who stepped out from behind the smiler and the coffee drinker. "Guten tag. We need to see your papers, bitte."

It was at precisely that moment, out of the corner of her eye, in the dark shadows down the riverbank under the tree, that Danuta saw a brief flash of light and heard the sound of a gun discharging...

22

Three pm. Wysznica. Time to inspect the new stock. Fischer said goodbye to Tina. "I'll be back in time for tea."

"And I will make sure something hot is ready for you!" she replied, shaking her chest provocatively. Schole turned away to give the commandant some privacy. He hated the way Tina flounced about like a cheap tart when he was around, flaunting her body, making it plain that the commandant belonged to her. But Schole knew her affection towards the commandant was not genuine; he was not stupid, and he hated the indignity of it all.

After Fischer's last trip to Berlin, Tina had been prancing about the house in some new French silk underwear, a gift from Baldric. Tina was not allowed to go to Berlin under any circumstances. Fischer's wife was there. The fat cow who gave birth to the two chubby, ugly children whose picture sat on his desk-the photograph Tina turned over so she could not see their faces when he took her from behind in the office.

She preferred sex that way, with him behind, so she did not have to look into his sweaty face or up his disgusting hairy nostrils. The filthy noises he made were bad enough and as for that stinking pipe of his and the habit he had of cleaning the spittle out of the mouthpiece by tapping it on the dining room table at dinner ... All that gunk and mucus spattered on her beautiful white linen tablecloth. How the camp laundry got the stains out was beyond her...

Schole held Fischer's jacket as he slipped his arms into the sleeves and Tina brushed the dandruff from the shoulders and handed him his hat. German officers traditionally took great pride in their appearance. Their immaculate and beautifully tailored grey uniforms had been produced by Hugo Boss, cut and sewn by forced labour taken from the ghettos and camps specifically for that purpose. Compared to the British, who paraded around in their one-size fits all baggy khaki clown suits, the Germans were to a man, doyens of fashion and elegance within the theatre of war. Even Fischer looked good.

Schole helped the commandant into his greatcoat next and then handed him his gloves, straightened his Iron Cross for him then placed his pipe on the mantelpiece. Schole liked to fuss over the commandant but Tina thought he was sycophantic, and she made sure Fischer knew. As far as she was concerned, Baldric had three wives. The fat cow back in Berlin, her and Schole. Fischer actually agreed and said that he thought Schole was the one who looked after him the best! If he had not been laughing when he said it, she would have slapped his face. Fischer once said he could not survive without Schole, but he had never said that about her.

***

Light snow was falling over the parade ground, and the women had been standing to attention, shivering in the slush for thirty minutes before Fischer arrived with Schole in tow. All around as they waited, the women observed armed soldiers watching over weary workers going about their business, loading tree trunks onto trucks, wearing only striped pyjama suits. They looked filthy, desperately cold and undernourished. It was clear that this place was some kind of work complex, surrounded by barbed wire and watch towers while smoke belched from two huge chimneys behind a series of timber huts ... In the background somewhere not too far away, they could hear a working sawmill, and the throb of machinery. During the journey to Wysznica, the women occasionally spoke of rumours they had heard in the markets and from shopkeepers. Terrible things about places that seemed all too similar to the one they found themselves in, and they were now trembling more from the fear that had wormed its way into their minds than the cold that had penetrated their bones.

Fischer inspected the two lines of women, starting at the back, walking between the rows. That was enough. It was too cold. During the inspection he placed his hands behind his back and nodded at one or two women quite amiably, in the same manner as the Fuhrer during his visits to factories and munitions plants. The women did not make eye contact but appeared respectful. He was pleased by what he saw.

Fischer stood in front of the line-up. "Women of Poland," he smiled as he began his address. "Welcome to Wysznica!" The snow continued to fall on the tremulous, wretched assembly as Fischer droned on about the glory of the Reich and the Fatherland. There was no doubting that in his mind, his dream was nearing reality and the mythical door to the bunker at Berlin was starting to open.

He thanked the women for volunteering. "Your offer to work for the Reich does you great credit", he said. When the war was over and Germany was victorious, he would himself personally ensure their contributions were acknowledged and rewarded. He spoke with a strong voice, authoritatively, standing upright and proud in front of them. Schole looked on in admiration, the women in fear.

Fischer had momentarily stopped in front of Ania during his inspection and looked her up and down. She thought she saw him raise an eyebrow. Or perhaps she had imagined it. There was a crowd of uniformed onlookers in the background, including the fat driver and Karl Braun, the skinny guard whose colleagues sometimes called the Greyhound; they saw what happened.

Fischer continued with his welcome speech. "For those of you who decide not to participate willingly in this exciting new project of mine, we do have other tasks of a less, shall we say, salutary nature. Look around you at those who wear striped suits, then compare their lives now to what you are about to be offered. You will soon understand. Women of Poland, the choice is yours." The commandant's inspection and introduction took no more than ten minutes, but it failed to lift the women's spirits. The German onlookers who knew only too well of the commandant's moods were surprised that he was not irritated by the apparent lack of interest. Schole knew why-Fischer was up to something.

23

Danuta was confused. No one stumbled or fell to the ground bleeding. Nobody clutched their chest or their guts as Krzys's shot slammed into their body. No one even ducked. But didn't the flash and the sound of the shot come from Krzys's spot under the willow tree? She fingered the gun in her pocket-what to do? One of the guards suddenly yelled, "Scheisse!" and sprinted down the riverbank towards the tree. A metal coffee mug clattered to the ground as another guard pulled his rifle from his shoulder and stuck it into Danuta's chest. She was told to stay exactly where she was. Moments later the guard who had run down the riverbank yelled, "Klaus, kommen, schnell, schnell!"

As Danuta waited nervously on the bridge she saw the two Germans struggling up the grass bank with a body, which they dumped unceremoniously on the road in front of her. It was Krzys.

Her eyes widened. Krzys's father may have taught him how to stalk and hunt but it seemed he had not learned how not to be stalked or hunted himself. There may well have been three guards up on the bridge, but there was also another somewhere else, and he had seen Krzys move into position under the tree on the riverbank. And now, Krzys's lifeless body lay on the road collecting snow as one of the Germans went through his pockets and the others tried to work out what to do next.

Danuta's eyes filled with tears as a tremor of fear spread through her body. She had never counted on this. It was not supposed to happen this way. Krzys had made it sound so simple. Yes, there had been some danger involved, but after the incident at the pig farm it seemed as if she and Krzys were invincible. She wanted to run to him, hold his head, kiss him back to life. How could he be dead? This was ridiculous.

The previously pleasant German did not appear as nice when he nodded towards Krzys' body. "You know this man?"

Danuta voice was quaking. "No. I've never seen him before."

"Then why are you crying?"

Danuta had not realised she was crying. What should she say? What should she do? Krzys always had the answers; he always knew what to say. A tear traced a path down her cheek and slipped into the corner of her mouth.

One of the guards prodded her with his rifle. "Well? Speak up. And put your hands up, hande hoch, hande hoch!" He seemed terrified himself, and his hands trembled when he spoke. They did not train him for this. They put him on a bridge in the middle of nowhere, where nothing was supposed to happen, and now he had a dead body at his feet and a very nervous young woman standing in front of him. Danuta looked at him-he was just a young boy.

"We should phone ahead and tell them what has happened here," one of the Germans said in an attempt to take control. Then he turned to Danuta, stepped closer and shouted, "You haven't answered his question, why are you crying? Why?"

Before she could say a word, a muffled crack came from the far side of the riverbank. The German who was holding the rifle at her chest was staring at her, then his head seemed to twitch slightly and without warning his legs folded beneath him and he slumped heavily to the floor, his rifle clattering onto the road beside him.

Several more cracks like fireworks came in quick succession, and the remaining Germans fell in separate crumpled heaps. One of them was moaning softly and blood was pulsing from a hole in his neck, pooling beneath his head. He stared up at Danuta as if he was confused. *What the hell is going on?*

Danuta was about to scream when a pair of gloved hands suddenly wrapped themselves around her face from behind. She could smell tobacco as well as another odour that was already becoming familiar. Cordite.

People were seemingly melting out of the shadows, all wearing black, moving swiftly, throwing the Germans over the bridge into the river, one by one. "This one is still alive!" A Polish accent. The hands fell from Danuta's face and someone whispered harshly into her ear. "Stay where you are. Do not move."

A tall man stepped from behind her and pulled a revolver from his pocket. She noticed that it appeared longer than the handgun she had seen in Krzys's possession, and it was only when he walked up to the moaning German and put a bullet into his head that she realised it had a silencer. Then, in a sudden rush, a van rattled across from the far side of the bridge, its side painted with the word 'Florist'. It skidded to a stop in the fresh snow, the rear doors opened and Krzys's body was bundled inside. Then Danuta felt someone behind her again and before she realised what was happening, a hood was pulled over her head.

She felt herself being pushed into the enclosed rear of the vehicle while in the background she heard a loud splash; the last German being ditched into the river. The rear of the van dipped as more people jumped in and

Danuta heard the doors slam. She could feel people breathing around her, smell their bodies, the damp of their clothing, cigarette smoke; four, maybe five people. The whole business seemed to take only a few minutes before the van clanked noisily into gear and shuddered as the wheels span in the snow and it fishtailed away. Danuta had no idea if she had just been rescued or abducted.

24

After Fischer made his exit from the parade ground, the women were herded up a small flight of stairs into a nearby building. They were taken into a freshly painted room. A small square table with a chair behind stood at the far wall, and a man in a white doctor's coat sat writing while a large, intimidating woman (the chief medical officer-CMO) stood at his side with her hands crossed over her ample bosom.

Neither the doctor nor the CMO looked up as Schroder pushed the women into two lines, standing to attention and clicking his heels when all was ready. The doctor finally looked up and coughed officiously.

He eyed the women with disdain, sighed, then pushed his chair back and stepped out from behind the desk. He was tall and distinguished and it was difficult to tell if his expression was one of annoyance or deep thought, but it was clear that everyone needed to be on their guard as he stepped forward. Ania noticed a stethoscope around the man's neck and several shiny medical implements peeping out from the top pocket of his white coat.

Herr Doctor walked silently along the first row. He stopped by one of the younger girls, who did her best to avoid eye contact, just as the older women had quietly suggested. The young girl's eyes darted this way and that, any direction other than into the German doctor's eyes. Ania knew her as Eva, a stunning Polish girl of fifteen who went to the same school, in what seemed like a lifetime ago. Eva gulped loudly and the doctor smiled pleasantly before moving on and coming to a stop again, this time in front of Ania.

He removed a pencil from his top pocket and placed it under her chin, moving her head from one side to the other. He seemed somewhat perplexed. Finally, with a pleasant voice he enquired, "Juden?" as he wiped the pencil on the sleeve of his coat.

"Nein, Herr Doctor, Polski," Ania said politely, and then she inexplicably shrugged and added, "I have a big nose." He smiled at her little joke and moved to his left. Ania closed her eyes and quietly took a deep breath. *How stupid was that? Where did it come from?* Cracking a Jewish joke with a German doctor who could have her killed on the spot? *Stupid, Ania, stupid!*

She heard the doctor's voice again, further up the line. He was talking to someone she did not know, an older woman, with fear in her eyes. The doctor asked her a question but she remained mute.

The woman next in line spoke up. "She does not understand German, Herr Doctor."

The doctor did not take his eyes off the older woman, who was visibly shaking and looked as if she might collapse at any moment. "Uh-hu," he said. Then he moved on to the person, the one who spoke up. The doctor took one look at her and the girl standing by her side. "Aha! Do we have twins here?"

"Yes, sir. Yes, Herr Doctor, sir," the girl said.

"Very good. Make a note of their names please, Frau Groepler." The CMO moved forward with a notepad and pencil poised. Her hair was pulled back severely in the form of a tight bun on the top of her fat, round head. Her jowls were flabby, eyes black and cold and she was solidly built with the firm, athletic body of a female shot putter or wrestler. Her severe expression instantly generated fear amongst the women.

The doctor continued along the line, did not stop again, but raised his eyebrows and flared his nostrils occasionally.

Three guards had quietly entered the room and took positions by the door. Ania saw Braun once more, even scrawnier without his coat but no less intimidating. When the doctor appeared to have completed his inspection, he returned to his desk, sat wearily then started to write his notes. Frau Groepler tore a sheet of paper from her notebook and gave it to him. The only sound in the room was the scratch of the doctor's pen on his notepaper. After a few minutes he placed the pen aside, screwed the lid back onto the bottle of ink he had been using, and motioned Schroder to step forward. The doctor whispered to him then looked across the room towards the women, nodding at Schroder, who pulled the two sisters out of the parade.

A second guard joined Schroder and they removed the twins from the room. The doctor then looked up at the CMO and spoke calmly. "That will be all for now, Frau Groepler. I am going back to Auschwitz. This has proved to be quite a fruitful exercise. Call me if another such transport arrives, will you please?"

"Of course," said the CMO. "I hope we will be honoured by your presence again in the near future, Herr Doctor Mengele.";

***

After Mengele departed, Frau Groepler also left the room. Braun reappeared a few moments later, scanned the lines of women until he found Eva, and pulled her out. Her face was etched with terror as he grabbed her hair, and her shrieks pierced the air until she disappeared into an adjacent room and the door slammed shut behind her. Within seconds, the women heard the terrible muffled sounds of Eva being beaten. They exchanged fearful glances, though they remained silent as the guards stood by, one looking at his watch, another yawning.

Several minutes later Frau Groepler reappeared, red-faced and a little breathless, adjusting her uniform before she addressed the women. "You are very lucky. You have been chosen to serve the Reich and if you do your job well, without complaint, you will be looked after." Her eyes were still racing after the exhilaration of joining Karl Braun in beating Eva to a pulp for failing to look at Dr Mengele when he spoke to her. She was disappointed that the frail young girl had succumbed so quickly, but she managed to get a few hefty kicks in herself before the girl's body was dragged away, leaving a long red smear on the cold, white floor tiles.

Back to business. Frau Groepler pulled herself together. "There is a lot to do before you begin your work, so listen to me carefully because I don't have more time to waste on matters of discipline." She spoke as if the incident with Eva had been one of those annoyances that you get in any job-the phone ringing at the wrong time, or being unable to find a file because someone had not returned it to the correct place. She paused for effect, then sighed somewhat theatrically as if she was composing herself for everyone's benefit. "It is time for you to prepare for your selection, so now we want you all to have a shower please, ladies." And she smiled like everyone's favourite aunt.

The women were now on their best behaviour, which was exactly what the CMO wanted. "You will follow me. Now!" The women quickly fell into line and followed Frau Groepler out of the room and down the hallway towards yet another door. They passed what appeared to be a series of small rooms, each with a curtain drawn across the opening-no doors. A few moments later they crossed a covered footbridge that took them into another building, where they found themselves inside a large, fully tiled communal washroom. The women had already heard the rumours about the so-called shower rooms at concentration camps, and they stood stone-faced and frozen to the spot, some gazing in horror at the showerheads, others uttering silent prayers.

"Kommen, rasch, rasch!" One of the German guards waved his arms. "Take off your clothes and get into the showers. Now! Hurry up, rasch rasch!" Emilie was the first to move, others followed. Braun had returned and was carrying a leather riding crop, which he flicked into the palm of his hand as he stared around the room. He seemed to have a few speckles of blood splashed across his cheek and his eyes were still racing after the exertion of beating Eva. There was a flurry of activity as the women removed their clothes and tried to protect their modesty. It was not long before a pile of dirty clothes had been kicked towards the door.

Braun opened the door and two men in striped pyjamas scurried in with their heads bowed. Their stench reached Ania on the farthest side of the room as they gathered the women's rags and made their way out under Braun's watchful eye. Never once did the men look up from their task.

The women shivered anxiously as they stood naked in the cold, tiled room. Some of the married women had not even been fully naked in front of their husbands, yet here they were, surrounded by nudity, trying to not stare at each other. Ania stood with one arm across her chest and the other clutched nervously between her legs as she whispered to Emilie, "What is going to happen to us?

Emilie smiled at the beautiful young woman. "You are safe my little one, believe me. With a body like yours, you will be fine. Just keep your mouth shut and cut the wise cracks." Cold water started to flow from the showers and an array of guards seemed to suddenly find reason to visit the room, including the fat driver, who took great delight in pointing out Ania to the others and making rude gestures.

The women stayed beneath the showers as long as they could, hoping the guards would disperse. The only woman who appeared to have no issue with her own nakedness was Emilie, who accepted the situation before most others. It was easy to see who had already gone through the rigours of childbirth-mostly the older women but a few younger ones as well. Their ages ranged from teens to mid-thirties in the main, and there was a good mixture of body types; fat and thin, robust and sporting, all of them strong country girls.

As she showered in silence, Ania was pleased to find what appeared to be some kind of disinfectant soap which she used to wash herself thoroughly, her hair too, and the luxury of the moment after the days of travelling in the back of a truck was not lost on her. After several minutes one of the women screamed and another openly sobbed as hot water suddenly appeared.

When Ania finally stepped out of the shower, a guard she had never seen before handed her a thin white towel, which was surprisingly soft. After drying herself as best she could, she wrapped the towel around her body and stood shivering on the cold tiles alongside the other women.

The guard who handed out the towels conducted a head count then instructed the women to follow him to another room. This room also had a desk with someone sitting behind it, only this time it was a uniformed German clerk. Directly in front of him was a box of index cards, several rubber stamps lined up to the right and an inkpad to the left. Ania was the first to be ushered in front him, and he spoke without looking up. "Do you have papers?"

"No, sir,"

"Why not?" The official wrinkled his forehead.

Ania managed to hold her tongue this time. "I was in my nightdress when I was take—selected, sir," she replied, wisely correcting her ill-chosen words.

"Oh, I see." He took a card from the index box. "Name?" he asked.

"Ania Burczyk," she stuttered.

"Age?"

"Seventeen, sir."

"Your last address?"

He wrote her reply carefully on the card, pausing only once to refresh the ink in his pen. After a few more questions, he looked up and stared deep into her eyes. "Religion?"

She never hesitated in her reply. "Catholic, sir."

"Family background?" he continued. She stared at her twitching toes.

The German raised his voice slightly. "Family background?" he asked again. "Where are you from, girl? Your family-where did they come from originally, your grandparents and their parents-your family background?"

"Polish, sir," she said with a huge sigh. "I didn't know what you meant, sir, I'm sorry, sir." She blinked away any possibility of tears and he grumbled under his breath and ran his finger along the top of the line of rubber stamps. After carefully choosing one, he stamped the card, then handed it to her and yelled, "Next!"

Ania was immediately ushered from the room and left shivering in the hallway, where a guard grinned and said, "Most of your kind don't come out of the showers with wet hair." Braun appeared and took Ania through a door marked 'Examination Room 1'. The room was bright and freshly painted stark white. There was yet another desk, more rubber stamps, cards, pens and ink. A long, thin bamboo cane rested on the desktop next to the writing paraphernalia, but the most ominous thing in the room was an examination couch, with a uniformed guard standing at one end.

Frau Groepler entered the room wearing a white doctor's coat. "Card." Ania nervously passed the document over. "It says you are seventeen."

"What?"

Ania felt a sudden stinging slap across her face. The shock brought tears to her eyes and left a painful imprint on her face.

"You call me Frau Groepler when you speak!" the CMO yelled. "Answer me respectfully."

Ania's apology was ignored, and she felt her bottom lip start to quiver. She refused to give way to tears-the Burczyk girls were known to be stubborn as well as flippant. After answering a few more questions, the replies to all of which appeared to be on the card already, Ania was told to remove her towel.

She glanced across the room towards Braun, then back to Frau

Groepler. It seemed that she had hesitated for too long and this time the cane whisked through the air and wickedly slapped her across her calves. "Get on with it, you Polish whore!"

Ania dropped the towel and tried to rub the sting away, but straightened when she saw the cane rise again. She was dizzy with pain when the Frau's huge round face appeared directly in front of hers, their noses almost touching. She could feel the German's hot breath when she spoke. "Bend forward."

The CMO picked through Ania's scalp in the same way that one monkey would groom another. "You are lucky. If you were in any other building in this place your head would be shaved. No lice!" she declared, and she walked to her desk and ticked a box on Ania's card. "It says here, colour of eyes, and someone has written one blue, one brown but they didn't give me a stamp with the word 'freak' on it!" She laughed at her own joke and nodded towards the examination couch.

As Ania lay on the examination couch the CMO forced her knees apart.

Braun leaned forward for a better view as Frau Groepler forced several fat fingers inside her. Ania gripped the sides of the bed and every muscle in her body tightened. The frau coughed and extended her free hand towards the cane, which she had conveniently rested against the examination couch. Ania relaxed immediately and the examination continued.

As she looked down the length of her naked body, between her raised knees towards her feet, the frau's ugly face suddenly appeared. "Still untouched, eh? Unusual for a Polish slut." She mumbled something inaudible, then walked back to her desk and wrote on Ania's card. She returned and took Ania's blood pressure, looked down her throat, into her ears, listened to her heartbeat.

Having ticked all the boxes and written several comments, Frau Groepler picked up a rubber stamp and thudded it down with such force that the table rocked and several stamps fell over. She nodded towards a door. "There!" Ania looked across room at the door.

"And take your disgusting towel with you!"

Other women gradually joined Ania in the adjacent room, wrapped in their towels, shocked and frightened by their processing at the hands of Frau Groepler. The younger girls were sobbing and one was standing with her knees pressed together as a small trickle of blood wound its way down the inside of her thighs. No one dared try to comfort her as she sobbed and sniffed quietly to herself.

Some women carried painful welts, bright red stripes criss-crossed over tender thighs and upper arms. Ania had positioned herself near the only window in the room. It was dark but the area outside was floodlit. She had not eaten nor had a drink of water since they left the village hall early that morning but so far, fear of the unknown had kept her hunger and thirst at bay.

Raised voices came from the examination room, the CMO and another familiar voice, a man. Obersturmfuhrer Schroder appeared at the door, holding a small white card covered in rubber stamp markings and handwriting. He walked up and down several times before stopping in front of Ania. "You, with the weird eyes. Follow me!" he said.

25

Danuta remained blindfolded in the back of the van throughout the one-hour journey, her legs occasionally brushing against Krzys's body. Because of the cold, she could no longer feel her fingers but was strangely grateful for the sack over her head: at least her breath warmed her face. Things were happening too quickly for her to mourn for Krzys. She was more concerned with staying alive and her instincts were telling her to stay awake and keep her mind clear.

The vehicle sped through the slush-covered streets of outer Krakow with no lights, guided by the driver's instinct and intimate knowledge of what lay behind the shadows in every backstreet and alley. They managed to duck and dive around several German checkpoints but knew the nearer they got to the centre of the city, the greater their chances of being discovered by a patrol or stumbling into a fresh road block.

The sounds of light armoured vehicles and motorcycles could be heard reverberating around the dark city, and several times the van parked and waited as German patrols rumbled by, mere streets away. Everyone was told to keep quiet, and usually, a few minutes would pass before Danuta heard the driver slip the vehicle back into gear and felt the wheels spinning in the snow as they moved onto the cobbled streets once more.

After yet another stop and what seemed like a longer than usual pause, Danuta felt a hand force its way under the hood and cram a foul-smelling gag into her mouth. She dry retched as she was pushed backwards and felt the bristles and warmth of an unshaven face against her neck. "Ssshhhhh" a man's voice said, "ssshhhh." She could smell stale cigarette smoke on his breath and they sat in silence for another moment or two before Danuta heard the unmistakable sounds of weapons being loaded followed by the rear doors of the van suddenly opening.

Strangely, the first thing she noticed was the smell of flowers and before she could think of anything else, she found herself being bundled out of the back of the vehicle and across what appeared to be a small cobblestone courtyard. She was then pushed inside a building. The door slammed shut behind her followed by the sound of several bolts hastily pushed into place.

Then a very different smell and a very different sensation. She was now in a room. A kitchen, she presumed. She could feel the heat from a stove, smell warm soup, wood in a fireplace, and finally a woman's voice above the familiar clatter of cutlery and stirring of pots. "Who is this?"

Danuta's gag and the blindfold were wrenched away and she blinked at the unaccustomed light. Several faces stared back at her and the woman spoke again. "She's just a child!"

"I am no child," Danuta said angrily, "and I do not appreciate this ridiculous cat and mouse game of yours. If you are going to kill me, do it. Get on with it."

She counted six or seven people, and every one of them was laughing. The man whose voice she recognised from the bridge put an arm around her shoulder. "Why would we kill you after we have just risked our lives to rescue you, little one?"

"Why wouldn't you? I don't know who the hell you are."

"She's feisty!" the woman by the stove said as she handed Danuta a bowl of hot soup.

The man spoke again. "You can call me Grabowski. And this is my woman, Wislawa, and then there's these other reprobates, my brother Jozeph, next to him is Eddie, then Jurek and his brother Jurek-yes, confusing I know, but you haven't met their parents, and the other one who doesn't want you to know his name because he is shy, I think?"

The shy man threw a bread roll at Grabowski, catching him behind the ear. Grabowski ignored the play and turned to Danuta. "Now you know who we are," he said, "but we need to know who you are and why you were on that bridge with Krzys Paderewski."

Everyone was staring at Danuta. Her mind was racing. Was she safe here? Who were these people? There was no way she could risk telling them her full story yet, so she lied a little. "My name is Danuta Szalek and I am from Orsa."

"Near the Russian border?"

"That's right. I was visiting friends near Lodz and got stuck there when the Germans invaded. That was how I met Krzys-at a market. He offered to take me to Krakow, and now I am here with you and I don't know what is going to happen next!"

***

They talked as they ate and Danuta learned that the people she was with had been returning from what they called a 'mission' when they heard a gunshot from the bridge and stopped to investigate. Danuta now assumed that she had been rescued by the Polish Resistance, but how was she to know for sure?

The cavalier attitude they had displayed and the fact that they had no problems killing Germans was a good sign, but they could still be Bolshevik sympathisers or dissidents just trying to do as much damage as they could to anyone or everyone.

As Danuta drank her soup she looked around the room at the men's faces. Krzys had warned her that the Russians were especially cruel to Polish women; violent gang rapes and murder were not unheard of. But she knew that she had been at her most vulnerable in the back of the van during the journey and no one had laid a finger on her. She had arrived safely enough after all. Maybe she was wrong about them being Russians.

***

The streets of the historic and beautiful walled city of Krakow were decorated with the black and red flags of the Nazis. Swastikas fluttered everywhere. The Polish Eagle remained on many public buildings, but the Germans had removed its Crown. The Eagle had been indicative of Poland's strength and the Germans had cleverly allowed them to retain it-in a modified subservient manner, a reminder of where they as a people now stood, beneath the jack-boot. Poland would eventually cease to exist in its own right; it would become an adjunct to

Germany, a provider of cheap labour, servants and slaves. Nothing less would satisfy Hitler.

One of the Jurek's had disappeared during the meal, and he returned about twenty minutes later with another man and spoke to Grabowski. "It's him alright. It's Krzys Paderewski."

Grabowski seemed genuinely upset. "I am sorry, were you close?" he asked Danuta.

"He offered me a lift, that's all. I told you." There was more to this; it was obvious when her eyes filled with tears. Wislawa put a friendly arm around her shoulders.

"I am sorry, my dear. We will bury him in a hero's grave. You may be assured he will receive full honours," Grabowski said.

The room was silent now, apart from Danuta's sniffing. "How do you know Krzys?" she finally asked Grabowski, wiping her eyes with a sleeve.

He put an arm around one of his men. "This is Tomasz, a cousin of Krzys's. We all work for Krzys's uncle, Slav Posluzny, a man of some importance here in Krakow. We heard about the problems at Zwinbrzych and expected that Krzys would be on his way to join our cause."

"How did you know for sure?"

"Let us just say that family always knows. Don't worry, my dear, you are safe with us. We got the German who killed Krzys and the other bastards on the bridge. Tomorrow we will take you to meet Krzys's uncle, and you will stay with him until we can make more permanent arrangements for you."

Danuta felt a sudden surge of anger. "But I want to fight, I don't want to be hidden away. I want to kill Germans, just like they killed my mother and my grandparents ... my sister also, I think ... and Krzys."

"Then you can discuss that tomorrow with the people who make such decisions. Until then you must stay with us. Wislawa will look after you."

As Wislawa shuffled her chair around to face Danuta, the kitchen door suddenly burst open. Several masked men sprang into the room, machine guns raised. Grabowski had no time to grab his own weapon, and the rest of his men were also caught off guard.

The intruders scanned the room, their eyes sliding left to right behind the slits in their balaclavas, and when they seemed satisfied that the place was secure, they moved aside and a colossus of a masked man stepped into the room, dressed in old faded brown corduroy trousers, a black jacket and a grey cloth cap. Others followed, including a man whose hands were tied, presumably one of Grabowski's men who was supposed to be on guard outside. They tumbled him into the room and he fell to the floor moaning.

The giant carried an over-large machine gun, big enough to down everyone in the room with a single burst. His face was concealed by a hessian mask with crudely cut eyeholes and a slit for the mouth. He looked like an executioner, and when Danuta saw the shock on her own captors' faces, their arms raised in surrender, she realised that Krzys had not been the only careless person in her wartime life so far.

26

Rolf Schroder was eighteen years old when he joined the SS. His mother cried and unbeknown to anyone, in the privacy of his study, his father shed tears as well. The Schroders were librarians and their only child Rolf had always been a studious boy with excellent grades, never interested in sports or outdoor activities. While his friends roamed the streets at night and joined political rallies, Rolf was more concerned with reading and studying.

There was no doubting the fact that the Schroders were good Berliners. They had followed the rise of Adolf Hitler with interest, along with Hindenburg's second run as President in 1932. It seemed obvious that Hitler's appointment as Chancellor was a shallow and lily-livered attempt to persuade Germany and the rest of the world that Hindenburg was still in control.

But by March 1933 Hitler was in command of the Reichstag, with dictatorial powers, ultimately leading to the invasion of Poland and beyond:

good things were happening, German pride was being restored. Unemployment figures tumbled and new wealth was created, along with an increased level of anxiety amongst racial minorities and those who disagreed with the Nazis.

Suddenly the common person felt good about being German once again. People had money in their pockets at last and they could see a future for themselves and their families. The fact that everything was founded upon fear did not seem to concern the general population.

The Jews had been a growing source of angst throughout Europe during this time, due in the main to their financial and economic dominance. If there was one thing that most true blood Germans like the Schroders knew, it was that the Jews traditionally traded amongst themselves and kept their wealth within their own communities, and that was not a good thing for the economy. They did not conform to the German way either, had their own religious beliefs and ceremonies as well as a ridiculous dress code. For all that, the studious Schroders did have one or two close

Jewish friends-serious, intellectual people they met through the library.

What surprised the Schroders most about the Rosenbergs was how interested they were in German history and philosophy. *But why* did they insist upon calling themselves 'German Jews'; why not just 'Germans' like everyone else. The Fuhrer had openly said that Jews could not be trusted-was he right?

When Kristallnacht happened in November 1938, tens of thousands of Jews were beaten up, murdered or sent to concentration camps. The Schroders were amongst the crowds that walked the streets to stare at the mess and misery Hitler and his Nazi party had created. They calmly walked with their Arian neighbours, surveying the results of twenty-four hours of looting and pillaging, when Jewish businesses and synagogues were burned to the ground and a whole race was finally dragged into the open so the baying masses could join in with the persecution.

As the Rosenbergs attempted to clean up the burned-out shell of their shop that night, Frau Schroder looked the other way and walked briskly by with one of her German friends. But Mrs Rosenberg saw her and their eyes met for the briefest of moments. For some inexplicable reason Frau Schroder suddenly developed a severe headache and had to go home. She remained in bed for two days, and when she eventually surfaced, she was deeply depressed.

A week later the Gestapo turned up at the library. They had with them, lists of approved and non-approved literature, and the Schroder's were told to ensure the non-approved books were piled in the street outside the library by close of business that day. They would then be audited and any books found from the "not permitted" list would be removed, along with Herr Schroder.

The Schroders and their staff worked through the day and into the early part of the night, and Herr Schroder was surprised at the size of the pile of books that ended up outside, occupying the full width of the pavement and spilling onto the street. Great works by Leopold Staff and Brecht, scholarly masterpieces about contemporary culture, scientific journals, even prayer books, it mattered not; they were all considered unhealthy influences on the German people. Like the good citizen he was, Herr Schroder stood straight-faced and tight-lipped when the Gestapo arrived and set fire to the huge pile, but his heart was not in it, and he cried for the second time in his adult life that night.

Behind closed doors, according to the now bitter Herr Schroder, every person with a modicum of intelligence knew that no good would ever come from burning books. The Fuhrer had made a huge mistake and the nationalistic fervour that had once bubbled away inside the Schroders' hearts was fizzled out, and they suddenly saw only bad things for the future. Take away books and you dent civilisation. The Schroder's were beginning to feel an unfamiliar emotion-the burden of guilt. The bad news continued when Rolf was sent to that cultural hellhole called Poland. "At least it is not the front. We must thank God for small mercies," his mother said as she waved him off at Anhalter

Bahnhof, Berlin's main railway station. Secretly, they were pleased with their son's lot. Working at a labour camp in Poland was no bad thing, and he could take pride in doing something useful towards the war effort whilst mercifully being kept away from the carnage and horror of the front line. Maybe he could help the Rosenbergs if he bumped into them? It would ease his parents' guilt if he did.

After Rolf left for Poland, his father's health deteriorated. He walked around the library mumbling to himself, looking at the gaps on the shelves and the crossings-out on index cards. He started to be rude to patrons and most of the time appeared preoccupied and distracted. His eyes had a distant look about them, and people often remarked that they no longer saw him smile. He could not speak out for fear of someone informing the Gestapo about his so-called subversive views, so he gradually died inside, a little more every day, bit by bit.

When Rolf arrived at the camp that was to be his home for the duration of the war, a few enquiries confirmed that the Rosenbergs had been sent to Bergen-Belsen. He did not know much about Bergen-Belsen, and some of the more senior men laughed when he enquired about the facilities there; was there a library, an orchestra perhaps?

Initially, Rolf was confused about the role of Wysznica and his part in it, but it did not take long before the atmosphere of cruelty pervaded his bookish mind. Atrocities happened every day. It was a way of life. People were disfigured, maimed, murdered and there seemed to be little if no accountability.

Rolf gave up questioning things after a while and it did not take long before he could justify the brutality. He then participated in its delivery. He was a perfect example of how easy it was to sway opinion and convince decent Germans that there was only one way to deal with seditious dissidents and Jews. After all, if everyone was beating them into submission, it had to be right, did it not?

Rolf became fascinated by the way the Jews queued for their turn in the gas chambers; and as ridiculous as it seemed, they even sheltered in the shade of nearby trees to escape the harsh rays of the summer sun as they waited their turn!

Once the war was over the world would be rid of every cripple, retard, mental case, Communist, Gypsy, homosexual, intellectual, subversive and Jew! The greater good was what it was about, and it was impossible not to be caught up in the fervour, even for Rolf Schroder.

***

The SS guards and officers at Wysznica were the usual mix of city and small-town Germans with the same thing in common—a love of the Fuhrer and the Fatherland. Many had come through the ranks of the Hitler Youth, as in fact Rolf Schroder had, and he was pleased to meet up with a friend from those heady days, Karl Braun.

During his school days Braun had been unnaturally skinny despite possessing a voracious appetite. It appeared that no matter how much he ate, he never gained weight. With his shirt off during the summer months it was almost possible to see every bone in his body-you could play a tune on his ribs and count every vertebra in his spine. He became the butt of jokes and an easy target for bullies. His only defence in those days was to run away. Because he was a fast runner, his athletics teacher gave him the nickname of *the Greyhound.* In later years, however, he liked to claim that he was called the Greyhound because of his build. *Karl, you are all prick and ribs* they used to say in the showers after training. Whatever the reason, the name stuck.

Braun vowed to one-day show the bullies what he was made of. Until then, he took out his frustration on animals, graduating from dismembering field mice to torturing the family cat and then his neighbour's noisy dog. He particularly enjoyed seeing animals squirm, twitch or howl as he worked on different parts of their bodies. One of his favourite pastimes was to catch a bird, tie its feet with fishing line and attach it to a wire fence. The hapless creature would spin like a Catherine wheel in its attempts to fly away. Of course, its feet were eventually severed, and it fell, flapping and gasping until it bled to death. Karl would sit and watch the whole process from start to finish while snacking on his favourite chocolate bars.

It was at the age of fifteen that Braun became tired of running from the bullies. He found himself cornered one time too many and learned that he could fight quite well. He was a dirty combatant, biting, spitting, kicking, gouging; anything to win. He seemed to enjoy inflicting pain on humans more than animals and to his surprise; he discovered that he liked to receive pain. Both of these aspects followed him into his relationships with women and he never managed to keep a girlfriend for more than a few months as a result.

Several years after leaving the Hitler Youth, Schroder and Braun found themselves together again at Wysznica: Schroder the swot and Braun the thug. Schroder had continued to grow intellectually (he knew *Mein Kampf* by heart) and he sought authority with a level of enthusiasm that left mere pretenders in awe. Power it seemed was the great motivator, but he wanted more than the dismal level of bureaucratic influence his father tried to enforce as a civil servant at the local library.

Always impeccably dressed, Rolf was the very essence of the SS: upright and idealistic, a no-nonsense soldier who followed orders to the letter, without question. He knew how to play the system and how internal politics worked. It was difficult not to notice him because Rolf Schroder had presence. The SS saw him as an ideal candidate for early promotion and Braun had no problems hanging on to his friend's coat tails and enjoying the ride.

***

Driving halfway across Poland had been a bit of a jaunt for Schroder and Braun, a break from the daily grind at Wysznica. It even provided some perks with access to the women-that was until Braun roughed one of them up. Apparently she did not want to participate in his bedroom games but she had already been signed in, so she had to be signed out! No problem-Rolf did the paperwork and it was all handled to Berlin's satisfaction in the end. SS teamwork at its best.

Fischer had provided a detailed portfolio describing exactly what he wanted for the Club. Youth was an important factor because Polish women did not age well. Good healthy country girls, farming stock, with rosy cheeks and strong limbs-that was the order of the day. The commandant supplied maps, the names of towns and villages and the identities of civic officers who would provide information on the whereabouts of such women. A total of thirty were required, and Fischer's orders were very specific.

The men who had been involved in the mission were now eating a hearty meal in the canteen, where most of the junior non-commissioned officers and general ranks gathered during their meal breaks.

News of the brothel had initially sent a buzz of excitement through the camp, but there was disillusion when it was discovered the women were only available to the prisoners!

It was to be the Kapos and the Sonderkommandos who were to benefit from the Club. The Kapos who maintained discipline by beating their own people, and those filthy Sonderkommandos who worked in the gas chambers and crematorium. Why were those scum allowed to enjoy fresh young Polish bodies when their masters were not? The cooks were in it too, and the firemen and the hut elders-anyone who had a role in the smooth running of the camp would benefit as long as they were not Jewish. But the likes of Schroder and his kind, the ones who risked their lives on a daily basis, were prevented from enjoying a bit of fun time?

It was not right, and the morale of the SS troops in and around the camp was substantially reduced when the Club's rules were circulated.

There were to be twelve women working at any time, from eight o'clock at night until midnight. The women were to be selected by the commandant himself, on advice from Doctor Mengele and his medical team. The women, so the memorandum stated, were volunteers, offering their services to the Reich, and they would be eager to reward those prized workers who did so much for the German cause under such difficult conditions.

"We have to find a way to get at those sluts," Braun said that night in the canteen. "They will be wasted on filthy Polish Kapos. Let's give them some real German meat!"

"I am told greyhounds are known more for their speed than their staying power. Why should two minutes with you be such an attractive proposition for a whore?" Schroder scoffed.

"Get fucked."

"If I do, I have a feeling it will be the only fuck either one of us will be getting tonight or any other night in this camp, my friend," Schroder replied.

"I think not, my dear Rolf. I think that this time you may be wrong..."

PART 4:
THE POLISH
RESISTANCE

27

Vodka flowed freely when Krzys's uncle Slav was introduced to Danuta that night. He was famous for making dramatic entrances, but with a machine gun and a hood over his head? Grabowski tried to weasel out of his failure to adequately guard the florist shop. "I could have killed you myself! What if that had happened, eh? What if I had shot the 'masked intruder'?" Grabowski said, slapping Slav heartily on the back.

"You were too busy telling this young lady how important you were, Grabowski." Slav put a meaty arm around Danuta's tiny waist. "Now if you really want to get to know a man of importance..."

"Perhaps you can introduce me to him when he arrives." Danuta's wit amused everyone, including Slav.

Soon after his surprise arrival, Slav was appraised of what happened at the bridge. Despite his love for his nephew, Slav had to admit he had died due to his own carelessness. "Let this be a lesson to you all, Grabowski. You must have eyes everywhere. Look how easy it was for me to get in tonight, for God's sake!" Slav signalled for everyone to sit down. It was time for business. Chairs were scraped into position, glasses topped up, and all eyes turned towards Slav. The mysterious person who had previously wished to remain anonymous took his place next to Slav, removed his scarf, hat and jacket, revealing that *he* was in fact a *she.*

The woman's long flowing blonde hair had been tucked inside her cap, and as she shook her head it tumbled onto her shoulders and she smiled at Slav. A truly beautiful woman. She was introduced to Danuta as Natalka and nobody seemed surprised by her disguise-it appeared to be a joke among them. She draped a long, elegant arm around Slav's shoulders to ensure that Danuta knew who he belonged to. Then the talking began.

"When the Germans marched through Warsaw in September, I was there on business—"

"That would have been monkey business, eh, Slav?" One of the Jurek's interrupted with a grin, prompting Slav to slap Natalka's perfectly rounded bottom.

"It probably was," he smiled, and everyone laughed except Natalka, who frowned jealously. Slav continued. "I tell you, my friends, I saw my fellow countrymen at their worst on that terrible day."

"What happened?" Danuta asked.

The great man paused and downed a shot of vodka. As he topped his glass up Danuta took the opportunity to take a closer look at him. His hair was tightly cropped and he wore a light beard that clung to his square chin like moss to a rock. His nose was wide and his lips full. *I have a mouth that was made for kissing,* he once said. *And for loving, as well,* Natalka added with a wry smile. But it was Slav's eyes that were his most captivating feature; infused with a twinkle that no woman he ever chose to bed had managed to resist. With his large head and solid frame, he was a formidable, charismatic figure; the type of man that people either stood behind or ran from.

"I had been watching what was happening to the Jews for a few weeks, studying them closely as the Germans moved them to the ghetto. Signs appeared on park benches, public toilets and trams overnight.*Do not sit here, Jews,* or *No Jews allowed.* They were no longer permitted to walk on the footpath, those Jews, and I saw a man clubbed to death in front of his wife and children by a German thug, for doing just that. And why did he step onto that particular pavement? Why? Because he was picking up a toy dropped by his child."

At this point the beautiful Natalka took his huge hand into her own, squeezing it tighter than he had ever squeezed her bottom. "And what was it that disgusted me so much?" Slav continued. "Was it the fact that he was killed in front of his family? No. Was it because the German wiped the blood from his rifle butt onto the man's coat as he lay dying in the gutter? No. What was it then? What disgusted me so much that I decided at that moment I would do everything within my power to avenge that poor man's death?"

Everyone knew it was a rhetorical question and Slav emptied his shot glass again before continuing.

"As far as I knew, the man was a nobody, neither famous nor important. A factory worker probably. Maybe he had a small business; let us say he was a baker. Whatever he did, he was a Pole *first* and a Jew *second!*" Slav's fist slammed down on the table, making everyone jump. "He was one of us for God's sake! Yesterday he was *my* neighbour, or *your* neighbour or your work colleague, your boss even. He was POLISH!" he screamed. "I watched Polish men and women spit on their own Jews as they made their way to the ghettos. And then I saw the same citizens running down the road with the spoils-that's right, they looted their abandoned Jewish neighbour's homes before the Germans could take possession of them!"

Slav paused again and angrily took a large swig from the bottle, having given up on his shot glass. "And now, here in Krakow, our home town where we grew up and where our children play side by side with our own Jews, here we are doing the same things; but here we are worse! What could be worse than what happened in Warsaw you ask, what?" He was met with a sea of blank faces, which his eyes explored, one by one, before he continued. "I will tell you what is worse and it is on our own doorstep. *The Factory of Death.*"

Slav spoke of Auschwitz. Just a few miles down the road outside Krakow. He told everyone that when rich Polish women shopped for food in the markets in Krakow's town square, their fur coats wrapped around them and their bags bulging with black market goods, the Jews, *Polish Jews,* were being lined up to enter the gas chambers at *the Factory.* Machinery and equipment had already arrived from Germany by train, and specialist builders were coming from Warsaw to build more chimneys and ovens. "Last year they built a fucking crematorium in the forest!" he yelled.

Then it was time to talk of the mission Grabowski and his team had been on when they stumbled upon Krzys and Danuta on the bridge. They had been charged with blowing up a train carrying equipment for the gas chambers at Auschwitz. For some unknown reason several explosives failed to detonate, and while they had caused a derailment they had done little more than prevent the materials reaching their destination for a few days. It seemed that everything was unloaded and trucked to Auschwitz anyway.

Slav told them their mission had failed disastrously. They had risked their lives for nothing. "I have come to the conclusion that we are going about this the wrong way. We are trying to disrupt the Germans from the outside when we should be working against them on the *inside*. We should be inside Auschwitz."

He spoke of his team of builders and maintenance workers who had permits to visit all areas within the giant Auschwitz-Birkenau complex, associated sub-camps and factories. Slav's company now maintained all the buildings, barracks, prisoners' huts-even the toilet blocks! Most of the timber they used came from the mill in Wysznica, so Slav also had unfettered access there too. What he wanted to do with Grabowski and his team was smuggle weapons and resources *inside* the camps. The Germans would not expect that.

Slav suggested that they could also smuggle in little treats to make life more bearable. "Can you imagine how much joy would come from a bar of soap? They have forgotten such things exist, things we all took for granted before the war." The Jews did seem to be making the best of it; they still made music, and taught their children the ways of their religion with its strange chants and ancient ceremonies. They had established schools and did everything within their means to live as decent, civilised people, despite being in that most dreadful of places.

The Germans let them get on with their so-called culture. Why should they care? They were all going up the chimney anyway!

And that was why working from the inside out was the best way. The Germans would never dream that the Jews were capable of such things. "Imagine if we could organise them properly, steal gunpowder from one of the armaments factories on the outskirts of Auschwitz, smuggle ammunition and small arms in, stockpile it among the building materials inside the camp."

With a well thought out coordinated attack from within, it might be possible to destroy the gas chambers and crematorium, kill many Germans, blow a huge hole in the wire fences and even knock out a couple of watchtowers. Hundreds could escape, thousands maybe if it coincided with arrival of a transport. Such a plan! It was a preposterous idea! *The Jews fighting back—who would have thought it?*

"That is not disruption, Slav. It will just be an irritation, that is all. If we are going to do something we should do something *substantial,* something the Germans would remember forever. Let's blow the whole place up and kidnap the camp commander in the process!" Jozeph was regarded as a bit of a hothead who often said stupid things without thinking. An act such as kidnapping a camp commandant would guarantee unthinkable repercussions for the communities inside and outside the camp. It would be horrendous.

There were times when Slav and Natalka were alone that Slav actually questioned whose side Jozeph was on. Natalka had never liked Jozeph; he was the black sheep, the one with the weak chin. She did not like the way he behaved when he had drink in him either, the things he said, the lustful way he stared at her sometimes. But he was Grabowski's brother, and Grabowski was Slav's second-in-command.

Jozeph was a complicated sort who had lost an eye in an accident as a child; he was full of resentment about the way the dice had rolled for him. He refused to wear a glass eye or patch-he wanted everyone to see how cruel life had been to him. So they stitched his empty socket closed, and he carried the scar defiantly, to show the world his misfortune. After all, wasn't Grabowski, his elder brother, the one who unknowingly threw the snowball that carried the stone that took his eye?

***

Slav reported directly to Stefan Rowecki, head of the Armia Krajowa, the secret Polish Home Army underground movement based in

Warsaw. Rowecki had sanctioned Slav's plan to put together a team of people *inside* Auschwitz; to arm them, reinforce their positions, train the strongest, teach them how to use weapons, how to set explosives, and all under the noses of the Germans. Secrecy was, of course, paramount.

"We must be careful, all of us. This new plan must not be leaked. If you have doubts about anyone working with us they must be brought to my personal attention immediately. We are all accountable."

Jozeph arrogantly said, "*We* may well all be accountable to you, Slav, but who are you accountable to?"

"Me? I am answerable to God!" Slav boomed as he slapped Natalka's bottom again. "God and this magnificent woman!" The room was filled with spontaneous laughter followed by vodka all round as the new plan was saluted in the usual way, several times. "Na Zdorovie!" Everyone gathered around Slav; everyone except Jozeph.

28

There was a frantic level of last-minute activity on the day the Club opened as men throughout the camp worked slavishly to win points to secure one of the valuable admission vouchers. Already there was a black market in trading points, which the guards allowed as long as there was something in it for them. Fischer had been told about this by Schole, who learned it from Schroder who indeed got the information from the Greyhound, who seemed to be overly interested in the whole business. The information pleased Commandant Fischer. As he had hoped, there was a level of prestige associated with the Club; demand was already evident, and that could only be good.

At five o'clock the Club women were assembled in a back room, awaiting Fisher's final inspection. Nerves were raw, especially among the younger girls, who had been told how to present themselves by the older ones-it was important to be selected because the alternative was all too evident-a brief look through any window served as a salutary reminder.

The clothing and make-up the Club women wore had been collected from Auschwitz. The Jews arrived with their suitcases full of belongings, and Schroder had been given access to a batch of luggage from the most recent transport but he had no idea what women wore or how they maintained their bodies. So he solicited help from an attractive young Jewess at Auschwitz, actually pulled her aside from a transport himself. She was about to head to a work detail or the gas chamber when Schroder chose her.

She enthusiastically opened suitcase after suitcase for him. *Here, sir, they will need this, sir. And this underwear, the men will love to see them in this; these shoes I think, very good, wonderful shoes, you can spiv them up with all these things, and thank you so much for giving me this opportunity, sir. Thank you. May God bless you, thank you, sir.* She worked tirelessly without a break, her enthusiasm never faltering. Schroder sat back and let her bring things to him; *put those here, the others over there.* After a while Schroder surveyed the piles of clothing and accessories. *Enough! That will do.* He signalled to one of the Auschwitz guards, a mere wave of the hand, and the woman was dragged away in disbelief, off to the gas chambers where she was processed with the last batch that very day.

According to Fischer, Tina had an excellent dress style-'*classy music hall with a touch of Berlin burlesque*'—was how he once described it and he charged her with ensuring that the Club women were appropriately attired.

After being washed and steam pressed the selected clothing was finally taken to the 'dressing room' where the Club women were allowed to pick several outfits each, as near to their own size as they could find. They were even provided with scissors, needles and thread to make minor alterations if they so wished.

The women eventually found themselves warming to the task. One of them talked of having been at a big city store with her grandmother as a child, where she experienced the frenzy of an end-of-season sale. Though there was no such rabid activity at the Club, the women finally relaxed as the significance of being allowed to wear civilian clothing sank in.

For a brief time, as the women dressed, applied powder to their faces, lipstick to their lips and brushed each other's hair, they began to talk openly. A fat farmer's wife from Oswicim surprisingly explained that for her, life could not be worse than it was at home.

"My husband was a miserable, drunken slob. The Germans shot him and I do not care. Things are better without him. At least I am going to get some sex now, and I tell you this, I reckon it will be better than I am used to, and hopefully it will last longer!"

No one laughed. "Come now, why so glum?" the fat woman continued. "It could be worse. Do you not see the walking dead out there? Fourteen-hour shifts shovelling lime or humping timber around in that treacherous weather, and for what? A bowl of insipid soup every night and a piece of weevil-infested bread? We will be fed and let's face it, there will plenty of German sausage for us too, eh, girls?"

Finally someone responded with a smile. "German sausage? Who wants a skinny little bratwurst? I prefer a good helping of Polish kielbasa myself, any day of the week!"

The unfamiliar sound of laughter echoed around the room until someone mentioned Ania. An exchange of opinions as to her whereabouts followed. Some said she was locked away against her will, others thought she was feathering her own nest-taking advantage of her looks and youth.

Whatever the reason, it did not help those who remained. They now had an opportunity to survive, and they all agreed they should do their best to look after each other during the difficult times ahead. A strange fellowship developed amongst the women as they dressed themselves, though it was evident that their newfound solidarity was as fragile as it was shallow. In places such as Wysznica, trust was as hard to maintain as it was to win.

***

Of the twelve women needed for the first shift, Fischer had gone for variety and chosen the six youngest, the three oldest, a thin one, another with a boyish figure, and one woman who was exceedingly large-the fat farmer's wife.

The women had been certified disease free by Dr Mengele and Frau Groepler, and were now suitably attired, ready for inspection. Fischer was determined not to waste the resource and after selecting the first shift, he had to decide the fate of the rest. One of the prettier girls was sent to the officers' mess to work as a waitress and the least attractive to the kitchens. The two youngest would go to Fischer's house where they would work alongside the existing staff of eight, cooking, cleaning and generally looking after his and Tina's comfort.

Of the remaining, only two would be on standby to cover for the twelve hostesses in the club in the event of something unforeseen happening. Those remaining were put to work in the laundry. Fischer explained it all to Tina that night over dinner and as he went through the list of who went there, she did a count on her fingers.

"That leaves one," Tina said. "You missed one."

"I missed no-one," Fischer said as he dismantled his pipe and tapped the mouthpiece on the tablecloth. "There are twelve cubicles in the Club, my dear, and did you notice at the far end of the hallway there is a door-on the right-hand side; a green door?" He reassembled his pipe and stuffed it with a fresh pinch of tobacco from the leather pouch he removed from his jacket pocket. "Did you hear me, my dear? The green door?"

Tina mumbled. "Yes, yes. The door. The green door. I saw it, so what?"

"That is the door to the Premier Room. The room where the very best of these women, the most desirable, will be accommodated." He held his wine glass up to the light. "The Premier Room will offer rewards that the others cannot. While the rooms with curtains offer certain, shall we say, common delights, the Premier Room will offer much, much more. Only a select few will be allowed behind that green door, but there will not be a man in this camp who does not want to sample its delights!" He lit his pipe, thoughtfully puffing clouds of aromatic Virginian tobacco smoke around his end of the table.

That afternoon, when Tina had herself viewed the final selection of women, she noticed that the girl with the strange eyes was missing. And now she knew why. If it were Baldric's intention to sample the delights of that room himself, it would be over the girl's dead body, or perhaps his partially dismembered one. There was no way Tina was going to share her man with that little Polish whore!

Tina had noticed the girl with the weird eyes immediately. How could she miss her? The shivering little bitch may have been barefoot in a nightdress and swathed in a filthy blanket when she arrived, but she was hard to miss. Her youth, her natural beauty, voluptuous body and most of all those fascinating sparkling eyes of hers-she stood out like a shining beacon in the slush on the parade ground.

But Tina knew that she herself still had 'it'. She may have been pushing thirty and her young daughter may well have been back home in Piaski with Babcia caring for her, but she knew how to manipulate Baldric, and while it was a dangerous path she trod in the bedroom, she had managed to keep him interested and excited since the outbreak of war.

There was always the promise of 'that thing', the one sexual act that she could not quite bring herself to do; even for him. So she kept him dangling and took the risk, promising that one day, when the mood took her, she might just let him do it. She had to get through the war in one piece, for the sake of her daughter; and if sleeping with a short, fat, disgusting German pig like Fischer got her there, then so be it.

Tina frequently told herself not to feel insecure. Gravity may have started to affect her body, but she had learned a few tricks to help disguise any flaws. The overhead light was always out, for instance, solving the problem of badly cast shadows, and laying a certain way or draping a sheet across her buttocks could cover a multitude of dimples.

Fischer was still talking about the Premier Room when the maid served desert. He was a little too excited about the girl with the odd-coloured eyes for Tina's liking. "Men will kill for the opportunity to sleep with her," he raved. "She is the find of the century!" He was still puffing at his pipe, slurping his wine, cramming mouthfuls of his favourite apple strudel into his mouth and talking animatedly about the green room to even notice that he was alone at the table. Tina had gone. She had heard enough about the girl with the strange eyes, but she most certainly had not heard the last.

29

It was eight o'clock when the Club opened for the first time; a dark, bitterly cold night. The wind sped eagerly around corners and between buildings searching for someone to annoy and prisoners huddled together in their bunks, hunched away from wallboards where the cold sliced through the gaps and wrapped itself around their bodies. They had long ago become numb to the filth and stench of those around them as they lay talking to each other about the old days and softly singing tunes from times gone by. The prayers of a few were heard by many, though some reacted with anger, feeling that God had abandoned them long ago.

Rough coughs and rattling chests confirmed that typhus and TB were hiding in the bodies of many, waiting to cheat the Germans. It would not be long before the dark night took them to a better place for a few hours so they could no longer feel the lice crawling over their flesh or the rats nibbling at their frozen extremities. Not everyone would wake the next morning-such a blessing for some.

But the misery of another bleak night at Wysznica was not everyone's lot, as the first lucky voucher holders nervously approached the steps at the front of the Club. There was an unusual level of activity around the building, as people seemed to legitimately break the curfew to watch the comings and goings of the voucher holders. Guards, Kapos, prisoners-they all wanted to know who was going to be first in and first served.

A guard was stationed at the front door. He examined vouchers under the yellow glow of the light above the doorway behind him as several nervous men waited in line, stomping their feet and slapping their arms around their bodies for warmth. The guard took his time, and why not? He deliberately left them in the cold and looked down his nose at each of them in turn, taking far too long to inspect their vouchers, hoping to find an early forgery or perhaps a reason to disappoint. Finally satisfied, he grunted and nodded his approval for the men to venture through the front door.

Once inside the men were surprised by the warmth, the smell of new paint and the unaccustomed lure of luxury-a tiny slice of heaven, right there in hell. On each side, down the length of the hallway, a series of curtained rooms awaited. Behind those curtains lay comfortable beds covered in crisp white linen adorned with bulging pillows stuffed with duck down. Everything would smell of the breezes from the beautiful fresh countryside, where the sun turned people's skin brown and the whispered promises of lovers made passing birds blush.

On those beds lay the most ravishing women that war ravaged Poland had to offer, ready to whisk the men away from their lives of misery and pain for the next thirty minutes. The stench of death would be replaced with the intoxicating musk of women waiting eagerly for love, and for the best part of their short visit, for the lucky voucher holders; evil would take a back seat at Wysznica.

But first they had to get past the formidable chief medical officer, Frau Groepler, who had positioned her desk inside the hallway, creating a barrier to where the women waited nervously behind her, in their little curtained rooms. A nursing assistant stood by her side.

"Yes!" Frau Groepler belched the word out as she shuffled her rubber stamps and straightened her lists before dipping her pen into a bottle of ink as she waited for the first man to step forward.

And so he did, hesitantly, attempting to pass a piece of paper to Frau Groepler, whose hands remained flat on the desk. Instead of reaching for the voucher, she just stared, and it remained in the space between them, in the man's shaking hand. He looked anxious, expecting her to say something, but she remained stone-faced and silent, her eyes resolutely locked onto his.

It was then that he realised he still had his cap on, and he removed it apologetically and nervously patted his greasy hair down after spitting into the palm of his hand. The CMO grunted her approval and turned her attention to the voucher. It seemed that he was a cook in the officers' mess.

He had worked three consecutive twenty-two-hour shifts to get his voucher, which showed on his weary face, though his eyes could not hide his excitement. It had been over four years since Marek Kowalski had lain next to a woman and felt the warmth and reassuring comfort of female flesh. "Shower, inspection, then make your choice!" the CMO shouted as she stamped the voucher and pointed towards a room at the end of the hallway. "Next!"

The water was warm. Another four-year first for the amazed Kowalski. And towels-actual clean, cloth towels! The luxury was too much to bear, and he lingered too long holding the towel to his face and smelling it before a sour-faced bitch in a nurse's uniform barged in and pulled him roughly aside. He stared at the top of her head as she knelt to examine his genitals. She looked up. "No disease. Choose carefully because once you are in the room, *you are in the room.* Slide the sign on the wall to show it is occupied. You will need this." As she handed him a small package a question appeared on his face. "It is a rubber, you fool, what the German military call a 'muzzle protector', though judging by the size of your weapon, there is not a lot to protect these women from. No kinky stuff allowed. Missionary position only. Your time starts now."

Kowalski padded down the corridor, passing other bewildered voucher holders, all craning their necks to see what they could when he pulled his chosen curtain aside.

The room he chose was occupied by the fat farmer's wife. She smiled nervously from the bed as Kowalski peered in at her. She had the same large flat bottom that he remembered spooning against the last time he lay with his own wife. This one also had huge, pendulous breasts, just like those he used to caress so lovingly all those years ago. His hand shook as he slid the sign on the wall from green to red and stepped into the room, pulling the curtain shut behind him. The sour-faced nurse looked up at the wall clock and scribbled in her notepad.

The other women waited anxiously behind their curtains, listening to the sound of footsteps, the occasional sharp retort in German and in the background, muffled voices. They had been told to be especially nice to these valued workers, to make them welcome and to ensure they left with smiles on their faces. It would not be hard to find other women willing to fill any vacancies behind the curtains. Insubordination or a lack of desire to serve was easily dealt with. After all, the perks were the best in the camp-hot water, two meals a day, fellowship, civilian clothes, make-up, even alcohol on special occasions. All the women had to do was satisfy up to fifteen men a shift. No one had ever had it so good at a German concentration camp, according to Commandant Fischer.

***

Within minutes of the curtain closing, Emilie's first visitor stood naked and fully aroused in front of her. Piotrek Karpinski was known for his brutality at the lime pit where he was chief Kapo and greatly feared. His methods were respected by the Germans and he provided them with workers who were much sought after by the armaments factories around Auschwitz where physical strength was considered a prerequisite.

Karpinski kept his teams working at a pace with no let-up, fourteen hours a day. If someone fell or tripped, they never did so twice. Only the toughest lasted on his shifts. He had no problems getting one of the first vouchers.

Despite having only been at the camp for a few days, the women had already heard of Karpinski, and Emilie's heart sunk when he told her his name as he closed the curtain. He motioned for her to remove her dress and watched until she was naked. His eyes moved over her body and he smiled, revealing a few blackened stumps of rotting teeth. As he crossed the room his penis swayed with each swaggering step until suddenly he was upon her, ripping her arms from her chest, prising her legs apart with his knees. She held her breath as he forced himself inside her, his disgusting body odour overpowering and pungent. Her eyes gaped in horror as she saw lice scurrying around the thick bristly hair that covered his shoulders; his first shower in four years was a complete waste of time without disinfectant.

He grunted with each brutal thrust, sending torturous pain up through Emilie's body and purple flashes across her eyes. One of Karpinski's hands closed around her throat and the other covered her mouth. She made a feeble attempt to wriggle out beneath him, but he was far too strong. The pain and lack of oxygen swept through her body and before she could protect herself, Emilie slipped into unconsciousness.

She woke a few minutes later with Karpinski still on top of her, panting like a dog and stinking even more from the exertion. "You enjoyed that you bitch, was that what you wanted, eh?" He then started to thrust inside her again, her body bouncing beneath his, the springs of the mattress forcing them into a rhythm as she prayed he would finish soon. But there seemed to be no let-up as he pounded into her, his shoulders rising and falling for what seemed like several minutes before she realised what was really happening.

Karpinski, the terror of the lime pit, was crying. "You bitch, you whore, you fucking Polish slut," he cried as he thrust into her again. A thump on the wall eventually signalled that time was up. As he dressed, Karpinski said, "Next time I expect you to stay awake when I fuck you, bitch. If I wanted sex with dead people I would work with Sonderkommandos at the gas chamber."

***

Ania had been allowed first pick of the clothes and make-up with a guard watching over her. She was then taken to the Premier Room and locked in after being given a meal with vegetables and real meat, on a white china plate with a red and black swastika in the centre. They even gave her real cutlery.

As the night rolled by Ania lay alone on her soft, comfortable bed, her mind drifting back to the time she used to spend talking to Danuta in bed. Her sister had been the first to experience most things, and she willingly shared what she had learned. She was the first to smoke and she then taught Ania. She was also first to taste alcohol and, of course, she smuggled some vodka into the barn for her little sister to sample. Despite a coughing fit, Ania liked it, especially the feeling of warmth as it slid down her throat into her belly.

And then there were boys ... ah the boys ... Danuta was first to try. Ania would have to wait, but the *wanting to try* made her ache sometimes. The things Danuta told her, the things her sister did; Mother would have killed her if she knew! Growing up together the girls had no secrets, but now they were separated there was one secret that haunted each of them-the whereabouts of the other. The pain of not knowing was tearing them apart, an agony previously unknown and never imagined. Ania needed her elder sister more than ever before. She did not know how to deal with the jealousy of the other women and worst still, how to cope with the guilt she felt about her promotion to the Premier Room. Outside, in the freezing huts, hundreds of people were dying of disease, malnutrition and the mind-numbing cold, yet she found herself alone, well fed, warm and comfortable in the room behind the green door. Why?

30

A crescendo of noise announced the arrival of another transport: a loud whistle from the engine with steam hissing from its boilers, the thud of heavy ramps dropped onto concrete followed by the rattle of huge cattle doors sliding open and hundreds of terrified people herded onto the platform. There was an immediate burst of activity as dogs barked, people screamed, babies cried and occasionally a gunshot burst through the clutter noise. It was difficult to sleep on the piss-soaked bunks at the best of times but when a new transport arrived everyone strained their ears and for once, tried to ignore the rats and bugs that scampered over their bodies. Despite the disgusting stench of those who shared their bunks, people still huddled close, searching for some human comfort at such times; so much suffering, so many people...

Ania was one of the lucky ones because she never heard transports arrive-the sound was drowned by all the comings and goings in the hallway on the other side of her door. Several times she heard groans from other brothel women, the occasional yell or a raised voice, and once or twice, the strange almost irreverent sound of laughter. It was like listening to an obscure radio show.

Not all the men were violent or abusive to the women. There were also charmers, like Kowalski, who did not want any sexual contact at all. He decided he just wanted to lie naked and spoon the fat farmer's wife. He spent his thirty minutes talking into her hair and smelling her cleanness, telling her how much he missed his wife's huge, white dimpled bottom, the likes of which he feared he might never see again-until now. A strange kind of bond formed between Kowalski and the farmer's wife that first night, for they were both captive, but in different cages. Before his time was up, both were in tears and when he left he did so with regret-his and hers.

Even though the night had started well for the fat farmer's wife, her run of luck did not continue. A worker from the sawmill saw to that, another shift leader who was known to be almost as cruel as Karpinski and much more energetic. This man also liked to degrade and humiliate a woman as much as he could during sex. Inflicting pain added to his pleasure and he would have fitted in well with the SS had he not been a Gypsy. Thirty minutes was a long time for any woman to spend with a man like that.

To her surprise, at one o'clock in the morning after her first shift finished, Emilie had another visitor. One of the truck guards, the smoker who stared at his shoes for the whole three days. How he got a voucher was beyond her understanding because the Germans were forbidden from visiting the Club women. Emilie reasoned that he must have bribed his way in, though it was impossible to imagine how he got past Frau Groepler.

Perhaps it just went to show that everyone had their price? The truck guard was surprisingly polite to Emilie when he closed the curtain behind him, clicking his heels as Germans often did, then grinning widely, giving her gifts of cigarettes and chocolate before he undressed. She made sure he finished his business quickly, and then they sat up in bed smoking and talking quietly about his life before the war. He never mentioned a wife and it seemed that he, like many, just needed someone to talk to, someone to listen, someone to hold. He kept apologising, but Emilie did not know what he was apologising for. For what happened during the journey to Wysznica? Something he did in his past or for what he was doing now. The war? For being German?

By two o'clock in the morning, the Club was finally quiet and the first shift was over. Ania could no longer hear taps running or women sobbing softly into their pillows. The moans and groans and the sound of bouncing bedsprings had been replaced by the creaks of the building settling and the snores of those already sleeping. By two-thirty it was so quiet that Ania could even hear the guard at the front door snoring.

She turned her lights off, assuming her night was over too, even though she had no visitors. As she lay quietly staring at the ceiling in the dark, she thought of her grandparents, sister and mother, even her sweet old dog, Cabbage. A blanket of gloom seemed to fall from above, and she closed her eyes and asked God to help her find a reason for all she had seen and for the unending suffering around her. Would he also please ensure that Danuta was safe? Her thoughts turned into prayers, which filled her eyes with tears and increased her sombre mood.

Her prayers were suddenly interrupted when she heard a key rattle in the lock. The door quietly creaked open and a narrow beam of light slipped into the room, slid across the floor and up the side of the bed, coming to rest on her body.

When her eyes adjusted to the light she saw Schole, swaying slightly, looking a little worse for wear standing in the doorway. "So, here you are," he slurred. "The commandant's star prize locked in a gilded cage waiting for her reward." Ania pulled the sheets up to her chin. "Ah, such innocence, such beauty," Schole said as he closed the door and made his way towards her.

He turned the bedside light on before making himself comfortable by Ania's side. She could smell the alcohol on his breath as he spoke. "Tomorrow you will be given a number. Here. Just here, on your forearm." He pulled her arm from beneath the covers. "You are a very lucky girl to have a number, do you know that?"

She shook her head. It seemed that alcohol and Schole did not mix; he looked as if he might vomit at any moment, but he managed to somehow continue. "The numbers they are going to tattoo on your arm mean you are a useful commodity here at Wysznica, my little bird." He gently stroked her cheek. "The commandant has determined that you have a value to the Reich, or to him, anyway. If you have no number then your days are very limited, very limited indeed. Having a number means everything for your kind in here."

She had seen Schole hovering in the background during the various inspections she had endured since her arrival, and he was always watching, always observing. He was like a child playing spies, pretending to be undercover, a secret agent. At this early hour, in his present condition, he looked far too young for any of this madness, with his round metal-rimmed spectacles and an acne-covered face.

Despite his apparent innocence, Ania knew she had to keep her senses about her. She had already learned that in war there was a time to talk and a time to listen, and she understood instinctively what to do now.

Schole's strange visit lasted less than half an hour. He spoke mostly about his dislike for Tina and warned Ania be careful of Herr Commandant's girlfriend, who was nothing more than *a money grabbing peasant slut from the backwaters of Poland.* He told her that Tina had her claws out, and she should be very careful.

As he stood to leave, Schole produced a small pile of vouchers for the Club's Premier Room. As he handed them to her he said, "You will need these soon." Without further explanation he left, locking the door behind himself. Ania was still looking at the vouchers when she heard a key rattling in the door lock for the second time in quick succession.

***

Fischer was in a state of high excitement when he arrived at the Premier Room, his jacket partly unbuttoned and a bottle of the very best Napoleon Brandy under his arm. Two glasses appeared as if by magic and he placed his ample body next to Ania and poured a large drink for them both.

"Tina is asleep at last, thank God!" he gasped, as if Ania had known all along that he was trying to get away. "We have matters to discuss, you and me," he said, patting his pockets and cursing because he had forgotten his pipe. Without it he somehow felt less articulate.

Ania had seen her sister naked several times, as they had shared the same bed and bath for most of their lives. Earlier that day she had also seen other women naked in the showers, but now she was about to see a man without clothes for the very first time. Despite what Danuta had told her, there were no shivers of anticipation travelling down her spine, no tingle between her legs. The prospect of seeing Commandant Fischer naked was indeed daunting, something that Ania was completely unprepared for.

He was grotesquely fat for such a short man, and with his upper garments removed his belly flopped over the waistband of his underpants. Tufts of hair seemed to protrude from every orifice on his body, and it luxuriated thicker on his back and shoulders than his chest. His whole body rippled when he moved, including the layers of fat hanging from his shoulder blades. At a quick glance, it seemed to Ania that even his breasts were larger than her own!

He poured more brandy, his second glass, her first still untouched. He told her to drink. The brandy was very different from the homemade vodka she had sampled in the barn with Danuta but it still burned its way down her throat making her cough, which gave Fischer an opportunity to rub her back. As his hands fell on her velvet skin he visibly quivered with excitement and gently tugged her nightdress from her shoulders. The more flesh he uncovered the more he shook.

"I will keep you safe in this room as long as I can," he gasped. "But it does depend upon a few things." His voice was almost trance-like as he removed her nightdress and buried his face between her perfectly formed breasts. "You need to learn a few things-things you will be doing to keep me happy. It will be better for you to enjoy these things too. Make me smile, Ania, and your life here will be rewarding and extremely comfortable." He stopped for a brief moment, as if he was going to tell her what would happen if she did not meet his expectations, but his expression changed, and a look of sincerity washed over his face. "I am being honest with you here. Let us have no secrets or misunderstandings about our relationship."

Ania braved a question. "What about Fraulein Tina, Commandant?"

"Ah yes, Tina. She should in fact be your second consideration, after my happiness. If she finds out I have been visiting you she will no doubt remove my testicles with a very sharp, rusty blade of some kind as I sleep. But not before she has killed you in a more horrific way, make no mistake about that." Fischer seemed buoyed by the possibility of such a conflict. "Tina can be a little feisty at times." He looked thoughtful for a brief moment, and then changed the subject. "You have the vouchers?"

"You mean these things?" Ania handed him the small pile of papers she had been given by Schole.

"Excellent. I knew Fritz would not let me down."

"What are they?"

"They are your alibi-mine too! If Tina, the camp inspectorate, or indeed anyone else of importance asks if you entertain in this room, show them the vouchers. Schole will update them from time to time-no-one can gain access to the Club without these vouchers-these ones are evidence that you are indeed a popular girl." He showed her where they had already been dated and stamped. Each one represented a 'visit' from someone in the camp. "It just means that to the casual observer, you are entertaining the best of our workers, just like the other women here, but on a more selective basis, of course, as befits your status in the Premier Room."

Fischer put the vouchers aside, dropped heavily onto the pillow by Ania's side and spoke to the ceiling as if he were dictating a letter. "There are a few minor rules that will govern our relationship. Follow them, and you will be fine."

There was to be no gossiping, no mixing with anyone apart from those she met in the performance of her duties, which were determined only by Fischer, of course. She was to save her 'special' self for him and him only. He repeated that he would try to keep her safe as long as he could, but she had to be complicit in the arrangements and the lies. He started to remove his underpants, which indicated to Ania that the conversation was over. Now it was time to get down to business. Finally, she found it hard not to stare at the commandant, as he lay naked before her, apart from his socks and their suspenders, which were emblazoned with red and black swastikas.

"Do we have an understanding, Ania, my dear?" Fischer was nibbling her ear and groping for her breasts.

She nodded nervously, her body tense. He seemed somewhat breathless already. "Tina does things for me that I like, but there are some things she will not willingly do. That does not matter now that I have you. You will do those things! I shall keep Tina for my day-to-day physical needs-routine relief, if you like. But you? You are my secret, my beautiful little treasure and you will be the purveyor of special treats for your commandant. You will soon learn what I like; I will teach you." His voice sent a chill through her body. "I urge you to enjoy it yourself too," he said enthusiastically. "It will be very much worth your while, believe me," he said enthusiastically.

Here she was, Ania Burczyk, about to have her first sexual experience with a man old enough to be her father. A man who, at a whim, could have her killed without any repercussions. It did not appear as if he would beat her, yet if he so desired he could and there would be nothing she could do about it. But why was he anxious about Tina? If he was so powerful what did it matter to him if she knew he had taken a mistress? After all, Tina was also a mistress herself, wasn't she? As Ania lay thinking things through, Fischer's fat fingers started probing, stroking and fiddling.

What to do now? Ania thought as she lay naked on top of the sheets. What was expected of her? How should she present herself? Her instinct was to retain her modesty and drape a sheet over her body, but Danuta had told her that *men like to look, they like to see.*

There may have only been two years between Danuta and Ania's ages, but there was a twenty-year gap when it came to life experience! Danuta was well past the fumbling stage before Ania received her first shy peck on the cheek, and she had a certain reputation in the village; she was, as the local boys said, a little on the *friendly* side. They were all chasing Danuta, and she enjoyed the attention. She would have a husband soon enough and judging by the way the boys queued for her attentions, she would have the pick of them.

The two girls were in bed one winter's night, six months before the German invasion, when Danuta told Ania everything she knew about men and their hunger for sex. *My God, it's almost primeval,* she said. Ania giggled and clasped her sister's hand to her chest, *tell me more, tell me more!* she squealed.

Danuta told her sister everything: what they did what they liked done to them, how they smelled how they looked and how they felt; *the way they grunt, their tight little buttocks in your hands as they thrust into you...*

Ania's eventual reality proved to be very different than her expectations-except for 'the power'. Danuta had talked of it often. *Oh yes, the power. You will know it when you lay naked with a man. There will be no doubt, no misunderstanding, Ania, my darling sister, you will have the power.*

Danuta was right.

Ania knew she had *the power* as she watched Fischer drool when he told her how beautiful her breasts were as he cupped, stroked and kissed them-his whole body was shaking with lust. She then saw an erect penis for the very first time, hidden beneath several rolls of fat, peeping out of a thick bush of coarse hair like the twitching nose of an inquisitive creature in a hedgerow.

When she stroked it, Fischer's eyes glazed over, his voice became hoarse and his breathing urgent. He shook violently when she kissed his nipples, every nerve in his body on fire. And just as Danuta had said, the more she touched, the more he looked as if he was about to explode- and when she stopped concentrating on his nipples and decided to explore a little lower that was exactly what happened.

31

The next morning Ania woke to find a maid in her room, delivering a magnificent cooked breakfast. Orange juice and toast accompanied two eggs and three rashers of bacon. Where it came from at a time like this in the middle of Poland, she could only speculate, but she enjoyed it thoroughly. After she ate she washed herself at the sink then dressed. Schole appeared, resplendent as ever, acting as if it was the first time he had been in her room and the visit he paid her the previous night never happened.

He politely escorted her to another building where she was photographed and tattooed with a number-five digits that would be with her forever-43798-on the inside of her left forearm. At the last minute there was a hitch, as Schole had to arrange for someone to travel to Auschwitz to collect a tattoo gun. Ania was given a hot drink as the courier seemed to have been delayed. Schole expressed his anger with those concerned, and then explained to Ania that the usual method of tattooing at Wysznica was by way of a metal stamp 'branded' onto the bony area just above the left breast. To allow her magnificent body to be marked in such a way would have been tantamount to suicide for him-the commandant would never forgive him. "He would send me straight to the Russian front!"

Eventually the marking was complete and Ania was escorted back to her room. During the return journey she managed to look through several windows and observe the activity outside. She saw the zebra people running barefoot this way and that through the slush and snow and always the brutality against them. Some prisoners were made to carry huge logs; others were pushing barrows overloaded with lime or gravel. All the time the guards were pushing, prodding, tripping and laughing at their charges. The wind was blustery out there, billowing around their bodies, buffeting them from different directions as if nature itself also hated the people dressed like zebras.

Ania felt relieved when she finally returned to her warm room, to be greeted by a small but decent lunch on a tray. Schole had hardly spoken on the walk back, saying only *'turn here or look straight ahead'*. He locked the door when he left and afterwards Ania noticed more surprises: as well as the food, she found several books on her bedside table, including a beautiful leather-bound copy of *Mein Kampf*. She spoke German better than she read, but she certainly knew how to work the gramophone that had also been put in her room, along with a dozen or so records for her personal listening pleasure.

As time progressed she found her relationship with Fischer deepening as little surprises continued to appear without notice. She never asked the maid or Schole where these things came from or why they had been left but she took them all and never once failed to weep at her good fortune and apologise to God for the greed she felt.

Later that afternoon, Schole turned up again and sat uncomfortably on the side of her bed as she made him a cup of tea at her small sink. He made light conversation, as if waiting for the right moment to broach a difficult subject. He then changed the subject mid-sentence, for no apparent reason, then stood courteously and launched into an apology for his drunken behaviour the previous night. He concluded his little speech with a bow and a heel click.

He told Ania that he had to go away for a while, only a week or so, no more, on personal business for the commandant. But he wanted to visit her again privately after his return, and promised he would never be drunk in her presence again. "If you are in agreement, Fraulein Ania, I would not impose, and I promise you will be safe at all times during my visits. I hope you believe me?"

***

That night as Emilie, the fat farmer's wife and the rest of the women received the next batch of lucky voucher holders, Ania sat alone in her room with her gramophone playing softly in the background, partly for company but mostly to cover the uncomfortable sounds coming from the rooms beyond.

At eleven pm exactly, her door swung open to reveal Obersturmbann-fuhrer Fischer in full dress uniform, complete with his Iron Cross (first class). He placed a bottle of excellent French Champagne and two beautiful crystal glasses on the bedside table then removed his cap.

After popping the cork and pouring two drinks he politely asked Ania if she minded him sitting with her, and enquired how her arm was, if it was sore from the tattoo? He also asked if Schole was looking after her. "He is the most dedicated member of my staff. He might seem a little strange and there are times when I don't know what to make of him myself, but I confess that I would be lost without him. It is a shame that such dedication cannot be rewarded when this is all over." He took a drink, lowered his glass thoughtfully then said, "Do you know, I do believe that Schole would give his life for me."

Fischer could not have been more frank, open or courteous, and he insisted that Ania call him Baldric because he only wanted her to call him Commandant in front of others and most especially, during moments of high passion. "Such as last night," he said with an expression that confirmed he had truly enjoyed their first encounter. The more champagne he drank, the more enthusiastic he became, and the bottle was soon empty. Ania's glass remained in her hand. Though she appeared to sip from it occasionally, the level barely changed.

Fischer apologised that her door had to remain locked. It was not to keep her in but to keep others out. She belonged to him, and no one else. "After all, as Shakespeare once said, *'to the victor, go the spoils'*" he misquoted splendidly.

Fischer told Ania that Tina unexpectedly had to go away for a while. "So now I can give you the attention that your beauty deserves," he said, his hand under her chin as he admired her face. It transpired that Tina was visiting relatives who were looking after her young child in Piaski. Fischer had spared Schole and a driver to accompany her and keep her safe.

Schole had been instructed to return the long way, the very long way, via Warsaw, to take Tina on a shopping trip as a treat and to stay in the finest of accommodations. With both her and Schole out of the way there was very little chance of his visits to Ania being discovered.

"Until she returns, I can teach you how to give me those little treats I told you about, my dear," he said as he reached around her waist.

32

The morning after the drinking session with Slav, things were quiet in the flat behind the florist shop. Danuta had stayed with Grabowski instead of moving in with Slav as previously discussed. Slav wanted his privacy with Natalka and anyway, there was plenty of space at Grabowski's. Danuta had a room to herself and was made to feel most welcome. She rose at nine and made her way to the kitchen where the man she had met the night before, the man with one eye, Jozeph, was cooking breakfast with Natalka.

They served fried tomatoes and sausage, and coffee that tasted like mud. Danuta was not hungry. The previous day's activities and the events that followed had taken their toll and she was still trying to process everything, especially Krzys' death.

"I'm sorry about the food," Jozeph said, "but Natalka is cooking. She may look good but believe me, she can't cook to save her life." A metal mug flew across the room and crashed into the wall above his head.

"I have more to offer than my looks and you know it. You wouldn't speak to me like that if Slav was here," Natalka said tersely.

"Of course I wouldn't, because if he was here, you would be in bed showing him exactly what you *are* good at!" This time a plate smashed into the wall above his head. Jozeph laughed. "She is not a morning person," he said. Then he changed the subject. "Grabowski is at Auschwitz with Slav." Natalka busied herself collecting the parts of the broken plate as Jozeph spoke. "He's supposed to be doing some work to the prisoners' huts but in reality he is recruiting for his new grand plan. Good luck with that eh? Apparently tonight we are going to hear how to smuggle weapons, ammunition and food into the camps." A look of self-importance spread across Jozeph's face and he narrowed his one good eye. "There are plans afoot that I can't discuss with you Danuta. Only a few of us know of them; Slav's closest confidants." He spoke with great authority, but the sound of Natalka deliberately dropping a pot on the stone floor echoed around the room and she gave him a stern look. "Slav and my brother only talk to those they can trust," he said.

It was a lazy day for Danuta, and she dozed for a while after lunch, but woke when a vision of Krzys's body flashed through her dreams. She made herself a cup of tea and read the newspapers that were lying around the apartment. She was not allowed to go into the florist shop at the front of the property, as Germans often called in to buy flowers for their wives and girlfriends. Wislawa owned the florist shop and she popped into the apartment from time to time to chat, although she did seem somewhat guarded around Danuta, just like Jozeph. Natalka and Jozeph seemed to be constantly bickering. Danuta's initial thought was that Jozeph was jealous of Natalka's relationship with Slav; they slept together every night so they talked-they were close as a couple. Maybe one-eyed Jozeph thought they were too close and Slav told her too much.

Slav and Grabowski returned at eight o'clock that night carrying a series of blueprint plans from Auschwitz and Wysznica. The documents not only showed details of existing and future buildings but they also mapped out where the sewers and ventilation shafts were located-the best hiding places. As Slav and Grabowski talked in detail Danuta helped make coffee and snacks. The two leaders appeared to already be comfortable with her.

"After we have recruited and trained teams inside both camps, we will start to smuggle small arms in. Participants will be rewarded with food and other treats and necessities. I have a huge works program at Auschwitz at the current time, increasing the number of levels in the prisoners' bunks. There are to be three levels when previously there were only two, and each level will now be a resting place for three prisoners, not two. That makes nine in each bay instead of four. Think about it, the same space but now nine miserable people. Unbelievable." He savaged a sandwich before continuing. "It's easy to conceal things. I can stow munitions and explosives among the materials I bring for the job." He rolled up the plan he had been working with. "The Germans cannot physically check everything I take into the camp, and as I get to know the guards better, the easier it will be to persuade them to turn a blind eye now and again. They love chocolate, cigarettes, of course, and good brandy. Best of all they like silk underwear for their girlfriends. The black market can supply it all, at a price, of course, and I am earning well from this job. It is no problem."

He said he was frustrated they could not do more, but as the war progressed he had no doubts that new opportunities would arise and he would be ready, no matter what. He raised a glass proudly. "My little accountant Jurek will make sure the money is available when it is needed."

"I hope he is better at cooking the books than Natalka is at cooking the food," Jozeph said sarcastically. Grabowski shot him a withering look, pre-empting an uncomfortable silence, which Danuta eventually broke.

"You spoke about expanding the bunks at Auschwitz, Slav. May I ask why they are doing that?"

"More Jews from Europe. There are thousands coming. Hundreds of thousands maybe, it is hard to tell. Every day there seems to be more of them. Transports arrive loaded down with the poor devils. I have seen them. Some die before they can get out of the cattle carts, which I suppose saves the Germans a bit of work." He seemed so matter of fact. "They can't kill them quickly enough at Auschwitz. There are too many now and it's becoming a real problem. I have no doubt they will be building more gas chambers and ovens soon though. Cost isn't a problem; it's the delivery that matters."

"Enough of this for God's sake!" Natalka suddenly burst into tears and threw her arms around Slav, resting her head on his huge chest as she sobbed. He caressed her face lovingly. "I am sorry, my darling, but that is what is happening beyond our backyards, here in Krakow. Let me tell you, let me tell everyone, Slav Posluzny will never be ashamed to admit he is Polish, but those who turn a blind eye and do nothing? They will carry the shame to their own graves and beyond!"

33

After three days it was considered safe for Danuta to walk outside the apartment. She now had a fine set of papers, in the false name she had given to Grabowski and Slav-Danuta Szalek. It was comforting that no one knew who she really was. Later that afternoon Wislawa decided to send her on an errand to collect some baking flour. On her way back she got lost and found herself walking through the back streets of Krakow, with night threatening to arrive and the curfew looming.

Danuta felt the beginnings of a wave of panic working its way through her body. If she was not back before curfew, what would she do? She asked several people if they knew of the florist shop, and they sent her in all directions, but she seemed to be travelling in circles.

It was then that an army patrol vehicle pulled alongside her and a German voice called for her to stop. Two soldiers jumped from the vehicle and accosted Danuta. "What do we have here Gunther, a resistance fighter maybe?"

"I can't see much resistance in this one, that's for sure," the taller soldier said, placing a finger beneath her chin. As he backed Danuta against a wall she noticed the curtains in a window opposite twitch then suddenly close, snapping out any possibility of help. The German shouted into her face. "Papers! Now!"

Danuta placed the bag of flour on the nearest window ledge then patted her sides, fumbled with her buttons, hands shaking as she anxiously searched for her documents.

The German was impatient. He displayed a level of confidence beyond his apparent age and rank, and his partner, an oafish-looking man, clearly enjoyed his company. And why not? Gunther Schulz was handsome and authoritative in his new uniform; his mother had told him often enough and the Polish ladies did appear to like him.

He gripped Danuta's jaw and she smelled the alcohol on his breath as she tried to twist her head away. "You see that, Hans, we could shoot her on the spot for that, resisting an officer of the Wehrmacht and trying to escape!"

"Shooting would be a waste of valuable ammunition. I think we should employ her!"

"Employ her?"

"That's right. She looks infinitely employable to me. Never have I seen a more suitable 'Wehrmacht warmer'. She is rather thin, though, so perhaps she can only warm one of us at a time, but who is to be first?"

"Ah yes, a man can do with a bit of warming-up on a frosty evening like this, eh?" Schulz started to fumble with Danuta's coat and she tried to shrug him away.

"Hold her for me, Franz, arms behind her back. This one needs to learn a few manners, I think." A slap stung Danuta's face as her arms were twisted backwards. She yelped and stiffened her body. Schulz had free rein now that his partner was holding her at bay. She felt another slap, hard enough to draw a little blood from her lip and leave an imprint on her right cheek.

"You can do this either way, you Polish bitch, the easy way or the hard way. What is it to be?" he hissed into her face. Danuta remained defiant and tried to twist away again but Schulz pulled her towards him and made a grab for her breasts. The oafish German held her tight and decided to join in the fun by sticking his tongue into her ear and kissing her neck.

Both men were laughing now, for it was all too easy. They had perfected their technique of harassing innocent, vulnerable Polish women over the last few months, and it had proved highly successful. It was easy to scare a woman into submitting to sex with them both. Who would she complain to and how would she prove that she had been raped and had not freely offered her services, as others were doing to all across the Krakow region.

With his partner holding Danuta tight, Schulz managed to undo his own coat and his pants, and despite her attempts to keep him at bay, he finally forced one hand down the inside of her pants. As she continued to resist he was thinking he might just have to slap her again, a little harder this time perhaps, when an angry voice rang out from behind. "What the hell is going on here?"

At that moment, a smartly dressed German officer appeared from nowhere and pulled Danuta away from the two soldiers.

Schulz, with his trousers at half-mast, spoke. "We were just teaching this whore a lesson, sir. The bitch insulted the Reich."

The officer looked at Danuta, and then at Schulz, who was trying to pull his pants up. "She is not alone then, is she? You have failed to salute a senior officer or acknowledge the Fuhrer!"

Schulz immediately stood to attention, attempting to click his heels but producing nothing more than a muffled thump as his pants dropped around his ankles. "Heil Hitler!"

"I suggest that you and your foolish accomplice here get going and take this as a lesson in diplomacy. I am sure that this young lady is going about her legal business and trying to get home before the curfew. You have papers?"

he asked Danuta. She nodded. The officer turned back to Schulz. "Your duty is to control the Polish population not harass them unnecessarily, do you understand?"

Both men clicked their heels and gave boisterous salutes to the officer. Schulz finally managed to pull his pants up and button his coat before he and his colleague sheepishly jumped back into their vehicle and sped off into the fading light.

"Now then, young lady," the officer spoke unexpectedly kindly, "let's take a look at you. Are you OK?" He reached out and gently pulled Danuta's coat around her shoulders. She thanked him and lowered her head, adjusting her clothing, tugging her lapels around her chest. "I think I should see your papers, if I may?" he said.

Danuta found them at the first attempt and handed them over. It was so much easier when she was not under duress. The German scanned them quickly and Danuta suddenly realised her new address was there all the time, on her documents! She smiled at her own stupidity and he noticed her change of expression.

"OK, Danuta Szalek, these seem to be in order. I think I should take you home to make sure you have no further problems as it is almost time for the curfew. You may only have to go around the corner, but it is better that I escort you. You never know who you might run into out here on these streets."

Danuta grinned again. The German had nodded up the street when he said it. *Just around the corner.* What a fool she had been! But she had to think quickly now because she could not let him near the florist shop. "I am not going home, sir; I am staying at my grandmother's house tonight. This house here, this door."

The German decided to engage Danuta in conversation. Like most German officers he was immaculately groomed. He removed his leather gloves and shook her hand. She noticed how soft his skin was, how well manicured his nails were, and how small his hands looked. He introduced himself as Arndt Nebe. Haupsturmfuhrer Arndt Nebe.

"That is Captain Nebe, for your information, but I think you should call me Arndt, don't you?"

Nebe was cultured and well educated, able to speak fluently in three languages. "I come from the beautiful city of Dortmund," he said with a disarming grin. He was extremely handsome, quite charming and by the time he kissed her hand to bid farewell he had already given her an embossed card, with a red and black swastika at the top and his address and contact details in the bottom left-hand corner. Danuta found herself staring into his beautiful blue eyes.

"I have to leave now, Danuta Szalek. I have some planning to attend to tonight. There are still Jews in this area and we need to round them up. There is plenty of space in the ghetto and it would be a shame to see it go to waste, don't you think?" He did not wait for her response. "A little tip for you, if I may? You and your grandmother should stay indoors tomorrow, because that is when our final round up begins! You know, I always enjoy that part of my job. It is most exciting because Jews can be rather devious and more inventive than you could ever imagine. I love the sound of the dogs baying, people running this way and that, guns going off around me and at the end of the day; a nice pile of dead Jews outside every apartment block on the eastern side of Krakow! The British have their foxhunting, we have our Jew baiting. Such sport never did a man any harm, don't you think?"

Danuta realised her hand was still in his and she pulled away quickly. He was too occupied to notice, his feelings of self-importance blocking everything. A silent scream was building inside Danuta's throat, her heart thumped in her chest and she felt the desire to vomit over his beautiful uniform and his disgustingly handsome German face. Instead, she found herself instinctively reaching forward and pulling him towards her in an embrace. "The least I can do is thank you for saving me from those thugs, Arndt. You are my knight in shining armour. God only knows what would have happened to me if you hadn't intervened."

What began as a seemingly polite hug turned into a passionate embrace as Danuta pressed her body into his. He felt her breasts against his chest as she nuzzled into his neck, the smell of her hair lingering in his nostrils. For the briefest moment she pulled away and stared into his face, held him between her hands then leaned forward kissing him passionately. They remained locked in the embrace for several seconds, and as their kiss lingered and his breathing deepened, Danuta carefully slipped her right hand into the pocket of her overcoat. It was then that she heard the sounds of a thousand bees inside her head; a roaring, buzzing noise that filled the cavity of her skull with an intensity that made her want to scream ... visions of Nebe running through the stairwell of an apartment block chasing terrified Jews around ... then she felt his hand on the curve of her breast, which he rubbed gently with his thumb, and she pressed herself into him even more, responding to his other hand which had slipped around her waist and down the inside of her skirt in search of the soft mounds of her buttocks.

Danuta instantly found what she was searching for in her pocket. She momentarily paused and gently pulled herself away from the German's embrace. "Goodbye, Captain Nebe, this is for Krzys." She took Slav's hunting knife from her pocket and punched it deep into the German's side, twisting it fiercely. Nebe turned towards her, gripping her tightly, his face frozen in shock as she pushed the knife further into him. Then his eyes widened and his mouth opened enough to let a soft gasp escape before he slumped forward onto her. She found herself supporting his entire body weight but managed to shuffle him around and lower his body to the floor, inside a door well.

Danuta stared at the crumpled body. One moment he was alive and the next he was gone. She suddenly remembered the knife in her hand and looked down, surprised that there was not much blood. It felt as if her heart was about to burst through her chest and a wave of panic started to well deep inside her body, she needed to run, to get as much distance between her and the dead German as she could. But then she realised that the sight of a woman in flight might attract attention, so she took three deep breaths, put the knife back in her pocket, picked up the bag of flour and looked up and down the silent street.

The curtain in the window of the house across the road twitched again and a slither of light slipped onto the pavement, the shadow of someone clearly visible behind it. She adjusted her clothing once more then threw the business card the German had given her onto his body and started to walk back to Grabowski's apartment and the florist shop, which turned out to be less than one hundred metres around the next corner. As she closed the front door behind her the clock on the kitchen wall ticked over to six pm-the start of curfew.

34

Ania learned to endure the camp commandant's regular nightly visits during Tina's absence. Tina returned loaded down with new clothes and cosmetics, blissfully unaware of Fischer's antics. He told Ania that regrettably, his visits would not be so frequent now that Tina was back, so she must prepare herself and be ready for random visits from him, any time of the day or night.

Schole also started visiting Ania, as he said he would. His visits were always late at night, usually immediately after Fischer had departed. As always, Schole was polite and apologetic. Ania felt as if he had a secret he wanted to share but he could not quite get the words out. Perhaps it was a matter of trust. He certainly needed someone to talk to and she seemed willing to provide an ear.

Fischer was enjoying Ania. "This is the best of both worlds for me and for you," he told her late one night as he lay beside her. "I get my stress relief from Tina, and I also enjoy special treats from you. In return, you are protected from the vagaries of life in the camp! What could be better?" There was no doubting that Ania had it good compared to the rest of the brothel women; the beautiful meals, starched linen and plump towels, regular deliveries to the room with the green door. Ania even had a personal guard. As far as the other women were concerned, there was no doubt what she was up to. While they were working in fear of their lives, Ania was deliberately trying to sit out the war in comfort. But the war would end one day, and when it did they vowed to deal with her in their own way. Ania occasionally saw them in hallways or through open doors, when they stared, spat or mouthed silent obscenities.

"I am concerned about the rest of the women, Baldric, they are jealous and I think they want to harm me. I need your protection," Ania said. Fischer turned and placed a hand on her cheek for reassurance.

"This war," he said. "It brings out the worst in us all, I'm afraid."

Ania was coping with the isolation and she felt secure enough for now. She was working hard to please Fischer and Schole. At night when she lay alone in the dark, that was when she was lonely, that was when she missed Danuta the most. She missed her touch, her smell, the sound of her sighing in her sleep, her voice and the gossip. Oh the secrets they shared! Ania's whole being ached for her sister and she was beginning to formulate a plan where, if she got close enough to Fischer or Schole she would ask one of them to locate Danuta for her. They could do it; they had influence and the connections. It would mean nothing to them, but so much to Ania. They were her only hope.

***

Ania was washing herself in the basin in the corner of her room after the commandant had just left late one night when she heard the familiar rattle of a key in the lock. She sighed and walked across the room to open the door, still wearing her underwear. "So what did you forget this time, your pipe or your watch?" she asked as she pulled the door open.

She was immediately shoved back into the room by Braun, who was wild eyed and spattered with blood. There was no time to scream before he put a strong hand over her face and forced her onto the bed.

It had been a very profitable night for the guard at the front door of the Club. Frau Groepler had long ago given up patrolling the corridors and supervising the ticket holders. Medical examinations had also ceased because they were too time consuming. Instead, the women were given boric acid to use as a douche and plenty of carbolic soap. Precaution enough, for them. Occasionally the CMO sent a deputy in her place (who was easily bribed) but most of the time it was the guard on the front door who ran things.

Voucher holders soon learned how to manipulate the system, but the Germans also wanted access to the women, so they devised their own scheme to ensure they got their share. Unknown to the camp administration, the guards that ran the front door had segregated two of the best women, Emilie being one. A barter system with a pre-agreed scale of black market goods was then put in place.

Now, every night, the guards' pockets were bulging with strange currencies, items of jewellery, plus the usual cigarettes and cigars-even an IOU promising to pay in beer once a favoured brand was delivered to the canteen. When Braun arrived unexpectedly at the front door that night he appeared agitated. He had a glazed look in his eyes and there was blood on his face and tunic; he was also jabbering frantically. Something had happened in the camp and the guard at the front door did not want to know about it. Wherever the Greyhound went there was trouble and tonight he looked crazy!

After a brief discussion, Braun dug deep into his pocket and forced a collection of scrunched-up bank notes into the guard's hand—then he asked for the key to the Premier Room.

"I don't think so, Braun. There is no spare key, only the commandant has access."

"Rubbish. I know that weed Schole visits all the time. I want the spare key." Braun was in no mood for protracted negotiations.

"Look. I cannot do it. If the commandant finds out I will be sent to the front."

Braun produced an American bank note. Fifty dollars! How did he get his filthy hands on US currency? He handed it over with a look that said, *there's more where that came from.* The guard held the note up to the light and examined it. There was no shortage of forgeries around with so many Jews in the camp, but this one looked real enough. It had a picture of the eighteenth President, Ulysses S. Grant on one side, and it was crisp and fresh looking, almost new in appearance. It had also been folded a great many times, presumably to make it small enough to fit into the seam of some filthy Jew's jacket. That was what convinced the guard it was genuine. Money was money, but Braun wanted a key to the green door? As the guard mulled things over Braun produced another US note-a twenty this time.

"Look, Braun, fifteen minutes only, OK? No more. She belongs to the commandant and it's more than my life is worth..." The guard held the key in front of Braun's face and he snatched it with a flourish and ran down the hallway towards the green door.

What a night it had been on the front door of the Club, and it was not over yet! Both segregated women were busy and now Braun had dropped that wondrous piece of American currency into the guard's hand-he could not believe his luck! Just after Braun disappeared the guard heard some disturbing noises coming from Emilie's room. He had visited her himself a couple of times in the recent past, and she had been extra nice to him, with the promise of more to come if he undertook to protect her from the visits of people she did not want to see. *Just tell them I am occupied—that is all you have to do.* She had told him who she wanted to avoid, but what could he do if one of them turned up with an offer that was too good to refuse? There was a war on, after all.

He was given a ruby brooch only a few days ago. Beautiful. Taken from an old Jewess during a selection at Auschwitz. The frail old lady broke from the ranks and desperately shoved the brooch at one of the guards. "Take me to the safe side. Please. Let me be with my grandchildren, please, sir, I beg you, sir. Please."

So what could he do? He did the right thing, of course, took the brooch, grabbed the woman's arm and hurriedly led her over to the area where the children stood. She was reunited with her grandchildren, mouthed *may God bless you* as she and they were escorted down the stairs to the gas chamber...

The guard at the door to the Club could still hear raised voices coming from Emilie's room as he tucked his US currency away. Such sounds were often heard, but for some reason this time, something seemed amiss. He stopped for a moment and listened, trying to make out what was going on. It was then that he heard the blood-curdling screams.

Suddenly there was frantic activity, curtains were pulled aside, people ran around in different stages of undress, swearing and shouting; the door of the Premier Room slammed, boots stomped up and down and Schole suddenly appeared from God only knows where. Despite the turmoil and confusion, the most puzzling aspect was that the terrible scream had belonged to a man, not one of the women.

***

Karl Braun had just finished raping Ania. She was barely conscious, bound to the bed and his hands were still around her throat when he heard the screams. He had been having a terrible day; sometimes the killing got to him; the faces of those pathetic Jews, Sonderkommandos and Kapos. He needed a woman's body to abuse, to take the brunt of his frustrations, and there was none better than Ania's. As soon as he heard that scream however, the Greyhound was up and out of the Premier Room in a matter of seconds, leaving Ania naked and still tied to the bed.

Schole had been working in an office nearby and heard the fuss. He was first on the scene and started issuing orders to all and sundry as people suddenly appeared in the hallway. He immediately unlocked Ania's room and found her bound and sobbing on the bed. He freed her immediately and asked what the hell had been going on. Where was the commandant, was this what he did to her during his visits? Did she hear any of the goings on outside? What did she know?

She was too distressed to speak but thankfully showed no sign of injury. Schole gave Ania a glass of water then went back outside to the furore in the hallway, locking her door behind him.

The frantic level of activity at the Club continued. The front door was immediately locked; an additional guard posted with instructions to let no one except the commandant or Schole through. Several armed SS guards also patrolled the hallway. The women were removed to another location and the curtains to every room were opened-except for one.

***

Early the next morning an officious looking Schole appeared at Ania's door, immaculately dressed as usual, but for some unknown reason he seemed different—officious perhaps. "There is something the commandant wants you to see. Kommen."

He stood aside as Ania jumped from the bed. "There is no time to dress. Just come in your nightclothes. Come now." Ania's eyebrows dropped to a frown and she reached for a dressing gown. Schole spoke again, with more urgency this time. "You must come now."

The ground outside was awash with slush and some of the roof tops and window ledges were still covered in snow. It was windy and bleak and Ania quickly found herself wishing she had grabbed a blanket to wrap around her shoulders. Her little room was so warm, yet here she was facing the reality of the cold outdoors again. How easy it had been for her to forget the misery and suffering of others.

She was led to the small courtyard at the back of the brick-built barracks complex. At one end was a large granite structure known as the Death Wall. It was here that firing squads executed nearly three hundred Gypsies in one day, a record that Fischer often boasted about.

The buildings formed a horseshoe shape around the courtyard, the Death Wall being slightly set back from the others. Access was through an archway between two adjacent buildings. Prisoners in striped pyjamas visited every day regardless of the weather, keeping the gravel pristine and level, free of footprints, ready for use at any time. As she followed Schole into the courtyard Ania saw several hundred prisoners in their zebra pyjamas, heads shaven, all of them standing to attention, shivering and fearful. She was taken to where the rest of the women from the Club were already lined up-the only prisoners not wearing zebra uniforms. No one acknowledged her, no one tried to make eye contact. Schole slotted her into position at the end of a line, next to a woman whose terrified face she did not know. Someone behind hissed through clenched teeth, "You cow."

Despite the number of prisoners in the courtyard, there was very little noise; no shuffling of feet or talking. A large assembly of heavily armed guards scanned the crowd and apart from the occasional rattling cough from somewhere deep in the ranks, the only sound that could be heard was the wind as it raced around the prisoners, daring them to move their bodies for warmth.

As Ania looked around, she realised that everyone was staring at a bulky grey blanket heaped in the middle of the gravel courtyard. Something was beneath it. It had to be contraband, seized during an early morning inspection. That was why there were so many people gathered there.

Fischer appeared at the arched entry and the guards snapped to attention. He was immaculately dressed in his greatcoat with his Iron Cross proudly displayed between the buttons at chest height. Two guards escorted him to the centre, next to the blanket. He barked out an order. "Bring her forward!"

From somewhere outside Ania's line of vision there appeared to be a brief scuffle and a guard half pushed, half dragged someone, a woman, into the courtyard and left her on her knees, next to Commandant Fischer.

The woman's hands were bound behind her back and her face was bloodied and bruised, streaked with tears, her hair matted and caked with blood. Blood had also congealed around the woman's nostrils, and one of her eyes was swollen and closed, the skin around her sockets and cheekbones bruised a greenish yellow colour. Her bottom lip was torn and hanging loose, and with several teeth missing her gums were visible behind the flap of skin. If she had not been wearing the familiar clothes of a Club woman, she would have been unrecognisable due to the beating she had taken.

Ania muttered under her breath to herself. "Oh my God, Emilie."

Emilie was alone, blood-soaked, quivering from head to toe but still defiant in the centre of the courtyard. A guard pulled her to her feet, cut the ties on her wrists then moved away.

The commandant stared at the assembled crowd then turned towards the blanket on the ground and said to

Emilie, "Remove it." She swayed slightly, hesitated for a moment then looked at Fischer. He slashed her across the face with a small leather whip. Every prisoner in the courtyard winced. "Remove the blanket!" he hissed. Emilie braced herself, determined not to cry, reached down and dragged the blanket aside with a blood-streaked, shaking hand.

There was an audible gasp around the courtyard-the body beneath the blanket was that of the fat drivers. His face was frozen in shock, mouth agape, left eye staring into nowhere. Sticking out of his right eye socket was a large galvanised nail.

***

The fat driver had been doing deals with the guard at the front door of the Club from the very first night. He wanted to get to Ania but the guard knew better than to allow a fool like Lange into the room with the green door-he did not have enough money, anyway.

Lange was known amongst his colleagues as a stupid man with a reckless streak, who they all knew would cause a major problem one day. Everyone laughed along with him at the canteen, but no one ever stayed for a second beer. Lange was not to be trusted; he was bad news, a person best avoided.

But Lange had a plan to get back at Ania, who he thought was hiding the fact that she was a Jew; hadn't she told him once, on the journey to Wysznica? He was starting slowly, working his way through the Club women, moving along the hallway towards the green door, night by night, woman by woman, room by room. Eventually the guard on the door would give up and sell him the key for a few minutes, and then he could enjoy himself with the girl with the weird eyes, the one who had become his obsession since he first saw her on that cold, Polish back road. For now he would take second best, the weird-eyed girl's friend, one of the segregated women, called Emilie.

Emilie was already exhausted the first time Lange pulled the curtain aside and stepped into her room. When he spoke she felt his spittle popping onto her face. His breath reeked of stale cigarettes and it was all she could do to prevent herself from vomiting as he tried to force his tongue inside her mouth when he kissed her that first time. "Be nice to me, Princess Poland," he sneered. He raped her viciously that night, slapped her around, left her on the floor bleeding and sobbing. She could still hear him laughing as he left the building.

Emilie offered herself to the door guard in an attempt to keep the fat driver away, but it only worked for a few days. Eventually Lange managed to worm his way back into her room, and the abuse continued. He told her his wife was frigid and too fat for his liking. She no longer looked after herself and did her best to avoid any sexual contact with him. He had been visiting prostitutes in various locations around his hometown, until thankfully, the war took him to Krakow and then on to Wysznica—heaven for him.

Frau Groepler was becoming increasingly angry about Emilie's bruises, cut lips, and black eyes, and she warned her that she had better shape up or she might just find herself shovelling lime in the snow instead of working in the warm Club. Men did not want sex with women who looked as if they did not look after themselves. If she was being slapped occasionally it would only be because her visitors were not happy with the service she offered. *Smarten up or be prepared to ship out* were Frau Groepler's orders.

The time soon came when Emilie could no longer face Lange's after-hours visits. She had enough to fear from other visitors without him adding to her burden. She noticed that the guards from Auschwitz, who were now in on the deal, were particularly spiteful. They had a stink about them, which if she had ever visited that place herself, would have easily identified as the smell of death.

So the time came after she spent several days considering the consequences, when Emilie had to take some kind of action to protect herself. She said her goodbyes to the other women, wrote a note to Ania apologising for leaving her alone, and gave it to one of the women who agreed to slide it under her door the next morning in exchange for some of Emilie's possessions. Then she lay on her bed and waited to see if the fat driver was going to pay her a visit that night. He did.

As Lange forced her legs open with his knees and shoved his disgusting fat greasy face between her breasts, she carefully reached beneath her mattress. Her fingertips found the nail that the old man had dropped in the village hall so long ago. Emilie had cleverly kept it hidden, even during a medical examination, claiming a severe case of diarrhoea, which was enough to dissuade Frau Groepler from examining that particular part of her anatomy.

While Lange licked her breasts and told her what he was going to do to her next she manoeuvred him onto his back and straddled him-*you like this don't you, eh?* It was then that she slipped the nail between her index and middle fingers, with the flat end resting against the palm of her hand. The fat driver easily mistook her grabbing a handful of his hair and pulling his head back, as passion. Before he realised what she was doing Emilie slammed the nail into his eye with as much force she could. She felt it pierce through the jelly of his eyeball and scrape against the bony socket behind before it sank into his brain and remained wedged in place, several inches deep, through his eye.

In a sudden state of shock, he fumbled around his face with a shaking hand. His fingers scraped against the nail that protruded from his eye, and a trickle of blood mixed with a strange grey fluid dribbled onto his cheekbone. He was caught totally by surprise, unsure of what had actually happened until he looked at the gluggy mess on his fingers. It was then that he let out a scream that echoed through the building. Then he rolled off the bed onto the floor where he lay twitching like a deranged epileptic for a minute or more, before he finally froze in position. Lange the fat driver was dead, and all hell broke loose.

***

Now Emilie was staring at the fat driver's body in the courtyard by the Death Wall and it seemed that half the camp was watching. Fischer had already completed the report for Berlin. He had had to be very careful what he said; after all, the Fuhrer himself was looking at the Club project and Eichmann and the rest of the High Command were anxious to discredit it. A problem like this could shut the whole place down before it had become properly established.

So the incident with the nail was put down as an 'industrial accident'. There was a sawmill at Wysznica where unfortunate events often happened. It was just bad luck that in this instance one of the guards had been involved, along with a woman who apparently worked on the bandsaw; at least, that was what was on the paperwork that was sent to the inspectors at Berlin and they seemed satisfied enough.

Braun now approached Emilie from behind. He wrenched her arms back painfully, then dragged her across the courtyard and placed her in front of the Death Wall. She stood shaking like a bare-footed waif, head bowed, one knee angled slightly in front of the other, trembling from head to toe. She managed to raise her head to look around-everyone seemed so strange through her blurred eyes with their insipid faces and shaved heads. Hundreds of big round eyeballs stared back, and even the furthest away saw the warm urine that now ran down Emilie's naked legs. She lowered her head and stared at the warm puddle growing around her feet, twisted her toes in the gravel, and finally started to cry. She looked up when she heard the sound of marching a few metres away. There was a line of nine soldiers in front of her now. Stern faces, shiny grey metal helmets and warm greatcoats, rifles by their sides. Then she heard Schroder's voice from somewhere in the background.

"Take your aim!"

The combined sound of nine rifles being raised in unison filled the air; leather straps creaking, metal catches rattling. "Load."

A loud clunking sound echoed around the buildings as bolts were pulled back and nine bullets were lodged into their chambers. Emilie had heard the firing squads several times before, in the background as she sat in her warm room in the Club, and she always wondered how many real bullets were used. Someone said that in the old days there was one live round only; that way no one would know who actually killed the person in front of them. *But what would the Germans care about such things, unless they wanted to save ammunition?*

Emilie had heard that the person facing the firing squad was always blindfolded. *Where was her blindfold?* She looked up at the row of rifles pointed at her, wondering which of them had the bullet-the one that would take her life. She tried to look straight down the rifle barrels towards the creased foreheads and narrow eyes at the other end. *Was it him? Did he have the live round? Or him maybe?*

"Fire!"

She heard a load roaring sound echo around the square; saw little puffs of smoke come from the end of the rifles pointing at her, then felt several heavy thumps like someone punching her body, the strange sound of bullets passing through her and bouncing off the wall behind; then a blinding surge of excruciating pain as her legs folded and the wet gravel against her face as she collapsed ... Then her world went black.

They turned Emilie over and laid her flat on her back as the rest of the prisoners were made to march past her body as they returned to their huts. They saw the agony on her bruised and battered face; her twisted limbs; her torn dress; some even counted the bullet holes in her chest. Nine.

PART 5:
DEATH
CAMP
HALT!
STÓJ!

35

1942
Wysznica, Poland

Obersturmbannfuhrer Fischer paced his office, puffing on his pipe, chewing the mouth-piece. He had been doing this for at least fifteen minutes as he waited for Schole, who for some unknown reason failed to pick up his phone when called. A messenger was sent. The commandant did not like being kept waiting.

For convenience sake, Schole had tried to persuade his boss to move into a suite of offices within the confines of the camp where he and everyone else worked, but no, Fischer preferred to work from his house, where Tina was always available to amuse or attend to his needs at a moment's notice. Running a labour camp was stressful work, and Fischer had been particularly stressed lately. He had been making more and more important decisions: dealing with staff problems, signing death warrants, trying to cope with an increased level of transports. Even small matters annoyed him, and his staff were wary of his moods and the increasingly harsh levels of punishment he ordered for minor misdemeanours. Everyone was on their toes.

Schole finally arrived and knocked loudly on the door.

"Kommen!"

He entered.

There was no time for pleasantries. Fischer was fuming about something. "I have received a communication from Berlin, Fritz. From the Fuhrer himself." He tapped a document with his pipe. "Sit down, sit down," he said. "Hoess has been promoted. He is now Obersturmbannfuhrer Hoess. A lieutenant colonel, can you believe that? The same fucking rank as me. Eichmann is responsible for this, you mark my words. It's ridiculous. He was only a captain when he arrived and now look at him. The man's a crook, he is poisonous."

Things had changed since Auschwitz opened its doors on 14 June 1940. Originally designed to take up to ten thousand political prisoners and enemies of the state, it regularly housed double that number and well over half of them had been processed within the first eighteen months. The plan was simple-they either worked until they could work no more and had to be processed or they were left to starve and die from disease. That is, if one of the many daily 'selections' or 'aktions' did not get them first.

Hoess had initiated some kind of human conveyor system for selections, and it worked better than he or even Berlin had imagined. It was murder on an industrial scale. Hoess was now lauded as a genius, and that rankled Fischer.

Because of Hoess' success, Berlin had decided upon a huge expansion program for Auschwitz. All the sub-camps around, Wysznica included, were being ramped up to accommodate and service the expansion, and it seemed that Auschwitz had become the jewel in the crown for Adolf Eichmann, whose popularity with the Fuhrer was rising in leaps and bounds. What Berlin had been calling the Final Solution behind closed doors was now openly acknowledged and prioritised. Jews were rounded up in greater numbers and placed into ghettos all over Europe. Occupied countries were being forced to give up their own passport-holding Jewish citizens as well. There were literally millions of people involved, and they all had to go somewhere for processing.

What were originally set up as simple labour camps were now being turned into factories of death, where human beings went in at one end and their dust came out the other. And there were plenty of value-added benefits for the Reich during the processing.

Schole adjusted himself in his chair as he studied Fischer's face. "And what is going to happen here at Wysznica, mein Commandant? What of you and your wonderful efforts so far? Do they appreciate you in Berlin?"

"Eichmann does not like me. It is a well-known fact. He is envious of my personal relationship with the Fuhrer."

"Indeed."

"But the Fuhrer is looking after me, be assured of that, Fritz. Oh yes! We go way back, as you know, and I think he has long-term plans for me that even that scheisskopf Eichmann doesn't know about. Wysznica will be expanding; we are part of the grand plan. Engineers will be flown in next week, an architect as well, I am told and we are to have new enhanced facilities here. If things go to plan we will be free of that jumped-up dwarf Hoess! We will no longer be a part of the Auschwitz apparatus, a cog in their processing wheel; we are going to be a machine in our own right!"

Fischer opened a file stamped in large red letters 'Confidential Top Secret'. With his pipe wedged firmly in the corner of his mouth and a somewhat ceremonial air, he removed a document and smoothed it onto his desktop. The Fuhrer's personal crest was on the beautifully embossed letterhead, along with the familiar black and red swastika.

"We are to substantially increase the size of our disposal rooms and double the capacity of the crematorium! We will still be less than half the size of Auschwitz, that is true, *but* we will outstrip Hoess, just you wait and see. We will process more units than he ever dreamed possible, and in quicker time too!" Fischer paused momentarily to ensure that Schole was paying attention. He was. He always was. There was nothing more inspirational than the commandant in full flight. Fischer read directly from the Fuhrer's letter.

"I expect nothing other than a continuation of the excellent results you have already provided the Reich and your Fuhrer, my dear Baldric." He picked the letter up and shook it, his eyes burning into Schole's. "You see that, Fritz? Signed by the Fuhrer himself!"

"I see it, Baldric."

"This is a mammoth task; it is going to take a lot of organisation. The technical, economic and administrative procedures we will be implementing must never be documented. This is the Fuhrer's personal instruction, you see. As well as the experts from Berlin, the architects and engineers who are attending to the processing equipment, we need to look at procurement and storage; we will need to build more huts and barracks. Even the administration block will have to be increased in size. Everything. This is a huge undertaking!"

"Should I speak to Hoess at Auschwitz?"

The mere mention of his nemesis's name made Fischer bristle.

"What on earth for?"

"Well, he knows the local trades. He has the logistics contacts. All we have is labour..." Schole shrewdly made eye contact with Fischer. "And the best administration in the whole network!"

"Yes indeed. OK. I agree. Look, you may speak to Hoess, but keep it discreet. I don't want him to know what I am thinking. Carouse with him a little if you have to, make him feel important. I understand he likes that kind of thing. I want his best builders *here, working for me,* as soon as the architects have provided their blueprints and plans! I shall be supervising all the work and trades myself. The Fuhrer expects nothing less. I am told that Herr Eichmann will personally inspect the works when they are complete, so I don't want any delays or issues. I want things signed off quickly so I can put Hoess in his rightful place!"

Fischer then opened his desk drawer and removed a bottle of brandy and two glasses. "This is it, Fritz, we are in this campaign for real. Everyone will benefit and I can see promotions on the horizon." He filled the two glasses and handed one to Schole.

"Heil Hitler," they said in unison as the glasses clinked together. Schole drank the brandy without grimacing. He was not a brandy drinker, but then there was nothing he would not do for his commandant.

36

Ania's door was unlocked at ten o'clock one morning and a stranger ambled in, unannounced, someone she had never seen before. "Dzien dobry." The man cheerily removed his cap and introduced himself. "It's nice to meet you. I am Slav."

Ania reached for a towel.

"Don't worry, Miss Ania, I am a friend," Slav said, though he made no effort to avert his eyes.

"You are the builder?" Ania asked. "How did you get a key?"

"Herr Fischer the commandant gave it to me. He asked me to call on you this morning."

"Have you never heard of knocking? I could have been engaged."

"I was told I would not be disturbing you." Fischer had used the well-known *wink and nudge* method of communication when he explained to Slav that Ania was 'special', not unlike the high-grade shredded Virginian pipe tobacco that Slav had somehow managed to find for the commandant through his black market connections. It was clear to Fischer that this man Slav, this giant builder who was well known and highly regarded by Hoess, was a man of the world.

Slav tucked his cloth cap into his belt and checked the hallway. The guard was on the front step outside, enjoying the cigar he had just been given. As Slav closed the door Ania said, "I have heard talk of you; good things. They say you can help; they say you help people in the camps."

"I try to. I am here to help you too. The commandant says you want a shower?"

Ania pointed to the corner. "I want my own bathroom. I have a toilet and sink as you can see, but I want better facilities. I have to be accompanied by a guard every time I want to shower and can only do so when the other girls are not around. I am not allowed to mix with them. It is all very inconvenient."

"I understand," Slav started scribbling in his notebook. "The shower is an easy fix."

Ania sounded a little hesitant. "They say there is nothing you can't do. The women talk as if you are some kind of saint." Slav smiled. He had never been called a saint before; usually women had more colourful names for him.

"A saint am I? Look, I bring medicines if I can, little treats, the occasional luxury; soap mainly, toothpaste sometimes and if I can, talcum powders. But most of all I bring hope. Not everyone in Poland wants all the Jews dead. There are still a few decent people in this country. Hope is what I trade in."

"So, you are a trader, eh?"

"I have connections. I know people ... on both sides."

"If I was to ask a favour of you, Mr Builder, what would it cost?"

"First of all you could call me Slav. Everyone does, even the commandant."

"Well, at the moment I will be the exception." Ania refused to be seduced by Slav's charm.

"Then I shall let you be the exception. You are far more beautiful than they said, much too beautiful to offend. They told me about your eyes, too. Amazing. So seductive."

Ania ignored the flattery. "Can you find my sister?" Her heart still ached for Danuta. The more time that passed, the more she realised it was indeed likely that Danuta never made it out of the house on that fateful day in 1940. But somewhere deep down, she kept a tiny flicker of hope alive, and it was that hope more than anything else, that maintained her through the dreadful weeks and months of confinement and abuse. She would never give up.

"You had better tell me more. If she is in a camp I will find her. If not, I think maybe it won't be so easy," Slav said.

Ania told Slav the whole story. He said he would try, he would put word out at Auschwitz first, of course, then the other camps and fan out from there. He had contacts everywhere. He would find her if it was possible.

"And what do you want as payment, Mr Builder?" Ania asked.

"Your relationship with the commandant, how close are you?"

"Close enough, thank you very much. Sometimes, I would say, too close."

"Then all I want from you is to know what is happening. Anything you can tell me, anything that could help me make people's lives safer and more comfortable here."

"That is all you want?" Ania stared at him a certain way.

Slav stared back. There was no doubt about it, she was stunning; full breasted, thin waisted, long slim legs, everything in perfect proportion. And that face-those eyes! She looked as if she had done a lot of growing up in a very short time, a tantalising mix of a young body and a mature mind; a delightful package. She was showing a little cleavage, enough for Slav to notice. She smiled as he stepped forward and reached for the towel that was loosely draped around her body. Ania never flinched, but instead of caressing her, Slav pulled the towel up over her shoulder. "You know, it is not always so easy being a saint," he said with a wry smile.

37

Schole had visited Auschwitz as agreed, and did an excellent job wining, dining and complementing Hoess. At the same time, Schole's most trusted operative, Rolf Schroder, visited the various departments and sectors to find out how things worked on a practical level. Schroder also had Braun with him.

While Schole drank champagne and dined with Hoess and his family in his villa, Schroder and Braun were busy trying to discover what made everything tick, looking at the hands-on issues, working out where the weaknesses lay. And more importantly, where the benefits were. Now they were back, talking in the canteen at Wysznica.

"They always seem to have trouble with one or more crematoria. Something is always breaking down. They claim sabotage but how? The Jews have neither the wherewithal nor the expertise to make something look like it has broken down when it has in fact been deliberately interfered with," Schroder said. "You know what I think?

I think they use the breakdowns as an excuse. They are inefficient. You know the ovens we saw? How many units were in each one, do you remember?"

Braun shook his head. "Two maybe?"

"That's right. Two. But there was capacity for three! If we got our Sonderkommandos to straighten the units out as soon as they were collected from the gas chambers, we could pile them three high and push them through much quicker. That means for every twenty units they put through at Auschwitz we could put through thirty! I am certain we can process over four hundred units in a ten-hour shift. It might take a little effort and ingenuity, but I would say it can be done."

"I saw at least a thousand units waiting to be processed outside crematorium three. And more were coming. They told me they had another shipment of ten thousand due in from Hungary tomorrow."

They discussed the problems associated with having stockpiles waiting for processing. "It's not healthy for us. We are the ones who have to breathe that fucking air," the Auschwitz guards had said.

"Those pigs smell worse when they are alive I tell you!" The Greyhound liked to use the word 'pigs' when he talked of Jews because that was what they were: pigs. Not rats like some of his colleagues called them. 'Rats' was a word that Propaganda Minister Goebbels had come up with. "These Jews are plain and simple *pigs*. They even eat shit-I have seen them with my own eyes. Only last week outside the latrines at Wysznica-I actually saw one of them eating shit. They are pigs, all of them!" Braun said.

"When our expansion is complete we will be overrun with pigs. Up to five thousand on each transport, more some days, that's what I am told by Rapportfuhrer Schole," Schroder said. "It is going to take a lot of administration. I hope the commandant and Schole are up to it."

But Schroder and Braun both knew they would have to step up to the mark themselves as well. Gone were the lazy days when they played cards and drank beer into the early hours. They had to stay alert at all times. Great things were expected of them, and there could be rewards heading their way as long as they could maintain order and discipline, but they needed help with that.

The Kapos at Auschwitz were men and women taken from the criminal classes. It was easy to spot them when new transports arrived; the ones who still looked relatively fit despite the terrible conditions in the cattle trucks, the ones who stood on the bodies of others so they could reach the ventilation shaft on the roof, the ones everyone else moved away from during selections.

Schroder explained how the system worked. "The Auschwitz Kapos parade around as if they own the place. The fools seem to think they are indispensable. Their miserable efforts may keep them alive longer, but how much longer, eh? One more week-one more day-one more hour-just as long as they are needed." Schroder laughed. "At the end of the day they will find themselves in the ovens regardless of what they do! No matter what happens, you can't keep them out!"

With all the talk about expansion it was easy to forget the realities of the war in Europe. Things were slowing down; the blitzkrieg was over. The Allies were fighting back now, thanks to the energy and resources provided by the Americans. It was not that long ago when it looked as if everything would just run its course and it would only be a matter of time before the war was over. But things were changing now. Perhaps it was time to think about the future-time to lay down a few alibis and feather a few nests. What they needed was a pension plan! Schroder downed his beer, Braun took the top off another and they both smiled at each other. "Are you thinking what I am thinking, Karl?" Schroder asked.

"Ja."

They tapped their bottles in unison. "Here's to Canada!"

38

Baldric Fischer read the memorandum for the fifth time in as many minutes. He finally screwed it up and threw it into the waste bin, then yelled for Schole.

"What is it, mein Commandant, what is wrong?" Schole knew by the tone of Fischer's voice that this was not the time for first names.

"It's fucking Hoess again. He's throwing his weight around as if he runs the whole of Poland. Berlin want more units, so he has come up with a plan to use *us* for his surplus units. He knows we are ramping things up so he wants us take his castoffs, to do his dirty work and all the difficult, messy processing while he gets all the glory!"

'Difficult processing' usually meant the very young or the very old. Not that fragile Jews caused much fuss-it was just the volume. And they caused as many issues when they were dead as they did alive. Fischer was convinced they did it on purpose.

"That's terrible, Commandant!" Schole saw the problem immediately. "What can we do? Can you write to the Fuhrer personally and pull a few strings?"

"He's a very busy man, Fritz. Things are difficult at the moment. The fucking Japanese are the ones that caused this pressure. If they had just got on with their role in the Pacific and left Pearl Harbor alone, the Americans would not have joined in and the pressure would not be so great. Now our troops are stretched to the limit and one of the biggest problems *we* have is processing all those damned European Jews. Berlin wants them dealt with quickly. Before Pearl Harbor there was some sort of structure in place, a coordinated method that worked like clockwork. It was not perfect but at least it was organised and took its course. But now? What are we supposed to do when the stream has been turned into a raging torrent?"

"So what is Berlin proposing?"

"They want to speed up processing in all camps. Did you read the statistics from Treblinka? Amazing! Last year they processed over two hundred thousand units and it's only a small camp-a twentieth of the size of Auschwitz. Half our size. We need to know how they did it. Fuck Hoess and his plans. I will ignore him and we will model ourselves on Treblinka, outwit him that way. We will take his overflow and more-it won't be long before *I am asking him* to send us *more* units because we are underutilised!"

"And you will copy the Fuhrer in on the correspondence, of course?" Schole asked.

Fischer rose from behind his desk and walked across to the fireplace, admired his pipe collection before turning and placing a heavy arm on Schole's shoulder. "At times like this I realise just how well you know me, my dear Fritz."

"You are a great man, mein Commandant, and it is an honour to serve you." The two men looked at one another for a moment, each unsure what they saw in the other's eyes.

Fischer was first to break the strange silence. "I can't trust this to anyone else, Fritz. I just can't." He sighed then continued. "Can you get over to Treblinka straight away and find out how on earth they do it? I will make the phone calls, organise the necessary permits and introductions. You can leave today?"

"Of course, Commandant. For you, of course!" Schole clicked his heels and sprang into a Hitler salute.

"In the meantime, I will write to the Fuhrer myself. Maybe I *can* pull a few strings, who knows? I think I still have influence in that quarter." And he raised his left eyebrow; a magician about to pull a rabbit from a hat.

***

What Schole found at Treblinka was impressive. They had perfected the art of killing and processing; the place was run like a manufacturing plant. A transport would arrive into what appeared to be a public railway station. It was, in fact, merely a stage set. After everything they had heard and feared, the Jews were amazed at what they saw when they stepped from the train. This place! So beautiful and the Germans, so pleasant as they gently helped the old people and children down the ramps and gathered them on the platform. There were no rabid, barking dogs, no machine guns aimed at them. Piped music was played as they were led through beautifully manicured gardens with neatly trimmed hedges. Every building had window boxes bursting with colourful flowers and it was all attended to by teams of smiling, uniformed gardeners.

The shocked Jews were then politely ushered into the shower rooms by softly spoken guards who gathered their possessions for safekeeping (so they could dress again after they had showered), reassuring them throughout the process that all was well. There was no panic, no fear, everyone cooperated and smiled at them. But when they were naked and the heavy metal doors unexpectedly clanged shut behind them, that was when then the killing began.

The Jews' screams were muffled by strategically placed landscaping, more loudspeakers and more piped music. Afterwards, the bodies were buried in mass graves. Layer upon layer, each body liberally sprinkled with lime. And Schole now realised why Treblinka had ordered so much product during the last twelve months! But not all the bodies were buried, there were too many for that, so the balance went straight into specially constructed burning pits. One layer of bodies, one of logs, another layer of bodies, another of logs, and so on until the whole pit was full. The logs also came from Wysznica! A splash of petrol next, and up they went! The air circulating between the layers ensured the whole lot continued to burn for hours-it was the construction and the layering that mattered-the technique. Unfortunately such precision work had to be done by hand, so who did it? The Kapos, of course-the Jews did it themselves! Amazing!

It was hard work processing such huge quantities through such a small site, but a bit of discipline and organisation proved it was possible. It was German efficiency and ingenuity at its best. The statistics were astounding, and it was statistics that made Berlin happy; numbers were everything.

But was it possible to adopt such measures at Wysznica?

They were a labour camp first and foremost; they had to produce their quota of lime and timber. A new pit was in the pipeline and the land was already being cleared, ready to take gravel from the ground. The whole place looked too commercial with its heavy machinery, equipment sheds, workshops, and everywhere, Zebra suited labour toiling away.

But Schole had drafted a master plan, and he went through it, step by step, slowly, deliberately with Fischer on his return.

***

Up to now, when transports arrived at Wysznica, the selection process was slow and cumbersome. Everything was recorded and documented. The process of selection itself could take hours, and that became a real burden in winter because the cold got to everyone; the dogs became hungry and irritable, the guards cold and trigger-happy. The whole process was burdensome.

After selection, those considered fit enough to work were taken away to be photographed and tattooed while those with no value were sent to holding huts to await processing. Of course, their details had to be recorded so there would be enough information available to schedule the occasional 'aktion' and clear out several huts, disposing of hundreds of units at a time.

After years of this kind of bureaucracy, Schole had devised a way to shorten the process. He said they would make everything more immediate; things would be less archaic.

"The children, the old people, the cripples-the residue-they will be immediately processed, as at Treblinka, through a garden area that will look like a pleasant, paved street lined with pergolas each side, some will have picnic tables." Schole spread a drawing onto Fischer's desk, pointing here and there as he spoke. "The units will be told they are in a transit camp, asked to undress and shower after they have their heads shaved-there were lice on the trains, so they will understand the need for disease control. They will be told they will be given clean clothes when they come out of the showers, ready for a good night's rest before boarding another transport the next day to be taken to a place where they can help the Reich with the war effort—making clothes, growing food, that kind of thing."

He unrolled another plan for processing the remaining units. What looked like a major building project at first sight actually only involved the manufacture of a series of simple facades, a bit like a film set. "That builder of yours, the huge fellow with the cap, he can do it quite cost effectively. When the units get off the train they will immediately see gardeners attending to plants, smiling faces, contented people, happy in their toil. And how about this? To welcome each transport; an orchestra!"

Fischer raised his eyebrows. This was sounding more ridiculous by the minute! *But then, why not an orchestra, we have a brothel do we not?*

Schole continued. "As the units progress along the fake street, which we will name *the pathway to heaven,* they will see happy people in their usual striped camp uniforms, clean and neatly laundered, of course. Some will be playing chess, others reading or painting, that kind of thing. Eventually they will reach here." Schole tapped the drawing. "The processing chambers, which will be disguised as simple shower blocks, complete with signs warning of scalding from the hot water." He paused to watch Fischer's face, then seeing that all was well, continued. "Their heads will be shaved at this point, and then they will undress and be taken into the processing room. Each unit will be given a bathing kit as they enter and these will be recycled time and again, no-one will suspect." Fischer could not help smiling at the ingenuity.

"Disposal of the units will commence here." Schole tapped the drawing again, pointing to the gas chambers. You see the chimneys, Commandant?" Fischer nodded. "They are not chimneys. They are in fact heavy-duty mesh tubes that extend through the roof and down to the floor inside the chambers. The reason there are so many is because we will use double the amount of Zyclon B. It will be quicker. I have a report here, addendum D, from the science department, confirming how many canisters are required to process one hundred average units. If we increase the number of canisters according to the formula provided, we reduce the processing time proportionally!"

"Speed things along, eh?" Fischer said.

"Correct. We speed things up substantially and the cost is minimal. Processed units will be removed by using these doors." He pointed at the drawing again. "And they will be taken by cart to the crematorium and beyond, where a new innovation will be used at Wysznica-burning pits. They call them 'roasting pits' actually-rather suitable, I think," Schole said, nodding his head appreciatively.

In a final review of the whole business, he spoke about the selections and how quick and easy they would become. Units would be far more amenable to what was happening. There would be no more wailing or splitting up of families. "We will just send the whole lot through in one blissfully ignorant queue, as soon as they arrive."

Fischer looked thoughtful. "You say it will be easier, Fritz, but are you sure? I mean, there are so many more units."

"I think we should make our selection process more direct, be less concerned about our administration and more concerned about a unit's ability to work or otherwise. Why do we need to record names, occupations and towns of origin? Surely we are past that and all we really need is a tick or a cross? It is that simple. Everything will work like a well-oiled machine you see. It will run like clockwork. Commandant, I can promise you a clearance rate of one hour from the time of disembarkation. One hour! Count them all and either give them a tick or a cross after head shaving-that is all we need to do. The reality is that they are all going up the chimney anyway!"

Schole continued. "We only need to keep a certain number of units for work details. The rest are surplus. We must make sure we only choose the fittest and the strongest, not the old, young or frail. The others? Unlike Auschwitz, we shall process them *the same day!*"

"The same day?" Fischer looked anxious for the first time. "We are talking about a lot of units here, Fritz!"

"It can be done, Baldric. Trust me."

"How will this work? It will be a terrible strain upon our resources, will it not?"

"Yes and no, Baldric. You see, we need no additional *paid* staff, that's the beauty of it." Fischer looked puzzled but Schole continued. "We will double the number of Kapos and Sonderkommandos with two levels of authority amongst them. Level one will be the general workers, the pushers and shovers if you like. Level two are the ones with the real authority. They will police everyone with vigour if they think they are going to live longer themselves. Let them think they are safe; give them more access to the Club. Maybe we will need to increase the size of the Club?"

"That is a 'maybe', but how on earth are we going to manage the increase in Kapos?"

"One of our men can manage fifty Sonderkommandos or Kapos in such circumstances, according to Schroder. Remember, these people are on the promise of a longer life. The better they do their job; the less trouble we have; the longer they live- or so they think."

"In a way it makes sense, Fritz." Fischer was warming to Schole's plan. "But what if we don't manage to process all the units you talk of, in the time scale you hope for? What of the bottleneck? I heard that log jams and delays are a constant source of stress for Hoess." Fischer thought he had Schole there. A university education and three first class degrees with honours were helpful, but they were not everything in life, they did not guarantee common sense.

"We thought about log jams. One of my most trusted men spent a lot of time at the Auschwitz crematorium when we were there. He thinks they underutilise their ovens. Based upon Schroder's findings I am confident we can get capacity up by thirty per cent, every shift, at no additional cost!"

"Thirty per cent you say? That is very good, Fritz. Very good indeed ... if you can make it happen..."

"I will fill you in on the details in due course, but believe me,

Commandant, it *can* be done. And that leads me to the spoils."

Fischer straightened his jacket. "The spoils you say? We love the spoils, do we not?"

Schole had saved this for last. Schroder had provided the information; Schole had worked out the detail. Schroder and his man Braun spent a whole day studying one particular aspect of the Auschwitz operation and they were convinced they could manage it better; more efficiently, more profitably. "Commandant Hoess and his team have an area they call 'Canada'. This is where they process everything the units carry with them from the ghettos. Suitcases, sacks, baskets and the like and, of course, the clothes they are wearing."

"Fritz, my dear Fritz. We do that already! This is not new; this is 'old hat'!"

"Put your old hats aside, Baldric, because I have a new hat for you to try on!"

Fischer fumbled in his pocket for his pipe, stuffed a fresh wad of tobacco into the bowl and lit it. "Are you saying there is a better way?"

"I am sorry to say this, Baldric, but there are some aspects of our processing where we could improve." It seemed that at Wysznica, at least according to Schole's findings, they were not thorough enough when the prisoners arrived. Processing took far too long and that gave units an opportunity to reconsider concealment. Valuables could be passed around, hidden better, bribes could be proffered.

At Auschwitz things were very different and far more efficient. They had whole rooms full of spectacles, which were repaired by Jewish opticians before being sold to support the war effort. Everything was recycled; clothes, artificial limbs, glass eyes, even trusses! Prisoners' heads were shaved at Auschwitz, but Schole wanted to shave their bodies as well. It would provide a substantial increase in revenue as the hair would be disinfected, bundled according to colour and grade, then woven into a kind of felt, which would be sold to the navy to make socks and blankets for U-boat crews. Plenty of cash was also found during the searches, and it was sent to the National Bank in Berlin under armed guard. But it was the Jews' teeth that were going to provide the greatest source of revenue at Wysznica.

"Teeth?" Fischer asked incredulously.

"Certainly," Schole continued. "I have never seen so many teeth and some of them carried gold inlays, for decorative purposes, I would imagine."

Fischer frowned. "Such vanity, these Jews. They live like vermin but have gold crowns?"

"Indeed, Commandant. But listen on, because when the Sonderkommandos remove the units from the gas chambers they crack their teeth and remove the gold fillings. Hoess has a room where the teeth are taken and a Jewish goldsmith melts the gold from them and turns it into ingots."

"Presumably they are sent to Berlin with the cash?" Fischer asked.

"Indeed, mein Commandant."

Fischer found another negative. "And the ingots are audited by the inspectorate also?"

"Of course. But do they know how many teeth are taken? One tooth, two, ten, maybe a hundred taken from every shipment? They would have no idea how many teeth there were, all they see are the ingots at the end of the process!" Schole appeared very intense at this point, and he licked his lips nervously. "Up to now our units have mostly consisted of Gypsies and dissidents, prisoners of war, so-called intellectuals-what do they have to hide? A wedding ring here or there, a watch maybe, a few bank notes, a bit of loose change. But now we will be taking more Jews, and Jews are rich, some of them are very rich and their cunning puts foxes to shame! They have money and all kinds of jewellery with them. It's not just the gold in their teeth, though that is the cream on the cake, the fruit on the sideboard, so to speak. They also have loose gems concealed wherever it is possible to do so! They call it 'portable wealth'. You name it, they hide it, it's like Ali Baba's bazaar at Auschwitz! The trick is to send enough to Berlin to keep them happy. Shoes, clothing, hair, photo frames, toys and the like, let them have it all, let them sell it! It doesn't matter. They need to see something, so we give them what they want and maybe even a little more. But we 'cherry-pick' the best and keep it aside for your pension fund, Commandant! I have to tell you, Baldric, if we do this the *right* way, you can walk away from this war a very rich man. Very rich indeed!"

Fischer's mind was working overtime. "There will be risks; theft, that sort of thing. We must install controls all along the chain and trust no one! We need dependable people overseeing the whole process."

"I have two such men," Schole said. "They will run our version of Canada with an iron fist! Schroder and Braun are my best men. They won't let us down. Your fortune will be safe after this is all over, Baldric. And don't worry about the camp inspectors either; I have an idea how to keep them off our backs. There will be two sets of books you see, which I will audit personally."

Fischer knew he could trust Schole. *Look at him! He's like a puppy dog at his master's feet! As long as he is serving me, Schole is happy.* Fischer never questioned where Schole's loyalty came from, but he sometimes thought he saw something in his assistant's eye ... no doubt Schole would want to be rewarded after the war, and that was only reasonable. There was no one in the lower ranks with a sharper mind and Fischer would deal with whatever Schole expected when the time came.

"I like it, Fritz! One for the Reich and one for me!"

"No, Baldric, one for the Reich; two for you!"

39

Being promoted to Unterscharfuhrer was a dream come true for Karl Braun. Where it came from and why it happened was beyond his understanding, but he soon took to the role of sergeant and was quick to bristle if he was not saluted by lesser ranks as he paraded around the camp like a peacock. Schroder had risen up the chain of command too; overnight he had become First Lieutenant. Obersturmfuhrer Schroder-his parents would be so proud!

Schroder and Braun were told they would be working together on an important new project for the commandant. Gossip in the canteen was focussing on an end to the hostilities, and Schroder privately reassured Braun that their future was now secure: he was working on a plan that would make them both rich.

***

In the coming weeks, Schole and Schroder worked together on the details of what was to be called Canada Two. Things had to flow smoothly and security was to be their watchword. No mention was made of Schole's plans for the commandant's secret pension, and Schroder said nothing about his scheme for himself and Braun.

The staff at Auschwitz had told them what tricks to watch out for during searches: false heels in shoes, rolled-up bank notes concealed in piping around lapels, hollowed-out artificial limbs, the linings of clothing and the soles of children's booties, even the concave arms of spectacles were used for concealment. Also, there was not a cavity on the human body that was not being used illicitly. If nothing was found before processing, it would be found after the bodies were prised apart and dragged from the gas chambers. Also, the dust and bone fragments would be scraped from the crematorium ovens, allowed to cool then sieved in case some of the units had swallowed something that could survive the intense heat of the ovens. They were certain they would find diamonds and other precious jewels.

There was never a shortage of workers for Canada Two. Human nature saw to that. Checks and balances were in place, all along the line. Motivation for the Kapos and Sonderkommandos would be in the form of vouchers for the Club and more significantly, the opportunity to extend their lives. Level one Kapos were dispensable. The Level two Kapos were highly trusted men, bursting with brutal self-importance; they would oversee the security of the camp and in theory they could last forever in their jobs. Not a bad incentive!

Discipline at all levels was the key to success and there was no room for errors or misunderstandings; Braun would see to that and he would to be well rewarded, according to Schroder.

Meanwhile, Schole would produce two sets of ledgers. One for the Inspectorate of Concentration Camps and the other, which was very much 'under the counter', was for Commandant Fischer. But unknown to Schole, Schroder had installed yet another set of ledgers for himself and Braun. An invisible third set. Braun was going to store the loot because Schroder, as the more senior of the two, would immediately be under suspicion if any anomalies came to light. Not being greedy was the key. Just a bit of 'cream' here and there. Nothing much, just enough *not* to be noticed. The volumes were going to be so high that their little slice could well be monumental by the war's end. A fifty-fifty division would ensure that he and Braun were set for life! If there was any finger pointing by the inspectors, it would surely be in the direction of that snivelling little clerk Schole. Schroder would see to that.

Schroder the bookworm had finally made it. He was now a first lieutenant and his financial future appeared to be secure. The twelve-year-old schoolboy whose system for recording library entries was still in use when he was twenty-six had made a name for himself in the armed forces. Not only that, he had established an under-the-counter pension that would far outweigh anything the army could possibly pay him. He would be able to purchase a house after the war, and perhaps set himself up in a small business. Life was looking good!

On the night of his promotion, Schroder tried several times to phone his parents in Berlin, eager to share the good news. The line was down. British Bomber Command had got to his parents and the library before he could.

***

It did not take long to establish Canada Two. Workers were chosen carefully, with the promise of rewards for the most diligent. Those who did not perform satisfactorily? There was always room for one more in the gas chambers, no matter how busy they were.

Braun established a simple procedure when workers at Canada Two came across cash or jewels. A large wooden box with a heavy padlock was placed within reach of each sorting table, and the women who were responsible for the searching were constantly monitored to ensure they did not steal the bounty themselves. They had to work naked, reducing the opportunities for concealment. Cavity searches were frequent and embarrassingly public, so honesty among the workers was not a problem.

They were looked after well, fed twice a day instead of once, given plenty of water and on cold days a heater was installed to ensure their fingers were nimble and their minds remained active. They were allowed to chat among themselves and encouraged to enjoy their miserable occupation. A loud speaker was installed and they were encouraged to sing along to the German music that was played throughout the day; an initiative that was frowned upon by Berlin but seemed to work at Wysznica.

Bodies that came directly from the gas chambers were rigorously searched. A gruesome job but the Sonderkommandos were keen to take responsibility; the most objectionable occupation carried with it the prospect of a longer life. There were those at Wysznica who were convinced that all Sonderkommandos were perverts. Indeed, among their number there were more than a few who relished the challenge of searching naked corpses.

Some even asked for the opportunity to work on such details.

With everything now in place, Fischer requested a large transport of Hungarian Jews be diverted from Auschwitz to test the new system. Two trains with ninety wagons in total turned up-over six thousand Jews. The commandant was delighted with the result. Everyone was processed in a single day, beginning to end! A huge party was thrown for those involved, and the Kapos and Sonderkommandos were each given a voucher for the Club, whose hours were extended to accommodate them. Alcohol was passed around to all concerned, and the guards also celebrated in the canteen, with Fischer leading the patriotic singing himself at one stage. Even the female workers at Canada Two were allowed several bottles of watered-down cooking wine and some stale bread rolls that were handed to them to distribute as they saw fit.

The big test, however, was with the Inspectors of Concentration Camps, who arrived stern faced the next day, with their clipboards. The good news for

Fischer was that they returned several days later with a tick in every box. Schole was more than happy with the commandant's under the counter haul and Schroder and Braun looked at their personal stash and could not believe their luck. Everyone seemed to have stumbled upon a gold mine, and that was from just one transport!

40

Overall, Fischer was pleased with the work of his builder, Slav Posluzny. There had been one or two setbacks; a few unfortunate 'breakdowns' that slowed production, but these were dealt with quickly and nothing was delayed for too long. The builder was on the ball with everything it seemed, except Ania's shower in the Premier Room.

"The mill cut the timber to the wrong size twice, Commandant, and the glass still has not arrived-there is a war on, you know? What do I do, make the glass myself? If I could, for you, Commandant, I would, but such things are outside even my means. You know that I put your jobs ahead of something I have been asked to do for Herr Hoess at Auschwitz. He doesn't like it, but I know which side of my toast has the butter and who is spreading it for me."

Fischer loved the fact that he was given preference, and he loved it even more when Slav referred to Hoess as 'Herr' and not 'Commandant'. This man Slav appeared to be a good find, but

Fischer still checked every job to ensure he was not cutting corners.

As they moved through the compound during an inspection, Fischer spoke disarmingly frankly. "I heard the guard at the Club has been diagnosed with lung cancer because of all the cigars you give him, and you have been back to the Premier Room three times to check the shower measurements, Slav. I hope that is all you are checking, eh?" He slapped the builder heartily on the shoulder before they moved.

"Any delays are only due to the weather, commandant," Slav said.

"Yes," Fischer added, "I understand that the cold may slow things down a little, but I can always turn the heating up for you..." he said with a wry smile as they walked past the crematorium.

***

Slav's visits between Wyshznica and Auschwitz were frequent. Every day he stopped somewhere, slapped a back or two, told a ribald joke, dropped off little gifts for a wife or a girlfriend, the guard's children. Slav was everyone's best friend and Schole had expressed concern that perhaps he was overly friendly in some quarters. "I think he can be trusted," Fischer said as he examined another batch of fine Virginian tobacco that had just arrived, courtesy of the builder.

Slav's workforce had recently been increased at his request. Fischer wanted the project completed ahead of time, so he was compliant and willing to accede to most of Slav's requests as long as he could see real progress. Jewish prisoners now toiled alongside Slav's own men, who secretly trained them how to handle a rifle, lay explosives and cut throats. The sound of someone hammering nails or sawing timber was sufficient to cover the noise that such activities generated.

The day finally came when the expansion at Wysznica was complete; ahead of time as requested. Slav had done a remarkable job and Fischer rewarded the prisoners who had worked alongside the builder's men with extra soup that appeared to have meat of some kind floating in it-a first! Time was of the essence as far as Fischer was now concerned and Schole was immediately tasked with redirecting transports from Hungary. Meanwhile, Fischer boasted to Berlin that his camp was ready for anything they wanted to put his way. It was during this frantic time, known to but a few, that Slav finally fixed a date for the uprisings at Wysznica and Auschwitz-7 October 1944.

***

Slav rarely talked of 'the girl at Wysznica', in front of Natalka. If the Gestapo ever got hold of Natalka, the less she knew, the better it would be. Slav's contact was very well placed and taking huge risks by passing him information, so he was determined to keep her name a secret.

It had been some time since Slav put the word out to his German contacts about Ania's sister. She was most certainly not in any of the local camps, and probably never had been. Danuta was such a common name-that was the problem. *Why, Slav knew several 'Danutas' himself—one even worked within his group!* "You see how common your sister's name is?" he said to Ania. But he promised he would never give up looking and was in the process of developing a relationship with an employee at the Department of Records in Berlin, where millions of index cards were kept, detailing the movement of people around Europe. He was convinced that it would not be long before those cards were searched and if Ania's sister could be found, it would be through his new contact in Berlin.

***

Slav called a meeting in his apartment to discuss some highly confidential information he had just received from his informant.

Grabowski and Wislawa, Danuta, Jozeph, Eddie, the two Jurek's and Natalka were gathered at the back of the florist shop. "There is going to be a slight change of tactics for our little group. It is a short-term matter and one of great significance." There was no vodka that night; coffee only, strong and black. "It has been a long time since we have done anything directly to upset the Germans, but I have been given some information that I passed to Warsaw and Stefan agrees that we would be foolish not to use it to our advantage."

Slav spoke of a small convoy that would soon be leaving Berlin. Its destination? Wysznica. It would consist of just three vehicles and one motorcycle outrider. Small enough for other road users to move out of the way, but not so large that it aroused interest. The front vehicle would be an armoured scout car with two SS guards; nothing unusual about that. The last vehicle a canvas-topped truck with several SS inside; again, standard procedure for a small convoy. It was the staff car in the middle that was of most interest.

"Why would that be so?" Jozeph asked, rolling his eyes at Slav's protracted introduction. How he hated all the drama that came with Slav's announcements. *Get on with it, Slav, get on with it!*

"As well as a hand-picked driver and one armed guard in the front passenger seat, the staff car will also carry a personal secretary and none other than the head of every concentration camp in Europe, Obersturmbannfuhrer Adolf Eichmann." A stunned silence greeted the statement as the enormity of the opportunity hit home. "That is not all, my friends. The head of the Gestapo and the SS, Chief of Security for the whole Reich, Obergruppenfuhrer Reinhard Heydrich, will also be in the car! Hitler calls Heydrich *Old Iron Heart* but he has less endearing nicknames in other places, believe me."

Grabowski whistled, Wislawa clapped and the two Jurek's looked at each other, somewhat bewildered. Slav continued, his eyes moving from one face to another, coming to rest on Jozeph's. "They are coming to check on the new facilities at Wysznica."

"Why do they not fly?" Jozeph asked.

"There is no landing strip near Wysznica and they are both fearful of flying," Slav said calmly.

"Train?"

"Eichmann doesn't feel safe in a train either; it seems that he feels vulnerable. That last job we did-the derailment that failed? It looks as if it was not such a failure after all, eh?"

Slav waited for the laughter to die down before he continued. He spoke of their current operations, the build-up of arms within the camps, ready for the uprising. But this visit by Eichmann and Heydrich presented an opportunity to impact the whole war. "This is our chance to strike a blow for Poland and re-establish our national pride. If we succeed in this, well, I think you all know just how significant that will be."

"What if it is a trap, Slav? What if that girl of yours, the informant, is deliberately giving you false information? It all seems too easy to me," Jozeph said. Slav recently had cause to speak to Grabowski about Jozeph's scepticism. It was undermining him. Grabowski had said, *Well, he's my brother. I know him better than anyone, Slav. He's fine, trust me. He's just a hot head who wants to feel important.*

Slav answered Jozeph's question. "Well, I believe this woman. She's young, she's scared and she wants to hurt the Germans as much as we do."

"How does she know about this-the details?"

"She's the commandant's whore. He has her locked away and visits her several times a week. I believe the expression is *pillow talk*." Slav smiled at Natalka, and then continued. "Look," he said earnestly, "we have to succeed at this. It is our most dangerous mission by far so let us remember that. We have an opportunity to influence the war in Europe by knocking out two of the highest-ranking officers in Germany's High Command at the same time."

"And if we fail, Slav, the consequences?" one of the Jurek's asked.

Slav looked up. His eyes said enough. "I think you all know ... we must *not* fail."

41

Fischer seemed anxious. "Obersturm-bannfuhrer Eichmann and Obergruppen-fuhrer Heydrich are due to arrive tomorrow afternoon, Fritz. They will tour the camp, all the new facilities. I want them to see everything, and then I will entertain them in the dining room here for dinner. We need to discuss the menu and I only want the best food and the finest wines-nothing but the best, you understand?"

"Of course, Commandant."

"I don't need to tell you how important this visit is. The Fuhrer himself told me in a conversation last week that he may visit us personally if Obersturmbannfuhrer Eichmann's report pleases him."

"Ofcourse. I understand." Schole was eager to impress, and was about to make a comment when Tina walked in, unannounced.

"Ah, my dear, are you ready for the big day tomorrow?" Fischer asked. Tina said she was. The caterers were on urgent standby awaiting approval of the menu. They wanted to know if any other of the visitors were vegetarian, like the Fuhrer. "The menu, ah yes." Fischer picked up a document from the muddle of papers on his desk, ticked a few boxes. "This, this and this I think. Followed by some of this. There, what do you say, my dear?"

"I think you are wonderful when you are making decisions, my darling Baldy. You are so powerful!" Schole decided to step out of the room when Tina sat on Fischer's lap, ensuring her skirt rose high enough for her stocking top to be seen. Baldy seemed to be losing his interest lately and Tina was beginning to feel insecure. He had reduced his demands in the bedroom, and that concerned her. Perhaps he was distracted; after all, it was not every day that such high-ranking dignitaries ventured so far out of the capital.

***

The dark was like a blanket that folded over Slav and his team as they waited beside the narrow road that wound its way out of the town of Auschwitz towards Wysznica. There was no moon, which was exactly how Slav had said it would be.

They had arrived on foot, moving across the fields separately from different directions, dressed as farm workers, carrying hoes, rakes and the like. Slav and Wislawa pulled a small hay cart under which was hidden several machine guns, rifles and grenades. It was going to be a long night, and thankfully it was not raining. As the light faded, their dark outlines melted into the surrounds.

As with all Slav's missions, everything was planned to the finest detail. There was a practice run the week before the convoy was due and they assumed their positions at the exact point of attack, made notes, drew maps, practised their signals and calls. Warsaw had reviewed everything and given the go-ahead. Now they were in position, sleeping under the hedgerows, ensuring they were ready before the allotted time. There was no room for error this time. It was not going to be like the time they blew up the railway tracks but missed the train because it had been delayed by five minutes.

Nothing was going to go wrong with this mission.

They woke just after sunrise to the sound of several motorcycles growling through the lanes, scouting up and down the narrow roads, pausing now and again to check this and that before speeding off again. A motorcycle and sidecar stopped a short distance from Slav's hiding place. The soldier in the sidecar relaxed and let the mounted machine gun in front of him spin away from his grip. He casually scanned the hedgerows and trees, looked at the scenery, seemingly bored, as his colleague urinated into a bush just metres from Slav. A few minutes later, they moved on.

After thirty minutes or so, the motorcycles were back. Six of them this time. It seemed that they had checked the whole route and were now returning to the start point, satisfied that all was well. Even for a casual onlooker it was clear that something major was afoot.

As soon as the Germans disappeared a series of pre-arranged signals from Slav confirmed all was well. The sun decided to make an appearance and dissolved the remnants of mist in distant paddocks, while a soft warm breeze wafted through the surrounding grass. It was going to be a beautiful day, heralded by the birds singing and insects buzzing around the trees and hedgerows. A small grey rabbit made an appearance, its ears swivelling and nose twitching as it fed on the lush grass not far from Wislawa's feet.

Despite the fact that they had been in position for quite some time, Slav's team were as alert as they were ever going to be. No one said a word; not even a whisper had passed between those nearest each other. The occasional signal, a hoot or a whistle, was all that was permitted, and Slav had never seen his team more disciplined or determined. Time was moving slowly but all eyes and ears remained keenly focussed on any unusual movements or sounds around them.

At nine o'clock precisely they all saw Slav raise his right index finger in the air, confirming there was just one hour to go. He seemed to disappear from view all of a sudden, before popping up by the side of each person in turn, a hand on a shoulder or a nod of his head to wish them luck. He slipped through the landscape like a fox; no one heard him arrive, no one saw him leave.

Nine-thirty. Slav's hand rose again and sliced slowly through the air, the convoy was now just thirty minutes away. During one final scout around, Slav was satisfied that all was well. The air may have been fresh and still, the scenery beautiful, but the atmosphere was tense.

Outwardly, Slav was a pillar of strength, as calm as a duck pond on a warm summer's day. Earlier that morning he noticed his hands were a little moist and right now he wished he could have lit up one of the cigars he had tucked away inside his jacket. He would have one later, for sure.

A quarter to ten. His arm rose again, hand turning to fist, and then falling again. Fifteen minutes to go. It was time to check the weapons. Several metallic sounding clicks echoed through the undergrowth. The rabbit stopped eating and looked up, nose twitching, eyes blinking, ears swivelling. A clunk as someone's ammunition magazine was pushed into place and the rabbit was gone. A cow called from a nearby paddock and a couple of crows cawed from their treetop observatories. Then all was quiet again.

As they waited, everyone reviewed the plan in their mind. They each had to be clear about their role-where they had to be, when they needed to be there and what they had to do when the time came. Nothing was left to chance. Just before ten their hands started to tremble as pulses increased, eyes blinked rapidly, and fingers tapped nervously against triggers.

Then, at precisely ten o'clock the rattle and hum of several vehicles was heard bouncing off the foliage and trees a short distance away. It was accompanied by the coughing of several motorcycles. Slav, with binoculars raised, held his right hand aloft and spread his fingers to indicate the number of vehicles. A second signal from his left hand confirmed how many motorcycle outriders there were but he didn't have a signal for the fact that the canvas-covered truck had been replaced by a second armoured patrol vehicle at the rear of the convoy. Slav thought about it for a moment and then cast the thought aside-if anything, it was indicative of the importance of the parties in the convoy. There was no need to abort.

Two nights before, Slav announced who was going on the mission. It was to be a high risk, frontline attack that would only present them with one opportunity. Danuta and Natalka were to wait at the florist shop and apartment. Wislawa was to be the only woman from the group involved in the ambush. She already had frontline experience and could almost work blindfold alongside the men, but it was too risky to have Danuta and Natalka there. Danuta had no battle experience whatsoever and Natalka was too precious for Slav to risk. The only action she had ever seen had been in Slav's bedroom, and there was no way he was going to risk her.

Natalka argued strongly for inclusion, and an hour later was still arguing, but Slav was adamant, and slept alone that night as a consequence.

The success of this mission was critical if Slav was to be taken seriously by the top brass at Armia Krajowa. Factions were forming and some were showing a degree of anti-Semitism which Slav found disturbing. They were fighting for a free Poland but *with no Jews?* During a recent strategy meeting Slav had nearly come to blows with a junior official who actually referred to the Jews as 'filthy Zyd'.

Stefan Rowecki himself had intervened and in a show of solidarity, went out of his way to ensure that the next issue of the underground newspaper, *Biuletyn Informacyjnye,* ran the headline *Help Fugitive Jews.* But Slav still heard the rumblings of disagreement from some section leaders. He knew he might have to go his own way if he was to have the slightest chance of helping his fellow countrymen-the Polish Jews. *That's right, you fOols, they are Poles first, the same as us!* His outburst shut them up, but for how long?

The morning before Slav and his team set off for the attack, Natalka made sure her man left with a smile on his face. She apologised to him for sulking, told him she understood why he refused to let her join the mission then showed him how much she loved him. It was a fond farewell.

Instructions were then given, and Danuta was told to wait with Natalka until the mission was complete and all being well, they were to regroup at the florist shop after lunch. Signals were agreed upon, watches were set and final farewells made. This time there were no smiles, just determined faces and raised, clenched fists.

On the morning of the mission, at nine o'clock, Natalka was in the kitchen anxiously preparing Slav's favourite golabki for his return. Danuta decided to take a walk to the flower markets to kill time. They both heard the bells of the town hall clock tower ring out at ten o'clock, and each of them paused, looked to the heavens as they said a small prayer.

***

Suddenly, from around the bend, two headlights bobbed into view, the front armoured troop carrier confirming to anyone coming from the opposite direction that they should move aside and let the convoy pass. All the vehicles could be seen now, snaking around the distant bends and hedgerows like a motorized lizard.

As the two outriders and the first vehicle passed Slav's position, the Mercedes staff car came into view and he immediately broke cover. Stepping out from behind a tree, legs astride and head held high, Slav opened fire with his machine gun. The blistering storm of bullets brought the Mercedes to a halt and the rest of Slav's team exposed themselves and attacked the remaining vehicles from both sides of the road.

Slav had taken out the driver of the Mercedes with the first burst of machine gun fire. It ripped through the vehicle, front to back, the occupants dancing in their seats like puppets in a crazed fairground show, the bullets tearing through their bodies and their seats, sending arms and legs into the air along with pieces of padding and fabric. Blood spattered throughout the inside of the car and every window shattered.

Eddie, Grabowski, Wislawa and the two Jurek's immediately broke cover and opened fire but the hand grenades that were supposed to disable the first vehicle and motorcycle outriders never appeared. Jozeph, who had been charged with the responsibility of rolling two grenades under the front armoured vehicle when it reached his position, could not be seen. The vehicle revved loudly and it suddenly span around with the side doors clanking open. A huge tripod mounted machine gun immediately rattled over 500 rounds into the surrounds, taking out Slav and all his operatives in a hailstorm of bullets, smoke and screams. In less than ninety seconds, six of the seven Polish underground operatives lay dead.

The clatter of automatic weapons stopped as suddenly as it had begun, and there was a moment's silence as the surrounding countryside held its breath. Then a crow cawed from a nearby treetop, mournful and sad, and the hedgerows came alive again. Insects buzzed and birds sang while other creatures returned to their day as the smoke from the machine guns slowly drifted away.

A door then opened in the rear armoured troop carrier and a Gestapo officer stepped into the morning air and smiled. He walked around the carnage and examined the Mercedes, its driver and passengers, who were slumped in a variety of positions, bleeding profusely and clearly dead. The chauffeur, secretary and decoy guard had been kindly provided by Obersturmbannfuhrer Fischer and they were kitted out in German uniforms for the occasion, though it was to remain a closely guarded secret that they were Jews. The dummies that occupied the remaining two seats inside the Mercedes wore replica uniforms of Obergruppen-fuhrer Reinhard Heydrich and Obersturm-bannfuhrer Adolf Eichmann.

***

Obersturmbannfuhrer Fischer, Titsy Tina and Rapportfuhrer Schole stood by the side of the recently hastily completed airstrip just outside the main gates at Wysznica. The grass had been removed, revealing a layer of gravel which had been levelled sufficiently to enable a light aircraft to land. As soon as this particular operation was over, it would become a fully-fledged gravel pit: the equipment was already inside the recently constructed shed on the western side of the camp.

Tina tried hard to keep her dress from lifting as the draft from the propeller of the Fieseler Storch threatened to reveal more thigh than she wanted. Adolf Eichmann was indeed a powerful man with considerable authority, and she would make sure he saw enough of her legs when seated next to him at dinner. For now however, more modesty was required.

Schole reached across the front of Fischer and discreetly straightened his Iron Cross as they waited for the door of the aircraft to open. Earlier that day, Fischer had said he was convinced this was the beginning of a new era for him; he was destined for higher office and promised to take Schole with him. Schole could not have been happier.

A few minutes later and Fischer stood to attention, coughed into his gloved hand then made a final adjustment to his cap. Perfect timing, as the fuselage door opened and Obersturmbannfuhrer Eichmann and Obergruppenfuhrer Heydrich walked out onto the aircraft steps to be greeted by a dazzling array of smiling officials and a small brass band playing 'Lily Marlene'.

42

1943

Things could not have been better for Fischer at the start of 1943. Not only had he been responsible for liquidating six members of the Polish underground while securing the safety of both Eichmann and Heydrich, he had also made amazing progress at Wysznica. His statistics far exceeded those at Auschwitz. Despite the huge number of staff at his disposal, Hoess was unable to get near Fischer's results and while the increased level of transports out of Europe caused no major problems for Fischer, Hoess was slowly sinking under the weight of numbers. Schole's master plans for Wysznica could not have worked better.

But there was one thing playing on Fischer's mind, nagging away like a toothache. Who tipped off the Polish underground about Eichmann and Heydrich's visit? It had to be someone on his team, of that he was sure, but who? Only a few people knew of the visit, but what about the servants, the maids and cooks, the prisoners who cleaned the windows or mowed the grass? Anyone could have overheard a conversation. It was difficult to ascertain or resolve so as a precaution he sent every member of his household staff to the gas chamber, and recruited new cooks, maids and cleaners. In addition he sent several SS units to the tiny village of Ciegloblin, chosen at random from a map on the wall in his office.

They slaughtered all one hundred and fifty-six residents: women, children, babes in arms and old people. Then the tanks moved in and destroyed every building before soldiers finally removed all signage. By the end of the day, the only evidence that even Ciegloblin existed was a place name on old maps.

The success of the dummy convoy and the retaliation against the local population had put pride back into Fischer's men. As well as foiling a significant assassination attempt on two of Hitler's most senior officials, a bonus came in the form of a British airman they found in the cellar of the church at Ciegloblin. He was badly injured, presumably when his plane was shot down, so they executed him and the priest on the spot-hanged them both from the rafters above the font; a wonderful sight according to those present. They then set about destroying the church, first with flamethrowers then a few hours later with two tanks that reduced the building to a pile of charred timber and stone.

Fischer was confident that by the time the reports of his successes got back to Berlin there would be no one at headquarters who did not know his name. Did they know who Hoess was? He doubted that anyone would care if they now knew of Hoess or not.

It was mid 1943 when the first cracks started to appear at Wysznica. The number of unprocessed units stockpiled around the crematorium seemed to be growing; it appeared that Schole's plan to put three units into each oven instead of the two recommended by Berlin was not working because it was taking far too long for them to burn. At first they managed four hundred units a day, but for some reason they could not maintain the pace. The burning pits and mass graves had long since been filled to capacity and now rats were everywhere; the last thing Fischer needed was his men going down with typhus or some other Jewish disease.

While Schole worked tirelessly around the clock to find solutions to so many problems, Fischer also had other issues-Tina's insecurities. She became increasingly clingy after overhearing Heydrich talking about the end 'being near'. She wanted more attention than Fischer could spare and at night she lay next to him whining, *you will still want me when this is all over wont you, my darling Baldy?*

Ania was also complaining now; apparently she was lonely! She had music, clean towels, good food and visits from the commandant himself, what more could a woman want? Schole suggested she should be given a little freedom, two days a week perhaps to allow her to socialise. Nearly all the original women had been replaced and there were now five Jewish girls working in the club, using fake documents supplied by Schole. It was a simple case of convenience and meeting demand by utilising the best stock available. The camp inspectors were unaware of the Jewish girls, so what did it matter?

Ania had befriended one of the new women, Zofia from Budapest, who offered a shoulder to cry on when Ania talked of her beloved sister Danuta. With Slav gone it now seemed to be impossible to locate her and Ania ached with the 'not knowing'.

Ania and Zofia took the opportunity to stretch their legs whenever they could, walking around the camp, talking, dreaming out loud and laughing sometimes too, though they admitted to feeling shame at being able to smile when there was so much misery around them.

A high fence topped with barbed wire separated the administration sector from the men and women's camps. The wire was electrified and sometimes-desperate prisoners hurled themselves onto it to end the pain and madness of their lives. Bodies were often left to rot as a deterrent though most zebra people no longer noticed them or their lingering stench, even in summer. Walking unimpeded around the camp gave Ania and Zofia a sense of freedom that neither had felt for a very long time. When they closed their eyes they imagined they were on a boulevard in Hungary or Warsaw, window shopping or chatting over coffee and cake in a trendy sidewalk cafe. Reality had a way of grounding them however, and when one afternoon they saw a bird skitting anxiously across the rooftops in search of a place to roost, they noticed that it never settled. Even the wildlife sensed the obscenity of Wysznica.

Zebra people were all around, either being moved from one workplace to another by the Germans or standing around in bewildered groups. When Ania looked at the prisoners she heard their silent screams. Their emaciated, diseased-ridden bodies were covered in scabs, and bore the evidence of SS brutality; noses bashed out of shape, missing teeth, split lips, swollen eyes and festering sores. They were more like shadows than human beings and when they did speak it was with great effort and purpose, as they struggled to pull enough air into their lungs. They had already been branded by Death and seemed to be waiting for Him to return to collect them.

As Ania and Zofia ventured deeper into the camp they noticed the condition of the zebra people worsened. Moving away from the administration block into the men's zone they frequently found themselves confronted by dazed people stumbling about with empty food bowls, hoping someone would put something in-anything, a blade of grass maybe, an insect, it no longer mattered. These prisoners were now emaciated, hollow shells.

A little further in and they discovered bodies stacked outside most huts. Some were heaped neatly, head to toe, others were not so organised. Dumped by Kapos, awaiting collection, they were in disorganised mounds with arms and legs randomly sticking out like branches in a bonfire. The zebra people in this area were no longer subject to roll calls or aktions. The Germans left them to die in their own filth. It was easier because there were so many of them. So many...

43

Karl Braun strode briskly towards the crematorium-long, angry strides- and anyone who happened to be in his way was knocked to the ground, where they lay covered in the dust of those who had gone up the chimneys before them. Whenever he was having a bad day, Braun went to the crematorium because it was a good place to take out his frustrations on others.

Controlling Canada Two was causing Braun problems. There was too much administration for his liking and not enough summary disciplinary action. The volume of units he had to process was becoming untenable and everyone, including him, was expected to cope. It was, after all, about statistics and nothing else. Numbers, numbers, numbers. Push, push, push, all the time. At such times all Braun wanted to do was hurt someone; that was how he coped. And right now, because of a dispute with an officer from the Inspectorate of Concentration Camps, he wanted to hurt someone badly. *Who do those inspectors think they are, the fucking Gestapo?* Where was Schroder when he was needed? Schroder had no problems with the inspectors.

Braun had been caught off guard by the snap inspection, and he was rude to the chief auditor, put him offside. Not a good start. So the jumped-up little clerk with the clipboard under his arm and the round wire spectacles balancing on the end of his bulbous little nose decided to turn a simple half day's work into a full audit. And that meant opening the vault, producing the ledgers for the last quarter, auditing everything, including the contents of the safe in the commandant's office. Fischer had not been pleased with the disturbance either and he made it plain to Braun that he would talk to him about it *when Herr Inspector had completed his important work.*

Fischer was always a little uncomfortable during an inspection. Only a year before, Hoess had been caught out on some minor matter and had been banished for a few months. Even though he was allowed back, there was something odd about the whole business and Fischer knew that if he was ever subjected to a bad audit his chances of making it to Berlin were gone.

The crematorium staff saw Braun coming: the Kapos, the Sonderkommandos. They stubbed out their cigarettes, buttoned their collars and started waving their arms about and swearing at the men around them. There was nothing wrong with giving someone a few lashes from the whip either, now that Braun was in sight. His presence always resulted in a flurry of activity.

A pile of corpses lay in front of the ovens, and three Kapos were trying to prepare the rigid bodies for the ovens, but arms and legs protruded where arms and legs were not meant to be and the whole lot was a mess. "Who is the head Kapo here?" Braun yelled. A nervous man scurried forward, removed his cap and bowed respectfully. Braun was not impressed. "What the fuck is going on? Why are there so many unprocessed units around?"

The Kapo stared at his feet and mumbled an apology. "We do our best, sir. The ovens are full at the moment, sir."

Braun turned to one of the guards standing nearby and sneered. "Don't these people know they are working on borrowed time and we are the ones who lend it to them? They have production targets to meet and if they fail, there are others who won't be so slack. There is no shortage of labour here."

Braun was convinced that everyone was on the make, at his expense. The Kapos, Sonderkommandos, guards, prisoners and even the inspectors from Berlin were trying to leverage something out of the misery at Wysznica! Wuttke, one of the dog handlers and a well-known canteen gossip said Braun had changed since his promotion. The Greyhound was snappy and irritable with everyone and could not be trusted. And now here he was at the crematorium, outside oven number two, holding an anxious Kapo by the collar as he addressed those around. "We need to teach this Kapo a lesson in productivity, prove to everyone that they must work smarter."

One of the guards tentatively stepped forward. "But this is my best man, Scharfuhrer. He is the only one who can get close enough to empty the fat from the trays beneath the ovens without interrupting the process."

Braun released the Kapo, who then shuffled from foot to foot, trying to avoid eye contact. "Is that so?" Braun asked. "What is your name?"

The terrified man spoke to the ground. "My name is Szymons, sir. Chief Kapo Szymons."

"Good. Then let's see just how near to the fire Chief Kapo Szymons can get today, shall we?"

Work had come to a standstill all around, everyone gawping and fearful of what was about to take place.

Braun nodded towards the oven. "Open the door." Szymons stepped forward, removed a stick from his belt and despite the searing heat crouched low and deftly flicked the door handle, jumping back as a blast of hot air burst from the furnace like an angry bull. Intense orange flames licked around the oven's framework and the heat wormed around the gaping rib cages of the two stark white skeletons inside the chamber.

"There's your problem you see," Braun yelled to one of the guards. "That is why you have so many units out here. You only have two in there." He grabbed Szymons and pushed him forward, forcing him to look into the oven. "Do you see? Do you see that? You should have three units in there, not two, dummkopf." The Kapo instinctively ducked in anticipation of a slap around the head, but Braun's demeanour suddenly changed. "Do you not think you could get another unit in there? There's room for one more maybe, what do you say, Chief Kapo?"

Szymons replied tentatively. "I think we may be able to get another in there, sir. Yes, maybe. Perhaps. Sir."

"You think you can, do you? Then why didn't you do it in the first place?" He waved his hand at two Kapos standing nearby, watching the whole episode. "Tie this man up!" The men appeared confused, so Braun repeated his instruction, "You heard me. You two, tie Szymons up. Now!"

Some rope appeared and the two Kapos hesitantly tied Szymons' hands and feet as Braun stood impatiently by. "Come on, be quick about it or I might change my mind and use one of you instead! Get him into the oven."

The men hesitantly lifted Szymons into a horizontal position, like a battering ram, at which point he started to squirm and scream pitifully. A dark patch appeared at the front of his pants. "No! No, sir, please, I beg you!"

Braun seemed to be enjoying the spectacle as he spoke casually to one of the guards. "You see this? Do you see how easy it is to get them to do what you want? It's a simple matter of motivation." He turned back to the two Kapos who were still holding Szymons. "In with him now, come on, at the count of three!"

The unbelievable was about to happen in front of a small, shocked audience. Szymons shaking body was inched towards the open oven door, head first. The two men holding him turned their shoulders to the searing heat as the skin on Szymons' face started to blister and his hair suddenly burst into flame. It was at that moment that Braun saw Ania and Zofia standing with their hands to their faces, eyes like saucers. Suddenly buoyed, he turned away from them, straightened his cap and shrugged his jacket into position, shouting at the two Kapos, "Put him in!"

***

"Do you know you are not supposed to be here?" Braun seemed calmer when he addressed the two shocked women ten minutes later.

Ania was the first to speak. "The commandant said we could walk."

"You have a letter of authority?" She shook her head, *no.* "Then you have no authority."

Zofia wanted to speak but no words came. All she could think about was the sight of the two Kapos swinging Szymond's towards the oven. He was frothing at the mouth and his scalp and face were badly burned. Braun's eyes were glowing. "On the count of three!" The corners of his mouth twitched upwards into a smirk "One!" The two men swung Szymons backwards. "Two!"

forwards he went, and back again as the momentum built. Then, just when everyone thought Braun was going to yell *three!* He called out, "OK, OK, put him down for God's sake. I will let your precious 'fat cleaning' chief Kapo live!"

The two Kapos rushed Szymons to safety and placed him on the ground, undoing the knots in the rope that held his hands and feet, apologising all the time. A bucket of water was tipped over him and he lay mumbling and crying while steam rose from his crumpled body.

"You women should leave here. Now. Go! This is not a good place for you. Stay where you are safe, behind your own boundaries. You could be swept up in an aktion at any time, then where would you be?" Braun laughed and looked up at the chimneys as Ania and Zofia hurried away.

44

Fischer had just returned after a flying visit to Berlin, and he was particularly enlivened when he called on Ania. He liked to see her at such times, and it was easy for her to pretend she had missed him. But this time he spoke not of his journey but of something Tina had said on his return. "Tina suspects I am visiting you. She had it out with me. She said she knew things about us and she threatened me in all kinds of ways!"

"So why are you so happy, my dear Baldric?" Ania asked as she started to undress the commandant.

"Because she has no idea! The times she insisted I was with you I was actually with Schole! I called him at home, did you know that? Got him out of bed, made him come in with his diary and sat him in front of Tina and said, 'OK, Fritz, tell her where I was on...'" Tina had snatched the diary, checked the dates and times herself then threw the book at the wall.

"I still don't understand, Baldric." Ania was undressing herself now.

"Can't you see how excellent it is? There is nothing like a woman who feels scorned or cheated. She swears she is going to catch us together. Swears it! You had better watch out for yourself, Ania. She's a dangerous woman. You know how Polish women are! Her anger makes her, how do I say this? It makes her more...?"

"More passionate?"

"Exactly."

"I am a Polish woman too, Baldric, and I hate the thought of you and her being together. It is like you are two-timing me!"

Fischer laughed at Ania's pouting face. "Talking about timing, have you seen my watch? I think I left it here a few days ago."

"You did. I found it by the sink."

Fischer shrugged as she handed him the beautiful timepiece. She must have been mistaken. He never left his watch on the sink because he always hung it from the bedpost so he could keep an eye on the time during lovemaking. He set the watch back on the bedpost once again, attended to the business at hand and this time, when he left twenty minutes later, he remembered to take the watch with him.

It was nine o'clock the following day when Ania first noticed the itching. She could not stop scratching and even left her underwear off. After the guard unlocked her door she called Zofia to her room. "I have an itch, Zofia, in a place where itches are not supposed to be. Can you look please; I don't want to go to that filthy cow, Frau Groepler."

"I love you, Ania, but this is a huge request! That place down there, it's not somewhere other women are supposed to go unless a child is about to come out."

"Do it for me please? I would do it for you."

Zofia paused for a moment. "You remember that French soap the commandant gave you, do you have any left?"

"You can have the soap. I will give you perfume as well, and I even have some stuff for under your arms if you like. Please, Zofia! Just look at my foofoo will you!"

A moment later and Zofia's face appeared at the wrong end of Ania's bed, staring up at her from between her knees. "Oh my God, Ania. Have you been to the beach recently? A secret visit you kept to yourself?"

"Very funny! What are you talking about, what's going on down there?"

"You have some little visitors from the seaside down here, my dear. I think you have crabs!"

***

The next day, Tina confronted Fischer in a blaze of anger so severe he feared for his safety. "When you got back from Berlin on Monday, these weren't the only things you brought back for me, were they?" She threw the pair of beautiful handcrafted leather shoes at him.

"What do you mean, what are you going on about?" he asked, trying to avoid the confrontation as he sat up in bed surrounded by files and loose papers. "I have the budgets to review, my dear, and I have to get the figures to Berlin in the morning. Leave me alone." He had an inkling of what she was talking about. He had been itching too.

"Crabs. I have crabs. You slept with me when you got back from Berlin. The same day."

"I was never unfaithful to you in Berlin, my darling. Why would I be? Why look at cheap jewellery when I have such beautiful diamonds at home?" He pushed his papers aside and patted the bed for her to join him.

"If you didn't visit anyone in Berlin, maybe you have a little friend you visit here, and you caught something from her? I have unwanted guests inside my underwear; I did not invite them and they came from you, Baldric Fischer. If I find out *who* you caught them from, blood will be spilled!" He could not placate her. She was still fuming half an hour later and after more shouting and histrionics, Fischer spent the night on the sofa in his study. He would visit his good friend Dr Mengele at Auschwitz the next morning, for a private consultation.

45

Danuta looked at the clock that was perched on the mantelpiece above the roaring fire she lit only an hour or so before. Dinner tonight was going to be golonka-pork knuckles and vegetables-a favourite. There was also one of several bottles of good French Bordeaux, which she had found in a kitchen cupboard in the apartment she now shared with her new German boyfriend.

They met the same day that Slav and the others died. She was in a cafe, waiting for the right time to go back to the florist's flat. A woman had burst in, in a state of extreme excitement, talking at a hundred miles an hour. A small crowd gathered around her. "There was an ambush this morning, the underground tried to bump off some high-ranking Germans in a convoy!"

The city was alive with the news but there was no real detail-only gossip. It was when Danuta returned to the flat that she saw the cars and the mysterious dark-eyed men in hats and long leather coats coming and going. A neighbour told her she had seen Natalka being taken away by the Gestapo.

Heaven only knew what Natalka was going through. Now Danuta understood why Slav was reluctant to share information. The mission had failed. An unexpected turn of events. Everyone knew the risks but when Danuta heard that they all perished her legs turned to jelly and it was all she could do to stop herself bursting into tears. Slav had always been so particular, planning everything down to the finest detail. He said his source was impeccable, but it appeared that he had been led into a trap by 'the girl' at Wysznica.

Danuta's life was in turmoil; she couldn't go back to the florist's flat so where could she go? She did not know anyone else! She decided to return to the cafe and see if the owner knew of someone who would rent her a room or give her a job. When she arrived a German soldier was standing at the counter ordering pastries and vodka. He kept looking at her a certain way. Before she knew it, he was sitting next to her.

This German was not at all cultured like Captain Arndt Nebe, who she had stabbed in some stranger's doorway in what seemed like a lifetime ago. He possessed none of Nebe's manners and was not the most articulate man either. He seemed broody, edgy even, but he was amiable enough and there was something about him. They ended up at his apartment that evening. Maybe it was the circumstances, the adrenaline, her sense of loss perhaps, but her new German lover made her laugh, and he could cook. She stayed the night and was still there three days later. Where better to hide than under German noses? Maybe this one could even help her find Ania.

It became immediately obvious that Danuta's new boyfriend was nothing like anyone she had met before. The more she got to know him, the more his sultry, moody side showed. He seemed to have huge highs and terrible lows. There were times when it was almost too difficult to gauge how to treat him or to know what to say. She was constantly walking on eggshells. She felt as if she was living with a human time bomb, and there was always the possibility of an explosion when he was having a bad day.

He was highly sexed and at times frightening in his demands. It mattered not if she had her period; when he wanted sex, he took it. That was the downside. But he paid the bills and money did not seem to be a problem. On good days he would throw her a handful of zloty and tell her to buy herself something nice. He often came home with wine or gifts; his access to the black market ensured she wanted for nothing.

Like most of the troops around Krakow, Danuta's German boyfriend worked at one of the camps and was often away for long periods. He would be off shift for several nights then back to the camp again three days later, for two weeks. In a strange way she felt secure. If she was ever stopped in the street and asked for her papers she could show the pass he had given her. And all the time, as she wandered around the streets and cafes of the city, she tried to discover what had happened to Natalka. But she had to be careful; if her new boyfriend ever suspected she had been involved with the Polish underground movement...

Her boyfriend told her he liked having someone in the apartment when he was working away. He was concerned about theft-people became desperate during times of war. But they were in a good part of the city and other Germans had apartments in the same complex-families too. Why was he so paranoid? Anyway, she reasoned, *so what?* So what if he only kept her there for security. Did it really matter if the relationship was one of convenience for him? It was convenient for her, also and she was safe; for now.

German soldiers and their Polish girlfriends were often seen around the city wining and dining, dancing, having a good time in the better bars and restaurants. But Danuta's man did not like to leave the apartment unguarded. He was tense and secretive, and his rages were becoming more frequent, although when he sulked he mostly kept to himself. He seemed to be insecure, and when Danuta jokingly said she might run off with someone when he was away working he squeezed her jaw painfully between his thumb and forefinger and said, "I don't think you will be doing that."

She failed to hear him let himself in as she prepared dinner that night, and when he unexpectedly put his arms around her waist she nearly upended the cooking pot. "Steady on," he said. "Am I that scary?"

"Of course not! I didn't hear you come in, that's all." She untangled herself and he stole a drink from her glass. "How was your shift?" she asked.

"Don't ask," he said, his eyes black with anger. "Here," she handed him a fresh glass of wine. "Drink this while I serve dinner."

They ate in silence and quickly polished off the bottle. As Danuta started to clear the table her boyfriend disappeared momentarily, returning with something in his hand. "Look at this will you?" he said, as he placed a gun on the table.

"It's yours, yes? The Luger?"

"Never mind what sort of gun it is, look at the handle will you?" It had taken a Jewish artisan three weeks to craft the gold inlay of a greyhound in full flight.

"It's beautiful, Karl, what an amazing piece. It's like a work of art!"

"I had a goldsmith do it-a Jew, of course. I still have him locked away nice and secure because I have one more job for him..." He handed her a small blue velvet bag, which she weighed in her hand. "What is it?"

"Open it," he said with a grin.

She tipped the contents onto the table and several items of jewellery tumbled out. A ring with a fine garnet stone, a pair of beautiful diamond drop earrings and a gold lady's signet ring engraved with the letter 'O', which his Jewish goldsmith would change into a 'D' for her-probably his last job.

She struggled to speak. She knew exactly what he meant about the goldsmith ... his last job ... She also had a pretty good idea where the jewellery had come from. "My God, they're lovely. Are they for me, Karl? Are you sure?" she mumbled unconvincingly.

"Of course they are for you! But you missed something; they must still be in there, let me look." He shook the bag and two more articles tumbled onto the table. She stared at them in horror—could not bring herself to touch them. The colour drained from her face, her head started to spin and she blinked her eyes quickly, swallowing hard to stop herself gagging.

"You should see your face! Come now, it's just a few teeth! I'm going to get the gold removed and made into something very special for you; whatever you want! I thought another ring maybe? Tell me what you would like? My little man will do it for you, he's a genius!"

Karl was like a child examining a new toy at Christmas. "If there is not enough gold in them what does it matter? We have another seven thousand units due in at the end of the week so I can pull a few out of that, I'm sure." Danuta wanted to vomit as she watched him roll one of the teeth between his thumb and forefinger.

46

Titsy Tina stared at herself in the mirror and smiled. It had been a great day. The end result could not have been better, as she now had Baldy back under her control. It had all crystallised when she saw his watch hanging from that weird-eyed bitch's bedpost during one of her secret 'personal inspections' when Ania was out walking. Of course, the little whore never knew that Tina had been nosing around her room; Tina was far too clever for that.

She had suspected the illicit affair for some time, but that worm Schole refused to confirm it, though he must have known. The guards also, though they were far too loyal to spill the beans. But it did not matter now because Tina had the evidence she needed. But what to do about it? What she wanted was for Weird Eyes to be out of the way, once and for all; out of Baldric's life and out of hers. But she had to be careful not to push too hard, because Tina knew she was easy to replace. There were plenty of younger, better-looking Polish women willing to take her place in Baldric's bed.

The filthy little slut with the weird eyes obviously had her claws into Fischer and Tina knew she had to do something soon. The morning she found his watch on the bedpost, she paced up and down Ania's room for a while and ended up looking at her own reflection in the mirror above the sink. Then it hit her!

She left the watch and ran back to the house, already working on the details of a plan in her head. It might prove to be a little unsavoury for her, but so what, there was a war on wasn't there?

When Fischer was in Berlin a few days later, at the personal invitation of the Fuhrer and still basking in the glory of Eichmann's visit, Tina decided to 'contract' a dose of something unpleasant. She got herself smashed on cheap vodka in a cafe then took the remains of the bottle around the side streets behind the city square, looking for a donor. It was there that she found a stinking, louse-ridden local trying to sell chess sets with hollowed-out pieces, used for smuggling black market goods. They got talking and finished the vodka. When his eyes started rolling she whacked him over the head with her bag, which had a brick in it. When he was unconscious she gingerly removed his pants and to her delight, discovered a colony of little creatures scurrying around his nether regions.

Her next move was simple enough-using a pair of scissors, she removed some of his pubic hair and placed a fine sample of genital crabs into a small jar. Goodness only knows what he thought when he woke some time later and discovered his new 'hair-do'. Tina laughed all the way back to the camp!

When Baldric returned from Berlin the next morning she knew without a doubt that as soon as he had dropped his cases off, he would want to visit Weird Eyes and get his watch back. No doubt he would also want to play around a bit. But Tina got to him as soon as he walked in; she did not even wait for the driver to put his bags away. She pounced in the lounge-room, blindfolded him as a tease and gave him a 'welcome home' he would never forget-literally, delivering an ample quantity of pediculosis pubis creatures to their new home. A few hours later he trotted off to see Ania, claiming that he had to get the latest production figures from Schole. He left Tina a wonderful present (the handmade leather shoes) and an hour or two later he also unwittingly gave Ania a gift.

The next day, Tina made the shock announcement that she had an infestation 'down below', and all hell broke loose. She had already insisted that Frau Groepler immediately test all the Club girls and when she was provided with the results, it transpired that one of them had crabs-Weird Eyes!

No wonder Tina looked so proud of herself when she confronted Fischer. He had been sprung in a major way. Frau Groepler and all the medical staff knew that Ania had 'visitors', so Fischer had no choice but to take action to prevent their spread. Weird Eyes was immediately scrubbed with carbolic and relegated to general brothel duties, and removed from her gilded cage! There was no way Baldric could visit her again, not with just a curtain to hide behind. Ania was forced out of the room with the green door and was lucky not to be drifting out of the crematorium chimney up into the sky above Wysznica.

Fischer realised how stupid he had been, allowing himself to be manipulated by Tina while he played her against Ania. What a fool he had been, letting his cock rule his head! How much did Tina know? Was she the one who tipped off the underground? And what about Canada Two? Everything had been going so well now that the transports from Europe were in full flow ... And Tina knew everything: his pension fund, the safe and the two sets of books-everything! My God, he had been so stupid!

With the end of the war looming, Fischer had been secretly planning to set Tina up in an apartment in Krakow where she could live comfortably with her daughter, and he would provide for them both. He could continue to lead a respectable life no doubt, as some kind of senior civil servant in the Fuhrer's new government. He would be seen as a fine, hardworking married man with a wife and children back in Berlin as he commuted between there and Krakow in his important new role. The future had looked rosy for Baldric Fischer.

Then he caught a dose of crabs from a whore! *Verdammte holle!*

***

Tina pretended to be upset for a day or two, but Fischer stood firm and refused to send Ania to the gas chamber. He wanted to keep his options open as far as the girl with the weird eyes was concerned. She was impossible to forget. Who knows what might happen in this fickle war? And she was younger than Tina, certainly had a better body, and she had no hesitation in sharing it all with him. How wonderful would it be after the war if he had her in an apartment in Krakow instead of Tina? But how did she get the crabs? Had she really been stupid enough to cheat on him when he was away? Never! Had she been raped without his knowing? Absolutely not-she would have told him immediately.

So how did Ania get infected? And when it came to it, what about Tina, she was also infected?

Fischer could only put it down to one thing. They got it from him. And where did he get it from?

Berlin!

***

What a night it had been in Berlin, being wined and dined by the Fuhrer's inner circle as a 'thank-you' for exceptional work at Wysznica. Such erudite figures as Goering, Minister Goebbels and the others could never be seen to participate in the final gesture of appreciation afforded to commandant Fischer that night, but they assured him that the Fuhrer himself had sanctioned the visit to Berlin's most prestigious brothel. Had Eichmann not told him so himself, when he dropped Fischer off in his own staff car that night after dinner? At the brothel there was more champagne, music, dancing and, of course, the women! Oh, those women! He was in bed with three of them at one stage, or was it four? No matter, they could not keep their hands off him!

It was his night of nights but never had he dreamed it would end in such a way.

He must have caught the crabs at the brothel. That was war for you: it was hard to find decent, clean girls anywhere in Europe now. Fischer had been a frequent visitor to many of Berlin's exclusive establishments over the years, and as luck would have it, this was the first time he had caught anything. It had been a good run that unfortunately ended badly.

But he had something else to occupy his mind at the current time, a matter far less fickle than women. Judging by the ledgers that Schole was showing him, he was amassing quite a fortune. As well as a large amount of currency and a significant quantity of jewellery and gold, a painting was discovered in the lining of a suitcase at Canada Two. Schole swore it was a Rembrandt, cut out of the frame but otherwise undamaged. That alone would set him up for the rest of his life. The finer things in life had always been just out of reach for Baldric Fischer, but now they were attainable, and it was all thanks to Schole!

47

With the blue velvet bag and its gruesome contents on top of the chest of drawers next to her bed, Danuta lay thinking about the people who had parted with their precious possessions minutes before going to the gas chamber. Those hidden trinkets and baubles were evidence of someone's existence and the very last chance they had to negotiate a way out of the line. That was hard enough for Danuta to think about, but the teeth?

For those victims' families there would be no Shiva, no period of mourning or sad farewell, certainly no headstones. There would not even be any identifiable ashes, for they would have come out of the crematorium chimney and drifted through the air over Krakow according to the whims of nature, falling onto someone's washing or the gutter of an apartment building. The jewellery they had concealed about their bodies had been removed either just before or just after their death, and now it was hanging off an SS officer's girlfriend's wrist, neck or ears. The very thought of it disgusted Danuta. In fact, she disgusted herself for putting herself in such a position. Ania would never have done such a thing, would she?

Karl had been spending a lot of time alone in his office at the back of the apartment, after dinner every night. He would slam drawers and occasionally laugh out loud like some kind of madman, only to reappear half an hour later as if nothing had happened! And why had he put a padlock on the door, threatening Danuta with the most terrible consequences if she dared go in without his approval. What was he up to, what was he hiding in there—more teeth?

He started asking Danuta about her past. He wanted to know who she was, why she had suddenly entered his life and where she had come from. He had her old papers checked-they proved to be false. *I need to know who I am sharing my bed with!* There was something about her, something vaguely familiar...

***

Karl often pretended to be asleep, with his back to Danuta in bed. Work was getting to him; not the acts of violence or the killing-he had no problem with them and never had. It was the volume, the huge number of units that arrived every day, and the expectations of those above him. And there was something else that was eating away at him: Danuta had recently asked if he knew anyone in the Gestapo, someone who could possibly trace a person for her. Why? What was she up to?

He had been trying to work out why she seemed so familiar, when out of the blue at the crematorium one day, he stumbled into the commandant's whore. She had tried to avoid him after the rape, but this time he deliberately engaged her, and that was when he realised the connection! The way she chose her words and put her sentences together, her elegant bearing and the shape of her mouth and the little dimple in her chin...

His mind drifted back to the cold day in 1940 at the small farm in Zwinbrzych, when he and Schroder had argued about the girl who was missing from the list. Was she in the wardrobe or not? Schroder then spotted her running across the field and he picked her off with his first shot. But had he killed her? Was it possible that this was her? He had seen the scar on Danuta's neck the first time they had sex, but she dismissed it as the result of a childhood accident.

He was going to double-check the records from that day at Zwinbrzych. He wanted to know the names of the two girls on the list. If they were Danuta and Ania that would be enough for him. If he was right, and he was certain he was, he was going to have to do something about his new girlfriend. And do it soon.

48

Ania was philosophical about the way things had turned out. As far as life went in the camp, she had enjoyed the better side of it up to now. The other women at the Club had resented her because she always had hot water and soft toilet paper, but now the room behind the green door had been turned into a store and she found herself in the same position as the rest of them. Perhaps she had misjudged Tina's hold over the commandant. Fischer had made it quite plain that Ania was a distraction, his plaything, a luxury, not a necessity. He would have carried on enjoying her, too, if Tina had not caught a dose of the crabs. But where had they come from? Ania decided that Fischer had been the carrier. It had to be him. It certainly was not her because she had not slept with anyone else. And it would not be Tina, would it? She wouldn't sleep around and put her security at risk, would she?

Life was now very different for the girl with the weird eyes. Gone were the nice meals and the fine linen. Fischer had occasionally given her perfume and French soaps, as well as silk stockings and underwear that he smuggled back in his luggage from his trips to Berlin. He enjoyed his clandestine relationship, and rewarded her according to her performance and enthusiasm. Despite her initial lack of experience she had found it easy to satisfy him. Her natural beauty and voluptuous body had been the key; together with her willingness to submit to the indignities that he so enjoyed. It was easy enough and it never took long before she had him lying back gasping for breath with a grin on his face.

But now she had to allow those stinking, filthy, overworked, women-hungry Kapos and Sonderkommandos access to her body. She soon discovered that the Sonderkommandos-the ones who worked in the crematorium-were the worst. Zofia once told her that her father had been a fishmonger and she remembered the stink that accompanied him; no matter how many times he washed his hands the smell of fish still permeated the air around him. It was impossible to be rid of it. And so it was with the crematorium workers, for they could never rid themselves of the stench of death.

The Club women had been talking a lot of the future. They knew that when the war was over, and there were already rumblings that it could happen soon, they would be judged harshly for their role. There would be no shortage of witnesses pointing at them in the street, trying to pull their hair and scream abuse. Shops would refuse to serve them and people would cross the road when they approached. Was the worst yet to come?

***

It was now 1944 and the allies were at last admitting that they were aware of what was happening in concentration camps around Eastern Europe. Spotter planes, out on reconnaissance runs looking for bombing targets had stumbled upon the factories of death. Prisoners and guards stared in disbelief at the planes circling above them, and the talk within the camps was all about liberation. They had been found at last and the Parliaments of the allies would surely set things in motion to free them from purgatory. The plans that Slav had made for an uprising in Auschwitz and Wysznica had not been shelved, in fact they were now moving forward at a pace. The camp rebels now had enough stocks of arms and munitions to have a real impact on the big day. In addition, they had enough fight in them to give the Germans more than just a black eye! Something both terrible and magnificent was soon about to take place at Auschwitz and Wysznica.

***

The lucky voucher holder nervously entered Ania's room and pulled the curtain shut behind him with a strange expression on his face. He looked around the room with sharp, bird-like movements, taking everything in quickly. That was why he was still alive-he missed nothing. His hair was slicked down and he had obviously attempted to wash himself, though he was still grimy and smelled of soil.

Ania may also have noticed the handprints on the back of his jacket where the rest of the men from the new gravel pit had proudly cheered their supervisor as he left for his adventure that evening.

The man stood meekly, cap in hand, and could not believe what he saw when he pulled the curtain back-she looked young enough to be his daughter! He had expected to see a battle-weary hag, a tired old sow wearing heavy make-up and cheap perfume to cover her own stench, lying on the bed like a beast of burden, smothered in red lipstick and powder, smoking a cigarette.

It was a brief, fumbled affair, and afterwards the visitor sat on the edge of the bed and conversed with his host. Ania had a somewhat resigned expression, not from boredom so much as *well, that is one more nearer the end of the day.* But as she stared at the man who had introduced himself as Szalbek, she saw concern in his face. "I'm so sorry to put you through this," he said. "You look like a fine young woman."

Ania knew that he was old enough to be her father, and here she was, comforting him after he had just had his way with her. She wanted to cry for him but could not. The pain of being in that place was a big enough burden for her to carry without having to share the guilt of others.

The man's thirty minutes were over quickly enough. Someone banged on the wall outside so he stood and pulled himself together, ready to boast of his exploits with the beautiful girl with the strange eyes when he returned to the gravel pit. He bowed slightly from the waist, and then thanked Ania again. As he was about to leave he seemed to hesitate. "Tomorrow morning, lie low. Be busy. Do not go outside. Whatever you do don't leave this room for any reason." The curtain suddenly swished open and a huge German soldier filled the space.

"Come on, you dirty old bastard. You have had your fill. There are others out here you know!" and Szalbek was gone.

***

"Out of the gloom sometimes comes light." Fischer was talking to Schole, a look of incredulity on his face. Obscured by the smoke from his beloved briar pipe, Fischer seemed to be reflecting upon something significant.

"What has happened, mein Commandant, are you alright?"

"It's the Fuhrer ... I don't believe it ... I can't believe it."

Schole did not understand. "Commandant, please..."

"Yes. Sorry, Fritz, but I think divine intervention has again stepped into the path of the Reich. Let me ask you, how many attempts have there been on the Fuhrer's life?"

"Five, six maybe, I don't know-nobody knows for sure."

"Well, on the sixth of June, my dear Schole, our enemies landed at Normandy to try to take from us the lands that we legitimately fought and died for. Our resources have been stretched to breaking point on many fronts, and our enemies have tried to take advantage of us when our defences are down. But the Fuhrer continues to lead us to glory and has no doubts that this invasion, the one they call the D-Day landings, is just a small obstacle on our path to victory."

"Of course, Baldric, there can be no doubt about that."

"Let us agree that the Fuhrer has made the occasional mistake. This is war after all and hasty decisions have to be made sometimes. The Fuhrer is courageous enough to make such decisions, no matter what the circumstances, as all great leaders in history have. But what if our leader was not there, Fritz, where we would be, who would make the decisions?"

Schole gulped. "What are you saying, Baldric ... The Fuhrer ... what on earth are you trying to tell me?" Fischer looked thoughtful and Schole suddenly said, "Oh my God. The Fuhrer ... he's not ... dead, is he, Baldric? Please tell me he's not dead!"

"That is my point you see, he most certainly is not dead." Fischer regained his composure, shook the mist out from his head. "He is as alive as you or I have ever known him to be! Mein Gott, he is so alive! There has been yet another failed assassination attempt, my dear Schole, in East Prussia this time. I can't believe it. Some fool from the High Command tried to exterminate the Fuhrer and everyone in the war cabinet."

"At the Wolf's Lair?"

"Yes. Where else in Prussia but the Wolf's Lair?" A tinge of irritation had slipped into Fischer's tone. "It seems that Von Strauffenberg was responsible. He and his team of traitors are being rounded up as we speak. The Fuhrer will address the nation tonight and Von Strauffenberg and his coconspirators will be hanging from the rafters of the nearest prison or backed up against a wall somewhere and shot before the Fuhrer speaks."

"I don't believe this, Baldric. Another attempt on the Fuhrer's life!"

"They did our great nation a favour!"

"They did?"

"Of course! They have woken us to the value of our Fuhrer yet again. The thought of life without his guidance, without him leading the Party, without him at the helm makes me shudder."

"It is without doubt incomprehensible to imagine where we would be without him, Baldric. His dream is our dream."

"Indeed it is. I actually like that, Fritz! I shall write to Adolf myself tonight, personally, and I shall say *your dream is our dream, Mein Fuhrer.* You don't mind if I steal that little gem from you do you?"

Schole straightened his back and clicked his heels. "I am honoured, Commandant!"

"You know, Fritz. There is something divine about the Fuhrer's survival after all these attempts upon his life. I truly believe it is a sign from God. 'He' has made a statement, 'He' has confirmed to the world that *right* is indeed on our side and *we* shall prevail. God is on Germany's side, Fritz, make no mistake about that!"

PART 6:
UPRISING

49

September 1944

There was nothing unusual about the start to that particular autumn day. At Auschwitz, Rudolf Hoess had breakfast with his wife and children in their villa before he set out for his office to attend a scheduled meeting. An inspection was due soon and he knew full well that he was still very much under the microscope. Someone had it in for him, of that he was sure. Maybe it was Fischer or perhaps it was someone else whose feathers he had ruffled? Hoess knew he had to be squeaky clean in the next inspection.

Meanwhile, at his house on the edge of the camp at Wysznica, Obersturmbannfuhrer Fischer asked Fraulein Krystyna if she had enjoyed breakfast. The window cleaner was busy making sure the sun could still be seen through the breakfast room windows-dust from the crematorium seemed to be everywhere and Tina hated it. When it rained the ground was covered in grey puddles, like watered down porridge. But the trees were clean again, a lush red and orange display that brightened the autumn day and put Tina in a good frame of mind.

Fischer was quite frisky when he woke that morning and he and Tina shared a shower together. Tina had already decided it was about time she went up to the balcony and sunbathed before the last warmth of autumn departed and another bleak Polish winter crept in.

"I enjoyed breakfast very much thank you, Baldy. I may be Polish but I do enjoy a little German sausage in the morning." She pinched her thumb and forefinger together in the air and Fischer reached over and playfully clipped her around the ear. Without further warning, he sprang from his chair. *Things to do!*

Of all the camps in and around Poland, Wysznica was so far ahead of the field with its production that it would surely only be a matter of time before the Fuhrer recognised Fischer's achievements and appointed him head of all camps in Europe. That was where he was going; he had finally worked it out. That had to be it. Eichmann's time was running out and that was why he was so irritable whenever he and Fischer met.

Rolf Schroder was at the vault by nine that morning and even though Braun was running late (if he *was* a greyhound he was never going to win any prizes for speed) everything looked to be in order-*above* and *below* the counter! His self-confidence was at an all-time high and Braun was the only one who seemed to be feeling the pressure. Everything was working to plan. Life was good.

In anticipation of the next inspection at Wysznica, a false floor had been installed in the new vault and thanks to two wonderful Polish craftsmen it was undetectable. The metalworker and carpenter had been processed as soon as the work was complete because Schroder did not want anyone other than himself and Braun to know about the new floor. It was amazing how much cash and jewellery could be hidden there; it far exceeded the stash at Karl's apartment. There was no doubt about those Jewish pigs-they were a devious lot, and the last two transports provided a haul way beyond Schroder's expectations.

The same morning, Danuta watched Karl kick-start his Zundapp KS 750 motorcycle outside their apartment. After dinner the night before, Karl had locked himself in his office and listened to the radio, as he had been doing every night for the last three weeks. She heard him stomping about, slamming things around and talking to himself until he joined her in the early hours.

There were so many steel ammunition boxes in that room that Danuta became concerned. What if the floor gave way because of the weight? He told her they did not have ammunition in them, so there was no need for her to be anxious. *So, what was in them?* She was told to mind her own business if she knew what was good for her.

Now thank God, Karl was gone for the day, for a few days in fact. Off to work. He could take out his anger on those poor Hungarian Jews-he had told her there was another transport due shortly. Up to seven thousand of the miserable souls were going to Wysznica, and over ten thousand to Auschwitz-Birkenau. Danuta wondered how many of them would still be alive by the end of the day and how many teeth would be pulled.

***

The first that Hoess knew about the attack was when one of the chimneys in crematoria number four fell. Bricks, dust, body parts and bones were everywhere after the explosion. The sound was heard across the camp and people stopped in their tracks to look up to the heavens to see if it was a signal from God. The next they knew, everyone scattered and indiscriminate gunfire peppered across open spaces and anyone wearing a uniform seemed to be a target.

Several Germans had been shot. Wounded soldiers lay moaning around the ruins of the crematorium as armed Sonderkommandos crouched behind piles of bricks, using corpses for protection while they took pot shots at their captors.

As they reloaded their weapons they managed to look at each other from their hiding places. They knew this was going to be the beginning of the end for most of them. They were waiting for the next explosion, when the camp perimeter wire would be blasted away leaving a hole big enough for hundreds, maybe even a thousand or more to make a run for it. Two watchtowers had to be knocked out as well, giving those willing to try the best chance of reaching the forest that lay tantalising close to the wire.

Back in Wysznica, Fischer's direct line rang in his office and it remained unanswered for a full six minutes until Schole decided to answer it. Just as he entered the room, the door to Fischer's personal restroom opened and he came out pulling his suspenders up, adjusting his pants. "If that is the Fuhrer tell him even I have to shit sometimes!"

As Schole listened to a voice screaming about a rebellion at Auschwitz, his face turned white. But before he could say a word, the first sounds of gunfire echoed across the camp at Wysznica.

***

Despite being short lived, the rebellion at Wysznica took its toll. Ten guards had been wounded, six of them fatally. Thirty prisoners had died too, though how many had been involved in the conflict was unknown.

As soon as he heard the first retorts from the rebels' guns, Schroder rushed to the affected area, and then quickly backed out again, happy to still be alive. It was worse than he thought, and he realised he was shaking. This was a real conflict, and he did not care for it!

The first thing to enter his mind was to ask how the prisoners got hold of their weapons. But the answer would have to wait because someone had to take control of the situation and stamp it out before it got out of hand.

At that moment, an excited Braun appeared at Schroder's shoulder. He then manoeuvred himself behind a vehicle to try to work out where the shots were coming from and what the strength of the opposition was. The Greyhound wasted no time. He had had a terrible night's sleep and an even worse start to the day so he was more aggressive than usual thanks to Danuta. Today was a bad day to take a shot at him!

"Cover me!" he yelled to Schroder, and he was suddenly gone. With bullets pinging at his heels he sprinted across the road and made his way around the rear of a storage unit and up onto the roof, where he got a clear look at the surrounding area. He could only see one tower from his vantage point, and the body of a guard was draped out of a window. The second guard was missing. It was then that he saw the two men in striped pyjamas doing something at the base of the tower. They were going to blow it up! He picked them both off in quick succession.

From his position above the storage unit, Braun could see little telltale puffs of smoke every time one of the perpetrators fired a round. He figured that the insurgents were unfit and inexperienced; many of them had probably never fired a rifle before and their aim was haphazard at best. From what he could tell, they were disorganised and disjointed, and it did not take long before he put a plan together in his mind, which started with him lobbing a grenade through the open window of an adjacent building.

It made sense that the combatants would have limited supplies of ammunition, which was soon confirmed by their sporadic gunfire. A standoff of sorts developed. Then, from inside a hut opposite, one of the rebels waved a hastily constructed white flag and with five others behind him, stepped into the road shouting "Nicht schiessen, don't shoot, nicht schiessen!" Braun took the top off his skull with one bullet, splattering his brains over his misguided colleagues behind him. As he collapsed, his pathetic little flag fell onto his face and turned red. Others then reluctantly stepped out from behind their barricades and hiding places. Weapons were thrown to the ground, hands were raised, the rebels were herded up. It was over almost before it began, thanks to Braun.

The uprising at both camps had been a great shock to the Germans.

How the prisoners got hold of their weapons no one knew, but it seemed likely that the explosives they used had come from a munitions factory outside the main gates at Auschwitz. A huge disagreement developed when Fischer blamed Hoess for poor security and Hoess blamed Fischer for providing him with a labour force consisting of thieves and rebels.

Fischer was clearly distraught over the whole affair. He would now have a stain on his record and after the damned war was over and with a New Order in place, he would have to work extra hard to reestablish credibility. All that work! All those years of planning, and for what? The Chief of Concentration Camp Inspectors had already been on the phone and Ober-sturmbannfuhrer Eichmann called personally stating that he expected a full report on the whole regrettable business within forty-eight hours. The Gestapo would assist with the enquiry and there *would* be repercussions. There always was when the Gestapo were involved.

***

Schole's biggest problem was how to make things look better than they actually were. If it had not been for Schroder and Braun, particularly Braun, God only knows what would have happened. At least the surviving rebels had already been hanged.

In addition, one hundred and twenty prisoners had been shot (ten for every German killed or wounded) and three immediate aktions had cleared the two largest huts, which held prisoners who had been at the camp the longest. Kapos and Sonderkommandos also perished in the gas chambers as a precautionary measure.

"The thing is, we must be seen to be handling this decisively, to prove to Berlin that we are aware of the gravity of the matter, Baldric. They will expect to see severe consequences for the prisoners, much more than just stringing a few of them up. Berlin will want to know that security has been tightened. Changes will have to be made, big changes. Privileges removed, punishments increased. The good times are over." Schole was quick to advise. The last thing he wanted was to see his boss's reputation tarnished in any way.

"I know what you are thinking, Fritz, but I find it hard to contemplate such a move. You know, after being such a resounding success—"

"But Berlin will want—"

"I know, I know. Berlin will want to see the withdrawal of benefits. I realise that. I have no choice, do I?" He looked up at Schole, hoping to see some optimism, but there was none.

"If you don't do it, Commandant, Berlin will do it for you, and that will not look good."

"Gott Verdammte. OK. I get it, Fritz. Close the Club!"

50

When Braun unexpectedly arrived home to change his torn and bloodied clothes that day he found Danuta sitting on a suitcase in the hallway of their apartment waiting for Natalka. By some miracle Danuta and Natalka had stumbled upon each other in the market that morning, and Natalka told her about the attempted uprising at Wysznica and Auschwitz. "You have to leave your German boyfriend today, quickly!" Natalka said when Danuta told her about Karl. People everywhere were already talking about the repercussions.

Stefan Rowecki himself had been instrumental in negotiating Natalka's release from the Gestapo after they found her behind the florist shop following the bungled assassination attempt on Eichmann and Heydrich. It had cost a small fortune but Rowecki was aware of how much she potentially knew. Fortunately, he had the right connections and he told her after she was released that if he had not been able to get her out on his terms, he would have had her assassinated inside the prison. Fortunately, she made it out in one piece, and would be forever indebted to Rowecki. She was not to know it at the time, but a chance to repay the debt was not far away.

It was mid-afternoon by the time Natalka and Danuta parted on the day of the uprising. Danuta went straight home and packed her belongings as instructed. "Just wait until I get there with a cart" was the last thing Natalka said. "I will be as quick as I can."

On her way back to the apartment Danuta thought about the trouble at the camp and prayed that Karl was among the casualties, or better still, the victims. But no sooner had she packed her cases and lugged them into the hallway than the front door unexpectedly opened and Karl stood in front of her, battered, dirty and very much unharmed.

She spoke first. "I have to go, Karl. I'm sorry. It's over between us.'" That was all she could think of saying. She had not left a farewell message-there was to be no note. She was just going to disappear. She had thought about staying one last night and making Karl another victim-another dead German to avenge her family's deaths. But Karl was no soft target, even when he was asleep. Living with him had turned her into a tired, anxious woman, and when she caught her reflection in a mirror as she packed, she was shocked by the person she had become.

What on earth had happened since January 1940? Krzys was gone, Grabowski was gone, Slav too and his people. Ania was also gone; she had to stop kidding herself about that and face up to reality. Apart from Natalka, everyone she ever cared for was now dead, and for what reason?

"So." Karl seemed quite calm as he put his keys and crash helmet down then closed the door. "So you think this is the best way to repay me, do you?"

"I don't mean it that way," she said, trying to explain.

But he would not let her speak. It was his turn now. "I took you in and gave you food and shelter. We had some fun too, some good times, did we not?" She knew it was a rhetorical question. "And now, you feel this is the right way to repay me?"

"Karl. It's not meant to be; you and me. Come on now, you can see that, surely?" She was clutching at straws and he had a cold, haunted look about him. He knew Danuta had been snooping around his office checking things out; the ammunition boxes and the safe. All of them crammed with foreign currencies, jewellery, gold and valuables of all kinds. There was no way he could allow her to leave after what she had seen. It was impossible. Of course she couldn't go, at least not standing up and conscious. Never!

"It's not a case of what is meant to be or what is not meant to be between us, Danuta. I simply cannot let you leave. I'm afraid you know too much." His rage rose in an instant and she never saw his right hand until the briefest of moments before his fist smashed into her face. She sprawled across the floor, blood pouring from her nose, her left eye already swollen shut. As she tried to blink away the blood he pulled her up by her hair and slapped her face with the back of his hand, bundling her against the wall. "You see, that's the trouble with you Polish. You never know when you are well off, do you? Why do you think Poland is always in a mess? Because it is a nation full of stupid people like you! If life is so bad with me here you can join your whore of a sister at Wysznica!" A well-aimed punch finally took the breath from her body and the light from her eyes.

Danuta was still unconscious as Karl's motorcycle roared away from the apartment a few minutes later. He had bundled her into his sidecar with no concern for what the neighbours might think. As they powered around the first corner they narrowly missed a small cart being pushed by a beautiful blonde woman with a concerned expression on her face.

51

The failed uprising at Wysznica left a scar that would never heal. Everybody felt the effects, from Fischer down to the lowest of prisoners. Previously it would have been impossible for the prisoners to imagine greater hardship, but a terrible new level of brutality swept through the camp as Fischer realised his attempts to reward his charges had been a waste of time and effort.

The Club had been disbanded and turned into hut two hundred and forty-six, filled with three tiers of wooden bunks, which were soon covered in putrid piss-soaked straw and excrement. The Club women were the occupants, along with others, and the day after they moved in, the rats followed, nibbling at their toes and ears when they slept and stealing hidden crusts of bread from beneath their bodies. Every dark corner seemed to be home to a pair of tiny red eyes. The stench became unbearable by the end of the first week, putrid by the second but tolerable when the third week came. It was unnoticeable by the time week four was on them.

All the women in hut two hundred and forty-six were allocated work in the sawmill. Fourteen hours a day. It would be freezing in the winter and appallingly hot in the summer, when all kinds of bugs were dislodged from beneath the bark of logs they pushed through the giant circular blades. Like those who were already working at the sawmill, Ania soon learned that the tiny crawling insects that initially made her cringe, would eventually have her licking her lips. She quickly discovered what she could eat and what would make her vomit. It was the worst form of protein imaginable, but it kept her alive.

Fischer dwelt on the uprising for months. He was personally affronted by the ingratitude of it all, could not understand how they could be so disrespectful when he had been so generous. "After all," he said to Schole during a moment of reflection, 'Poles and Jews? What are they? They are nothing other than vermin. You show them a little kindness and they bite the hand that feeds them. Believe me, it is a life lesson well learned."

After the initial recriminations and reprisals, Fischer no longer acted like an amiable, bumbling headmaster. Now there was an air of ruthless efficiency about him. A tired, no-nonsense attitude pervaded every decision, and the same spite and brutality that had always been evident at Auschwitz now pervaded every aspect of life at Wysznica.

Summary executions became commonplace. The size of transports increased and huts were overflowing with people wearing the yellow Star of David. Disease and dysentery were rife. The Jewish prisoners had become restless. Gone was the desire to live passively. With many parts of Europe now clear of Jews, Fischer formed an opinion about what was left. "Only the dregs remain, the Jews who would willingly murder their own just to survive another day; the worst kind of Jew!"

It was not unusual now for a hut elder to report several deaths during the night, though rarely were they recorded as suspicious. Homemade weapons proliferated and the hut elders, who had power over life and death within their domain, began taking younger men-boys-as their bed warmers. The rumours of homosexuality and paedophilia became a reality. The huts were no longer the place of sanctuary they once were and when darkness fell, in some quarters, the level of fear and misery increased.

***

Braun had Danuta placed in solitary confinement in the prison block at Wysznica; she had been arrested as a subversive and possible member of the Armia Krajowa. The Gestapo arrived and viciously interrogated her, and much to Braun's surprise it did not take long for her to admit having lived at the apartment at the rear of the florist shop. That connected her to Slav and Grabowski and that was enough for the Gestapo. It was a close call for Karl-he had not been implicated and the investigating officers agreed that he was just an innocent bystander-foolish it is true, but innocent. *You would be best advised to never again mistake your genitals for your brain,* he was warned.

After another beating they left Danuta in a small, damp cell seething with cockroaches and fleas where her cuts festered and her bruises refused to heal. Despite her punishment, her mind remained fixed on the last moments before Karl knocked her unconscious and put her into his sidecar. And it was his last words to her that prevented her from giving up and gave her the strength to resist crawling into the corner of her cell and dying: *If life is so bad living with me here, you can go and join your disgusting whore of a sister in Wysznica.*

Ania was alive!

***

Karl's life was better. It was cheaper to stay at the camp during the week and eat at the canteen. If he wanted entertainment, there was always plenty to do at Auschwitz, which was virtually a town in itself, with a cinema, sporting clubs and a variety of organisations designed to keep the Germans occupied when they were off duty.

As well as the prostitutes who proliferated around the centre of Krakow (if you knew which clubs to go to, and Karl did), at Auschwitz there were plenty of women working in the canteens and officers' mess. But it was the female guards and nurses that Karl chased. Many were hard-faced, brutal women who enjoyed either inflicting pain or watching it being meted out, and they were not averse to the kind of nasty sex that Karl enjoyed. It was true that the Polish whores were better looking, but they were always on the take, wanting to stay the night, wanting this, wanting that ... always wanting.

When at home in his apartment, Karl hid away in his small office, like a pirate with his treasure boxes at his feet, drinking copious amounts of beer. With transports in excess of eight thousand units arriving almost on a daily basis, they provided on average, six thousand pieces of luggage a day. And all those bodies, all that clothing, those cavities and so many teeth...

It seemed that things were breaking down on every front in Europe and it was just a matter of time now. A few months perhaps, no more. Karl knew that the last thing Berlin wanted was for their troops to tune in to Edward Morrow and hear the truth. It may have been a crime to be a German soldier listening to the BBC, but it was stupid not to.

When the war was over, what then? A house in the country was first on the list, and then he would find himself a good German wife (no more Polish women), have a couple of children ... and why worry about work? He realised that money bought a great deal more than possessions, the most important thing being time. There was no doubt about it, Karl Braun, the Greyhound, the no-good dumb kid at school, was now rich beyond his dreams.

As well as planning for the future, Karl liked to listen to the radio.

52

Danuta woke to the sound of her cell door opening. She had no idea how long she had been in the tiny cell or how much time had passed since they took her out for her last beating; a couple of weeks maybe, a month? The Germans had given her just enough soup to keep her alive-why?

She was certainly in a bad way, barely able to breathe at times. Her nose had been broken during the first interrogation and her eyes were now so swollen she could barely see. In addition, her top lip was split, and her face was covered in sores, caked with dried blood from the beatings.

Despite the fact that her clothes were saturated with excrement and urine, Danuta failed to notice the vile smell any longer. Her only company had been the cockroaches that scampered over any bare flesh looking for an opening to deposit their eggs. She no longer cared where they crawled, as she lay in her own shit and vomit, sometimes delirious, always muttering, praying and shivering. During rare times of clarity of thought, Danuta dreamed of the old days in Zwinbrzych with Cabbage on the bed as she and Ania talked long into the night. She refused to allow herself to cry in that cell, and somehow she always found the strength to hold her tears at bay. To fail would have been the end of her because she knew that when she was finally empty of tears she would also be empty of the will to live.

There was only one reason to stay alive, and that was for Ania. From what Karl had said, Ania was at the camp somewhere. If only she could hold her precious little sister once more, she knew the pain would go away.

"Out, bitch! Schnell, schnell!" The guard was shouting, a handkerchief covering his face. He did not want to touch Danuta's filthy body, as the stench was already too much to bear. When he realised she could not stand, he had no choice but to help her to her feet.

Holding the crook of her arm so she could gain her balance, he pushed her against the wall, his knee in the small of her back to keep her upright as he pulled her arms behind her body and secured them with handcuffs. Finally, he pulled a hessian sack over her head and she felt strangely comforted by the earthy smell. The guard led her through a hallway, reluctantly taking her weight as she hobbled blindly towards the defused light in the distance. The journey seemed to be never ending, with the muzzle of the guard's gun pressed against her spine as he cursed about her stink under his breath.

One of the guards, a vindictive young man with chronic acne, had told her about the Death Wall when she was first taken to her cell. The number of executions there, the blood that had been spilled in the last few years-he told her all about it and laughed at the misery that had been dished out there, the fear when people stood in front of a firing squad, how they pissed their pants; some even shit themselves! Danuta refused to give him the pleasure of showing fear. Why would she when she never felt it?

She was finally manoeuvred through an open door into the courtyard behind the cellblock where the worst political prisoners and dissidents were housed. It was a dull, overcast day but some light managed to filter through the heavy grey clouds that hung low above the surrounding rooftops. Danuta's legs finally stopped working. They were too heavy to put one in front of the other, so the guards dragged her across the courtyard, leaving deep gouges in the freshly raked surface. They dropped her when it appeared they were at the journey's end. She knew she was not alone, kneeling in the gravel. She could sense someone close to her-facing her, in fact. She could hear their breathing.

And then Braun spoke. It was if he was in a distant place, not just a few feet away. Danuta was now deaf in one ear with only partial hearing in the other, but somehow she recognised his voice. Braun was relieved that his little dalliance would soon be over. He should never have got involved with the bitch in the first place. Schroder had warned him. Polish women? They were bad news. Christ! She had actually admitted knowing members of the Polish resistance during her interrogation-he had had to talk fast to convince the Gestapo that he knew nothing of her past life. She was just someone to cook and clean, someone to fuck. Thankfully, Schroder spoke up for him, and it was Schroder who actually issued the warrant for today's little ceremony, thank God.

Danuta was suddenly blinded by a burst of light as someone wrenched the sack from her head. She turned away, blinking rapidly. In the cell her eyes seemed to be glued shut by the congealed blood and muck that was stuck to her face, but now they were open. She squinted, blinked again, tried to focus through the swelling and the pain. Her vision gradually returned, as if she was inside a goldfish bowl full of dirty water, looking out.

And then she noticed the shape of a person kneeling in front of her, on the wet gravel. That's all it was to begin with, just a shape, but eventually Danuta's focus briefly came into play and she realised the shape belonged to a woman. She stared at the woman, and the woman stared back-a question immediately appeared on both their faces. Despite the pain when she squinted, Danuta was able to see more clearly. The woman in front of her did not appear as malnourished as the majority of prisoners at the camp, there were no scabs, bruises or swellings on her face. And she had long black hair-her head had not been shaved for some reason and even though she looked weary, she was not yet worn out. This woman was different yet familiar. Very familiar, and she was staring back at Danuta with equal intensity, her head tilted to the side, eyebrows forming a deep 'V'.

There was a jolt of recognition, as the woman with black hair was suddenly able to see through the blood and bruises of the broken person in front of her. She blinked several times, shook her head and looked up at Braun. *Tell me I am wrong; tell me it is not her. Tell me!*

Braun looked smug. He already knew what the dark-haired woman now knew, and he watched through cold eyes as her shoulders heaved and she raised her hands towards the heavens and cried aloud, "Please, dear God, please, no!"

Braun had stepped behind Danuta, the Luger with the gold inlayed greyhound carved into the handle in his right hand. He let the women stare at each other for a moment longer. Trembling all over, the one with the dark hair slowly reached forward and stroked the other's cheek, wiping away the tear that had slipped down her battered face. The beautiful dark-haired woman was also crying, and in that brief, fleeting moment, Danuta's vision somehow cleared and she managed to open her swollen eyes long enough to clearly see who was in front of her.

It was then she heard Braun's voice for the last time. "Say goodbye to your sister, bitch." And in that exact moment the courtyard was filled with a loud explosion. Danuta's head jerked backwards and a plume of blood arced into the air like water from a burst pipe. She heard the unusually melodious clink of the shell casing being ejected as she slumped forward, blood pulsing from the hole in her skull. With her hands still tied behind her, Danuta remained on her knees, her legs folded beneath her body and her head slumped on her chest as if she were praying, and the last gasp that came from her body carried with it one word: 'Ania'.

53

Tina disappeared within ten minutes of Schole arriving with the message from Berlin, advising Fischer that it was time to evacuate the camp. One minute she was there, the next she was gone! Her wardrobes still contained most of her clothing but her jewellery, bags and handmade shoes-the expensive gifts that Fischer had given her over the years—were missing. Other things probably disappeared too, but this was not the time for an audit. Fischer had no idea where Tina had gone or how she got out of the camp, and his hurried enquiries were met with blank expressions. But right now he had more to think about than her whereabouts.

The instructions from German High Command were plain enough. Make sure there were no survivors; all prisoners were to be marched to Auschwitz to join the forced evacuation west. Fischer had been provided with a detailed exit plan that looked as if it had been prepared some months in advance. It even told him how to protect himself if he was captured. It was crucial that no secrets fell into enemy hands because this was not the beginning of the end or a retreat, the instructions said; it was a matter of regrouping.

Fischer told Schole to organise the immediate evacuation of the prisoners; just leave a few trusted men behind to destroy camp records and process any stragglers unable to join the march.

"Mein Commandant, what about you? What about *us?*" Schole had a strange expression on his face-not one of an administrator concerned about security, more a nervous child. "Mein Commandant?"

Fischer managed to hide his annoyance. He did not want to spook Schole at this stage.

"I will be fine, Fritz, and you'll be fine too. You're coming with me! Things are already in place; I started preparations some time ago after discussions with Hoess. As much as I have always despised that poisonous dwarf, we will forever have something in common. At this moment I need you to start the evacuation so I can attend to things here." Schole felt a sudden rush of pride in the reassurance; it was good to see the commandant taking control of the things.

As Fischer rushed into an adjacent room to gather documents from the safe, he continued shouting instructions through the open door. "Get a small team together, Fritz, no more than five men. Keep a dog or two here as well, that will help. Report to me in fifteen minutes. Come now, on with it quickly, schnell, schnell!"

Schole clicked his heels together and slipped into gear. Right now he had to find someone capable of carrying out the commandant's instructions, without question. Someone he could trust implicitly.

***

Schroder chose his team. The orders were clear enough. All documents were to be destroyed; every scrap of paper was to be burnt. All surviving prisoners were to be executed except for a handful of the disabled and diseased-*those who clearly only had a few days to live.* Leaving them around would help give the appearance that the remaining guards were assisting survivors. It would stand them in good stead when the camp was liberated-that was assuming they were unable to get away themselves before the enemy arrived. *Kapos, Sonderkommandos?* Schroder was to keep a few trusted men until the end, then process them as well; there were to be no witnesses.

With the evacuation underway, Schole ran back to Fischer's house. Fischer knew that even though the words 'war crimes' had not been mentioned in the message from Berlin, there was no doubting the implications that he and Hoess had repeatedly discussed in recent times.

An hour later Fischer was outside the administration block, comfortably seated in his Mercedes staff car, along with his driver and Schole but without Tina, who was still missing. Schroder was standing stiffly to attention by the side of the vehicle, his uniform immaculate, jacket fully buttoned to the neck, helmet gleaming. Fischer issued his final orders through the rear window as two Kapos loaded a hamper and several bags into the back.

Ten minutes later, with a red and black swastika fluttering from the roof ornament, Fischer swept out of the gates of Wysznica for the last time, accompanied by two motorcycle outriders. He felt a tinge of sadness for not being able to complete the job. There were still a large number of units yet to process, and he had no record of how many had already started the march to Auschwitz-that was sloppy and he would talk to Schole about that at another time.

The small motorcade slipped along the slush-covered country roads, past row after row of barefoot prisoners trudging forlornly through the snow. Several times they passed guards dealing with stragglers, beating them with coshes and rifle butts, leaving their crumpled bodies on the side of the road, the fresh white snow now stained with their blood. The guards were keen to get to Auschwitz. For them there would be safety in numbers.

Fischer was busy studying a map in the comfort of the rear seat of his car as it moved smoothly past the snake-line of human misery. A hundred metres further along the road was a 'T' junction with a signpost that clearly said Oswiecim-Polish for Auschwitz- and an arrow indicated a left turn. As they reached the junction, Fischer instructed his driver to turn right.

***

Schroder was busy directing operations back at Wysznica. "How many Kapos did you keep back?" he asked Braun.

"Enough," Braun had no time for conversation as he ushered a ragtag group of anxious-looking men up the stairs to the first floor of the administration block. They were to concentrate their activities there initially, where most of the statistical records and intake details were. During the first few years of the camp's operation, every prisoner was photographed and his or her personal details were recorded in a card index file. It was only after the camp's last major expansion that they decided not to track every intake, and once Scholes' wonderful new plans had come to fruition things changed rapidly. They processed tens of thousands a day. No more tattoos, no more photographs, no more index cards.

As for as those who had already been processed? From the moment they entered Wysznica they only existed in the hearts and memories of their loved ones. They had been reduced to a mere tick or cross on a form affixed to a clipboard; at the bottom of the page a count for each column. There were hundreds of crosses for each tick.

An upstairs window creaked open and Braun yelled down to Schroder, "I'm going to throw things down from here. Stand clear until we finish, then pile it up. One of my men is on his way to the garage for some petrol to use as an accelerant, OK?"

Schroder signalled that all was well and he instructed his Kapos how to deal with the paper and card index files that had already started fluttering down from the upstairs windows.

It was not long before large stacks of files and clumps of cards were piled up. Occasionally a whole wooden filing cabinet would crash onto the ground and burst open. Desks and chairs were also added to the bonfire and within an hour, the first-floor record and archive room was empty.

Schroder and Braun stood to the side as two Kapos scurried around collecting the loose papers that had drifted away during their descent from the upstairs windows. When Schroder considered everything was ready one of the men poured petrol over the top of the pile and a match was thrown. The mound erupted.

After an initial roar from the ignition, the fire quickly settled, allowing remnants of partly burned documents containing the details of hundreds of thousands of lives to rise into the air. They rode up with the heat haze until the breeze took them over buildings, across the camp. There they joined with the ashes of the dead, which continued spewing from the crematorium chimneys. Human ash and paper cinders, lost lives and their documented remnants fluttered to the ground like gentle grey snowflakes, forever gone but never forgotten.

Braun and Schroder had been watching the fire for several minutes when Braun announced that he was going to have one final look around upstairs before starting on the ground floor. "I want to make sure everything is clear up there."

He was gone for fifteen minutes and returned rubbing his left arm. There appeared to be blood on his sleeve and when Schroder asked what happened he said he had accidentally cut himself on some broken glass. It was not serious; nothing to be concerned about when there was so much to be done. But he had an unusual look about him, a nervous edge that made Schroder feel uncomfortable, though he could not figure out why. For some reason, Braun would no longer look him in the eye when they spoke and he seemed to keep his cap pulled extra low over his face.

Braun started to kick any loose cards and documents back into the fire after the draft had dislodged them. He stopped now and again to examine the occasional index card. Schroder watched out of the corner of his eye as Braun discreetly slid one of the cards into the inside pocket of his tunic.

"I'll be back soon," Schroder yelled above the crackle of the fire, and without further comment he vanished upstairs into the administration block, three steps at a time.

***

During the confusion as the Germans rounded up any prisoners capable of walking to Auschwitz, Ania and Zofia managed to hide deep inside hut two hundred and twelve. This was where the old and infirm women were situated until it was deemed to be at capacity, then there would be an aktion and the whole lot would be herded down to the gas chambers. Schroder had decided it was impossible to march the women from this particular hut across the road, let alone to Auschwitz, and he said he would deal with them later. They were hardly going anywhere!

Ania and Zofia had arrived breathless and anxious as they searched for a last-minute hiding place. The most putrid stench imaginable engulfed them, but they managed to control the urge to vomit and stepped through it. There were several holes in the roof at the far end of the hut, which allowed snow to enter and pile up against some of the bunks. The holes also provided enough light for them to realise that most of the bunks were occupied. Haggard grey faces peered out at them, three or four in each level.

The frail old women looked like witches from a Hans Christian Anderson fairy tale. A withered hand mysteriously started waving and a cackling voice called out, "Here, quickly. Up here!" Ania and Zofia obeyed without question and vanished into the rancid depths of the hut.

Outside, all was panic: urgent instructions shouted by the Germans, gunshots, dogs at the leash, barking and snarling. Added to that now, close by, the sound of truck engines, massed feet tramping through the snow, a motorcycle coughing and backfiring; all kinds of sounds that said things were happening! *Rouse, rouse!*

Just one hour later outside the hut, everything was quiet except for the eerie sound of the cold wind whistling around corners searching for life. A light dusting of snow had fallen but it stopped just as quickly as it started, as if it too were unsure if it should be there. For now just the cold breeze remained and the only detectable movement inside hut two hundred and twelve was the strangely anonymous blinking of huge expectant eyes from the shadows deep within the bunks. Everyone was waiting. But for what?

What was going to happen next? When would the next roll call be and who would carry the dead outside so they could be counted and ticked off the list on the guard's clipboard? The hut elders had to report the deceased as well as those still alive, and they hated the job. Bodies were carried out as proof that they existed and it was hard work, standing there in the early morning cold as the Germans attended to their paperwork.

There was only one thing worse than roll call. Aktions. The Germans appeared to impose them on an arbitrary basis but there was in fact, nothing random about them. Someone actually read all the reports, and they knew which hut had the greatest number of sick, frail or aged. And every so often, an aktion would happen just before morning roll call: a rush of activity, flashlights like lances piercing the dark. In would go the Kapos, accompanied by snarling dogs, as the German guards stood outside smoking and talking. The sick and the elderly, and those deemed incapable of work were dragged from their bunks by their arms, their shoulders, their hair. Wrenched out rudely and dropped onto the cold compressed dirt floor where they were beaten mercilessly before being thrown outside and left to pick themselves up and stand in line.

Frantic screams came from the ones who suddenly decided they were now fit to work. "Not me, I can work, I can help, let me make my own way outside, let me!" But the genuinely sick were pleased to go. Their time had come, and they were so very tired. The end was on its way at last, thank God. *Make it quick for me please, Lord, make it quick and clean.*

Ania and Zofia stayed hidden inside their lice-ridden nest with several old ladies silently watching over them; their last act of decency within an indecent world. As the gloom of the afternoon moved in, more faces seemed to appear at the end of the bunks. No one spoke. *Could they speak?* No one smiled. *Could they smile?* They just breathed softly and blinked those huge round eyes. They saw everything yet there was nothing to see. They were waiting for whatever came next; and the Germans, the ones who always determined what *would* happen next. Where were they?

54

Fischer had two black and white striped prisoners' uniforms in the boot of his Mercedes, secretly commissioned a few weeks previously. Schole knew nothing of them. There was also a hamper containing food, some superb cheeses, brandy, an excellent bottle of French Champagne, some glasses and blankets. In the back seat, alongside the commandant, a briefcase crammed with various denominations of foreign currency, his smoking paraphernalia and several maps.

As the vehicle slowly rumbled along, he busied himself with various top-secret memorandum and dictates issued by German High Command: *only to be read when authorised.* In an inside pocket, a handgun, and in the left-hand pocket of his jacket, his fob watch.

The contents of the vault had been removed the previous night under Schole's supervision. He was the only one who knew its new location apart from the Kapos who had loaded and unloaded the trucks, but they had since been 'urgently processed'. Schole could not help but smile at the thought that he was the only person in the whole world who now knew where the commandant's treasure haul was located, and how to access it. He was safe. He had a future.

In his top pocket Schole kept a small notebook, and written in the notebook a seemingly random address-the location of the commandant's fortune. If someone stole the book or it accidentally fell into the wrong hands, they would have no idea what the address meant. As a precaution, it was also locked in Schole's memory. Should the notebook be lost, the only person in the world that Schole would give the address to, was the commandant-his commandant.

Shortly after the right turn at the signpost, the two motorcycle outriders were ordered to circle back and catch up with the guards and prisoners on their way to Auschwitz. Now there was just the Mercedes with the driver and Schole in the front seats, and their lord and master in the back with his maps, diaries and paperwork.

Fischer took a brief moment to look up from his documents and study the road, calling to the driver, "Hans, pull over there, in that clearing ahead, and open the boot!" The car purred to a halt on the side of the dirt road and Fischer indicated that the motor should be turned off. Fortunately it was not snowing and by the time he reached the rear of the car, the boot was already open and the driver was standing to attention awaiting further instructions. The commandant rifled through the picnic box, appearing moments later with a chicken leg between his teeth, a bottle of fine French Champagne and two glasses in his left hand.

Only two glasses.

The driver watched as Fischer popped the cork of the Champagne bottle and inside his heart he felt a little aggrieved. Surely the commandant could at least share a drink with him at this late hour. After all the loyalty he had displayed during the last four years, being at his master's beck and call twenty-four hours a day, seven days a week, transporting him safely across Poland on so many occasions? He even drove him to Berlin several times a year because Fischer hated flying.

And that stupid girlfriend of his, that Titsy Tina who used to sit in the back seat pouting, ensuring he could see her chest in the rear view mirror while he drove her to Krakow or Warsaw on another extravagant shopping trip. After all the shit he put up with, surely he deserved just one glass of French Champagne with his boss.

The driver heard the pop of the cork but failed to hear the click of the safety catch, moments before Fischer shot him in the back at point blank range.

Fischer seemed totally unmoved as he stepped over his loyal driver's body. He took a final bite from the chicken leg and threw the remains into the adjacent bushes before handing Schole a lead crystal glass and filling it with Champagne, as if they were enjoying a day at the races.

Schole accepted the glass and tried to act as if the driver's killing had been no big deal. He reasoned it out quickly enough, and realised why it had to be that way-so there would only be the two of them left: him and the commandant. That was the reason; of course it was! He was happy to be the only one in Fischer's life now, the one he depended on. The only person the commandant trusted enough to keep by his side. It now seemed not to matter that Fischer was changing the order of the things they had discussed prior to the evacuation. He was the commandant after all; everything was fine.

Ten minutes later, with the bottle half empty, Fischer took a bag from the boot and excused himself, stepping behind some bushes, where he hastily removed his uniform. He kept his long winter undergarments on, and squeezed himself into some striped pyjamas. He was now one of the zebra people.

Fischer had recently secretly ventured into the stores and selected two sets of brand-new striped pyjamas. The largest suit he could find was much too long in the leg and a little too tight around the belly, but the Jewish tailor he kept from one of the early transports managed to do a reasonable job modifying it. It was still a little tight, but it would do.

With the new zebra suit on, Fischer's alibi was ready: *He had only been in the camp for two days after having been wrenched out of his place of work in Krakow and accused of racketeering by the Gestapo. He was a trader and the war had been good to him; he thrived because of the black market—that was until the damned Gestapo took him to Wysznica.* That would explain his somewhat healthy disposition compared to other prisoners'. Fischer's story was so convincing he almost believed it himself!

Fischer felt his well-practised Polish accent was just about passable now, and the only gap he could see in his plan appeared to be a lack of documentation. But then, was that so unusual? He could always say the Gestapo had taken his papers, couldn't he? Yes, he would say that. He was confident that with a fair wind and a bit of luck he might just get away with it. That was why he let Tina run; after all, the last thing he needed was someone around who might disclose who he was in an effort to save themselves. She knew all about his secret stash of treasure, his pension, but Schole had moved it so now she could not prove a thing-she did not matter.

Anyway, her time would come, and it would come very quickly. Retaliation against known collaborators like Tina would be swift and merciless. Just like Fischer and all members of the SS, she would want to keep a low profile.

Fischer finally stepped from behind the bushes, a prison blanket around his shoulders to keep out the cold. "It's bloody freezing, Fritz, go and get changed now and hurry up about it. I left a pair of pyjamas back there in the bushes for you. We will burn our uniforms together. I think I have some brandy stored away somewhere, some good cheese too. We might as well be comfortable before we set out, don't you think?"

The British were known to be 'gentlemen' even during times of war, and Fischer knew they would treat decently any prisoner (or anyone they assumed to be a prisoner) who had managed to escape the confusion of a German evacuation from a concentration camp.

Fischer also knew the British were not as clever as they thought. He was convinced he would get away with his little plan because they had all those Jewish bodies to keep them occupied. The worst that could happen to him was the Russians picking him up. He would have to duck and dive a bit to avoid them or he could end up in a death camp himself-if he was not randomly executed on the side of the road first. As Fischer saw things, the Russians were his main risk, but what choice did he have?

He was going to remain under cover until a unit belonging to the British military came along. It could be a lone car, a tank or even a convoy, who knew, but if anyone could pull the wool over British eyes, it was Baldric Fischer!

Schole had already made his way into the bushes, slightly tipsy from the Champagne and strangely intoxicated by the possibility of a future with Fischer. The commandant seemed to have it all planned; he had even got him a pair of those dreadful striped pyjamas so they could be liberated together!

Fischer seemed to trust Schole implicitly. Maybe he was pleased that Tina and Ania were out of the way; a part of the grand plan? The commandant had been distancing himself from everyone except Schole recently, although Schole had noticed that Fischer and Hoess had been as thick as thieves, dining together at least twice a week, and phoning each other daily.

Schole had managed to read a personal note that Hoess had sent over by courier just two days ago. He saw the word 'tribunals' but Fischer snatched the letter off the desk and put it in his inside pocket when he realised that Schole was trying to read it upside down.

Back in the bushes, as Schole hopped around on one leg trying to pull his pants over his boots, he heard the whoosh of the car as it burst into flames. There was an eruption of thick black smoke and he could smell the fumes as a huge balloon of fire mushroomed into the air. The heat was intense and there was no mistaking the sound of breaking glass and crackling foliage as he finally managed to manoeuvre himself into the ridiculous zebra clothes.

As he pulled the jacket over his head his fingers ran along the edge of an extra piece of fabric, a patch sewn onto the jacket. It was a triangle made from pink fabric, stitched to the left side of his chest. The blood drained from his face. His mind raced to a million places but before he could gather his thoughts he heard a branch snap, and when he turned to investigate he found himself face to face with Fischer, who was pointing a gun at his head.

"Commandant!"

"Relax, Fritz, relax. You'll be fine. Everything will be OK. I just want your notebook with the location of my little pension fund." Fischer sounded calm and friendly. But he had a gun. And his eyes were cold and black. His mouth tight. "I want that address, Fritz, and don't mess around, OK?"

"It's in my uniform jacket, Commandant; I haven't hidden it from you. I have never kept anything from you," Schole said, as he ran his fingers over the pink triangle on his chest.

"I know Fritz. That is the problem, you see. Perhaps you should have kept some things from me, don't you think? Anyway, for now, I just want the notebook. Throw it over to me, there's a good fellow."

Schole reached down and fumbled through his jacket but his eyes never left Fischer's. He knew that somewhere in his uniform was his service revolver, but he realised he wouldn't have a chance if he made a grab for it. But why should he worry? This was ridiculous. Everything was going to be fine; after all, the commandant had provided the zebra pyjamas he was now wearing, hadn't he? He would not want to harm him, would he? But why had Fischer felt the need to ask for the location of his pension fund under such duress? Why was he threatening the one person who always championed his cause? Schole found the notebook and threw it across the gap between them.

"Thank you, Fritz." With the gun still in his hand, Fischer flicked through the pages and stopped at one that caught his eye. He held it up and turned the book towards Schole. "Is this the address?"

"Please, Commandant. Please." Schole pleaded but Fischer waved the gun at him dismissively. He didn't have time for all this, Schole could see that. "Of course Commandant! It's written in reverse, that's all."

Fischer stared at the page but remained silent, a puzzled look on his face. Schole spoke again. "The street address, Commandant, it says number 1201 Onzrowaj?"

"Correct."

"The actual address is actually number 1021 Jaworzno. It is in reverse, like I said." Schole raised his eyebrows. "The town is correct, Krakow, but the street name has been reversed."

"What on earth for, why would you do that?"

"To keep your future secure, commandant. No other reason. I told you about it, didn't I; we have no secrets between us, Baldric. Not after all this time."

"There is one secret, Fritz, and it is yours. Or should I say, you *thought* it was yours?" Fischer waved his gun at the pink triangle on Schole's chest.

Schole felt his face redden. "When did you know, Commandant?"

"Do you think I am blind? I always knew, you damned fool. That is why I have to do this." Before Schole could say another word, Fischer calmly pumped four shots into his body and watched him fall to the ground, bleeding profusely from his chest and shoulder.

Schole coughed painfully and a dribble of blood formed at the corner of his mouth. "Why, Commandant? Why have you done this?"

Fischer stood above him. "There is no room for people like you in the New Order, Fritz. Do you think for one moment that the Fuhrer will allow you to continue your life the way you want when I go to Berlin, to the bunker? He hates people like you. He does not differentiate between perverts or subversives, you know that. You disgusting fucking queers have no place in our world, Fritz, the Fuhrer has always made that quite clear." Fischer raised the gun a final time and again discharged two shots into Schole's body.

A look of disbelief spread over Schole's face as he looked up at Fischer. He closed his eyes and muttered, "Mein Commandant..." then was gone forever.

Fischer shrugged. He had left it too long to deal with Schole, but the man had a fine mind and was the best administrator in the Reich. What a waste.

He looked at the gun in his right hand, heavy but trustworthy, a relic from the first war; an English Enfield MK1 revolver, 0.476 calibre. Fischer loved it. Like his pipes and his fob watch, another little luxury that he treasured, another marker that defined him as the man he was. Most of Fischer's colleagues in the SS sported the latest technology, Lugers or Walther P38s, but not him. They may have laughed at his old Enfield, but he now had a body count of two to attest to its efficiency. But he was supposed to be a prisoner from a concentration camp now; how was he to explain being in possession of a gun? He had no choice other than to hurl the weapon as far as he could into the forest, along with the remaining ammunition.

For a brief moment, Fischer felt strangely vulnerable, stripped of his power and authority and now unarmed. He was no longer making life or death decisions, and there was no one running around in circles to please him. He had no quotas to fulfil, no budgets and no schedules, no one to report to yet in a strange way, he also sensed freedom.

He gathered his and Schole's SS uniforms and placed them over Schole's body, dragged a few more logs and broken branches across the top and went back to a small clearing where he had left one last can of petrol. He tipped the contents over and around Schole's body, and then set fire to it. A large flame whooshed into the air and he shivered, wrapped a blanket around his shoulders, then made his way back through the bushes towards the road to wait for the British.

55

The BBC had been broadcasting details of Allied victories across Europe for several weeks. Allied troops were already inside Polish borders, and the Russians were into Germany at a pace. The end was near for everyone connected with Wysznica. Braun had known for several weeks that he should start thinking about his future. It did not take long for a plan to materialise, and Schroder inadvertently helped when he asked him to stay behind to destroy the camp records, giving him a perfect opportunity to fake his disappearance.

Later, as he looked into the pile of burning files and documents, a face caught his eye. It looked more like a gentile than a Jew but the word Juden *was* stamped on the card in red ink. Braun was certain no one saw him pick it up. The scratchy photograph looked a little like him; scrawny, with a shaved head, high cheekbones and deep-set eyes. A snarl on the corner of his lips too-you could see no fear in this face, only contempt. There was indeed a resemblance between Braun and the person with the concentration camp ID number 27944; the man called Pawel Michalik.

Braun stared at the card for a moment or two before cramming it into his pocket. He then yelled at Schroder that he had to do something then scampered away upstairs.

Braun found that it was not easy to tattoo himself. Instead of scratching, the needle seemed to carve lumps out of his skin. But he soon had the numbers 27944 on his forearm. It was not meant to be a work of art, and a splash of ink would give it some credibility. Then he decided to rub the whole thing with a handful of dust from the floor. That pretty well stopped the bleeding. The next thing he needed was to find a set of hair clippers.

By the time he returned downstairs to the fire, his cap pulled low over his freshly shaved head, Braun could tell that Schroder was suspicious. *What had the Greyhound been doing upstairs and why was he holding his arm like that? What is going on?* Braun tried to continue as if everything was normal but acting was not his strongpoint. Schroder became increasingly suspicious and he himself then disappeared, leaping up the stairs three at a time, giving Braun a backwards look as he brushed past a Kapo.

It only took a few minutes for Schroder to find the tattoo equipment and the hair in the washbasin. He quickly put two and two together, but by the time he sprinted back downstairs Braun had vanished. The Kapos claimed to have seen nothing; they had their heads down as they toiled at the fire. Where was the Greyhound?

***

Braun had already considered that he might have to do more than cut his hair and scratch a few numbers on his arm. If he was going to dissolve into the remaining prisoners he would also have to alter his complexion. Even though he was naturally skinny he still had to do more to completely fit in with his surroundings. As he ran towards the crematorium, he realised how deserted and quiet it was but he did not have time to waste-he needed a body quickly! The further into the camp he went, the more corpses he found. Skeletal faces stared at him from every corner.

Braun stopped outside a hut with a pile of bodies conveniently nearby. He stripped off his uniform, took a handful of cold dirt from the road and rubbed it all over his naked body: into every crease of skin, inside his ears, between his toes, everywhere. A fetid stench enveloped him and it did not take long for him to note the irony of using Jews' ashes to age his puny white German body and naked scalp.

Time was of the essence, as Schroder would have already started to search for him. Braun stood alone and naked now, teeth chattering and the extremities of his hands and feet tingling as the numbing cold took hold. What next? Clothes! The bodies he found were dusted with a thin layer of snow, higgledy-piggledy, arms locked into legs, heads wedged between thighs, sunken guts, jutting shoulder blades and rib cages, empty eye sockets in pale heads. Some among this pile of dead still wore the zebra pyjamas.

Braun grabbed an arm and tried to pull a body from the heap, but everything was tangled together, like a gruesome puzzle. This arm was connected to that shoulder but the head seemed to belong over there, and the foot that he pulled next was attached to someone buried deeper inside the terrible pile. As he stood for a moment trying to work out what went where, he saw an arm twitch. He watched it slip back into position after he had attempted to pull it away from the tangle-a deliberate movement.

He stepped back in shock.

It was alive!

The arm was alive!

That meant someone was in there, someone in that pile of dead people was still breathing! He pulled another limb, a leg this time, a surprisingly light, brittle structure that seemed to belong to an abandoned string puppet. With two hands he gave it a tug, wrenching and twisting in the same manner as if he were pulling a leg from a turkey roast at Christmas. Something split as he rotated it first one way, then the other and it gave way...

The skin gaped at the joint but no blood flowed. The wound was purple and shocking with stark white bone now disgustingly conspicuous. He released his grip and the limb fell back onto the tangle of body parts. A putrid smell wafted towards him in a vaporous cloud. He turned his head to stop himself retching. This had to be done; he had to find some clothing, but how to tell the living from the dead? Then he wondered how the hell they managed to separate the bodies and their various parts at the crematorium and fire pits before they burned them. Who was still clinging to life and who wasn't? Braun realised it probably did not matter to the Sonderkommandos. A pair of apathetic eyes suddenly blinked at him. They must have belonged to the living arm! Two tiny round opaque eyeballs, set into the deep sockets like caves on a bony face starved of flesh, blinking as if sending a signal in Morse code. They looked upset. *How dare you disturb me here. Cant you see I am dying? Leave me in peace, damn you!*

Braun attacked the pile of corpses with renewed vigour. He put aside his disgust as he rummaged around the remains of those filthy Jews, finally finding himself staring at an exposed body on top of the much-reduced pile. And it was alive. He tried to remove its striped jacket but amazingly it resisted with a piteously laboured attempt to retain some dignity.

Braun yelled. "For God's sake, let go, let go!" And before he knew what he was doing he felt his fist connect with the fragile face in front of him. It was like punching a piece of wood. There was no cushioning beneath the skin because the flesh was gone. It was all over before it began. There was no battle between the two parties, no seesaw struggle, no fight back. Braun quickly stripped the body and dressed himself in its stolen, striped costume, oblivious to the stench coming from the obdurate fabric. The head he had punched was laying at a strange angle to its body, still alive, a large bony lump having risen beneath the cheek under its right eye.

A wave of disgust swept up from Braun's belly and he vomited loudly on the floor. He wanted to kick the head and its intermittently blinking sorrowful eyes, to stamp on it, to jump up and down and smash it to a pulp, but then in the background, somewhere not too far away, he heard the sound of baying dogs. The afternoon light was beginning to fade. Shadows crept from beneath huts, stretching across the roads like a seeping liquid looking to swallow any remaining light patches on the ground. It was usually the wind that brought the night at this time of year, but now there seemed to be something far more sinister going on.

No one wanted those shadows to fall on them more than the remaining bodies that were still clinging to life. They knew that the crippling cold would take them with it when it disappeared as the morning sun returned the next day. The shadows were about to gobble them up, the night would suck the life from them and leave them where they lay on their abandoned, human rubbish tip, staring into space, no longer blinking. No longer waiting.

Braun estimated the dogs were about four blocks away, straining at the leash by the sound of it, chasing his scent. He found his discarded uniform, ran around the corner to the crematorium and threw it into an open oven where three skeletons crinkled in the bright yellow radiant heat. He paused for a moment and watched the uniform being devoured by the flames.

There were plenty of piles of snow around, but these were not drifts that had been pushed into corners by the cold wind. They were in fact piles of the dead, covered in ashes and snow. Occasionally an arm would protrude where the sun had melted its covering, poised mid-air as if it were about to catch a ball that a child had thrown. Braun stared, almost expecting a body to slowly unfold from the snow and stand up in front of him, shake itself down then casually walk away.

More dust and ashes were needed to help disguise his scent. He ran around looking for a spot where the mud was visible and he rolled on the floor, then patted himself down. The smell of death wafted up again from his jacket, rudely invading his nostrils as he bent to pick up more Jewish ash to scrub into his face. He worked it into his scalp, ears and nostrils until they too were ingrained with the filth and stench of those already gone.

To his right side, just across the way, were more bodies. So many corpses lying around like piles of leaves in autumn. But strangely there was no smell in this place. Perhaps it was the cold that froze it within the confines of the corpses, or maybe there simply was no flesh to rot, just skin and bones and a few eyeballs for the rats to pick at.

He had not noticed the rats at first. Then, out of the corner of his eye something moved from one pile of bodies to the next. Then he saw part of an intestine being dragged like a line of sausages across the ground, and up the side of a building to disappear into the rafters beneath the tin roof of a nearby hut. It was then that he realised the rats were everywhere: pinpricks of red, in pairs, blinking occasionally, watching patiently for an opportunity to allow them to do their disgusting work. He used to enjoy taking pot shots at the rats when he was drunk, but there was no time to reminisce now.

Braun pulled at a pile of skeleton-like bodies a few feet away from the crematoria, one of the neat piles, all laid out ready for placing on the trays that railed them into the flames. The dogs were much nearer now ... He pulled four, five, six bodies quickly aside, his heart pounding, eyes flickering as they scanned the adjacent buildings for any movement. The dogs were howling, eager for their quarry, keen to tear him limb from limb with Schroder looking on-*that will teach the skinny bastard.*

Braun managed to bury himself among the mound of corpses, several beneath, more on top, leaving a small gap between the jumble of limbs and body parts so he could see what was happening around him.

Just as he finished manoeuvring himself into position he saw them bounding around the corner, four dogs straining at the leash held back by two guards-one of them Schroder.

Schroder was screaming instructions, trying to make himself heard above the baying dogs, when one suddenly broke free.

The ground rumbled as the huge Doberman bounded straight to Braun's hiding place. Braun closed his eyes, held his breath, and tried to stop his teeth chattering as the dog started to push its huge head into the pile of bodies around him. He could actually feel the dog's disgusting breath on his face as it wormed in towards him. A deep guttural growl greeted him when he opened his eyes and found himself virtually nose to nose with the massive salivating beast.

56

Walentina Wilk laid a large plate of schnitzel in front of Rolf Schroder. She had been retained to cook until the job of destroying all records and processing the remaining prisoners was done. Schroder now had the added burden of finding the Greyhound, and that would undoubtedly be the hardest task.

Walentina had learned to say the right things to the right people at the right time. Cooking in the officers' mess for three years had taught her that, if nothing else. The staff at Wysznica liked her and her food. She felt safe for the time being, but what did they plan to do with her when the job was finished? She had to keep her wits about her.

"Did you see that fucking dog running around with an arm in its mouth?" Meike Wuttke from the canine unit spoke with a mouth full of food. "It's mad I tell you. It dived into that pile of units by the crematorium and came out with a whole fucking arm! Ran around with it for ten minutes, like the stupid hound it is! We should have

Shepherds, not Doberman. You might as well have a fucking poodle than a Doberman!"

Schroder laughed aloud, emptied his sixth bottle of beer and threw it over his shoulder where it slammed against the wall and shattered into a hundred pieces. "What I really want is a Greyhound, not a Poodle or a Doberman. Where is he, huh? Where is that fucking Greyhound of ours?"

"He's gone to dog heaven I suppose. Vanished into thin air without a trace!"

"I don't think so Wuttke, my friend, oh no. He is still here. I can sense it. I know the Greyhound better than anyone and I have no doubts that the sneaky bastard is hiding somewhere. And I will catch him, you mark my words, Wuttke!"

"So you've caught him? So what? What will you do with his scrawny body then?"

Schroder looked thoughtful for a moment, stuffed some food into his mouth and spoke again. "I am going to kiss him then take him on holiday!"

"You're going to what?"

"I am going to take him away from here, keep him safe, look after him and make sure the Russians don't find him. He has my share of the loot hidden somewhere, and until I get it, he will be safe, I assure you of that!"

"And when you eventually get your hands on your treasure trove, what then?"

"A traitor is always a traitor, my dear Wuttke! Listen, I tell you what, if you find him alive before I do, I will cut you in. How does ten per cent sound?"

Wuttke slurped his beer. "It sounds less than twenty per cent!" His fat cheeks wobbled greedily and for the first time since he joined up and was put to work in the canine division, he was smiling. It looked as if this war was going to have a decent ending after all. "How long have we got do you think?"

"Two days. Three at most, maybe. No more."

"And when they arrive, the Russians?"

"They won't shoot us. We will be unarmed and won't present a threat in any way. I have some Red Cross armbands somewhere. We will be caring for the sick, doing our best to get things ready for the liberators. By then there will be no one capable of calling our names out in a line up. No-one to point at us and tell the Russians what we did."

"Except..."

"...except the Greyhound."

***

Baldric Fischer made his way aimlessly through the frozen forest tracks, feeling cold, vulnerable and very alone. He still had his briefcase but wished he had not thrown his gun away, which was a huge mistake. If he had a weapon now he would not feel so exposed. His war was not supposed to end this way. He was meant to be sticking coloured pins into maps and arranging troop movements from the Fuhrer's side in a warm Berlin bunker, not scrambling over fallen trees in a snow-covered Polish forest. He decided to stop and make a small fire, just beyond one of the larger dirt tracks-as good a location as any to wait for the British.

He managed to find some dry twigs and small branches beneath a tree, untouched by the snow. In the background somewhere, he occasionally heard the distant boom of heavy artillery, then the pop pop pop of a machine gun, but that was all. A deer startled him once and he suddenly started to think about wolves. Did they have wolves in the forests in Poland? Schole would have known.

Fischer had several tiny capsules of cyanide hidden in the seams of his especially made zebra suit and he rolled them between his thumb and forefinger as he sat on a log, wrapped in his brand-new blanket. He did not want to take the cyanide, but the directive from Berlin was clear on that point. Under no circumstances were they to talk about the Final Solution or let vital records fall into enemy hands. But there was something far more incriminating than documents; personal statements. All camp commandants had been given firm instructions that they were not to speak of their roles or any directives they had been given if they were captured. That was what the cyanide was for, to protect the integrity of the Fuhrer's plans. After all, even if Germany lost the war it would only be a minor setback. The Fuhrer would return, stronger than ever, wouldn't he?

As he sat by the crackling fire trying to warm himself, Fischer's mind drifted back to his glory days at Wysznica. The parties, the accolades, all those units he processed-he even gave Hoess a run for his money in the end! Then ... the women. Oh yes, the women. Tina; very experienced and she knew how to please a man, but she was very demanding and needy. And then along came beautiful Ania with her mismatched eyes and that wonderful body of hers. And didn't she learn quickly, wasn't she keen to please? They were great days, great times.

Now all Fischer had to do was get through the next month. Four weeks. That was all he would need to establish his new identity and convince the English that he was a legitimate concentration camp survivor, a victim of the war deserving of a second chance. After that he would collect his treasure, find another Tina or look for the beautiful Ania and give her a second run. He told her he would come back for her one day. It was a promise. He knew that with his newfound wealth and her beauty, even if they lost the war, together they could achieve something great in the revitalised Europe.

He poked the fire with a stick and took another swig from his hip flask, shivering as the cold leached through his scant clothing and started to scratch at his bones. There was no food left and he ached for a fine steak with some of that beautiful mushroom sauce that his cook used to make. There he was with a briefcase full of money by his side, yet he could not buy a decent meal. Life could be so unreasonable sometimes.

As Fischer sat gloomily thinking about his plight, over his shoulder, he heard voices. He dropped his wooden poker, kicked the fire out, doused the smoke and strained to ascertain what nationality the voices were. *Please be English. Please be English.*

There they were again. Loud and clear. This time they were not coming from beyond the bushes. This time they were immediately behind him—two men with guns pointing at his head. In broad Russian they said, "Hands up, you fat pig. Be quick about it or you will have yourself a second arsehole!"

Fischer raised his open palms to the sky and in his best Russian said, "Comrades, please. Comrades at arms!"

***

It was not until it was completely dark that anyone in hut two hundred and twelve moved. Ania heard the ghostly sounds of people moving around, padding about in the dirt, their shadows like a carefully scripted slow-motion ballet as they gathered to whisper in the darkest corners. The dead people were planning something.

"Where are you from?" The toothless old lady who had allowed Ania and Zofia to shelter behind her that day was the first to speak, though her voice was hushed and croaky, her words constructed from dust.

"I will not lie. We were from the camp brothel until the commandant closed it." The old lady had only wanted to know where in Poland Ania and Zofia had come from, before the German outrage began, but for Ania there was no *before.*

"You don't have to justify what you do in times of war, little one. I know what you did, and more importantly, I know why you did it. If I was your age and looked like you, I would have done the same-I would have done more, probably. In such times, you do what you do, no less than that. If that is enough, you get through it, if not...?" She shrugged her bony shoulders like a disconnected string puppet.

Other shadows came forward, manifesting like spectres, hope long ago drained from their eyes. Dreams for the future meant nothing; it was memories from the past they clung to. The old days kept them alive, the hardships they had endured in years gone by, the countless never-ending days of working in the fields with a baby still attached to the breast. During those days they thought that life could never get harder.

Now? Now they wished they were back amongst the luxury of still having their loved ones around them and knowing there would be a tomorrow, no matter how wet, cold or miserable they may be.

They exchanged names, details, ages. One of them had gone to the same school as Ania. She spoke gently, a great effort. "Not the same year as you," the old woman wheezed through dried lips. "I was a year behind you."

Ania stared at her, one year younger but looking fifty years older. "I'm sorry." That was all Ania could think of saying as a wave of guilt washed over her for having had it so good while these women suffered so much.

"It's OK. You know, I heard that last week, your sister died yet it was not that long ago I chased her around the track at school. She won the one hundred metres. She was a gazelle, that one, a gazelle." There was no emotion in the woman's voice; she spoke only of facts, in flat tones. "Yes, she was a freak. And how we hated her, but you know, we hated you more." The woman raised an arm and playfully poked Ania in the breast with a claw-like finger. "You Burczyk girls were the envy of us all; you had everything. Look at you, look!" Her bony hand shook. "There was not a boy in the school who didn't dream of touching your body. Teachers too."

***

The shadow women talked of liberation. If the English came-they would be cared for. But the Russians? The Russians hated the Polish almost as much as they hated the Germans. "The fresh young fruit that still hangs on the tree is what the Russian soldiers will pick first. They are a retaliatory people and they want revenge for their losses. It will not be safe for you two if they arrive and discover that you worked in a brothel. They will see you as collaborators." The old lady paused and looked deep into Ania's face. "So, what do you do, stay or go? You have a decision to make, Ania Burczyk. What is it to be?"

PART 7:
LIBERATION

57

30 January 1945

When the snarling dog shoved its face into the mound of corpses, Braun felt certain his number was up. He thought about jumping out and raising his hands-surrendering to the mercy of his best friend, Rolf Schroder. The Doberman was only inches away from his face, its teeth and gums bared as it salivated, snarled and nuzzled its snout towards him.

Somehow, Braun had managed to locate a loose limb in the pile of bodies around him. He wedged it between himself and the Doberman just as the giant dog lunged forward. With a sickening crunch, the huge animal latched onto the arm and wrenched it from its dead owner's shoulder. Then with a yelp it pulled backwards, and with the arm still in its mouth ran across the road with Schroder and the other guard in hot pursuit like some kind of sick music hall sketch.

It had been a narrow escape, but Schroder and the dogs never returned. Braun waited until the grey sky had turned inky black. There were no sounds and no lights, just the sickly glow from the ovens as their grisly fuel continued to burn down to a fragile white ash that would continue to crumble until nothing but powder remained. He had been lying among the hideous corpses and their partly exposed skeletons for over an hour, and it was only when the adrenaline retreated that he felt the cold and started to shake uncontrollably. As he pushed his shoulders up to make space to slide out from his disgusting hiding place, his eyes fell upon the gaping purple slit where the dog had ripped an arm from one of the bodies. Maggots tumbled onto his cheek and a disgusting stench filled his nostrils as he sprang to his feet screaming. "You disgusting Jewish pigs. You filthy stinking scum!"

Braun sprang from his hiding place, stumbling and gagging as he ran to the nearest hut and squirreled himself into the furthest, darkest corner. Shaking and babbling like a madman, he managed to find a piss-soaked blanket and pulled it up over his body.

The voices in his head stopped and all around was still, the only sound being the thump of his heart and the sound of the wind whistling around the hut. Then out of the shadows, a voice, a strange accent, thick and foreign. "You have ten seconds. Either you move now or you never move again. Ten ... nine ... eight..."

He was out by the count of six and found himself in the centre of the hut, eyes straining to locate the place the voice came from. He had been certain the hut was empty but as he stood between the sets of bunks that ran down each side he realised he was far from alone. It was then that he was suddenly grabbed from behind.

***

"So you never read Charles Dickens you say?" The strange voice had not stopped since the Jews in hut ninety-eight tied Braun's hands behind his back and threw him onto one of the lower bunks.

"Why would I read Dickens? He is English isn't he? I would no more read him than I would read Tolstoy," Braun said sarcastically. "I mean, I tried to read Polish writers first but got no further than Staff, I'm afraid." He had not read any of the literary greats from Poland, but Schroder the librarian had told him about Staff, a great poet, a long-time hero.

The voice continued. "Dickens understood Jews, you see. He wrote about a man called Fagin, and Fagin was a Master survivor among London's Jews. The greatest of all survivors. He would have endured here in Wysznica, or in Auschwitz or even Treblinka! Why do you think the Jews here call me Fagin, eh?" The voice cackled, more to itself than to Braun.

The self-proclaimed Fagin finally climbed down from one of the bunks and stepped out of the shadows. He said he was thirty-five years old when he arrived from the Lodz ghetto, but looked nearer eighty to Braun. He still had a mass of hair and a pointed beard that protruded from his chin in true Dickensian style. But Dickens could never have imagined *this* Fagin's dark eyes, for they hid the worst of secrets: crimes he had committed to stay alive-rapes, threats, bashings, murders even- and all against his own kind.

From the time he took control of the black market in the Lodz ghetto to the moment that Braun stumbled upon him in hut ninety-eight, Fagin was looking for a deal. He had with him two henchmen, who in their day could have meant business; but to Braun, who was still wiry, fit and fiercely determined, they would present no real problems when the time came to overpower them. And now that he knew there was only this Fagin character and the two others to deal with, that time was not far away.

"We survive when others die," Fagin said proudly. "When we are cold, I provide warmth. When we are hot, I find water to quench our thirst. When we are in fear of our lives, I arm us." One of the henchmen waved some kind of weapon in the air. "And when there is no food, I feed us!" He pulled a small tobacco tin from his pocket, opened it and removed what looked like a cockroach, placed it between his disgusting teeth and bit down. A trail of thick yellow pus squirted from the end of the creature and Braun heard a crunch as the man started to chew, his mouth open so his disgusting meal could be seen.

This Fagin, this strange, ridiculous caricature, this survivor amongst survivors-he would not be so easy to take. Not because of his physical strength but because he was so devious. It was obvious from his darting eyes and ever twitching fingers that not only did he always seek the best advantage, he also knew the way out of every situation. Survivors usually did, and usually at someone else's expense.

Braun had never seen Fagin around the camp, even at roll call, and had never heard mention of his name. He was positive he would have heard of a mythical figure with a name like Fagin. Now he knew why Minister Goebbels called the Jews 'Rats'. Rats were famous for jumping overboard before ships sank and even after the bombing of Hamburg and Dresden thousands upon thousands of rats were seen scurrying around the ruins, surviving on human remains, dragging entrails from the shattered bodies of the dead and the dying. Rats somehow always survived, whatever the circumstances, whatever the cost.

Braun did not feel threatened by Fagin; he was more intrigued than anxious. He felt that this filthy creature, with his bearded, dirt encrusted face and bony fingers would never die. On the gallows the rope would break; in front of a firing squad the guns would unexpectedly jam; and if you had him cornered he would disappear in a puff of smoke. The question was, should Braun finish him off there and then, overpower his two henchmen and kill this character once and for all or should he attempt to join forces with him? Was Fagin a step in the right direction or was he an obstacle?

***

The preceding night had been starkly cold, long and wearisome for the remaining German guards at Wysznica. When the morning finally arrived there was no hooter to announce roll call. In the canteen, Rolf Schroder and Meike

Wuttke sat at a table snoring, their heads resting in their dinner plates, surrounded by a large quantity of empty beer bottles. The singing had stopped at around two-thirty. Wuttke was the first to collapse into the remains of his dinner; Schroder, being senior in rank, followed once he was satisfied that he had outdrunk his colleague.

At best estimate the night before, Schroder had worked out that they had two to three days before liberation, which was going to be a dangerous time for them. However, the world would eventually find a new 'normal'. People would have new jobs, businesses would open again, markets would flourish and families would reunite.

Annual reunions would follow for those who survived the conflict and beer would be consumed in great quantities with the volume of lies being all that would exceed it. The war may have been lost by Germany but no one could ever take away the fellowship and good times they had along the way. But was that enough? Schroder would happily trade the prospect of such glorious reunions for a future life in exile-so long as it was luxurious. And it would be if he managed to locate the hoard that the Greyhound had stashed away.

In the early hours of the morning, Walentina Wilk had waited patiently for the two Germans to fall asleep. When she was satisfied that it was safe, she loaded herself up with food and disappeared into the women's camp. As arranged, she went to the hut with the broken flowerpot outside. By the light of the candles she had taken from the kitchen she discovered the dreadful sight of the shattered bodies of the women who had previously agreed to shelter her. They had been waiting in the hut all day, hidden in the far reaches of their bunks, covered in filthy blankets and stinking straw. The other women had been herded out for the march to Auschwitz but six of them managed to hide themselves away. Then two German guards returned moments later and strode up and down the length of the hut, spraying machine gunfire through the bunks.

The six women who had somehow managed to avoid every aktion for the last two years died. Now, at the point of liberation, when the Germans were abandoning the camp, their luck finally ran out.

***

Ania and Zofia slept that night, but the shadow women did not. For the last year they had dozed only during the daylight hours, when the Germans were busy supervising their labour and no longer had time for aktions.

While the few people who remained alive at Wysznica prepared for the arrival of the morning sun, Baldric Fischer was unsure if he should be counting his blessings. Sitting on the snow-covered grass shivering, tied to a tree, he knew his war was well and truly over and his worst fears had been confirmed. He had been captured by two lone Russians, lost in the forest on their way to Wysznica to meet up with their unit.

The Russians had argued between themselves about Fischer, resulting in a bet. One was convinced the commissar would tell them to shoot their suspiciously overweight pyjama-clad prisoner and the other claimed he would want to hold him for interrogation.

The winner? The winner was to get first choice of either the briefcase (which seemed to be full of fake money) or the best-looking woman they found at the next village. And to add insult to injury for Fischer, one of the Russians had actually taken a shine to his pipe and was trying unsuccessfully to light it in front of him. Fischer would have killed him with his bare hands if he could have got to him. Fortunately the Russians had not found his little notebook with the location of his 'pension fund' and he still had his fob watch to bargain with. How far would that get him?

Back in Fagin's hut that night, the Greyhound had taken less than ten minutes to untie his own hands, though he left the rope seemingly in place in case one of his captors decided to take a look. As far as he knew, the Fagin character was not armed but his two so-called henchmen had homemade knives. Braun already had plenty of blood on his hands and killing intrigued him. He liked to see the expression on his victims' faces as he turned the blade or pulled the trigger and he often discussed such things with other SS men. Like his colleagues, when the killing was frenzied and less organised, he sometimes realised he had an erection, and that was the ultimate thrill. It was during these times that he liked to rape; indeed, the night when he bribed his way into Ania's room and raped her he had just got back from the crematorium where he had dealt with several Sonderkommandos who had been a source of annoyance to him for quite some time. They were lazy and talked back to him, overly confident and too sure of themselves. He had taken a bayonet from one of the guards and set about the idle Polish bastards with gusto. What made it worse was that they just stood there as he ran them through! They surely did it to anger him, because that was what Poles did sometimes. They knew they were going to die so they tried to intimidate and humiliate him by going quietly. Braun actually jumped on top of one of them and in a moment of frenzy, almost severed his head. He felt as if he was going to burst as he ran amok that afternoon, and when he eventually shook himself free of the devils inside him, he found blood all over his tunic, bits of intestine and brain matter on his leggings, dead Sonderkommandos and Kapos everywhere. That was when he decided to bribe his way into Ania's room and it was lucky for her that he was interrupted when the fat driver visited Emilie that night...

Fagin's two henchmen were asleep now, the sound of their laboured breathing rumbling through the dark hut. Braun was certain he could also hear Fagin snorting and grunting somewhere in the background, but he could not pinpoint the location. All Braun had to do now was stay awake and wait for the faintest hint of light to appear through the partly open door so he could finish them off.

58

The northern gates of Wysznica were already open and the sun had been up less than an hour. It was going to be a perfect, crisp winter day, setting the scene for a typically dramatic entrance for General Leon Martov of the Russian 47th Army when he rode his white charger Dimitri into the courtyard. The ground shook all around; the huge beast pounded the paving as if competing in a Moscow dressage arena. As the horse and its rider made their appearance, skeletonised bodies jerked into doorways and pairs of large saucer-like eyes peered behind grainy windows.

General Martov was triumphant. He stared back at those gawping at him, and with a dramatic sweeping gesture of his right arm, called out in his own version of Polish, "You are free, free to leave. Go when you please. You are free. All of you. Free."

The prisoners who had managed to make it outside stood in confused huddles and stared at each other like stick figures that had to come to life from a child's drawing. *Free? What does he mean, free?*

At the southern end of the camp an equally momentous occasion was taking place, in a far more pragmatic way. A Centaur tank flattened the fence and two open-topped armoured troop carriers followed, stopping beside the gas chambers and crematorium. An eccentric British officer, Colonel Richard Snapes of the 11th Armoured Division, stood in the front passenger seat of one of the vehicles, adjusted his beret and said, "Now then, what do we have here, chaps?"

By the time Snapes had stepped down from his lofty position, his adjutant had a clipboard and notepad at the ready. Within ten minutes, ambulances and medical staff were on the way and sappers were checking for mines and booby traps. "I have a terrible feeling we're going to need some heavy machinery," Snapes said as he looked around at the huge number of corpses. He had the same experience at Bergen-Belsen when he was involved with the liberation there and the only practical solution was mass graves. They were needed urgently, before the snow melted and the warmth of spring started to work on the bodies.

As Snapes studied the maps that had been spread across a table, a huge white horse ridden by a Russian officer came into view.

Leon Martov smiled to himself when he realised that at least twenty British rifles were aimed at him as he made his way towards the person who looked to be in charge, the one wearing the ridiculous hat.

Martov thought his entrance was appropriate, but as the English officer said, it had in fact been *downright ridiculous.* "I mean, after all, what if we had opened fire on you, General? It could have been the start of world war three and we haven't finished mopping up this one yet!"

"If you had fired at me, Dimitri here would have shit on you and your silly little guns and that would have been the end of it. He does not like being shot at and neither do I," Martov replied in fractured English. The two men turned and looked at the rear of the horse, where a huge mound of dung sat steaming on the frozen ground.

"I see what you mean," Snapes said without as much as a flicker crossing his face.

Then the negotiations began, but not before Martov agreed to a cup of tea and Snapes to a shot of the very best ninety-eight per cent proof Russian vodka.

"So you want this one, do you?" the Russian asked, enquiring if the English wanted to claim it was they who liberated Wysznica.

"We gave you the biggest, Auschwitz-Birkenau, didn't we, General? I stepped aside on that one and there will be far more glory for you and yours there than there ever will be for us here. Come now, old chap, you can see that can't you?"

It was true that the Russians' limited humanitarian resources were stretched at Auschwitz. But now that the Red Cross was there, along with others, it had freed Martov to continue through Poland towards Berlin, where other prizes lay waiting to be claimed.

"Here is the deal, Colonel," the Russian said. "You can have this camp, but any SS belong to me. Everything else is yours, including the glory."

Striking a deal about prisoners of war somehow seemed inappropriate to Snapes. After all, there were other more pressing matters such as burying the dead and preventing the spread of disease. Bickering over a few SS guards hardly seemed right. "Let us be realistic about this, General. We all want the Germans brought to justice; we will never disagree on that point. But the method of justice applied seems to be a point of contention between us. Would you not agree?"

"That is true, Colonel, but what you call 'justice', your English definition of it, does not match ours. You have your ways, we have ours. Give me the SS and you take the rest. What does it matter to you? Are you going to carry on squabbling about such petty matters or can I get on with my war?"

***

The light from the open door of hut two hundred and twelve was suddenly filled with the outline of a British soldier. "Anyone here?" The man stepped inside, seemingly oblivious to potential risks from booby traps or enemies lying in wait. Deep within the hut, Staff Sergeant Jim Maurice saw movement among the shadows. "If you're German you had better make yourselves known now, or I shall be forced to toss a grenade in there and you will be coming out far quicker and in many more pieces. Your choice. Hurry up now. Schnell, schnell."

The old lady who had sheltered Ania and Zofia shuffled forward, squinted at Jim Maurice through tired eyes. She called over her shoulder. "It's the British! We are safe. God must be awake at last."

Ania and Zofia climbed down from their bunks and helped the old lady outside where they all blinked at the sky. Jim Maurice stared in amazement as more skeletal figures tottered out of the shadows to join them.

These strange creatures with sad, pathetic faces fell to their knees with their hands clasped in front of them, praying and sobbing, looking up to the cold blue sky. The women from the hut had been joined by a few men from elsewhere and a small silent, confused group started to gather around Jim Maurice, including a naked, emaciated man holding a spoon; another with a battered tin cup tied to a length of string looped around his neck; one whose battered nose seemed to be healed now, like a strange smudge of gristle above his twisted, toothless mouth. On all their faces the same question: *what happens now?*

A naked woman, all skin and bone, suddenly tottered around the corner. Maurice could have circled her thigh with one hand. Every bone was visible when she walked-shoulder blades jutting out like epaulettes, hollow cheeks, flaps of skin where her breasts once were, knees as large as car hubcaps and huge feet with disproportionately long knobbly toes.

She looked at Maurice with a blank expression, a dull gaze; nothing to say. Then she turned and slowly strode away. Every loping step seemed to invoke pain, and she lurched along with peculiar, giraffe-like movements, leaving

Maurice certain that if she stumbled or fell her body would simply rattle apart, leaving a collection of bones on the floor.

Maurice shook himself back to reality and called for more medical staff. It was not long before stretchers arrived. Nurses too, people to care for these fragile creatures who still defied rational description. The old lady who had sheltered Ania and Zofia suddenly collapsed. As she was stretchered away she raised her head pitifully and tried to speak. It was clear that her last moments were not far away. Ania rushed to her side.

"What does she want? What does she need?" Maurice was clearly moved by the woman's condition. She somehow reminded Maurice of his sister back home in Dorset, whose dream of marriage to her RAF fighter pilot fiance fell from the sky just like he did during the battle of Britain. It was the old lady's eyes, her mannerisms, but mostly her stoicism during such adversity that most reminded Maurice of his sister.

Maurice was typical of a British Army staff sergeant: gruff and voluble, a cane under his arm, the peak of his cap highly polished and flat against his forehead. He struck fear into the ranks beneath him and garnered respect from those above. Ania's tiny hand rested on his arm as she whispered into his ear. He nodded then slowly removed his hat, put his cane aside and removed his jacket.

Then he lifted the frail old woman from the stretcher as she had requested, held her gently, careful not to break her brittle bones, pressed her to chest and folded her within his broad shoulders. Her tears came immediately. She was safe at last, cocooned in a man's arms, someone who was not going to let anyone hurt her again. Strangely, she wanted the warmth that came from Jim Maurice even more than she craved food or drink. Humanity was to be her sustenance.

Maurice held her for ten minutes. The soldiers around, men hardened by battle and the dreadful things they had seen, turned aside and gave them space. When the old lady finally said she was ready to leave Maurice tenderly wiped her face and gently lifted her almost weightless frame into the ambulance. The moment stayed with Maurice for the rest of his life, overshadowing the carnage he had witnessed during frontline actions. He spoke to no one of the event, keeping it as a personal moment, one shared with the God he suddenly found after being convinced time and again during this dreadful war that God did not exist.

***

That afternoon a movie camera suddenly materialised and a man in a British Army uniform held a microphone in front of his face and tried to find the words to describe the scene at Wysznica. But how could he capture the stench of disease, the odour of death that permeated the air, the eerie atmosphere. For those liberated, the joy had turned to anti-climax, an emptiness, a void where people knew that time was now standing still to allow Death to finish his grisly task. When the clock eventually started again, it would do so in slow motion for quite some time until those who survived had the strength to pick themselves up and start again. Even the air seemed hollow.

59

The Greyhound finally broke cover and stepped out of Fagin's hut. He had been watching everything from the partially open door before deciding to join the prisoners outside. Some of them danced while others sang and a few found the strength to cry while most just stared into nowhere, seemingly puzzled by the sudden absence of Germans.

Braun left the two henchmen inside hut ninety-eight. He was not sure if they had actually died from the wounds he inflicted on them during their brief struggle, or if they had succumbed to shock. He did not care either way. What did interest him most was Fagin, who had disappeared during the fight. A quick search revealed nothing. Fagin had vanished.

***

After ensuring that Dimitri was being cared for and fed, General Martov decided to look at the suspicious prisoner two of his men had brought in for questioning. The man appeared well fed, and claimed he was an industrialist who had been unfairly arrested by the Germans a few days ago. They had not even had time to tattoo his arm or shave his head, and when they abandoned the camp he managed to escape into the surrounding forests.

General Martov did not believe him. "So, what do we have here? I can see that the Reich ate well while Poland starved! What is your story?"

"An administrator, that is all sir, just a cog in the machine." Fischer meekly changed his story as soon as Martov came on the scene. He was not going to risk trying to bluff a General. He had to play this carefully. One incorrect word and he could find himself hanging from the wrong end of a rope.

Martov playfully rubbed Fischer's belly and burst out laughing. "It must have been well lubricated, this machine." Those around him laughed too, especially the two who had captured Fischer. Martov spoke again. "There are two ways to deal with the likes of you. One will be painful for Germany, the other painful for Russia."

"Painful for you Russians, General? How so?" Fischer tentatively asked.

"Our pain comes from knowing you are still alive, you fat German pig!" Martov's gloved fist caught Fischer beneath his right eye, sending him and the chair he was tied to sprawling across the room. Two guards wrestled the German back into position. "You see what I mean? It hurts me knowing that I didn't split your guts open with a bayonet instead of playing tippety-tap with your ugly fat face."

Fischer did not appear particularly affronted by Martov's comments. Perhaps he was being honest when he said he was just a minor clerk or administrator. "General," Fischer had already regained his composure. "Please, General, if I may. I have a gift that perhaps might help us get along a little better."

"You have a 'gift' do you?" the Russian said incredulously. "I hope it is wrapped."

***

Schroder and Wuttke had missed everything so far, sleeping soundly at their table in the canteen as all the excitement took place outside. Despite agreeing to leave the camp to the British, several Russians had taken it upon themselves to look around for souvenirs. The noise they made as they ransacked the rooms adjacent to the canteen finally woke both Schroder and Wuttke, who instinctively took cover under a table the moment they heard Russian voices.

Schroder scampered across the room on all fours, reached up and turned the lock on the canteen door then made a hasty retreat back to his hidey-hole to decide what to do next. Finding the Greyhound had taken a back seat for now. Staying alive was now the priority.

As the two Germans sat under the table trying to work out what to do next, unknown to them, two Russian soldiers watched their every move through the glass panel of the door to the kitchens.

***

"So, what do we do with you and this wonderful ... what did you call it ... fob watch?" the Russian general asked as he examined Fischer's treasured timepiece.

"You could always accept it with the good grace that officers of the Red Army are famous for," Fischer said. The Russian was amused by the German, who seemingly had a lot to say for a mere clerk. "There is also the matter of my briefcase, General."

"Your briefcase?"

"Yes, General. Your men took it from me, and I have to tell you that it is full of American and British bank notes. I found it not far from where your men and I first became acquainted. I am of the opinion that some high-ranking German official must have abandoned it as he attempted to make a hasty retreat prior to your arrival. There was a burned-out staff car as well, and I think I saw a body or two there but I did not hang around to check it all out. I would like you to keep the money, General, as a gift for you and your lady wife." Martov raised his eyebrows. "There is another thing, General, if I may? My pipe? Is it possible for it to be returned?"

"Your pipe?"

"One of your men seconded it."

"So, you are a pipe smoker eh? Very unusual. An overweight junior clerk, a briefcase full of bank notes, an expensive watch and a pipe smoker to boot?"

"General, in Germany, many working-class people enjoy tobacco this way. It is not so much a matter of status as I believe it may be with the English, but there are many famous German pipe smokers. Beethoven, for instance."

"Ha, Beethoven you say? A pipe smoker? That accounts for his music! So much shit! Terrible. Rimsky-Korsakov, now there was a real composer, and if you gave him a pipe he would not know whether to put it in his mouth or stick it up his ass!" The Russian was in great spirits.

His laughter was interrupted by the arrival of a messenger who whispered in Martov's ear and then departed. Martov turned to Fischer once more. "Back to business, my fat friend. I have decided to give you an opportunity to prove your claim that you were just, how did you say it, a cog in a wheel? What did you say your name was?"

"Schole. My name is Fritz Schole," Fischer said a little too quickly.

"OK, Herr Schole. I presume you have a rank?"

"Of course, General. My rank is that of Rapportfuhrer."

"Wasn't your man Hitler a Rapportfuhrer once, a corporal?"

"No, sir. A corporal is a Rottenfuhrer. A Rapportfuhrer is a humble, lowly rank beneath that of corporal even, though one day I would have hoped to have made my way up to the same exalted status as you. A man should always dream, do you not think?"

The large Russian general laughed expansively yet again. A little flattery never did any harm and anyway, he was enjoying playing with the German. He ordered one of the guards to untie the prisoner. "Come along," he said to Fischer. "Come with me."

Fischer was led through a shattered glass-panelled door into the canteen. On the floor were two German bodies lying in a pool of blood. "My men found these two heroes hiding under a table like a couple of mongrels. I want to know who they are."

"They have papers on them?" Fischer asked.

"Of course," the Russian replied, "but I want to hear what you have to say about them."

Fischer looked at the bodies of Schroder and the dog handler Wuttke sprawled across the floor, riddled with bullets.

"The one on the left, his name is Friedrich; he's the camp commandant's driver. I knew him well. He has false papers though I do not recall whose name was used. I think it was someone from the canine unit."

"And the other one?" the Russian asked, narrowing his eyes.

"You seem to have hit the jackpot, General. He will be carrying the false papers and documents I had been told to arrange for him during the course of my duties. They will show him as Lieutenant Rolf Schroder."

"And his real identity?"

"He is none other than the camp commandant; his name is Obersturmbannfuhrer Baldric Fischer."

60

A few days after liberation, British intelligence officers commenced the task of weeding out any SS members hiding among the prisoners at Wysznica. It was a routine already established and tested in other liberated camps.

It was known that members of the SS had their blood type tattooed beneath their left armpit, a typical act of Germanic efficiency that proved useful in the heat of battle when someone of significance was injured.

All inmates capable of walking were made to pass in front of a medical examiner with their left arm raised. It was easy enough to spot imposters. But sometimes Kapos and Sonderkommandos and even nurses hid amongst the crowd, and they were not so easy to identify; however, they all claimed innocence, insisting they were forced to perform their disgusting duties under threat of death.

The Russian general seemed to be satisfied that Fischer was indeed just a clerk; the humble right-hand man of the camp commandant no less. He was handed over to the British for imprisonment, and would be returned to the Russians in due course, along with any other SS they discovered.

Now the British were checking everyone, and they had a little help from the list they found in a filing cabinet at the camp hospital. It showed name, rank and blood type of all SS personnel at the camp. Fischer did not know for sure, but if his blood type differed from Schole's, who he was pretending to be, his game would be up.

The line moved slowly with one or two near misses, a doubtful suspect here or there because of a strange birthmark or an unusual scar. Fischer had positioned himself towards the end, and several people were already eyeing him with suspicion, perhaps thinking about exposing him to save themselves-he certainly stood out among the crowd.

Braun had managed to change his appearance radically. He was naturally so skinny that his ribs protruded from his chest and his shoulder blades stuck out like coat hangers-he definitely appeared to be a legitimate camp inmate. When he first reported to the British medical team he looked malnourished and reeked of death. The tattoo on his arm, showing the blurred digits 27944, matched the record of the prisoner named Pawel Michalik, whose index card he handed over, stating that he found it among the pile of burned documents in front of the administration block. It all looked genuine. The damaged photograph on the card was a good enough likeness in the circumstances. Braun had done it! He had fooled everyone with his makeover, and luck had been on his side so far.

The biggest test came when he unexpectedly crossed paths with Ania. Fortunately she did not seem to recognise him when they passed each other at the canteen. He realised that his transformation had been successful; with his shaved head, dirt-encrusted unshaven face and filthy zebra pyjamas she seemed to have no idea who he was. But as he stood in the queue now, waiting to pass the identity parade he cursed himself for not doing anything about the tattoo under his arm...

***

As he waited for his turn, Fischer looked at the faces around him. Some appeared as anxious as he felt, and he was certain he recognised one of the women further ahead in the line-a nurse with excellent legs that he would know anywhere. But she did not seem to notice him; perhaps she was nervous. That was good! But there was someone else a few people back, a skinny bastard in a zebra suit, who Fischer thought looked strangely familiar. The man was hollow cheeked, edgy, bony and rat-faced, but Fischer could not quite put a name to him. And he realised he was staring a little too intently because when he looked again, the skinny rat was certainly gawking at him...

***

Fischer finally found himself face to face with a British medical officer, who instructed him to raise his left arm. The officer examined his list and asked

Fischer for his name and blood type. Fischer kept his head down, mumbled something inaudible and was asked to speak up. "What is your name please?"

"Schole. I am Rapportfuhrer Fritz Schole," he replied.

Braun was still trying to think of a way out for himself. He had seen Fischer ahead of him in the queue, caught him staring a few times. Then he heard Fischer tell the British officer his name was Schole. The opportunity was heaven sent! Braun leapt out of the line and yelled, "This is not Schole. This is the camp commandant, Baldric Fischer!"

Someone else joined in. "Yes. It is him alright, it is him! It's the commandant. It's Fischer, this man is Fischer!" The place suddenly erupted.

"He is mistaken. Who is it that who accuses me? Ask the Russians, they know me; I am Schole, Fritz Schole! I have papers, look at my papers!" Fischer patted everywhere on his body in a futile attempt to bluff the British. A soldier arrived at his side and took hold of his arm. Fischer struggled to free himself.

A loud, chattering group started to jostle the fat German, so Braun gave someone a shove. Another prisoner retaliated and pushed the person in front of him. A chain reaction began up the line so Braun stepped into the fray, yelling and elbowing other prisoners as he tried to reach Fischer. Someone screamed at Braun to stop pushing in, so Braun punched him. Several prisoners jumped onto Braun and he found himself sprawled on the floor, still yelling and pointing. "Leave me alone, get the commandant, get Fischer!"

A British officer eventually pulled a battered Braun to his feet. "Can you swear that this man is the commandant of Wysznica?" he said above the melee.

"Of course. I would know the evil bastard anywhere!" Braun said in his best Polish. "Look what he has done to me! Look at me!"

Someone took offence. "Look at you? What about me?"

Braun screamed into the man's face, "Fuck you!" Another punch was thrown. A mini riot broke out and several more British soldiers dived into the melee. Braun took the opportunity to manoeuvre himself into a vulnerable position, and he soon found himself on the ground a second time, rolling beneath the crowd as they surged over him, swearing and kicking, trying to get to Fischer and everyone else.

Eventually things calmed down and the British took control. An officer pointed at Fischer. "Take him to the cells!" Fischer was led away, still pleading his innocence. Braun was wincing and hobbling on one leg. "Are you OK, are you hurt?" the officer asked.

"I think I may have damaged my ankle, someone kicked me. I am still frail after being here so long," Braun replied, doing his best to appear injured. The officer issued another order. "Take this one to the medical tent!" Braun was helped away.

The queue was reorganised. One of the British said, "Now where were we before all that happened?" He looked at the next person in the line, checked under his armpit and moved him along. Within ten minutes, Braun was having his ankle bandaged. The line-up had been forgotten. He was safe.

***

Ania heard later that day that the camp commandant had been arrested trying to pass himself off as Schole, so she made her way to the administration desk, spoke to an officer and asked if she could help. She knew Fischer better than anyone, she said. They told her that the prisoner who had made the initial identification during a procedural inspection was now in the hospital with a damaged ankle-possibly broken. He was going to make a statement in a few days, but they wanted other witnesses, more statements, more evidence.

Ania identified Fischer, and when she stood in front of him he looked at her fondly, hoping to gain some sympathy. He managed a weak smile, a twitch in the corner of his mouth, a glint in his eyes. *Remember the good times, Ania?*

There were no good times for me, Ania thought, and she turned to the soldier in charge and nodded grimly, confirming Fischer's true identity. Fischer bowed his head. This time he knew the game really was up.

***

Three days later Ania received the news that the old woman who had sheltered her in hut two hundred and twelve had died. She had given up and life had fluttered out of her body on gossamer wings. She had departed with the knowledge that her very last act had been one of the utmost decency by hiding Ania and Zofia.

There was confusion about the large number of deaths after the camps were liberated. Surely, now that the people were free the dying would stop? There was no need to die now, was there? But many prisoners could not eat, no matter how nourishing the food appeared to be. The British medical team eventually developed a form of porridge that the shrunken stomachs of the prisoners could actually digest.

The movie cameras recorded the amazing sight of thousands upon thousands of bodies being bulldozed into huge pits, the drivers covering their mouths with handkerchiefs as they attended to their grim task. There were so many bodies tossed and turned, rolled this way and that in a haphazard, undignified manner like broken rag dolls. The whole scene hardly seemed real. A bulldozer to bury the dead?

During the liberation of Wysznica, the charred remains of the camp records and statistics were found in the courtyard of the administration block. They discovered enough partially scorched documents to confirm that Fischer had not quite beaten the astounding record that Treblinka had set by murdering over three hundred and twelve thousand people in a little over one month; ten thousand murders in a single day, every day, for a month.

As he sat alone in his cell, Fischer thought about the news the guard had just given him; he was going to be handed over to the Russians in ten days. Things were going from bad to worse. Fischer's zebra suit had been taken from him and he was now in some kind of British prison uniform. When the zebra suit vanished, so did the cyanide tablets and his opportunity to take his own life. He would soon be at the mercy of the Russians.

But there was hope. There was always hope for Baldric Fischer! The Russian general had sent his pipe back in a moment of weakness, along with his tobacco pouch and matches. The soldier who stole it could not light the damned thing anyway, so he willingly gave it up.

Of course he could not light it! The stem was blocked with diamonds that Fischer had put there himself. Now he guarded them zealously. His notebook with the location of his unofficial pension fund also disappeared with the zebra suit, so all he had left was the diamonds in his pipe. There had to be a way out of this mess now, there just had to be!

61

The Polish Home Army heard about Jim Maurice after Wysznica was liberated. Their local section leader was a beautiful young blonde woman, a Krakow local who deliberately befriended Maurice and gained his confidence. The Armia Krajowa was not officially recognised by the Allies, but it did not take long for Maurice to understand their purpose and appreciate their sacrifices during the conflict.

The blonde woman told him the war was not yet over for the Polish people. Justice had yet to prevail. She told Maurice about the atrocities inflicted by Fischer and his men, the maiming, rapes, the torture and the summary executions. For the blonde woman, the war seemed to be a very personal issue.

"Don't worry about Fischer, he will be dealt with by the Russians in a couple of weeks, you may be certain of that," Maurice told her.

"Believe me, it will not happen," the blonde woman replied. "Your Colonel

Snapes? I have it on very good authority that he will soon be called to London for an important briefing. The Russians will never get their hands on Fischer because he will be transferred to Spandau Prison in Berlin to await trial for war crimes, along with other key SS figures. There is talk that the trials will be held at the Nuremberg Palace of Justice, and many people fear that most of the accused will escape with light sentences."

Two days later, Snapes was indeed called back to London, and on his return he briefed his men about a pending series of trials, the first of their kind ever in the world—crimes against humanity. Snapes' most prized prisoner, the Commandant of Wysznica, Baldric Fischer, was to be transferred to Berlin under special guard to await trial.

***

It was a particularly cold afternoon in February 1945, when Snapes was in Warsaw discussing security for Fischer's transfer to Berlin, that the Armia Krajowa managed to get a small party of operatives into Wysznica. They were disguised as Red Cross inspectors, with fake id's and documentation authorising them to conduct a snap audit. Holding cells were included, and they had authority to interview every prisoner held on suspicion of war crimes to ensure they were being treated according to the Geneva Convention. A few minutes after six that evening, Fischer was found hanging in his cell, a collection of loose diamonds scattered on the floor beneath his body.

No one saw or heard anything suspicious during the audit, not even Jim Maurice, who was responsible for security in Snapes' absence. He was totally exonerated for what was recorded as a suicide.

***

It became apparent that Fischer's biggest secret had passed with him—his hold over Adolf Hitler. The Fuhrer had enjoyed an illicit affair with his young half-niece, Angela 'Geli' Raubal, several years before the outbreak of the war. She suicided at the age of twenty-three, a direct result of her uncle's attempts to control her. Hitler managed to stifle the German press; if Geli's accusations about her brutish, perverted uncle had been made public, perhaps Hitler's attempt at world domination would have been thwarted.

Geli's family were close friends of Fischer's wife, and Geli herself was a regular visitor at their home. Baldric Fischer used the opportunity to spoil Geli, hoping word would get back to Hitler that he was a person of value. The closer Fischer and Geli became, the more she confessed to him.

On the day she suicided, Geli sent Fischer a highly damaging handwritten letter detailing everything that had happened between her and her uncle—the Fuhrer. Fischer hid the letter, and eventually found the right moment to tell Hitler about it. The document and its terrible secrets were safe, he assured Hitler, and they would not be uncovered unless his untimely death made it necessary-instructions had been left. It was a huge risk, blackmailing the Fuhrer, but it worked. Of course, Fischer assured the Fuhrer that immediately after the war he would personally deliver the letter to Hitler;

but between times the document became his meal ticket to an Iron Cross (first class) and a promotion to lieutenant colonel along with a comfortable life at Wysznica.

Despite many attempts by the finest minds in Berlin, no one was able to establish the connection between the Fuhrer and Fischer, and even a top-secret investigation by the Gestapo failed to uncover the hidden secret. It was one of the great mysteries that eluded everyone in Hitler's inner circle. The reason they never found out was because the letter never existed. The friendship between Geli Raubel and Fischer's wife did. Fischer made up the rest.

Another mystery that was to surface many years later was how Karl Braun, also known as the Greyhound, came to be in America in the year 2000.

PART 8:
THROUGH
ANIA'S EYES

62

Despite the years that had passed it was during the quiet times, before Anna dropped off at night, that the camp came alive in her mind. Though she was warm and comfortable in her New Jersey bedroom, Wysznica was as real as if she were lying on a mattress of piss-soaked straw in a wooden bunk, surrounded by the stench and fear of hundreds of other women.

After liberation the survivors needed love and warmth, closeness and touch to sustain them not just food and medicine. And they were grieving. Nothing was as painful as the memory of watching your family being dragged away to the gas chamber.

It was soon after Wysznica was liberated that the British rounded up a large number of civic dignitaries, holders of high office and wealthy Polish people who did not appear to have been touched by the war. They collected them from surrounding towns and villages, including Oswiecim (Auschwitz). Some came from as far away as

Krakow. They were taken through the camp and spared nothing. They were forced to stand inside the gas chambers as one of the British soldiers shut the doors on them. The survivors who had gathered to witness the spectacle enjoyed seeing the panic on their faces and listening to their disgusting language when they were eventually let out.

The visitors were then taken to the crematoria, and they stood stiff and pompous as they stared at the bleached skeletons still inside the ovens. They were shown a mountain of bone particles and human dust waiting for disposal, but it was too big to seem real. Most just stared and shrugged into their fur coats and handmade woollen suits.

To the huts next, so the mayors and the grocers, the butchers and the jewellers along with the council officials and all the other self-important members of Polish society could smell the 'living quarters'. The women covered their faces with lace handkerchiefs when they walked through, masking their senses against the damp, the cold and the disease-ridden stench of the place. One of the men in line was heard to say, "It's not that bad. What is wrong with these Jews? It's not the Hotel Bristol but I could sleep here for a night or two." And one or two others actually laughed at the comment.

The British had collected tens of thousands of bodies from every corner of the camp. Some were frozen into grotesque positions, their faces distorted by the agony of their deaths; open mouths, staring eyes and gaunt faces-a scene from *Dante's Inferno.* The bodies were in huge piles, like mountains of broken mannequins, and the visitors were forced to walk among them, to look at the lice and insects crawling through their gaping eye sockets and ears. The putrid stench was accompanied by the scent of copious amounts of cheap perfume and homemade rose water, which people used to try to mask the smell. Many years later Leo would complain that Anna wore perfume to bed, but she never tried to explain why. With Leo, it was rarely worth the effort.

The British had killed thousands of rats-poisoned them, shot them, trapped them- and they too were piled up for inspection, before being doused with petrol and set alight to rid the camp of the diseases they carried. Strangely, that was the only time that the visitors seemed repulsed by what they saw.

The warehouse that was known as Canada Two at Wysznica was piled high with personal belongings that had been taken from prisoners. Suitcases, shoes, spectacles, hairbrushes, undergarments, even artificial limbs. The most distressing sight of the day seemed to be the pile of children's clothing and toys; the worn teddy bears and dolls that had provided so much comfort had been wrenched from the hands of those innocent, terrified children, and now the Polish men were angry that their wives had been forced to confront such sights. It wasn't their doing, so why were they forced to look?

Several hours later, the dignitaries finally left. Some heads were bowed in reflection but most were held high with anger in their eyes. And the women? Yes, some were distraught, but many were determined to retain their dignity, wrapping their fur coats around their bodies as they walked defiantly back to their transports. There was no shame, and no-one offered comfort, solace or regret to any of the gaunt looking onlookers during the inspections. Not one person stepped out of their ranks to express sympathy to the survivors.

Staff Sergeant Jim Maurice was disgusted by the reaction of the dignitaries, the people of influence who looked the other away as the Germans murdered hundreds and thousands of people in their backyards. *"Look at you. Look at you!"* he shouted as if he were trying to pull a line of recruits together on the parade ground. "You are a disgrace! This happened in your towns and villages, just beyond your back fences and you did nothing to help these poor, innocent people. Shame on you, Poland. Shame on you all!"

It was midnight a few days later when the terrifying sound of gunfire again woke people in the camp. The fuss seemed to die down quickly, but the next morning the survivors were asked if they could identify a body that had been placed in the parade ground for inspection. A man had been caught trying to dig up corpses, searching for loose gems the Germans may have missed. It seems that he had been seen sieving through the ashes at the back of the crematorium a few days earlier and had been warned that if he came back he would be shot. He came back.

Jim Maurice pulled the sheet off the body. "Does anyone here know this coward? He has no papers or identification."

Someone stepped forward. "I know him. His brother was a great friend to this camp, part of the resistance. This man? He was in the resistance too, but he was a traitor and a coward! Good riddance to him and his kind, I say." The speaker spat on the body and muttered, "May you rot in hell, you one-eyed bastard!" That night they put the floodlights on around the perimeter of the camp, the mass burial sites and the crematoria, and they were to remain on every night for the duration of the British occupation. The noise from the generators made it hard to sleep, but they kept the cowards and scavengers like Grabowski's brother Jozeph away.

***

There was still a curfew at the camp after liberation and survivors were allowed to go wherever they needed to, during daylight hours. Ania had been told she would remain at Wysznica until the Allies had completed their investigations, issued her with papers and travel documents, and verified that she was fit enough to be released. Like everyone at Wysznica, Ania had no idea where to go, because Europe was full of displaced people. So she spent her days walking around the camp, reliving the memories, trying to exorcise them from her mind.

As she stood near the gas chambers one day, a warm coat around her shoulders, courtesy of the Red Cross, Ania saw a pair of pigeons on the grass. It was a cold day (it was always cold at Wysznica) and one of the birds, the male of course, was fluffing himself up and prancing about-*look at me, look at me* -like men do when a woman is around. The blue feathers that circled his neck caught the light, like a beautiful silk shawl, and he had a fine time, cooing and parading about. Suddenly, in a flutter of feathers like a storm cloud, the pigeons swept into the air and were gone; the space they had occupied filled by one of the Sonderkommandos Anna had seen working around the camp during the occupation. He too had been drawn back to the gas chamber, reliving everything, running the same film over and over in his head, praying for the sights, sounds and smells to leave him-knowing they never would.

Ania approached him and silently placed an arm around his shoulder. It was then that he spoke. His voice was a strange monotone, almost matter of fact, as if he could not believe what had happened to him during the war years. Surely, he had not played a part in this strange production. He? Surely not? He had been a butcher before the war and told Ania that was why they made him a Sonderkommando-because he was used to death. Now he needed to talk about everything he had seen and done, to reason it through with someone nodding, not judging. "A person cannot keep such things inside him, he has to let them out ... The things I did. It is very hard for me to live with the memories. One day I shall explode because my head is so full of it all."

He talked of the things he saw when he removed bodies after a gassing. Worst was the children, always the children, he said: tiny tots, babes in arms, innocent little things, enemy to no one and capable of causing no damage whatsoever to any state or government.

He told Ania that he would always remember the smell; not just the occasional waft of gas but the stink of faeces, urine and blood. "Women miscarried in there. People shat themselves as they fought a hopeless battle with Death." As he talked to Ania, tears trickled down the Sonderkommando's face, leaving a track over each hollow cheek that you could follow with your finger. The British cleared him of committing any crimes, but for him it did not matter. It was too late. He suicided the day after he was personally exonerated.

***

After the Sonderkommando killed himself, Ania regularly visited the spot where they had talked. It was while she was staring into the open doors of the gas chamber that she saw a movement inside and someone climbed out and made his way up the steps. He looked at her and shook his head sadly. It was not to be their only meeting.

63

Ania learned of Hitler's death while on the high seas in April 1945. Europe was finally free of the scourge known as the Nazi party. It would be some time until the Americans ended the war at Hiroshima and Nagasaki, but for the survivors of Wysznica, the hostilities were well and truly over- and Ania was a married woman!

She was married in every sense apart from the legal, documented way. She now had a husband and had taken his name, shared the same bed and lived like man and wife, but they had only met a few weeks before-when she saw Leo Brenewski stepping out from the gas chamber shaking his head.

It was during the formal registration at Wysznica, as the survivors lined up to obtain new passports, travel passes and other documentation, that Ania found herself face to face with Jim Maurice again. They recognised each other immediately and both smiled. Ania knew that Jim Maurice was going to help her, and he did. It was then that her famous party story about Owstralia was founded: foreign governments were giving priority to married couples who wanted to start a new life in a new country after the war. Just as Ania tried to explain her position to Jim Maurice, Leo appeared from nowhere, put an arm around her waist and apologised for being late.

"Oh yes? And who might you be?" Maurice asked.

"Ania's husband of course, *the* husband, Mr Leo Brenewski," Leo said in broken English.

Jim Maurice looked at Ania. "I thought you said your name was Burczyk?"

Leo quickly interjected. "I believe you call it the 'maiden' name in England?" he said. "A simple misunderstanding."

Maurice looked up at Ania again, an unspoken question on his face. She shrugged and nodded so he put a line through her last name on the document, changed it to Brenewski, then ticked the box that said, 'Married'. She was now able to jump on a boat to Owstralia with her husband!

But Ania did not want to go to Australia; she wanted to go to the United States. The next day, she and Leo found themselves sneaking onto a ship bound for New York. They were never discovered on the crowded vessel, and when they arrived they pretended they could barely speak English and suddenly became the most distressed and confused migrants ever to step foot on Ellis Island!

They were eventually allowed to enter, and after many years, made a home for themselves in Jersey. Leo drove cabs and Ania (or Anna as she became known) found a job at a nursing home ten minutes from their apartment, which was above a dry-cleaning shop at the time.

After a few years Anna discovered that she could not have children, due to the damage caused to her body by the Germans during the war. To satisfy her maternal instincts, she purchased a dog and called it Cabbage. Every dog thereafter carried the same name. Anna and Leo got on with life, eventually buying a small, comfortable home a short distance from the apartment they had previously rented.

When she first met Stella, Anna's heart seemed to miss a beat. She discovered that they had so many common views and opinions, and it was not long before the two women became inseparable. Though she was a few years younger than Anna, Stella was an only child, and did not have a relationship with her parents or extended family. She was lonely and so was Anna; the two women soon filled the void in each other's life. Anna had a 'sister' again.

Stella and Anna's most common bond was their husbands. It appeared that both men *needed* their wives but neither appeared to *value* them. Anna and Stella knew how to cook, how to work the washing machine, iron and how to keep a clean house. They made themselves available in the bedroom, managed the household finances and paid the bills, organised their husbands' lives and listened to their constant bullshit without complaint. "We replace their mothers in every room except the bedroom!" Anna said.

Joe was very much the typical Italian man; he liked to think he was in charge but everyone knew that Stella ruled the roost. Joe asserted his authority by controlling the money, and Stella was often heard to say that she thought he was more Jew than Italian because he hated parting with cash. It was not that Joe did not like spending because he always had plenty of notes in his billfold-it was just that he did not like *anyone else* spending it, especially Stella who, according to Joe, seemed to waste money on needless things such as food and the mortgage!

Joe's attitude to money was a running joke between the two families, and Leo liked nothing more than to tell his neighbour that he would make a great partner for a faggot because *there is nothing another faggot likes more than a tight-ass!*

Despite his bravado and big talk, Leo was no better than Joe when it came to money. Anna paid the bills, the mortgage, bought the groceries and whatever, and it was only when she ran out of her own money that he chipped in. Leo liked to drink, preferring the company of his buddies at the Polish Club to his wife most of the time. He told Anna in no uncertain terms that he had earned the right to do with the rest of his life whatever he wanted. He had survived the war and just because he did not have a five-digit number tattooed on his arm did not mean he had not suffered any more or any less than her. But when it came to anything else related to the war, he refused to talk. *It's over. Forget it. Get on with your life!*

*****

Anna first realised she could cry again on Christmas Eve in 1946. Refugees were still struggling to integrate and their strange food, ceremonies and clothing were often eyed with suspicion by Americans. Some thought their suburbs would be turned into ghettos because Polish and Italian migrants had decided to gather there. For the newcomers, however, there was comfort to be found amongst familiar accents. As far as New York was concerned, it was the Lower East Side where people like Anna and Leo, Stella and Joe decided to settle and lay down the beginnings of a new life.

The problem for most migrants was that everything was so American! Who knew what was in those strange hotdogs; were they not made in a machine, thousands of them at a time? Where were the fruit barns and delis? The newcomers could not buy a decent kielbasa for love nor money. So they set about creating their own food, growing vegetables and herbs in pots on their balconies, or if they were lucky enough, in their or other people's backyard. Smokehouses also popped up in the most unlikely places, and 'homemade' or 'home smoked' became watchwords for some New Yorkers. It was hard to start with, but eventually they made a place for themselves, and America was all the better for it.

The church that Anna and Leo visited that Christmas Eve had a surprising number of East Europeans; those clipped accents were comforting. There was to be more reassurance when the singing started because it appeared that the Americans knew the same hymns and carols as the migrants. The priest spoke about God that day, and the fact that the war was well and truly over. It was a time for new starts, perhaps a move towards the seemingly incomprehensible task of forgiveness, though such an act was hard to imagine at that time.

But Anna could never forgive the Germans. They had taken her whole family. How could she possibly forgive that? It was when she closed her eyes to talk to God that Christmas that she said she would never forgive Him for what happened at Wysznica. He had deserted so many people in the war, even though they called his name when the pain became too much to bear. As she stood singing carols after prayers Anna felt the salt from a tear in the corner of her mouth for the first time in many years. She did not realise what it was for a brief moment, the little dribble that ran down her cheek and slipped between her lips. But the first tear was followed by many more that night, and many since. Leo asked her why she was crying. "For the war, Leo. For my family and for all those who are no longer with us."

"I tell you before, woman, *move on,*" he said. *"It's over now; it never happened."*

Anna was not allowed to talk about the war, so she bottled everything up. It was only when she met Stella that she found someone willing to listen; someone who wanted to hear what she needed to say. Stella was like a sister.

It took a while, but Anna gradually cleansed herself of the guilt she had harboured for her participation in the brothel; the disgusting things she did and allowed to be done to her to remain alive. But there was one level of guilt she could never shift, and that related to Danuta's execution. The pain was unbearable at times, creeping up when she least expected it, reaching deep into her marrow. "It should have been me, it should have been me."

Anna never told Stella how Danuta died, but she shared many other secrets, and was never judged. Leo did judge her however, and the fact that she was young at the time did not help sway his opinion. She took the easy way out; never tried to escape, never attempted to sabotage her captors. Leo had been caught cheating a German officer on a black market deal and was sent to Wysznica to be executed along with other black marketeers, but the liberation intervened. According to Leo, he at least tried to get back at the Germans by pissing in their illicit whisky. But Anna, what did she do? She cooperated.

Some women did suicide rather than suffer the continued indignities the Germans forced upon them. Anna saw the fat farmer's wife's body hanging on the electric fence at Wysznica; the never-ending cruelty and humiliation had been too much for her in the end. Anna put her own failure to join the farmer's wife down as cowardice. The thought had crossed her mind many times, but she just could not bring herself to leap onto that fence and end it all.

Life finally moved on for Anna and Leo in Jersey. Like most married couples, they had their problems from time to time, but no more than others in those years immediately after the war. They gradually built a foundation and settled into a workable routine that suited them both. There was no love between them, but there was no desire to seek it outside the relationship either. They had a vacation or two over the years, saw a bit of America and eventually paid the mortgage off. Their life was good, but it did not stay that way.

***

Mr Ramez, the general manager at the nursing home, was a gentleman. He was 'old school', always wore a collar and a tie, stood when a woman entered the room, held the door open. But being summoned to his office still made Anna nervous, despite the fact that Ramez was known to prefer to avoid conflict if he could. He was a large man, softly spoken with huge sad eyes beneath a set of large, fluffy eyebrows. He had a nervy look about him and certainly did not appear too comfortable in such a lofty position.

After Anna made herself comfortable, Ramez started talking about the weather, the humidity-*terrible for this time of year* -how quickly the grass was growing and, of course, those Yankees.

Anna knew nothing about ball games. "I wouldn't even know which end of the racquet to hold on a baseball court!" Eventually, Ramez spilled the beans, in one long nervous sentence, with hardly a breath between the words. He sounded as if he had been rehearsing for days.

Anna was stunned. "Am I being fired, Mr Ramez?"

Ramez's eyebrows lifted like shutters. "Hell no, Mrs Brenewski. You are being retired!"

The rest of the conversation was lost to Anna, and she walked home in a trance. It was when she started cooking dinner that the tears came.

What was she going to do? It was not the money; they were comfortable enough-the mortgage was paid out years ago and they had some savings. It was because the nursing home was her life. And what about Stella? They would no longer walk to work together when their shifts coincided, and would only meet over the fence on washdays now, or at family functions. Without the nursing home, Anna's life looked bleak.

They arranged a farewell drink for Anna on her last day, a somewhat subdued affair, with no one wanting to see her leave. Even the frumpy shift manager, Elaine Brinkworth, seemed sad, though she and Anna had sometimes had brittle moments over the years. With the promise of an invitation to the staff Christmas party later that year, a bunch of flowers and a beautiful crystal vase Anna left the Paterson Manor Rest Home for the last time. Leo was waiting in his cab as promised for a rare ride home, but he swore he had left the meter on by accident when Anna spotted the clock ticking. They had arranged to go to dinner together that night to celebrate the occasion, but Anna called the Polish Club and cancelled when they got home. She was too miserable to sit with her husband and listen to his drivel.

Anna spent the next few days shuffling around the house, still upset and already lonely. When the phone rang that morning she almost did not pick it up, but when she did, after the seventh ring, she was surprised to hear Elaine Brinkworth's voice. It appeared that Mr Ramez and the Board had finally found some money in the budget for a library trolley. They had been talking about a library service for years and now the new owners were going to put a few dollars back into the business. The investment was not that great because they wanted the trolley to be operated by volunteers. To be more precise, *a volunteer.* Then Elaine said, "So what about it, Anna? Are you interested?"

It was not long before Anna turned the library trolley into a thriving little business, and what started as a part-time job blossomed into four and a half days a week. Everyone was delighted with the results and Anna enjoyed dealing with the local library and the bookshop in the shopping precinct. She had to arrange for large print copies of latest releases as well as audio books, and was keen to introduce speakers from time to time-local authors who would be invited to talk to the residents at Paterson Manor. Anna's life was back to normal ... or was it?

64

Mr Croft, the resident in room number twenty-four, had remained in bed longer than usual one morning, and Stella nipped in to see what he was up to when someone remarked that they had not seen him at breakfast. She found him with a breakfast tray still on the bed; his head was at a funny angle, his dentures were almost hanging out of his mouth and he had a rather surprised expression on his face.

His eyes were wide open, but Mr Croft was gone.

The nursing home was a real home for most who resided there, but it was also a business, and a significant one at that, part of a large group. So Mr Croft's room was cleared out and a week or so later, after a quick lick of paint, a new occupant took up residence. A man from sunny Florida, they said, though why he came all the way to New Jersey no one knew for sure. He apparently had a connection with the Catholic Church, but for some reason he was not going to one of their homes. The new resident was eighty years old and the staff were warned that he could be cantankerous. Elaine Brinkworth gave everyone the news during an early morning briefing. She seemed rather excited about the new occupant of room twenty-four, as if he was someone of notoriety, and when she said, "If anyone has a right to be cantankerous in his remaining years then it's this man!" it was clear that she was impressed with the new resident.

She told the staff that he had been some kind of hero at a concentration camp during World War II, and had even had his memoirs published. Anna listened with interest as everyone was making a fuss about having a war hero at Paterson, but she would have preferred to have seen a retired bus driver moving into Mr Croft's old room. It seemed that for once, Leo's words had some validity: *the war is over, forget the war!*

Human nature being what it is, Anna soon found herself making an excuse to trundle past room twenty-four with her library trolley. Maybe she could get a glimpse of the new occupant. The door was locked when she arrived, but Mr Croft's name card was already gone and a freshly printed replacement was there in its place. The procedure at Paterson Manor was for a person's nickname or preferred name to be shown first; a personable and friendly approach to aged care, just like the Mission Statement said. And there was the man's name on the door: *Polak,* it said in bold print, beneath which was the full name of the new occupant-*Pawel Michalik.*

***

Stella met him first. Like everyone, she was keen to meet the hero, so she stuck her head around his door at the first opportunity and introduced herself. "He's a miserable old buzzard," she said during lunch. "But he brightened up when he started talking about himself, as most men do."

Anna mumbled over the top of her coffee cup. "He's Polish. What do you expect?"

Stella looked surprised. "I thought you said you hadn't met him."

"I haven't, but I did see his name card." Anna had a strange expression on her face.

Stella continued with her assessment. "You know, he kinda spoke down to me as if I was the help. I honestly thought he was going to shout at me at one stage. And he had a look in his eye, you know the one, girls ... I certainly wouldn't want to get on the wrong side of the bed in his room!"

'*Getting on the wrong side of the bed*' was an expression the female staff used to describe being groped by 'dirty old men'. It had long been noticed that most female residents lost their sex drive with age, but it was not unusual for men to still find themselves '*in the mood*' well into their eighties and sometimes beyond. Female nursing staff, auxiliaries and cleaners often felt a stray, shaky hand on their ass when they tucked someone in, so it had long ago been legislated that they were to wear pants on duty.

Stella recalled the day when she was chased around a bedroom by a fully aroused, naked elderly gentleman resident. She managed to get to the emergency alarm button before he got to her, and a doctor arrived just in time to see the old man collapse with heart palpitations. His erection remained stubbornly in place for quite some time, but Stella put some dignity back into the situation by upending a plastic flowerpot over the top of his erect penis and popping a plastic daisy in the drainage hole.

Even Dr Mahmoud found it funny, and he was not known for his sense of humour. The resident survived the incident and Elaine Brinkworth confiscated the Viagra she found in his bathroom.

"It seems that one of his stupid pals slipped him a tablet during a visit, but it could have killed the silly old buzzard!" she said with a rare grin.

***

The staff were gathered around the lunchroom table the day after Polak arrived, reading an article from a Florida newspaper. Polak's story had been serialised in two parts and a copy had been passed around by Elaine Brinkworth. Everyone was suitably impressed with the story, which claimed that Polak had survived several years inside a concentration camp and then sought revenge by personally killing several SS guards and bringing others to account after liberation. Anna tried to appear disinterested, and was about to leave the room when Stella said, "The camp was called Wysznica, somewhere in Poland. Was that anywhere near where you were, Anna?"

***

Anna mumbled something inaudible and headed outside for some air. Her head was spinning and her mind racing; she felt a sudden surge of anger so great that she wanted to punch something- or someone. Instead, much to the surprise of a passerby, she looked up to heaven with tears in her eyes and screamed, "Why? Why now?"

The name Pawel Michalik ... She racked her brain but it meant nothing. She could not recall him from Wysznica but according to the newspaper article, he had been there the same time as her. There were several hundred survivors, so why should she recall the name of one in particular? A sense of foreboding crept up on her as she sat in the sunshine trying to gather her thoughts, and she realised, like it or not, she was going to have to face this man called Polak, sometime soon. The past had returned in a most unlikely way for Anna.

***

Anna decided not to tell Leo about the new resident. She knew what he would say, and he certainly would not have been interested in listening to her. She slept in fits and starts and the restless nights showed on her face. For the first time since she started at Paterson Manor, Anna did not want to go in to work the next day.

Anna found herself mumbling out loud as she made her way to Paterson Manor for her next shift. She was weighing up the various options open to her. Common sense said it would be impossible to avoid Polak. So, should she perhaps go out of her way to say hello and get it over with, or should she let it happen naturally, perhaps by a chance passing in a hallway or during dinner, in the dining room? While the prospect of meeting Polak was daunting, Anna took comfort in the thought that perhaps he was only at Paterson temporarily. After all, Elaine had said he had a Catholic background, a connection with the Church, so maybe he was waiting for a place at one of their homes. That would make sense.

The inevitable happened much sooner than Anna expected. There was a message in her pigeonhole in the office when she arrived that morning. A pink slip requesting the library trolley's services as soon as possible, in room twenty-four.

***

Usually, when residents were bed bound or just having a lazy day, they kept their doors open so they could watch the world pass by, but Polak was the type of person who liked his privacy. His door was shut when Anna arrived with her trolley. She knocked tentatively, waited a few seconds, braced herself, then nervously entered. A frail old man in expensive looking black and red pyjamas was sitting in bed staring at her. "Who told you to come in?" he snapped.

"You did. You coughed. I assumed that was a signal to come in." Anna was determined not to be intimidated by Polak, who was surrounded by newspapers, magazines and other bits and pieces, some of which he appeared to try to conceal when she arrived.

His skin was pallid and grey, flecked with age spots and a few lingering freckles. Out of all his features, his eyes disturbed Anna the most. They were not red rimmed and milky like most people his age, but sparkled black and cold from somewhere inside their sockets, like two angry little creatures waiting for a victim to pass by. It was those eyes that sent the hackles up on Anna's neck-she would have known those eyes anywhere.

65

"You are the library woman, yes?" Polak spoke as if demanded an answer.

"And that makes you Pawel Michalik," Anna replied, trying to avoid his eyes.

"Polak! That is my name. Everyone calls me Polak. That is what you call me! It is written on the door. No?" he barked. His tone of voice was still familiar after all those years. If Anna had had any doubts about who he was, they evaporated when his beady eyes started undressing her and the corners of his mouth, shiny with saliva, twitched. Being in Karl Braun's presence again made Anna's skin crawl and she felt contaminated and itchy, in need of a shower.

Polak had a piece of paper in his hand. "I want to order some books. Here ... the list." As Anna reached forward he churlishly pulled it away. "Be careful," he said. "You might catch something!" And he burst out laughing then thrust the paper back towards her.

"These are all about the Holocaust," Anna said as she studied the titles.

"Have you not read my book, *Survivor?* I am researching the sequel at the moment."

"No, I never read it. Things like that do not interest me. Personally, I think they belong in the past and that is where they should stay. Sorry."

"Sorry? Why would you be sorry?"

"Because you won't be getting any royalties from me, will you?" "Huh, that's typical of you Polish. Too miserly to help an old man. That's the real story of my life; always, I have to help myself."

***

After her first meeting with Polak, Anna became increasingly irritable and restless. It was as if she was back walking through the corridors of the Club at Wysznica. At night, as she lay in bed, she felt the weight of someone upon her, and if she closed her eyes the sight of the fat farmer's wife hanging on the electric fence appeared. The flashbacks were brutal and terrifying, dragging her back into the hell she thought she had left behind. Leo's heavy footsteps in the hallway turned into jack-boots, a car backfiring in the street outside was a gun going off. The nightmare had returned.

Very occasionally, a sense of reason would kick into Anna's thoughts: could she have it wrong about Polak being Karl Braun, the Greyhound? Maybe he really was who he said he was; after all, it had been over fifty years since the war and her memory could be playing games, couldn't it? Perhaps she had made a mistake?

***

Anna thought about contacting the authorities to resolve the matter once and for all. If Polak was a war criminal, they would deal with him appropriately, surely? But if she did call the cops what would they do? What could they do? They could hardly arrest him on her say so, could they? Perhaps the Simon Wiesenthal Centre would be interested? They had a file on every Nazi and member of the SS who ever lived. They would know how to prove or disprove Polak's identity. But what would happen in the meantime? They wouldn't take him away while he was being investigated? Of course not, and Anna would be stuck at Paterson Manor with him while they delved into his background; that is, if they were willing to try. The more Anna thought about it, the more she realised that calling in the authorities would be a waste of time.

Day after day, night after night for a whole week she thought about Polak, and she kept returning to the same conclusion, the same logical response to her dilemma. *She* was going to have to prove who he was. She might not be able to bring Danuta back, but she could ensure that Polak-Karl Braun-was somehow brought to justice for the crimes he committed at Wysznica during World War II.

***

Anna took the opportunity to take an unofficial look at Polak's file when everyone was in a staff meeting: there was mention of dementia and Alzheimer's. The old man did seem a little vague at times, but he could be faking-was it possible to fake these things? There were times when Anna saw laughter in his eyes when he was questioned about his war life and he seemed overly confident most of the time. Arrogant and egotistical. But some of the staff had actually said they felt sorry for him-*such a wonderful man and to think, it has all come to this: dementia.*

Anna still said nothing to Leo. The last thing she wanted was him reminding her that she was a German's whore during the war. During a drunken rage he once told her that her ugly past would return to haunt her. Perhaps he was right. So Anna remained insular and self-absorbed most of the time, as she tried to think of a way to expose Polak. Her nightmares increased in intensity and she found herself waking during the early hours, sweating and shaking, screaming at one of the guards in a dream. Leo turned in his sleep and mumbled, "You OK?" but before she could reply he told her to keep the noise down and dropped off again. He had no idea of what was going on in Anna's head, he never had.

***

The more Anna thought about Polak and his newspaper story, the more she realised it did not add up. He said he was Polish but, in many ways, he gave the appearance of being German, though nobody else seemed to notice; most Americans did not know the difference between the two countries and their people's accents. Polak was a fake and Anna knew, but the bigger question remained unanswered for now: did *he* recognise *her*?

Polak had not appeared too interested in Anna after their initial meeting-there were no questions about her past or background, no probing or sounding out when they chatted. He seemed not to care anything about her as the days passed, and she was beginning to think that maybe his dementia and Alzheimer's could be real after all. But no—she reminded herself time and again who Polak really was—just to look in his eyes was enough. Was he playing a game of cat and mouse with her, and if he was, who was the cat and who was the mouse?

***

Anna decided to take the first step in trying to prove if Polak was the real deal. She engineered a seemingly innocent situation where she found herself alone with Polak in the TV lounge when he was watching a replay of the England versus Germany World Cup football final from 1966, on Fox Sports. It was probably the most contentious final in the long history of the competition, the first serious meeting between the two sporting nations after the war.

Most Americans know very little about the sport they call soccer, but coming from Poland, being married to Leo and living next to football crazy Stella and Joe, Anna was pretty well informed about the game. Germany lost the match after extra time but there had been a great deal of controversy over one of the English goals. Polak asked Anna what she thought about it: *was it a goal or was it not?*

"I don't follow football. I'm a baseball girl myself," she lied, as she fussed over some magazines and scatter cushions.

"Ah yes, the Americans and their sport. They are the champions of the world in baseball, but only American teams play in their World Series!" Polak's laugh still made Anna's skin crawl. He pointed at the television set. "Did you see the third goal? The English cheated. They must have paid the referee off because the player Hurst, Geoff Hurst for England, his shot hit the crossbar and bounced back *into* the field of play. It never crossed the goal line! And the game was at Wembley Stadium in England, in front of an English crowd! They cheated. They never play fair. That is a known fact. The English cannot be trusted, I tell you."

"But didn't England get another goal a few minutes later? Wouldn't Germany have lost regardless of the disputed goal?" Anna certainly remembered the game. England won by four goals to two. Leo had been enthralled all the way through and they both ended up watching the extra time together.

"England won fair and square, I think. Germany lost," Anna concluded.

Polak's eyes narrowed. "Germany never lost. Victory was stolen from us!"

Polak seemed to have no idea about his slip-*victory was stolen from us,* he said! Anna tried to hide her delight and pretended that she never noticed. If only she could get him to say something in front of a witness, to admit he was German. What she needed was an accomplice, someone who wanted to know the truth about Polak as much as she did.

The person she needed was nearer than she thought.

***

Polak was full of self-importance and as obnoxious as ever when he took his place at the dinner table that evening. He seemed to be primed and ready for a scrap after his dispute about the football.

Anna knew from experience that if there is one thing men like to talk about, it is themselves. *They are all great drinkers, amazing lovers, fantastic fathers, great sportsmen and war heroes, all in the same sentence. Just ask them!* And that evening Polak was regaling everyone with his opinions about what was wrong with the world today and how it could be fixed. As usual, he had his hip flask at hand and when he thought none of the staff were watching, he offered it around; he called it a 'survivor reviver'-a shot of schnapps, of course.

Most of the diners turned their noses up, and when Anna happened to walk past he called out to her. "Hey, Polish? Will you join me in a reviver, two old Poles drinking together?"

Anna replied, "You know very well I can't touch alcohol when I am working, Polak. Are you trying to get me fired?"

Joanie Nevin immediately jumped into the fray. "Come now, Mr Polak. You should not try to force Anna to drink that dreadful muck of yours, and you know it." She peered through the spectacles that balanced at the end of her nose. Two sparkling eyes jiggled beneath her raised eyebrows, and her mouth was turned up at the ends in a joker's grin. She was in a feisty mood, either looking for trouble or just having fun. She had always been a forthright lady who, if she had something to say, would have no problems saying it. She was certainly nobody's fool and Anna had noticed that she had become a little edgy since Polak arrived, uncomfortable in his presence, which was unusual for Joanie.

Polak snapped back at Mrs Nevin. "Nonsense, old woman! She is a volunteer, we all know that! You can't sack a person who is not employed!" He waved the hip flask at Anna again, but she explained that she really could not join him in a drink. Out of courtesy, however, she poured some water into a glass and raised that in salute.

"Cheers!"

Polak nodded in return, and then took a large swig from his flask. Anna decided to tease him a little. "You know, I have been thinking about that football match, Polak. It was a good job Germany weren't playing Poland or the controversy would have been even greater, don't you think?" She raised her glass of water once more, and tapped it against his flask.

"Poland beat Germany? Ha! Impossible!" he sneered.

"Na Zdorovie!" Anna said in her native tongue. *Cheers!*

"You talk such rot, Polish. But anyway, here's to your rot!" Polak raised his flask and without hesitation said, "Prost!"

Joan Nevin's face lit up like fireworks. Her nostrils flared and her mouth puckered into a determined grimace. The flush on her face contrasted with her white hair, giving her an almost witch-like countenance as she slapped her hand onto the table in glee. Anna was not alone in her thoughts about Polak's identity!

***

A few years previously, Joanie Nevin and Anna had been busy with a tricky jigsaw puzzle, and she and Anna sat looking for one of those almost impossible to find pieces of blue sky when the old lady decided to share something very personal. She talked of her Jewish background. It had been with some relief that she took the name of her husband, Richie Nevin, an Irish

Catholic, when they married a few years after the war's end.

They were not blessed with children, so the obvious dilemma of religion never arose, and anyway, Mrs Nevin let hers slide after the war. It had been a wonderful relationship, Joanie and her accountant husband, spanning many years. Now she was in her nineties and alone in the world.

Even though her mind sometimes deserted her, there were times Joanie's memory and sharpness of thought returned. "Here is the thing, Anna my dear; in my life I have seen everything I wanted to see, and I have heard most everything I needed to hear. I regret only one thing: I never had the opportunity to say goodbye to my parents and grandparents. They went up a chimney at Dachau concentration camp, you know, and my belief in God followed them. Oh yes, it was a long time ago, but I will never forget. Goodness me no. I will never forgive either. I will go up a chimney myself someday soon no doubt, but it will be an American chimney, and it will be one of my own choosing."

66

The next morning, as Anna was hanging some washing in her backyard, Stella popped her head over the fence. She looked upset, said she had not been sleeping well. Then she asked Anna if everything was alright; she was very concerned that she may have upset Anna over something. She said she had asked Leo if he knew what was wrong, why Anna had suddenly changed, and he told her he had no idea and didn't even realise something might be awry. *"What change? She cooked dinner last night, complained about the ironing..."*

Anna told Stella she was fine except for a bit of a headache that she could not shake. She said she would have a chat with her doctor if it had not gone by the end of the week. Stella had to rush off, but it was obvious she did not believe Anna. Something *was* wrong, but what?

Leo had been thinking about Stella's question during the day, and that evening, in his usual subtle manner, he asked Anna if she was alright. "What's your problem, woman?" Anna shrugged and said she was feeling hormonal. Leo grumbled under his breath as he walked away. "Women! It used to be that time of the month, now it's that time of life..."

The next day there was uproar in the dining room at Paterson Manor. Things were said, a chair was upturned and blood pressures were raised to seriously dangerous levels. Polak was behind the drama, and he seemed hell bent on antagonising Joanie Nevin. Had he somehow discovered that she was from a Jewish background? A fight was in the air.

Anna arrived shortly after they started at each other, and Polak was in full flow, telling everyone about the wonders of Hitler's Germany. "After the first war, the war to end all wars, Germany was on its knees. Then Hitler rose to power, and he gave the country back its pride. No-one else could have done that, not even the Kaiser." He looked at Joanie, "You can say what you like about him, old woman, but Hitler was a visionary, a political genius, an amazing orator *and* a charismatic leader."

"He was scum!" Mrs Nevin spat the words out, along with some half-chewed food particles, which spattered the table like shotgun pellets.

Polak's lips parted in a sly, fox-like smile. She was hooked and it was on!

"Volkswagen would not exist if it was not for Hitler. Imagine that, the people's car! A Fuhrer's vision," Polak continued.

"Hitler was not Europe's answer to Henry Ford, Mr Polak. Ford was an eccentric genius. Hitler was an evil asshole." Joan's mouth was set and her knife and fork were standing upright in her tiny, white-knuckled arthritic hands. She may have been shaking from head to toe but she gave no quarter.

Polak seemed equally resolute and he was clearly enjoying baiting the old lady. He was itching for a fight as he sat confident and upright, directly across the table from her. "Autobahns? Let us talk about them. Hitler gave us the autobahn or highways as they call them here."

"Like I said. Hitler was a bastard. And so are you."

Polak ignored the insult. "The jet engine, that was another one of Hitler's." He crammed a forkful of food into his mouth and continued talking with his mouth open, the grisly contents on full display. "And the rocket, Hitler was behind the rocket all the way. Just ask the people of London because they were on the receiving end of those doodlebugs."

The old lady's eyes narrowed a little more, like a snake about to strike. As they stared each other out, she stealthily put her cutlery down and started gently tapping her fingers around the table in front of her, searching for the sauce bottle, which she knew was somewhere nearby.

Polak noticed none of this; he was too busy enjoying the staring contest. "I must say, though, Hitler was not responsible for the concentration camps," he said with a smirk. "The British invented them during the Boer War I believe. Adolf Hitler merely perfected them!"

A stream of ketchup suddenly shot across the table, hitting Polak's face. Splat! The tablecloth and the wall behind became collateral damage, but most of the sauce ended up on Polak's head and shirt. The old lady leapt to her feet. "And that is for you and your friend Hitler, Mr Polak, you German cunt!"

***

The effect was immediately felt by the refined gentle folk enjoying their meals at adjoining tables; there was uproar in the dining room. But there was more to come, as both combatants angrily pushed their chairs aside. Despite her advanced years, it was clear that Joanie Nevin, the old white-haired Jewish woman crippled with arthritis, was actually going to square up to Polak. It took three staff ten minutes to return her to her room. She was still fuming, still wanting to fight Polak to the finish.

When she was gone, Polak tried to make light of the sauce-squirting incident. In fact, he looked especially pleased with his final remark as they took Joan away "You want to be careful, old woman; I hear that Germany is still looking for somewhere to send the gas bill!"

Joanie Nevin had lost her parents, all six of her siblings and her grandparents in the Holocaust. Only she and an aunt survived. "They call it Jew baiting," she told Anna later. "The Germans and all the Jew haters did it throughout the war and they are still doing it today. Bastards! They are all bastards, and this Polak? He is no more Polish than I am Scottish. I can smell a German at a hundred yards, and the minute I saw him I knew he was a sausage-munching Kraut!"

Management decided that Polak and Mrs Nevin should be kept apart whenever possible, at least until the matter blew over. When interviewed by the resident psychologist the next morning, Polak claimed he did not know Mrs Nevin was Jewish and he had no idea he was being offensive. He claimed not to remember much about the incident at all. He may have fooled the psychologist but he did not fool Anna or Joan Nevin. And now, other people were also starting to ask who Polak really was.

***

There were no locks on the inside of residents' doors at the Paterson Manor Rest Home; it stopped the old folks locking themselves in, either by accident or on purpose. The lack of a lock was Anna's biggest concern a few days after the ketchup incident, because she decided to pay an unauthorised visit to Polak's room when he was away at the dentist.

Anna's cover for the unauthorised intrusion was to say she was searching for a lost library book if she was discovered. She told Mrs Nevin she was going to look for evidence to prove that Polak was an imposter and the old lady immediately volunteered to stand guard. "Listen, if you want me to take a dump in one of his shoes, Anna, you just let me know!"

The residents' rooms were not spacious, just enough for a few sticks of furniture. There were not many decent hiding places either, and it did not take long for Anna to find Polak's treasure box, a small metal container about the size of shoebox. On his bedside table was an old music box that played 'Lily Marlene' when the lid was raised. Anna looked inside and found a watch, several brass-collar stiffeners and the key to that metal box. Old people were also not very inventive when it came to hiding things.

The treasure box was crammed full of paperwork and press cuttings, and in amongst it all, Anna found an American passport in Polak's name. There was also an Argentinean passport that had the same picture (his) but a different name. There were several letters from an address in Argentina, but they were not written in English, bearing a watermark and a religious symbol, a picture of Jesus next to the embossed address. There was also some correspondence from a bank in Switzerland, but it was in a language that was not familiar to Anna.

She found what she was looking for, inside a large brown envelope-the original document from Wysznica with Pawel Michalik's face staring defiantly into the camera. The photograph itself was brown and brittle, damaged in parts and scorched around the edges. This was the same picture that appeared in the Florida newspaper, the record of Polak's internment at Wysznica, which he claimed to have snatched from the fire when the Germans were trying to destroy camp records.

Anna examined the picture closely. It certainly looked like a younger version of Polak, but it was grainy and dirty-at a glance it really could have been any skinny concentration camp victim from the time, and now, with age on his side, it was even easier for Polak to validate his claim that he was Pawel Michalik.

Anna continued looking through the contents of the tin and discovered an SS cloth patch that seemed to have been cut from a uniform. No doubt Polak would lie about how he came to be in possession of that. There was also a teaspoon with an SS insignia on the handle, a souvenir, probably. Red and black were the colours of the Swastika as well as Polak's pyjamas.

And then the real proof Anna needed suddenly materialised! The metal box appeared to be unusually heavy when empty, and when she shook it, a dull rattle confirmed that it had a false bottom. When she worked out how to access the hiding space, Anna found something that she never imagined she would ever see again...

67

The night of Stella and Joe's wedding anniversary, Anna was unable to sleep. Leo was already in bed, dead to the world, and Anna lay awake watching the digits click over on her bedside clock. She waited until 12.30am, and realised it was decision time.

Earlier that day, with Joanie Nevin standing guard outside Polak's room, Anna had found the very same gun that had killed Danuta inside Polak's treasure box. The Luger with the engraved handle bearing the gold-embossed streaking greyhound was actually in her hand, which was shaking uncontrollably. She also found a full clip of ammunition and several loose bullets. A terrible thought flooded her mind; she could end everything right there and then and how fitting would it have been if she did it with the Greyhound's gun? But would killing herself help bring Polak to justice? Of course not, it would just leave too many unanswered questions. As Anna stood thinking with the gun in her hand, Joan Nevin started coughing in the hallway outside-a signal that meant someone was coming.

The cough turned out to be a false alarm, but Anna had managed to smuggle the gun and bullets out without Joan knowing. "I didn't find anything, dear, but I won't give up, believe me. We will pin something on that man, if it takes forever." The old lady stared at Anna, unsure whether she should believe her or not-she looked far too shifty to have come out empty handed.

Back in the kitchen at 12.35am, Cabbage was shuffling around on Anna's feet as she sat at the table writing. Over the course of the preceding weeks, she had written letters to Leo and Stella, thanking them for everything they had ever done for her. Then she started on her biography, the story of her life at Wysznica and beyond. At times it was difficult to see the page through her tears, especially when we she went back to the day that the Germans arrived at her grandparent's farm. She included as much detail as she could about the camp, because that was the real reason she was writing-to provide an eyewitness account of Karl Braun's crimes. She eventually concluded with a request that people should not judge her for her actions during the war. It was surely up to God in heaven to pass the final judgement on her life.

Anna knew it would be difficult to prove Braun's crimes in a legal sense; she was the only eyewitness and she had no documents or other tangible evidence to support her. It was her word against his. But she had found the gun, and she could say that he had fake passports in his treasure tin.

There was now little doubt in Anna's mind that Polak was Braun. She decided, therefore, that if Polak were to be brought to justice to account for his crimes, it would have to be done outside the court system. Natural justice would have to prevail and she determined that she would become judge and jury.

She had already given an account of his crimes, so in the interest of fairness, Anna stated the defence case, using the same reasoning that almost every Nazi used at the Nuremburg trials: *I was acting under orders.* The document she created, showing the evidence for and against Polak, ran to fifteen pages, and finally she turned to a fresh sheet of paper and wrote the heading: *Verdict for the case of Ania Burczyk versus Karl Braun.* It was followed by one word, in large capitals: *GUILTY.*

***

Anna knew the local priest well. He visited Paterson Manor from time to time to attend to the Last Rites of Catholic residents in the final hours of their lives. Father Pat was Irish of course, a prerequisite for a priest in New York. He was younger than his predecessor and well known for his gentle and caring manner when attending to those in need. Anna wondered if he would be so accommodating at five-thirty that morning, when she knocked on his door.

He was. He said he was happy to listen to Anna's confession, but needed a heart-starter at that time of the day. For such a young man, he was shrewd enough to see beyond her words, and he knew that there was more to Anna's visit than she initially said. After failing to work out how to use the new-fangled machine that had been donated by a grateful parishioner, he reverted to instant coffee. "The machine is too complicated, Anna. Operating this thing is like flying an aircraft! If the Lord wanted us to make coffee this way he wouldn't have given us Nescafe granules, now would he?"

They made small talk as the kettle boiled and then Father Pat wagged his finger in the air. "I know what it is! I have been looking at you and asking myself why you look different this morning, Anna, and now I know. You have odd-coloured eyes! One is a different colour from the other. I have never noticed that before!"

"That's because I usually wear contact lenses, Father, to make my eyes look the same, not to improve my sight. But today? Today I want to be myself. My real self."

They drank their coffee in a comfortable silence then walked across the garden to the side door of the church. Father Pat fumbled with the keys. "I have to lock it, I'm afraid. Vandals. Three times last year. I think enough is enough so I lock up at night and leave a note asking anyone who needs access to the church to text my mobile phone or email me and I will come down and let them in. How things have changed in this world of ours, Anna."

"You can work out how to text and email on a mobile phone but you can't switch a coffee machine on, Father?"

"The Lord works in a mysterious way, Anna," he said as the door swung open. Moments later he took his place in the confessional booth, with Anna the other side of the screen.

"Is this when I do a limerick, Father?" It had been a long time since Anna had been so flippant, but then it had been a long time since she had been in front of a priest.

Father Pat tried to put her at ease. "You know, people have told me about your limericks, Anna, and I am led to believe they are truly terrible. Is that perhaps why you are at the confessional?" That little Irish lilt in his voice helped, and Anna gained comfort from his presence the other side of the divider.

Fiddling with her wedding ring, Anna said, "Father?"

"Yes, Anna?"

"Is it wrong to come to confession before I actually commit what I know to be a grievous sin?"

"You are *thinking* about sinning? Is that not a sin in itself?"

"I suppose it is."

Father Pat spoke softly. "Anna, you are very nervous, and I think that maybe what you have to say has been on your mind for a while. Why don't you just say it? Get it off your chest and let me deal with it. That's why I am here, you know?"

"I know, Father; I know why God put you here."

"Then tell me why *you* want me to be here, Anna. Don't be concerned; there is nothing you can say that will shock me. If I wasn't a Catholic priest, I would be a Swiss watch."

Anna took a deep breath. "I am going to kill someone today, Father."

Anna heard Father Pat swallow, followed by the sound of his chair scraping on the floor. "Are you still there, Father?"

His voice came back, a little higher than before. "Are you sure you wouldn't rather tell me a limerick, Anna?"

***

Father Pat took Anna back to the kitchen for more coffee, to discuss her 'little problem' on a more personal level. His immediate thought was that Leo had upset her over some trifling matter that had grown out of all proportion, and like many wives at some stage during their marriage, she wanted to kill her husband! His attempt at humour stalled as soon as Anna told him the real reason.

She calmly told him about her war years, about Polak and what she was going to do to him that day. The Priest listened, spellbound, shocked beyond all understanding. More coffee followed, and still they talked. The housekeeper arrived and they realised it was nine-thirty. "Father, why did you want to leave the confessional, and why didn't you talk to me inside the church?"

"You told me that you felt God had deserted you all those years ago, Anna. I do not want to insult you and have you thinking I am pushing Him down your throat at a time like this. I do not want you to feel that I am trying to sell you a Bible. I am here to listen, not to judge, and hopefully I can persuade you not to continue with this vengeful action because no-one will win, no-one will benefit, least of all you or your dear departed sister, Danuta."

Father Pat could not find an answer when Anna asked him why God was not there for all the innocents who suffered in the concentration camps of Europe. "It wasn't a volume thing was it?" she asked. "You know, too much all at one time. Too many souls, as it were?"

He said he thought that God was at the camps, suffering with them, but he had no answer to why so many had to go through so much for so long. It was beyond his understanding too, but he was certain that God would have hated seeing what his creation-mankind-was doing. He told Anna that he thought God was still in her heart and that was why she had decided to knock on his door that morning. "Kill him and you hurt nobody other than yourself, Anna. Sure, this man that you call Polak, he will be dead, but why not let God judge him? The only life you will ruin will be your own, can't you see that?"

"Father, my life is already ruined. I am already dead; the Germans made sure of that a long time ago. I have had some joy since, but it has always been overshadowed by what I went through at the hands of the SS. I do not seek revenge, Father, I am only after justice. What do I have to lose?"

"Your life, Anna. You will lose the most valuable possession that God can give you."

"Like I said, Father, I lost that the day the Germans walked into my grandfather's house."

They talked more. Drank more coffee. Father Pat listened, then had his say again. Anna heard him, then spoke once more. The conversation went backwards and forwards for another hour, and finally Anna said she had to leave. "I want you to have this, please, Father." And she handed him the sealed envelope containing her life story, the legal document she had drawn up and her letters to Stella and Leo.

"And what is this, may I ask?"

"I want you to read about my life and my reasoning behind the decision that you have helped me change this morning. I still need to think about talking to the authorities about Polak, and perhaps when I have thought about it I can come back and talk it through with you, seek your guidance, as it were, Father?"

"Does this mean you are not going to kill anyone, my dear, today or any other day?"

Anna smiled and her face finally relaxed. "It does indeed, father. My life and the lives of others are safe today."

As Anna walked away at ten-thirty that morning, it was with the knowledge that she had just lied to a priest for the first time in her life.

68

Anna changed into her work uniform after a stroll around the garden with Cabbage. She had created that garden from scratch; there was just grass with a washing line in the middle when they bought the house. Now it had flowerbeds, a highly productive vegetable patch and even a couple of silver birch trees as a reminder of home. It was a little piece of heaven, a tribute to her grandfather, the farmer.

As she walked to work, Anna had to keep moving her bag from one shoulder to the other. It was much heavier than usual, though it still contained the clutter of a hairbrush, tissues, credit cards and some cash, bits and pieces of make-up, keys and so on. The difference lay in the bottom of the bag, beneath everything else-the Luger handgun and ammunition she stole from Polak's room the day before.

Anna was probably the only person alive who was aware of Polak's evil crimes and the lust he once had for killing. She had no doubts that he was

Karl Braun, the Greyhound, but if she were to bring it all out into the open, who would be interested? No one. Everyone at Paterson Manor had seen him watching German television and reading German newspapers-he even had German magazines delivered every month, but still no one asked why. The answer was simple: no one cared.

For so many years, organisations like the Simon Wiesenthal Centre had worked tirelessly to bring German war criminals to justice, but people were now beginning to say *leave them alone; the war was a long time ago. Forgive and forget. What is there to be gained?* The few surviving Germans who initiated and participated in those atrocities were now frail and old, time had moved on. *Live and let live. Let them get on with their lives while they had some of it left.*

There were still times when Anna cried for those she had lost, and for the innocence that was taken from her. But she cried alone now. People like her were becoming fewer every year, as indeed were those who had treated them so cruelly. Was it time for her to let go?

Several things that Father Pat said to her that morning had stuck in her mind. If she killed another person who was a known killer himself, did that not make her as bad as him? Should she not *show forgiveness, take the higher ground and be the better person? There was no justice in performing an injustice—and murder of any kind, no matter what label you gave it, was itself an injustice according to Father Pat and the bible.*

By the time Anna reached the locker room her head was spinning. She ignored several greetings as she entered the building, and her mind had switched into autopilot now. All she could do was focus on the task ahead. As she retrieved her library trolley she caught sight of her reflection in the mirror. Was there any difference between her and those German guards at Wysznica? Every day, they walked into their staff rooms and opened their lockers, just like she was doing now. And when they had their nice clean uniforms on they stepped into the workplace, as she was about to. But Anna was on her rounds, delivering books; the Germans were going about their day, delivering death.

Human beings had killed other human beings, not because they threatened their livelihoods or their families or indeed their own lives. No, they were killing them because it was their job, because someone above them in the chain of command told them to. To the Germans, killing Jews became no different than cleaning gutters or laying railway tracks-they got used to the smell of blood and the occasional splash of guts on their clothing. To the guards at the concentration camps across Europe, a job was a job, and they got on with theirs.

But every so often, among the drones of workers in the German killing factories, there was one who had a different look in his eye when he performed his duty. The sort of person who relished the undertaking at hand, who appeared to actually enjoy watching another human being suffer and die. Maybe it was to do with power, or perhaps a sick mind. Today they attach a label to people like that, say they are ill and give their illness a name to help them come to terms with their shocking deeds. They would certainly provide counselling and psychiatric help. The perpetrator becomes a victim, and his lawyers would blame his actions on a mind distorted by childhood abuse or bedwetting or some other clinically justifiable act.

***

Stella was in the corridor as Anna made her way to room twenty-four. They stood facing each other like gun fighters, Anna's trolley between them. Stella was first to speak. "Anna, can we talk please? I need to talk to you." Her eyes were brimming with tears.

Anna's voice was a monotone. "Of course, after lunch maybe?" She avoided eye contact as she pushed past Stella, but when she was a few steps beyond she stopped and called out. "Stell?"

Stella turned, her voice full of hope. "Yes, Anna?"

"I love you, Stell; please remember that, won't you?"

Stella started to cry. "What's going on, Anna? Are you OK? What is this all about, what on earth is going on? Have I hurt you in some way ... how can I fix this?"

Anna knew she had to stay focussed. If she let the mask slip it would all be over and she would not be able to continue. She opened her mouth to talk but words failed her. Eventually she managed to say, "After lunch eh? Let's talk then." Then she turned and walked away without looking back. She felt Stella's eyes burning into the back of her head, knew she was crying because she thought it was her fault that Anna was upset. Stella would know what it was all about soon enough. So would everyone else.

69

As Anna stood outside Polak's room trying to steady her nerves, her mind drifted back to an argument she once had with Leo. He was drunk and wanted sex but she was too tired. He mentioned the Germans then, some nasty comment about her never being too tired for them. He was right of course, because she never said no to the Germans, but how could she? A refusal could have led to a severe beating or worse-a one-way visit to the gas chamber. But Leo never acknowledged the reality of the position Anna had been in all those years ago. As far as he was concerned, Anna was a collaborator, and there were times when he seemed to relish reminding her; the older he got the more it seemed to eat away at him.

"Are you OK, Miss Anna?" Anna turned to find Joanie Nevin leaning on her walking frame next to the library trolley.

"I'm fine, dear. Why don't you go back to your room? You look tired."

"I know what's going on, Anna. I have been watching you these last few days. You know all about Polak and his wicked past, don't you, you found something in his room, didn't you, something incriminating?"

"I have to go, Joanie. It's time for me to visit Polak," Anna said softly.

"Then you must do what has to be done, Anna Brenewski. Do that and do nothing less than that." The old lady smiled sweetly then turned and trundled away as silently as she had arrived, her parting words lodged in Anna's mind.

Anna took a moment to gather her senses before knocking on Polak's door and quickly stepping inside. It was almost a relief when the door clicked shut behind her, because now it was just her and him, Karl Braun and Ania Burczyk. "I have the book you wanted, Mr Michalik," she said as she pretended to search her trolley.

As usual, Polak was in bed, propped up on his pillows in his favourite red and black pyjamas. She felt his eyes burning into her. "What? What did you say?" He was irritable.

"I have that book for you," Anna repeated, "the one about the Holocaust."

When their eyes met Polak spoke gruffly. "The only thing you have that I want is what you stole from my room yesterday, Ania Burczyk."

***

Polak looked well prepared, as if he had been practising what to say. His face was expressionless, his voice calm. "I see you have removed your contact lenses now. That was a very clever move, disguising the colour of your eyes! He raised his forefinger. "That threw me, I must admit. It took a little longer to place you because of those lenses." Anna placed her hands on the handle of the trolley. She had spent enough time being scared of this man. These were different times; this was another place. She was not going to let Polak know she was shaking.

"It is a real shame that I have bumped into you here," he continued. "I was at least hoping to see my time out peacefully in this shithole. Anyway, I would like my gun back please. You stole it yesterday, but it is no good to you-not with dummy bullets! If you want to hurt me, you would be better off hitting me with it; it's heavy enough to do a little damage to an old man's head." The sound of his laughter took Anna back to the Club. He had been laughing then, when he raped the commandant's woman.

She took the gun from her bag and lay it cold and heavy in the palm of her hand. He smiled when he saw it. "That's it. A nice weapon, yes? The artisan who carved the dog into the handle-I still remember his name—Solomon—a good solid Jewish name don't you think? You have no idea how many strings I had to pull to keep him alive so he could do that work for me. I had to pull a lot of teeth too, but when it was done, so was he." Polak shrugged his shoulders. "That's how it was in the good old days." Anna saw his hand slip beneath the sheets and for a brief moment she thought he had another weapon—one she had missed when she searched his room. But when his hand reappeared he dropped a handful of shiny bullets onto the bed.

"These are the real bullets, Ania," he said. "The ones you have are blanks."

***

He had only been playing up to now, teasing Anna, but a look of contempt had spread across his face. "You are all the same, you Polish people. You have no idea, do you?" He was out of his cage at last; his black eyes dancing with anger. "Do you really believe that I would leave live rounds of ammunition in the same place as a gun? Come now, give me some credit, will you? If you had looked harder you would have found the real ammunition in my wet bag, wrapped in greaseproof paper, nice and secure in a waterproof soap container, just waiting for a day like today."

Anna tried to remain calm. "Why do you have so much hate inside you, Polak? The Jews and us Poles, why do you hate everyone so?"

"Don't forget the Gypsies; I hate those filthy bastards too. And your so-called university professors and the lies they perpetrate about our beloved Reich. Oh yes, then there are the cripples, those with defects-I hate them almost as much as the Jews."

"Why?"

"Because they are impure. Can't you see that? The Fuhrer was right about them. The world had to be cleansed of their kind; all of them. They were a drain on society and they needed to die. Someone had to do it and did it really matter how it was done? The problem was, there was so many of them. It was hard work, do you know that? Ridding the planet of human vermin was damned hard work."

Anna shook her head in disbelief, amazed at Polak's cruel, misguided comments. How could so much spite and vitriol survive inside one person for so long? He interrupted her thoughts. "So, what is plan B, Ania Burczyk? Are you going to tell the authorities about me? Is that it?"

She ignored his question and asked one of her own. "Would you explain something to me?"

"Why not? Go ahead and ask whatever you want. Say your piece."

"How did you get to America after the war? How did you manage to escape detection for so long?"

He told her how easy it had been. After the liberation he somehow convinced the authorities that he really was Pawel Michalik, a concentration camp survivor. Perhaps it was his emaciated look and the number tattooed on his arm. And he had that piece of paper he claimed was a record of his admittance into the Wysznica. It all seemed to add up. So in the end they issued the appropriate documents and let him go. Once free he recovered his ill-gotten gains and went about establishing a new life. But then he came unstuck. The real Pawel Michalik's relatives tracked him down with help from the Red Cross, who were working tirelessly to reunite dislocated families after the war. Pawel Michalik had been registered as a survivor by the British, so he was eventually tracked down. His family knew that Braun was an imposter immediately, and before anything could be done to expose him, Braun had disappeared.

Nazi sympathisers within the Catholic Church had established what became known as the Rat Line, an organisation for helping right wing anti-communist war criminals escape justice. For a price, and the promise of future favours, 'Michalik' was issued with a Red Cross visa and appropriate documentation to get him safely to Buenos Aires.

As soon as he arrived, he was teamed up with Dr Mengele, who had managed to escape from Auschwitz and was already leading a comfortable life in Argentina. It was Mengele who introduced Braun to Adolf Eichmann, who was known as Ricardo Klement.

The three ex-SS men established an import and export business funded predominantly by Michalik. He may have been a low-ranking soldier during the war but he had money now, and there seemed to be plenty of it.

His wealth brought him a good life in Argentina, but by the late 1950s things were changing. Authorities around the world, including the Germans, were on a witch-hunt, pursuing ex-Nazi war criminals like Eichmann, Mengele and even small fry like Karl Braun. By a quirk of fate both he and Mengele had a near miss when Mossad, the Israeli secret service, unexpectedly turned up in Argentina and captured Eichmann in 1960.

Mengele escaped to Rio and Braun found himself on the run again, eventually establishing a new life in the United States, using the same name, Pawel Michalik. It may be a small world, but there were no computer checks on passports and visas in those days, so it was a lot easier to disappear if you had money.

"I have lived well. I had a wife and children in Florida, did you know that?" A look of pride slid across Polak's face, and he spoke as if he had been a genuine refugee who built an empire from nothing after the war. His wife had died shortly before he moved to New Jersey, but it was not her death that prompted his relocation. Some nosy reporter had been poking around, asking awkward questions, delving through old records. A lot of wartime information was freely available in the public domain by the year 2000 and he was anxious that the reporter might track his children down and tell them the truth about their father. So when his wife died he put himself into care in New Jersey, far away from his children, to live the rest of his life in peace.

"My kids don't need to know about my past, don't you agree? They are innocent of all that. I always knew there was the possibility that something like this could happen, but not so soon; maybe after I had died."

His tone of voice had softened now; the anger had momentarily left his face. "Why don't you put that gun away now, Ania Burczyk? Put it down, come now, let's talk sensibly about this, shall we, just you and me, two survivors, eh?"

Anna caught on quickly. "What? You want me to put *this* gun down, the gun with the fake bullets? The starter's pistol? You want me to put it away, do you?" Polak's eyes narrowed and he swore under his breath. He had been bluffing! If the gun only had blank ammunition, why was he concerned about it? He must have seen Anna's expression change when she realised the truth about the Luger. As he cursed for the slip-up, Anna watched his knuckles turn white while he gripped the bed sheets. She decided there had already been too much talking and it was time to do what she had come to do. She raised the gun and shut her left eye, extending her arm fully and looked down the barrel to the sights at the other end, which were focussed on Polak's forehead. She had never fired a gun in her life, but felt certain she had it worked out. It looked simple enough on the television, after all. "It is time for you to atone for your sins, Herr Braun," she said.

It was then that Polak yelled. "Put the fucking gun away, you idiot! Put it down I tell you!" His was momentarily back at Wysznica, shouting orders, threatening instant death to anyone who dared disobey him. Anna knew she had him right where she wanted, and so did he, but he had not given up yet. "Don't do anything you will regret, Ania. You know who I am. Be sensible now." He could see that nothing was changing. The gun was still pointed at his head. "I told you to put the fucking gun down, you Polish whore!" he screamed.

70

Someone barged into the room without any warning. Anna heard the door open behind her, followed by a sharp intake of breath, then it closed. She knew instinctively who it was. Stella scanned the scene in front of her; Polak in bed looking decidedly nervous and Anna standing in front of him, shaking like an idiot. An idiot with a gun in her hand! "Anna, Father Pat phoned to see if you were OK. He was talking to Elaine for ages, something about a letter you left for him to read. We are all worried about you. What's going on in here, Anna?"

"It's him, Stell, I knew it all along," Anna said. Polak's eyes moved from Anna to Stella then swiftly back again. He was like a coiled snake, just waiting for an opportunity to strike, but Anna and the gun were out of reach.

Stella did not understand. "Look, Anna darling, please put that gun down. Let's take it easy shall we? We don't want that thing going off accidentally, now do we? Put it away dear, please."

Anna started to feel nauseous. What the hell was she doing? Was she actually going to kill another human being? Of course she was! Someone had to make sure that justice was served, didn't they? If she didn't do it, who would? Nobody, that's who! Polak would continue to live the rest of his days without fear. When Anna was at Wysznica, she would have loved to have lived one day without fear-one hour even.

Anna spoke again, this time to Polak. "Your crimes will be exposed, Karl Braun, can't you see that? It's time for you to pay for what you did to my Danuta and everyone else." Something strange happened inside her at that moment. *My Danuta* ... As she said her sister's name, Anna suddenly felt like crying. A huge wave of emotion barrelled up in front of her, threatening to swamp her where she stood.

Here she was in a nursing home in New Jersey, pointing a gun at the man who murdered her sister in a concentration camp all those years ago. The actual weapon he had used to kill her was in her hand now. This was ridiculous! What did she think she was going to do? She could no more pull the trigger than she could fly to the moon. What was happening to her?

When Polak next spoke he looked first at Anna, then at Stella, as if trying to convince them both of his innocence. "I have nothing to atone for. I know nothing about what you speak. You are mistaken. Look at you; look at the state you are in, Ania!" He looked at Stella again, who simply did not understand what was going on. "Didn't you women read the Florida papers? I am not who you say I am. I am a war hero, a survivor just like you. I am Polak!"

Anna started to laugh. She realised she sounded like a loony, yet somehow, to her, the laughter belonged to someone else. She had to get herself back on track. "You are right, you *are* Polak. But you are *also* the Greyhound. You are Polak *and* the Greyhound!" A noise from the hallway beyond the bedroom door disturbed Anna's thoughts. She realised that her time was fast running out. Right at that very moment, news of what was happening in room twenty-four at the Paterson Manor Rest Home was spreading rapidly.

No doubt everyone now knew that she had a gun. She could hear people running about, someone shouting. *The cops are on the way, they'll be here any minute!* She had seen sieges on television before; the TV crews hastily assembling their equipment in the car park, huge rolls of cable being rolled out, cameras on people's shoulders, reporters holding microphones in front of their faces being dabbed with makeup, waiting for a cue to start talking. Very soon there would be the sounds of sirens in the street and helicopters buzzing overhead. This would be the story of the year, spread around the world in a few hours, because Anna was calling to account, Karl Braun, the Greyhound, the evil murderer from Wysznica concentration camp.

Polak broke the silence again. "There is still time for you to get out of this, Ania. There is nothing to be gained by killing me. Look, look at me, I am an old man now. Let bygones be bygones."

"He's right, Anna." Stella decided to jump into the conversation. "This can be fixed. Everything can be fixed. Whatever he has done, let the authorities deal with it, eh? Come on now my love, put the gun down. Let's go home together and have a nice cup of tea. Let's go and talk, eh?"

Polak sounded smug this time. "Your friend is right, Ania. Look at you; look at your hand shaking. You are not going to pull that trigger. You don't have it in you."

***

"Shut up! Shut up all of you. Let me think!" Anna was waving the gun around. The bloody thing could have just gone off at any time; she had no idea what she was doing! Then the strangest thing happened-she could smell urine, the unmistakable stench of piss.

After all his bluff and bluster about fake bullets and telling Anna that she didn't have the guts to shoot him, the old man had peed his pants! And when he realised that Anna knew, everything changed. An Oscar-winning performance as Polak broke down and started to cry. Anna watched the tears roll down his face, saw his shoulders heave as he sobbed and pulled the bed sheets up to his chin like a frightened child. "Please. Please don't do this to me," he sobbed pathetically.

A buzzing sound started inside Anna's head, a swarm of bees trapped inside her skull, and everything around her started to close in. A thick fog descended in front of her face. She could still hear Polak crying, could still smell his piss, and Stella was also gabbing away about something in the distance behind her. Anna's eyes started to sting and she realised she was also crying now, but for a very different reason than Polak. She tried to focus the gun beyond the fog of her tears, blinking fast to clear both her mind and vision. She wiped her face with her forearm. It became increasingly difficult to keep her aim steady because the gun was getting heavier by the minute. Then through it all, with everything going on inside and around her head, Anna heard Polak's voice once more. "Kill me then! Go on, bitch, kill me and you will end up in prison."

That was it! How dare he say that! *She would go to prison?* Ha! "I have been in prison since January 1940, you stupid old fool! I have nothing to lose now because I don't give a damn what happens to me. All I care about is what happens to you!" Anna raised the gun level with Polak's head, focused along the sights once again and watched him peeking out from behind the sheets like the coward he really was. Anna shook her head, shrugged her shoulders, took several deep breaths; she had to focus, she had to concentrate.

And that was when the faces started to appear.

Swirling in front of her, through her tears Anna saw Emilie first. "Look what I did for you," she said over her shoulder as Anna watched her walk off into the thick fog, hand in hand with Rolf Schroder. The hackles on the back of Anna's neck rose when Fischer suddenly appeared, grinning like an unwelcome uncle at a nervous child's bedside. She felt sick at the very thought of the things he made her do, and there he was, with a stupid grin on his face. Her grandparents appeared next, their eyes empty-dead people's eyes. Then her mother came; the same eyes, the life gone from her as well ... Anna's vision was now full of hollow faces floating in front of her, swirling about, jumbled up with Fischer and other Germans in the fog around her.

Behind it all, in the distance somewhere, Anna thought she could hear Polak baiting her, testing her resolve. "You can't do this, can you, Ania? You don't have the guts, do you? You are a gutless Polish whore." And then everyone in Anna's mind's eye seemed to move aside as Polak's face appeared through the mist. "Pull the trigger, go on, shoot me now, why don't you?" His tears had been replaced by a newfound confidence. His whole demeanour had changed. He was in a uniform again, a German uniform, and behind him in the background was a brick wall.

Red bricks, stretching up to the sky—the crematorium chimney at Wysznica with flames roaring out the top. And within the smoke Anna could see thousands of people drifting around-old women, babies, children with fearful faces and questioning eyes, all of them wanting an answer to the same question: why?

Now a person seemed to be yelling through a megaphone; in the room maybe or the hallway outside, behind the window perhaps. What were they saying? Was it the cops or was it Stella again? Anna could not make it out ... *Put the gun down, Anna, put that gun down* ... Then in front of her, like a faded old black and white film, the Greyhound appeared in his full SS uniform once more, that familiar expression on his face. He was walking up and down behind a row of people kneeling in wet gravel, their lips mumbling in prayer or a last-minute plea ... He smiled as he walked the line, and when he reached the end he looked up at Anna and raised his arm, then-bang- and the person in front of him fell forward—they were dead! Another bang—another body. Anna could recall the sound that followed every loud exchange, a strange, tinkle as an empty cartridge case was ejected from Polak's gun.

Each time the weapon went off, Polak turned to Anna and grinned. "That's how you do it, Ania. Just pull the trigger!" Another bang! "See?" He looked around and realised there was still one person kneeling in front of him. She turned and looked at Anna through desperate eyes. Danuta! Anna watched as Danuta silently mouthed the word 'Ania'. Braun strolled behind her, still smiling, his top lip curled in that familiar, spiteful way. Then he raised his gun to her head. "Let me show you again, this is how you do it, Ania..."

There was another bang inside Anna's head and she saw Danuta's body slump forward. Anna sucked in a deep lungful of air, then exhaled a long, calming breath as she raised her arm and pointed the gun towards the figure of Polak. She was grinding her teeth, squinting her eyes. Behind her, Stella winced and covered her ears. She never heard Anna say, "This is for Danuta..."

And suddenly it happened; an explosion in the room, a canon's blast that filled the air with a deafening roar. The shudder almost wrenched Anna's arm from its socket and momentarily threatened to knock her off her feet...

Stella screamed. Other voices joined in. Chaos as the door burst open and people in blue uniforms raced in waving their arms around, shouting. The fog immediately lifted from Anna's eyes and she felt a veil of calm descend in its place. Someone grabbed her from behind and prised the Luger from her grip. Everything in the room was happening in slow motion now, and as Anna was pulled aside, she turned back towards the bed and saw the blood for the first time-the Greyhound's body slumped to one side, a small round hole between his eyes.

ABOUT THE AUTHOR

Steve Matthews was born in the UK in 1953 and migrated to Australia in 1985. At the age of fifty-five, he sold his business interests so he could fulfil a lifetime's ambition to write full time. Since then, Steve's children's books have been published in Australia, the UK, Canada and the USA, and his work in children's literacy at home and abroad has been acknowledged in the Australian State Parliament. *Hitler's Brothel* is Steve's second novel for adults. He is also the author of *The Skinny Girl,* published by Highlight Publishing in 2018.

www.stevematthewsauthor.com

AUTHOR'S NOTES

In a past life, many years before I became involved in the world of writing books, a friend told me he was going to visit his family in Poland. On his return, I asked how the trip went, did he manage to meet everyone, what were they like? It was then I learned that he never *met* his relatives, he only *saw* them-their pictures were on a wall in Block 6 at the infamous Auschwitz-Birkenau concentration camp.

It transpired that only a few family members survived World War II, among them his father and mother, who were children at the time. At the risk of their own lives, strangers sheltered them, saving them from the death camps and the SS.

The Holocaust has haunted me ever since and I have now visited Poland and Auschwitz twice in search of a story. Each visit moved me to tears but failed to ease my feelings of guilt: knowing that other human beings designed and ran such places in a dedicated attempt to eradicate an entire race of people still leaves me horrified, bewildered and ashamed. However, it was someone in Australia who inadvertently put me on the trail of *Hitler's Brothel;* Stephen Bourke, who has my undying thanks.

In addition to my visits to Poland, I have read tens of thousands of pages about the Holocaust. I have also seen several hundred hours of documentary film and interviews and I have no idea how long I have spent ploughing through the internet. I even managed to find a few people to talk to who had experienced the war first hand.

I eventually realised that I wanted to write about an aspect of the concentration camp system that very few people even know existed.

Anna Brenewski's story is about a woman who lived through one of the most shameful events in human history. Not only did she suffer greatly herself, she also witnessed unimaginable horrors. Despite all this, after the war she somehow managed to find a fragile kind of peace in America.

Hitler's Brothel is a work of fiction, so I have woven fictional events around real happenings in this story. Most of the characters in this book are fictional, apart from some Germans who will no doubt be familiar to most readers: Adolf Hitler, Rudolf Hoess (the real camp commandant at Auschwitz), Himmler and Mengele.

Some of the events that are key to Anna's story are based on facts I gathered during research. For instance, while Wysznica as a camp did not exist, a great many of the facilities provided and events I describe did exist in German concentration camps around Europe.

There was indeed a brothel at Auschwitz, in block 24. There was also a warehouse facility for sorting victims' possessions, which was named 'Canada', and one camp did actually have an orchestra on the arrivals platform to play beautiful, calming music when transports arrived and during selections. The SS even arranged for prisoners to send postcards to their relatives from the fictional town of Waldensea, assuring them all was well. Cruel German propaganda at work.

The dietary controls mentioned during the German invasion of Poland are also true, and there is plenty of evidence to support Hitler's affair with his 'half-niece' Geli Raubel, the knowledge of which my fictitious Commandant Baldric Fischer used very much to his advantage. During my research, I found it difficult to put an accurate figure on the number of attempts on Hitler's life, but there certainly were many, all of which as we know, regrettably failed. The mind-numbing statistics from Treblinka (312,000 murders recorded in one month alone) and their disgusting method of luring their victims to death in the gas chambers is also considered to be true by historians.

Polak hid behind the cassocks of the Catholic Church at one stage in this story, and there has been plenty of dialogue around the world giving validity to the possibility of the Catholic Church helping members of the SS and Nazi party after the war.

The unenviable dilemma faced by Kapos and Sonderkommandos is also true. None of us know how we would have reacted had we been given the choice of instant death or working in the gas chambers and crematorium-beating up our friends and disciplining them being the least unpleasant of our allotted tasks. It is noted by some historians, however, that Kapos were selected from the criminal classes, and some were said to relish their newfound authority.

The Polish Home Army (Armia Krajowa) also existed, and I was shocked during my research to find evidence of their anti-Semitism.

I found records of people trying to dig up the corpses of victims in an effort to salvage any hidden jewellery the SS may have missed in their last crazed days of killing before the camps were liberated. It was also interesting-and devastating-to learn that people continued to die after liberation, as it took a while before the Allies developed a food that the emaciated prisoners could safely digest.

The common defence used by most Nazi and SS war criminals during legal proceedings after the war (including the famous trials at Nuremburg) was that they were 'acting on orders'. It is worth noting that some of them did in fact wear the now familiar striped pyjama camp uniforms to mingle with prisoners at the war's end.

Russian reprisals are also well documented; in addition, other Allies were known to have their own methods of justice.

Many aspects of my story are true. For those keen observers of history who find inaccuracies in any of the war-related facts, I apologise. I sometimes deliberately changed circumstances and events to suit the story. Just be assured that I have always tried to remain true to those who fell and those who survived that most terrible time.

For ease of reading, I have shown all dialogue in English, despite the different nationalities of the characters in this book.

I have no doubt that my words and all the millions of words written on the subject of the Holocaust so far inevitably fail to adequately provide the real picture of the true horrors suffered by those victims who entered the concentration camp system. However, I do hope that this book goes some way to helping us all understand the extent of what happened to the victims behind those metal gates, barbed wire and electric fences.

Thank you to the Simon Wiesenthal Centre for all the amazing work since its formation after the war. Their resources were invaluable. In addition, I would like to mention the superb book *Auschwitz—the Nazis and the Final Solution,* written by the distinguished writer, producer and historian Laurence Rees. It is in my opinion, the definitive document on the subject. Praise also to the BBC/PBS series *Auschwitz* that is based on Laurence Rees' book. Finally, of all the biographical works I have read on the subject of the Holocaust (and there *are* many!) it would be remiss of me not to mention the best-selling haunting memoir *House of Dolls,* written by the survivor Ka-Tzetnik 135633, first published in Great Britain in 1956 after being translated from the Hebrew. My thanks and admiration to you all.

Finally, after reading this book I hope you are prompted to ask what you would have done had you found yourself in Ania's position-at both ends of her life. I can tell you that I have thought about it a lot, and I am not proud of the conclusions I came to.

War is never over for those who experience it first-hand. This story is for all the Anna Brenewskis who suffered in the concentration camps of World War II-may your God bless you, and may you have finally found peace-whether you sleep beneath the ground or above it.
Steve Matthews

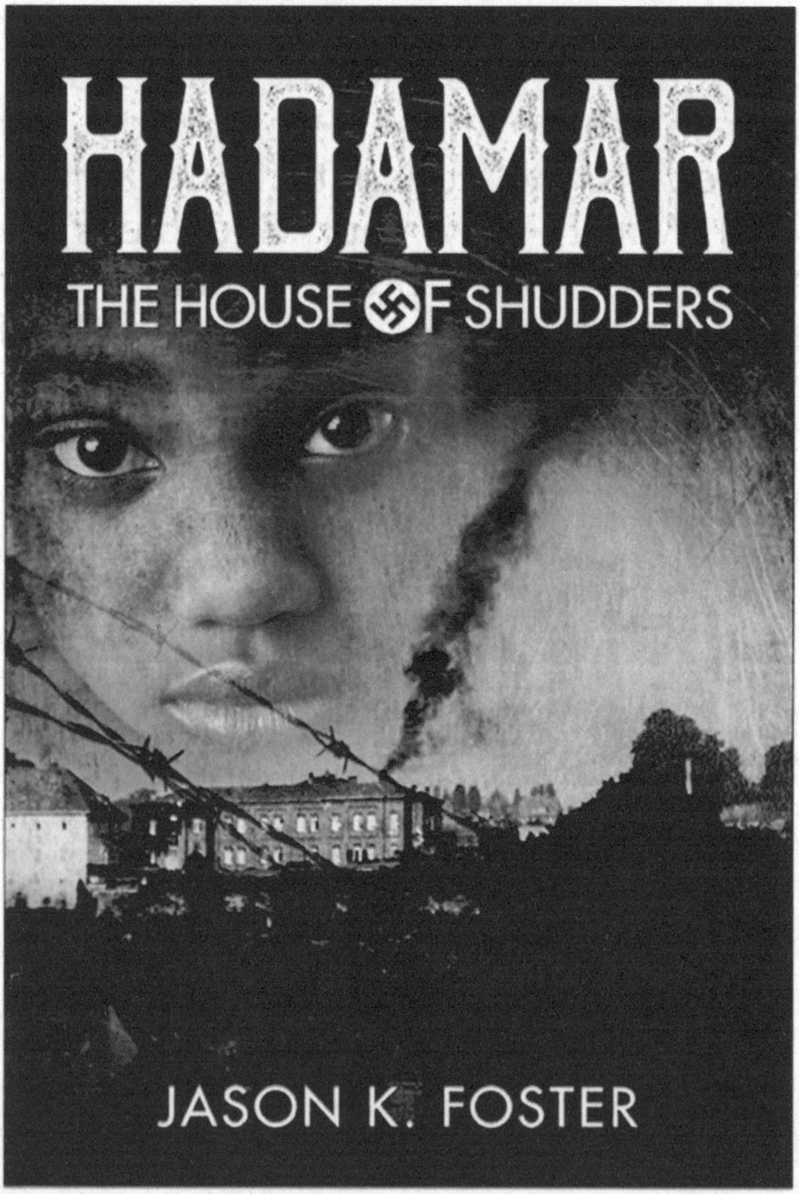

BACK COVER MATERIAL

Can a young Polish woman survive the horrors of a German concentration camp, rebuild her life and find the courage to exact revenge?

Two sisters are brutally separated by war in tragic circumstances. Ania is imprisoned and forced to endure the atrocities of a Nazi concentration camp. Danuta's search for her sister leads her into the dangers of the Polish Underground, Each will do what they must to survive long enough to find each other. Their dream of being reunited is crushed in shocking circumstances.

In an astonishing twist of fate, the opportunity for revenge presents itself 60 years later. But faced with the ultimate decision what will be the outcome ... seek justice or revenge?

Spanning decades, _Hitler's Brothel_ is a tragic and gripping tale of deception, courage and survival.